BOILED PEANUTS

By John Patrick Doyle

John P. Doyle

COPPERHILL MEDIA
A DIVISION OF COPPERHILL TECHNOLOGIES CORPORATION
http://www.copperhillmedia.com

BOILED PEANUTS
By John Patrick Doyle

Published by
Copperhill Media
A Division of Copperhill Technologies Corporation
158 Log Plain Road
Greenfield, MA 01301
USA

Copyright © 2011 by John Patrick Doyle

Cover Design by Copperhill Media

Image: Boiled Peanuts coming out of the can
Copyright © iStockPhoto.Com
Contributor: Juanmonino

Image: Looking Down On A White Board
Copyright © bigstockphoto.com
Contributor: Yuri_Arcurs

Disclaimer: All characters appearing in this work are fictitious. Any resemblances to real persons, living or dead, are purely coincidental.

No part of this publication may be reproduced, stored in a retrieval system or transmitted in any form or by any means, electronic, mechanical, photocopying, recording, scanning or otherwise, except as permitted under Sections 107 or 108 of the 1976 United States Copyright Act, without the prior written permission of the Publisher.

ISBN-10: 0-9832800-6-1
ISBN-13: 978-0-9832800-6-4

Printed in the United States of America

http://www.copperhillmedia.com

DEDICATION

To my wife, Mary, the comma queen, who punctuates my life with grace and who bears with sufferance the question from our townsfolk, "Is he a peeping Tom?"

- John Patrick Doyle

Prologue

Normally Paul was good, quietly rebelling against the tough kids at school whose bravery scared him. He didn't like trouble, and his sneakiness in opening her mailbox had puzzled him, but he'd found her name and that was the key. In the weeks since she'd moved next door, he'd seen how alive and pretty she was. Adopting Sarah Jenks as his mother was like warm buttered toast.

He'd rushed his homework so he could watch her house and imagine life with her. Between his fingers, he twirled his pencil like a revolving door hurling twilight off its sides. Even holding it just before his eyes the pencil couldn't hide her bedroom window from him, but, at ten, he was old enough to work out that shutting an eye stopped things doubling. With the pencil dancing ghostly between his blinks, he shifted his view from her empty bedroom down to the lit kitchen. He outlined her shining blonde hair on his window, the pencil-point tracing down her sides as she washed dishes. It was chilly in his room. His breath frosted the glass, and his fingers ached as he spiraled them over the pane to rub her into view again. He ought to grab a blanket off the bed to huddle in, but watching pulled him more.

Angrily, his bedroom door shook, rattling the room. The door-base boomed and his wad of papers shot from under the door. He froze as the door opened. "Damn thing," his dad grumbled, swaying in like a heavy tree, planting and uprooting its feet. If he got slapped at, he'd throw himself on the floor and be harder to reach. "Y'er wanted," his dad said.

Grateful his dad was going downstairs, Paul trailed the stink of sour whisky. He edged through his mother's door and closed it gently, hoping not to wake her if she'd gone to sleep. The window curtains were pulled, the room dark. Low lamplight puddled around her bony face, the nasty waspish orange bars of her electric heater buzzed near the floor. Her head turned to him, creaking like brushing twigs. He didn't understand why, but she was caking and cracking like river mud with the tide gone out. "Lo paw, ki," she strangled out. Obedient, he put his lips on the cream covering her flaked cheek. Its jasmine smelled of decay.

Focused on his mom's brown eyes, large in her shrunken face, he told her about 'Smelly' who was gawky and picked on by the rougher kids who'd been hauled to the principal's office for calling him names. "I should have defended him," he told her, but he hadn't. He felt better, telling her the boy wasn't really smelly. Sometime during his story, she'd fallen asleep. Soothed by his confession, he left her heated room for his bedroom. He jammed more papers under the door, pushed his small desk under the window and climbed on it. Wrapped in a blanket, he sat with the angle of the window frame wedged against his right shoulder.

With his legs pulled nearly to his chest and his notepad balanced on his knees, the sky went inky purple to charcoal as he worked on his picture of Mrs. Jenks. When he quit pressing his face closer, he brought the pad under his blanket and wrapped his arms around her. It's a long time, from winter's dark to grown-up bedtime. Needing adventure, he raised his pencil through the blanket crack, waving King Arthur's sword. Laying its tip on his tongue, he bravely twirled its lead. Sucking on it, sniffing the sweet wood, smelling clean hay and the beams of his Great Hall, he was surrounded by his knights. Perched on his desk he dreamed and dozed hours into the night.

Blearily aware of her bedroom light, he rubbed the sleepy film from his eyes. He clamped his tongue between his teeth and squeezed hard. She was already undressed, facing him, framed by the red curtains that barely covered a quarter of her window. Mr. Jenks was behind her at the back of the room. Paul could see her large breasts as she sat on her bed pulling over her head a cloth nightgown, white with blue flowers. She climbed onto her bed and he thought himself a younger child, sharing her pillow, warm beside her, sinking into her cuddle. Her bedroom went dark. Drooping with fatigue, he clambered onto his cold sheets, the blanket dragged over him, and he was asleep.

CHAPTER 1   SATURDAY

Paul leaned against the rough bark of the magnolia tree, firmly surrounded by its lower branches. He caressed the felt on the undersides of the large leaves. Light from the nearby house glinted on the outer leaves, and, from the center of his darkness, he imagined his tree a castle and the reflected lights his few townsfolk still awake that late. Mulch, damp from the afternoon rain, released its heady fragrance, jolting his brain with the smells of his Pittsburgh childhood--gravel dust, the hot tar of road repairs, diesel fumes--aromas he perversely categorized as bracing. Inhaling deeply, wrapped in the sensuous odor of the earth, he observed the family in their living room, cherishing his secret intimacy.

While he watched, he dwelt in a reverie of another time, in a story, told by his old English teacher who'd grown up in wartime London. Her attributes had faded to a caricature in his memory; a spinster of some severity and angularity who loved precision and took care to criticize his compositions. Vividly, he recalled reading in front of the class, and her correcting his misuse of 'bifurcation.' He replayed her childhood tale, 'You'd hear the doodlebugs overhead, and if the two-stroke engine noise stopped, you knew the bomb was falling. We dawdled past each shelter with our teacher, hurried to the next, and lingered again as we passed that shelter.' He'd never asked what he wanted to know, 'what were the children doing, out beneath the bombs?'

Abruptly, a crash of splintering glass pierced his dreaming state. In the older parts of Lexington the street lamps stood aloof, their cones of yellow light forming the rims of black valleys between, and there, dimly-lit, less than twenty yards ahead, two young men had smashed the window of a car. A sense of unreality split him from his body. He seemed to float above the street, observing himself blended into the bark, pinned to his tree. The men looked around. One reached in and opened the car door. Paul would have liked to shout, were he able. Then, to this tableau was added the deep snarl of a dog, and Paul re-focused on his closer danger. Disturbed by the activity in its street, angry, crouching low, the dog growled its warning. Paul had been bitten as a boy, riding a bike, his white legs flashing--an undoubted attraction to be sure--and since then he'd avoided confrontation with any angry creature. This one was poised to attack, and Paul's desperately whispered, "hush" and "there, there" failed to appease. It sprang. Paul lashed through the leaves, tore from the confining tree and ran. Man and pursuing dog fell in unison upon the pair of delinquents who struggled from the maelstrom and were chased beyond the street by the excited, yowling dog.

Transposed from peaceful seclusion to an exposed sidewalk, with his knees torn and his face abraded, Paul lay bewildered on the concrete.

Tentatively, he pulled himself erect by the side of the car. A large garden rock rested on the driver's seat, surrounded by broken glass.

"Are you all right?" exclaimed a woman who'd rushed from the nearby house.

"I'll help you," offered her companion, his arm needlessly about Paul, assisting him to stand.

"Goodness, you're injured," she said. "Come in and we'll fix you up."

Their attentions confused him. His murmured mild protests were ignored by his forceful helpers as they ushered him up the steps and through to the kitchen at the rear of the house.

"How brave you were!" she said, ministering to his inconsequential wounds. "Rudy heard the glass break, and we saw you tackling those hooligans and their dog. You were amazing." She turned to her companion. "Rudy, call the police, will you. The phone's over there." She dabbed Paul's forehead with antiseptic cream as they listened to Rudy's conversation with the dispatcher. Assistance was promised in a few minutes, he reported. "But not likely," he added acerbically. "They'll be busy with drunken college students this time on a Saturday."

"I'm Pat," she said, "and this is Rudy. It's my car they were after." Her brow furrowed. "I'm worried I left my purse in the car. Be a dear and look, will you, Rudy?" Rudy left, and Pat excused herself for a moment. Paul glanced about. It was an elegant, older house, high ceilinged with plaster cornices, wainscoting in the dining room, a chandelier above the dining table. The kitchen, where he was perched on a barstool beside a stone-covered island, was modern, with gleaming appliances of steel. The loud music from the front room was silenced. Pat reappeared, armed with bottles.

"Funny," she remarked, "a small university town, and, like half the place, my front door's unlocked with nobody bothering it. Lock the car door and someone heaves a great boulder through it." Paul nodded mechanically, full of the oddness of being wrenched from outside to inside. "Oh well, my own fault," Pat said, looking at Rudy who came in flourishing her purse. Turning to Paul she said, "Let's finish introductions."

"I'm Paul," he dutifully supplied.

Pat began pulling glasses from a kitchen cabinet. "What can I get you? Scotch? Would you like wine?"

His desire to leave outweighed by the need to be inoffensive, Paul said, "It's not really necessary, but some red wine, thanks." Pat showed him the wine rack. He selected what he hoped was an inexpensive bottle.

"My last ex-wife did that," Rudy said, "visiting cousins of hers. We drove to some ancient church on a Sunday morning. While the service was on, somebody smashed the passenger window and stole her purse. It certainly makes you doubt religion. Said she put it under her seat, but even so, tempting fate, leaving it there."

"Very true," Pat nodded, "but Paul prevented any great disaster." Suffering this praise, Paul drank his remaining wine. Pat refilled his glass and asked, "What do you do, Paul?"

"Well, I'm a librarian, at the public library."

"Have I seen you at the Episcopal Church?"

"I go sometimes. I like the music at the 10:30 service."

"I thought so, though I usually go at eight o'clock. It's shorter and more contemplative. In and out, and on with the day, that's me. I'm a retired school principal, but, retired or not, there's so little time."

It was difficult, matching this efficient and reflective ideal with the Pat before him. Sixtyish and slightly plump, much tanned, her bleached hair stylishly tousled, with enough red lipstick for several lips, she seemed roguish and chatty; a kind, if somewhat scattered, person. Though a school principal must have some steel in her. Rudy, on a barstool at the other side of the kitchen island from them, was significantly younger than Pat. He appeared fit, his skin so bronzed it looked hot to touch. His eyes played with hers, their glances meeting over their drinks as they sipped. Uncomfortable within these ocular embraces, Paul concentrated on his glass.

"I don't often get to the library," Pat said. "I do know a couple that are on your library board, Melissa Coombs and Daisy Fox." She gurgled at her thought, "They're actually not a couple, you understand." Paul nodded numbly. "And are you married?" she asked.

Lacking the technique to end Pat's friendly examination, he answered, "I'm divorced, about four years."

"And is there a girlfriend?" she asked.

"I'm afraid not."

"Same here, Paul," Rudy said. "On the divorce part, that is. I've been divorced three times."

"Rudy and I met six months ago on the Internet," Pat explained. "He has relatives here, but lives in Florida. We only set eyes on each other yesterday." She smiled broadly at Rudy. "Our first date was dinner at the Depot Grille, thirty miles away. Tonight, as you see, I was more trusting."

"Goodness! This is your second date. I should leave," Paul said, trying to stand.

Pat put her hand on his arm. "No, please don't. The police will want to talk to you, and we're truly delighted having you. Let me refill your wine, and we'll get better acquainted." A dazed bird brought to a gilded cage, he abandoned his feeble efforts to escape. Entertaining her reluctant guest, Pat's fountain of words flowed on. "We're all of us divorced, then. I was the trophy wife. The jerk dumped me for an even younger woman, but a tidy settlement got him where it hurt." She looked playfully at Paul, and lingeringly at Rudy. "And now I prefer my men younger." She turned back to Paul, "So, tell us how your divorce came about."

Paul didn't attempt to skirt the issue. Feeling his excess of alcohol and unpracticed at evasion, he said, "Amanda found someone else. In fact, she found herself another woman."

"How delightful," Pat gleamed, which she immediately changed to a doleful expression, "but distressing at the time, no doubt. Does Amanda still live here?"

Paul nodded. "She's an instructor at the Fitness Center. We get along okay. I do odd jobs for her when she needs help."

"Helpful as always, I'm sure," Rudy said. Paul detected sarcasm. He felt the awkwardness of coming between Rudy and his plans.

Responding to the flashing blue lights from the street, Pat and Rudy rose together. Not wanting to be left behind, Paul trailed after them.

"Evening, officers," Pat said. "Two police cars. We do feel special. But what will the neighbors think!"

"Good evening Ma'am. I'm Sergeant Driscoll and this is Officer Pruett from the Lexington Police Department. You've had some excitement, we understand." Pat led them into the living room. Paul sank into an overstuffed couch, wishing he'd chosen a firmer seat. Nervously waiting to be grilled, he focused on the ceiling light.

Officer Pruett flipped open his notebook, readied his pencil, and Sergeant Driscoll spoke. "An accident to the car, was it?"

"No accident, unless it rained chunks of rock," Rudy said. "Probably kids up to mischief. They smashed a window."

"Anything missing?" asked Officer Pruett.

"It's my car, officers," Pat said. "I'd left my purse there, but they didn't have time to take anything. Paul, here, was our hero and tackled them to the ground."

Sergeant Driscoll turned to Paul. "Is that so? And how did you come to be there at the time?"

Paul, everyone attending to him, felt the difficulty of squirming upright, sunk as he was into a marshmallow. He firmed his spine and responded, "I was out for a walk, heard the breaking glass, and before I knew it I was mixed in with them and they ran. It was nothing, really."

"Your pants are torn at the knees and your face scratched. There must have been a scuffle," observed Sergeant Driscoll. Paul had entered the melee blindly and could only say that, from glimpses, he thought them younger than his own age of twenty-nine, possibly eighteen to twenty-two. Not wishing to muddy the logic of events, he offered nothing as to his trespassing under a magnolia or the dog chasing him. To his immense relief, the interrogation concluded without a gimlet question exposing his falsity. Sergeant Driscoll promised to examine the car on his way out and suggested, with rain coming, that the gentlemen cover the car window.

Pat found duct tape and black plastic garbage bags in the kitchen, Rudy and Paul went out to work on the car. The police had left. A chill wind gusted and the air smelled of rain. A sliver of moon had risen, showing clouds massed on the horizon.

"It was foolish of you, getting involved," Rudy said.

Had his heroism been real, Paul would have agreed with Rudy. As it was, Rudy's opinion was annoying. "Everything worked out well," he said.

"For you certainly," Rudy grumpily replied between biting off strips of duct tape to attach to the plastic bags. "Maybe you'd like to be useful and take a bag to collect the broken glass?"

Paul removed the rock from the car. With the aid of the car's interior light, he collected shards from around the driver's seat. One plastic bag inside the other couldn't entirely contain the sharp glass, and he felt guilty that blood from his fingers dripped on the driver's seat. He took the glass to Pat's garbage can and, released from obligation, was anxious to depart. "Please say goodbye to Pat for me. I'll get home before it pours."

"You should go," agreed Rudy. "Good night."

Glad to leave his adventure behind, Paul hurried away. Despite the threat from the fast-moving clouds, he soon slowed and took the longer way home through Woods Creek Park where the path snaked beside the stream and little man-made light reached. It was a struggle to see and to stay on the path. When the clouds weren't covering the moon, he looked above and followed a pale strip of sky between the darkness of the overhanging trees as though he walked along the Milky Way. When the moonlight failed, he pushed blindly on, feeling the path's surface beneath his feet. He had found the steps leading up from the park to the road, when the rain, that he knew would come, did. The cold water, striking at him and biting into his cut fingers, was exhilarating. The deluge saturated his clothes, forming a soggy husk about his body, but Paul felt happy, and free of constraint, as he beat uphill against the pounding rain.

CHAPTER 2   MONDAY

What Paul wore was of no significance as the only work clothes he possessed were khaki trousers, several shirts of solid, plain colors, and two pairs of brown shoes. He was proud of that efficiency, of being heedless of his clothes. He dressed and walked outside his ground-floor apartment calling for his cat, Spook. On the path, a shrew lay on its back completely unmarked. He pitied the creature's fright-filled end, suffering for Spook's amusement. He squatted and touched the shrew's side, feeling its sleek, immaculate grey-blue fur. Its teeny tongue peeked out as if it would speak, its miniature fingers curled as if it would grasp what its perfect-looking eyes no longer saw. The shrew was beautiful but out of place on the concrete path. He nudged it into the grass with the tips of his fingers. Spook came running, Paul picked up his newspaper from the dewy grass, and they went in to breakfast.

At 8:20 he cycled to work. His bicycle wasn't new or even well maintained, with dirt embedded here and there in old oil, and its wheel rims and kickstand rusted in spots. He thought of this as his anti-theft device, as he never locked the bike. In his backpack was the library book he'd read over the weekend and the same lunch ingredients he packed every workday: an apple, banana, carrot, Roma tomato, and a small bag of mixed nuts. Lexington, in its own declivity within the Shenandoah Valley, was prone to mist on spring mornings before the sun burned the vapor away, and this morning was typical. "Let's go roamin' in the gloamin', with the heather on the hills," he mumbled in his tuneless way as he cycled on a bracing morning through the muffling mist of his own Brigadoon.

Paul let himself in the library's rear door. This morning, before anyone came, he needed to reclaim space on his desk. Whenever he found useful Internet sources, he printed their homepages, tossing the papers in a pile for later investigation. Sadly, there they languished in archeological layers and periodically he'd have to shovel the mound's lower level in an armload to the recycle-bin. These repeated failures vexed him, but he'd never found a solution, consoling himself that attainments naturally fall below high aspirations. His shameful task accomplished, he turned to the mundane gratification of reading new book advertisements. After fifteen minutes of quiet industry, he raised his head. Ruth and Tim had arrived, chatting at the back door.

"Good morning, Paul," Ruth said, smiling.

He responded to her, and echoed Tim's perfunctory, "Morning." They hung up their jackets, busily replaying the North Carolina game. He wasn't even sure what sport they were discussing, which secretly pleased him. He didn't like competition and, as someone's victory was always the other's defeat, competing seemed, on balance, pointless. He wished that viewpoint left him feeling less remote. He knew his ignorance made him vanish into a conversational void. Sighing at his neurotic mental processes, he went to open the front door.

During the morning, he was on duty at the reference desk in the center of the adult reading area. From there he could observe most of the library. When Ruth was swamped at the circulation desk, he was able to help her. When he looked her way, she often sensed it and smiled at him. At times, he glanced to his left, at the row of public computers. One of his uncomfortable duties was to remind the occasional offending patron as to library policy on sexual content. He himself was not immune to the various charms of women, and he knew how distracting that all was. From his station, he enjoyed the young women who came into the library, their smells, their shapes, their movements, the modulation of their voices. This poor self-mastery he excused with the thought that voyeurism is natural to a man.

It was late morning when he saw Ida Perkins enter the library. She was, like many library patrons, an avid genealogist, and Paul pictured himself her partner, searching for grains of gold. He approached her enthusiastically. "Mrs. Perkins, how are you? We have a new database called HeritageQuest. We can look at census records through 1930 to trace that great-uncle of yours."

"Thank you, Paul. That's wonderful." They sat together at a public computer. Ida said wistfully, "I do wish I'd asked my mother about the generations before her." Paul knew little of his own ancestors and that disinterest disturbed him, but, in self-justification, his mother had died when he was eleven and his father, by then, was lost to alcohol. "At my age I don't know why I care," she said cheerfully. "Any day I'll pass on and can ask them all the questions I want, in person." Paul chuckled at her wit. A long way from thoughts of death himself, he found her bravely stoical. Privately, he imagined Ida his affectionate great-aunt. Unfamiliar with the homes of old people, he pictured her occupying a small, dark-curtained living room, antimacassars draping the backs of chairs and sofas, her companion a parakeet.

They were deep into the mystery of Uncle Herman's departure from Chillicothe in the 1920s, when Charlotte Roth, the library director, came behind them. "Paul, I had a call from Melissa Coombs, a library board member. She told me about your bravery on Saturday night at Patricia Brazier's house. It's wonderful you're bringing such credit to the library." Ida, plainly startled at this revelation of Paul's heroism, looked at Charlotte who, to Paul's distress, retold of his exploits. He stared at the swirls in the carpet pattern, thinking of Pat informing Melissa, who passed the story to

Charlotte, and now Ida. He feared that many more retellings would fabricate the Battle of Thermopylae and he, the sole surviving Spartan warrior.

"No, really, it was more of an accident," he said, interjecting when he was able, but despairing of being heard. "It's nothing, truly."

"And modest, too," said Ida.

"Why don't you go to lunch, Paul," Charlotte suggested. "I'll assist Mrs. Perkins."

Grateful to escape her praise, and his discordantly meager claim to it, he retrieved his lunch-bag and went to the staff lounge. Tim and Ruth sat at the lunch table. Ruth moved over a chair so he could sit without squeezing past her. He pulled a paper towel from the dispenser at the sink. Using it as a plate, he spread his food. Breaking his carrot in two, he began to eat, as he usually did, from the larger end.

Ruth, a vegetarian, had cooked a veggie-burger in the microwave. Paul's stomach growled at the scrumptious mushroom smell. "You have such a virtuous lunch," Ruth said. Paul smiled at her. Packaged in its own skin, his was a lunch of convenience. And virtue, he knew, could be dull. He might have enjoyed microwaving some delicious lunch, but he'd never done that at work and change aroused the curiosity of others. It was irksome having his motivations prodded and poked.

"You should see the dinner he has when he goes home," Tim said. "Mountains of meat and gravy."

"Oh, Tim, leave him alone." Ruth smiled apologetically at Paul. "Charlotte told me you defended yourself against attackers over the weekend and acted courageously. Is that right?"

"What! He was in a fight?" Tim exclaimed.

"No, it was nothing like that," Paul retorted, immediately regretting his sharpness. "I'm sorry, Ruth. I've been badgered by the whole thing. I'd just like it to go away."

"That's okay," she said, "Buddhists don't approve of violence anyway, but it's necessary sometimes, of course." Everyone knew that Ruth was Buddhist, but being quiet, sensible and good, her eccentricities were easily pardoned. She was a young lady who loved nature, unafraid to be outdoors without a hat even though she browned unevenly in the sun. With her front teeth a little square, her brows thick and black, and no make-up, she was not a beauty, although she had character, and smiled as much as one could ask.

Paul, who liked Ruth, felt the need to amend his abruptness. "The redbud are beautiful," he said of the branches in a vase on the lunch-table.

Tim made a derisive "Yehmmph" noise.

"I didn't see you bring them in," Paul continued, "but they look like your arranging. Very Japanesey."

"Thanks. They are attractive, aren't they? I cut them this morning in the garden. The tree won't miss them." After a pause, she continued, "Paul, I wondered, if you would like--" but her hesitant question was interrupted. At the end of their lunch-table stood a young man in jacket and tie, evidently come on business.

"Sorry to disturb your lunch. The library director said I'd find Paul here. I'm Ned Rayburn from the News Gazette." Paul knew Ned, having helped him with library research on some of his stories. "Paul, is it okay if I go over a few facts with you? Won't keep you long." Paul looked at him tetchily. Ned continued. "I spoke with Officer Pruett about the fight on Saturday night. He told me your pants were ripped and your face roughed up. Is that true?"

"Doesn't sound like our Paul," was Tim's opinion.

"Oh, Paul, that's terrible," Ruth exclaimed. "Were you badly hurt?"

Paul hesitated, hoping to field some response against these cannonades he mustered only a resigned, "Yes," to Ned's question.

"What's the scoop? You went from mild-mannered to super-hero?" pressed the incredulous Tim.

"Tim, can't you see he doesn't want all this attention," Ruth said. "Were you trying to help someone?" she asked sympathetically.

"As I understand it," Ned said, "you saw these youths throw a rock through the window of Patricia Brazier's car. You confronted them and got pummeled for your pains. Is that right?"

"Yes," supplied Paul, reluctantly.

Information failing from Paul, Ned said he was off to talk with Pat Brazier. He thanked Paul and left. Tim finished his lunch and squeezed between the wall and the chairs on his side of the table. "You were the tight-lipped one," he said as he left the lunchroom.

Paul was disturbed and abstracted. Ruth said no more on the taboo subject, allowing him to munch mechanically through his lunch. Her hand moved toward him but crept back without bothering him. Re-focusing, he became aware both of Ruth's attention and of his rudeness in ignoring her. "You're off work on Thursday afternoon, aren't you?" she asked. "Are you doing anything special?" He said he wasn't, and Ruth moved to her question, "Would you like to visit the Buddhist temple with me then?" and being vulnerable, Paul assented.

Chapter 3   Thursday

Soon after the library opened, Ruth came to the reference desk to confirm their afternoon trip to the Buddhist temple. "I brought the picnic in," she told Paul. "I couldn't get hold of Mr. Robson about opening the temple, but I left him a message. Hopefully everything will work out."

"I'm sure it will. I'm looking forward to it," he replied politely.

"The weather might spoil our hike. The radio was saying possible storms this afternoon."

"Whatever happens we'll have a good time."

Ruth smiled in agreement and returned to the circulation desk, leaving Paul to his work.

At noon, his shift ended, and he saw Ruth heading his way. "I'll get the picnic from the fridge," he said. They walked to the staff lounge to load Ruth's provisions into his backpack.

Tim was playing a game of solitaire on a laptop and eating his lunch. Watching the preparations, he delivered his verdict to Paul, "You'll be in at work tomorrow wearing a yellow robe and chanting."

"I'd be more colorful, at least," Paul responded mildly as they left by the back door.

In the parking lot, Ruth asked, "You don't mind my driving?"

"It's great. I only drive when I have to."

Ruth drove her old station wagon up the winding road into the Blue Ridge Mountains. They crossed the Appalachian Trail at the crest and descended a few minutes before turning off on a dirt road that, after half a mile, opened onto a clearing at the temple. There were no other cars. "Mr. Robson isn't here," Ruth observed. "We'll have to break into the temple."

"Are you serious?"

"We'll see," Ruth said, smiling. He was relieved that she was joking. "Let's walk around," she suggested. Admiring the mountain scenery, they strolled along the edge of the clearing. "The community owns fifty acres," she said proudly. "The views are great in winter, and when the trees are in leaf it's quite secluded." It was a few weeks before the trees would be fully green, white-blossomed dogwoods covered the slopes, purplish redbud floated above them among the trees. He gulped greedily at the crisp air.

"It's spectacular," he said, "and the temple is striking." They walked toward the simple, rectangular log building, an Allegheny Mountains oriental hybrid with its low-sloped, red-painted tin roof. High in the temple walls, three small windows were open to the elements, well sheltered by a generously overhanging roof.

"I'm afraid you're up here on false pretenses," confessed Ruth.

"That doesn't sound good."

"It's not actually a temple, you see. I think it's because there's no shrine. It's called a 'center' but that's so bureaucratic." Paul assured her it looked like a temple to him. Ruth considered the windows. "I can get in there. The door opens from the inside. I just need to stand on your shoulders."

"It's pretty high up," he said. If anyone was crawling through windows, it should be him, but standing on Ruth's shoulders wasn't a possibility. "There's nothing's lower?"

"It's the same on the other side, and the front windows don't open."

The other matter was Ruth's legs. Her short black skirt covered a fine pair of legs. He visualized those knees elevating past his head and those legs heaving and squirming above him, and he was mortified at his weakness. "I don't think we should. Let's wait for Mr. Robson."

"There'll be no trouble," she said, taking off her shoes. "Give me a boost." More hesitation would be feeble. He cupped his hands for her foot, and she held his shoulders. "Heave away," she commanded, and he dipped and straightened. She stabilized herself with her hands on the log wall. Her skirt covered his face, the inside of her thigh pressed warmly on his cheek. He lifted her slowly, her weight shifting from his hands until she stood with both feet on his shoulders. Her shapely legs and blue underwear overwhelmed his view and that familiarity caused him anxious guilt. Before he could look down she said, "I don't have enough leverage, can you push some more?" Paul grasped her heels, arched his head back and elevated her. Unavoidably licensed, he admired her long legs as they receded from him. She shouted, "That's it. I'm there." Her belly on the window frame, her legs kicking wildly, she thrust forward, grabbed the side of the frame and turned to a sitting position. "Phew! That was harder than I thought."

Ashamed at being safe below, he asked, "Can you get down okay?"

"It's not so far on the inside." She slid into the building. The door opened, and she appeared, triumphant. "That was fun. Come in, but leave the shoes outside." Paul set her shoes by the doorway, untied his and placed them neatly beside hers. Uneasy at their illicit entrance, he looked around; a pile of mats and cushions in one corner, a few Buddhist wall hangings, white-plastered walls and ceilings, the floor wooden. Ruth spun about in the center of the room. "See the floor. It's hinoki wood. It's pretty isn't it?" He agreed that the pale honey color was striking. "It's cypress," Ruth hesitated, "or maybe it's kind of a cedar." She laughed, admitting her ineptitude as a tour-guide. "The hangings are Tankas. From Tibet." They admired the antique cloth paintings hanging low on the walls. "The larger images are the Buddha, and those around him are gods, or important monks, I'm not totally sure. They're full of symbolism, but it's so foreign." Paul nodded in agreement. Ruth ran to the corner and dragged out two blue mats. At the center of each was a round, three-inch-deep cushion. "Not many of us are good at sitting cross-legged so we have these cheat cushions. Try one."

They sat facing each other. Paul watched Ruth cross her legs. "Should we try meditating?" she asked.

Her black skirt had ridden up, exposing her bare white thighs. "Sure," he said, doubtfully.

"Relax and I'll repeat a mantra. If your mind wanders off, bring your thoughts back to the sound." Afraid his mind would be shepherding rambunctious goats, Paul crossed his legs, shook his shoulders to release tension and closed his eyes. Ruth intoned, "Om shanti shanti shanti" several times. 'Shandy' was Paul's first cat and that similarity in sound completely barred his herd from reassembling.

The sound of a car interrupted their meditation. They went to the porch to greet Mr. Robson, a slight, bald-headed, black gentleman in his mid to late sixties coming agilely toward the building. He hailed them, "Hi Ruth, Paul. Got your message, but I was held up." He came on the porch and took off his shoes. "Delighted to meet you, Paul. I'm John Robson."

"Paul Kirk," he said, shaking John's offered hand.

"I see you had no trouble getting in," John said. Paul looked for Ruth's response.

"Paul boosted me through a window. It wasn't easy."

"It's a good thing we're isolated up here," John replied. He explained that the building had no electricity and was unheated. "We like to hear the wind in the trees through the open windows and be one with the world. Though we make a concession and run an oil heater in the colder months to keep from meditating on our frozen toes." Changing the subject he asked, "Are you attached to anyone, Paul?"

"Not at the moment."

"You're well on your way to Nirvana, then," he said, approvingly. He allowed Paul's confusion to stand for a moment before clarifying his obscure remark. "I'm joking. Buddhists work at eliminating attachments, you see. Attachments to our selfish motives. But you didn't come for Buddhist philosophy. You're here for a pleasant afternoon." He grinned at Paul. "We Buddhists love to give lectures on the right path, and to listen to them, too. There's a story of two monks who come to a fork in the road. The signpost points one way to Nirvana and the other way to a lecture on Nirvana. They go to the lecture."

Paul laughed. "I'd be happy to learn something about Buddhism."

John pulled over another mat, and they all sat. "There aren't many Buddhists in this area," John said. "We're a small lay group, all converts from something, and we love to spread the word, but I'll give you the thumbnail version without inflicting too much torture."

"We tried meditating on the sound of 'Om shanti shanti shanti'," Ruth said.

"That's good. 'Shanti' means 'peace.' Did you find that it brought you any?"

"I'm as fragmented as ever," Paul replied.

John smiled. "The Buddha's message is that we suffer in life. We can enjoy relationships, but everything is impermanent and we mustn't be overly hungry for sensual gratification."

"No drinking wine or admiring women?" asked Paul.

"We're abstemious," John replied, "but Buddhists, like anyone, want pleasure. The key is not to crave it. Right thought, ethical conduct, mental discipline, that's the Buddha's prescription. We need to remember that our life is the creation of our own mind."

They sat with their thoughts a moment until Ruth spoke. "Mr. Robson, we should be going on our hike. We brought a picnic lunch, and I bet Paul's hungry."

"Certainly. I apologize, Paul, if I assaulted your ears. We meet on Sunday mornings at ten o'clock for meditation and then a social hour, if you'd ever like to visit."

"Thank you, Mr. Robson. It has been interesting." In truth, the cavernous mismatch between this talk of mental discipline and his own disordered life did stir in him some need, but he set that aside for the moment. He and Ruth put on their shoes, returned to the car for his backpack and waved to Mr. Robson. They started on what Ruth promised would be a gentle hike.

Single-file, Ruth allowed Paul to lead on the gradually ascending trail. "I've been this way a few times," Ruth said. "In a couple of miles a stream crosses the path, and there's a small meadow where we can picnic." Except for a few clouds on the horizon, the sky was clear and the air mildly warm. The mountains stood clear of haze, and the birds warbled their cheery spring notes. They conversed a little on the scenes they passed; the shapes of tree branches, the mossy rocks, the wildflowers that neither was good at identifying, but they could name or guess a few. April was too early for the woods to carpet their way with color but the violets were plentiful enough. Ruth exclaimed at finding a cluster of Virginia bluebells and joyously nosed into them, "Oh, aren't they pretty! Little clusters of trumpets." He enjoyed her happy enthusiasm, so unlike her restrained demeanor at the library. He envied that release from constraint.

With no more than rocks and exposed roots to step over, the walking was easy. After forty minutes, they heard a fast flowing stream fall on rocks around a bend in the trail. By a mossy slope, Paul stopped to show Ruth a wildflower he knew. "See, those are Dutchman's breeches." On the slope, six feet above them, the pendulous flowers clustered, white with a yellow base. "Mentally turn them the other way up. You'll see a pair of baggy white pants."

"That's so cute. I see it."

He enjoyed displaying this knowledge, aware that his impulse to impress was a little foolish. "Mind you," he said, "it's as much like the root of a tooth, but 'tooth root' wouldn't be the best name for a flower."

A few more paces brought them to the stream. "We cross to there," she said, pointing to a grassy area a short distance upstream. The water wasn't deep, but it churned around the flat rocks that lay as a causeway over the stream. Paul stepped out and turned, waiting for Ruth to step onto the first rock. When she did, she immediately slipped. His hand shot out to steady her and Ruth seized hold. They crossed in an arch, his arm high and rigid, Ruth hanging on, as if to a commuter strap on a train. When she reached safe ground, he dropped his arm and she thanked him.

At the clearing, beside a picturesque scene of water tumbling, frothing around large boulders, Paul said, "All that hissing and turmoil reminds me of my cat Spook socializing with the neighbor cat."

"How long have you had Spook?" asked Ruth.

"About seven years. Amanda, my ex, let me keep Spook." He smiled ruefully. "She kept most everything else."

"I love cats. Maybe I could see Spook sometime?"

"Sure. Let's eat, I'm starving." He removed the food from his backpack, and Ruth spread their feast. "What's that?" he asked, pointing to a container of grayish, blobby material like tuna salad. He was confident Ruth didn't eat tuna.

"That's tempeh salad: mayonnaise, onions, dill, and celery with chopped-up tempeh. And we've got sprouts, hummus, and pita bread."

"Looks great. I could eat a …" He stopped, confounded for a moment. "A large radish." Ruth laughed at his attempted humor. From the plastic bag of utensils, she took out paper napkins, put them down for an eating-place and passed a knife and fork to Paul. "This isn't my standard lunch so I've a feeling we're not in Lexington anymore," he said.

"But different is good?"

"Oh, very good." Their meal passed in temperate pleasantry. Paul finished his lunch with an apple. He munched around the core, popped it into his mouth and chomped down.

"You didn't just do that, did you?" protested Ruth.

"I've always eaten the cores. And now," he said, drinking some water, "I'm watering the seeds." Often suspecting himself of dullness, any quickness pleased him, but he did wonder if humor was like a nervous tic, erupting when the protagonist in his play didn't know the script.

"Men never grow up." As she spoke, Ruth glanced at the sky with concern.

Paul nodded. "Let's move," he said urgently. She threw their remaining food out for the animals. He shoved everything else in his backpack. The wind had risen. The sky was darkening. They crossed the stream focused on the trail ahead, Ruth stepping lightly over the river stones. Before they'd gone a hundred yards, they felt spatters of rain. "Looks like a downpour," he said with concern. "I saw a rock-overhang some ways along the trail. Let's jog and see if we can find shelter." The roots and rocks on the trail, barely noticed on their walk, turned hostile as they ran. The wind drove a sheet of rain toward them hung from the clouds. Paul imagined helicopters ascending the mountains, their rotors threatening, the poor resistance fighters zigzagging the mountainside, about to be spattered with machine-gun fire. Large plops of rain began assaulting them.

Pointing ahead, Ruth shouted, "I see it." As they raced, Paul pulled off his backpack. They scrambled up the slope and flung themselves against the moss and ferns of their meager refuge. A cave would have been welcome. This was a concavity in the hill beneath an overhanging rock ledge. Ruth hooted with laughter, and Paul was obliged to hold her arm or she'd slide down the hill. Scooting up as far as they could, they kept their feet above the splashing rain. Paul had felt the wetness of Ruth's blouse and clearly saw the thinness of her bra. It was difficult, diminishing his awareness of her nipples. He shivered, his own shirt coldly wet.

Thunder growled about the mountains. Lightning flashed to earth nearby, and they heard a tree crack. Secure, in their tenuous way, and thankful not to be sheltering under a tree, they pressed against the hill watching the exuberant lightning play across the sky. "I just remembered, I tossed in a jacket in case of weather," he said. Reaching into the bottom of his backpack, he removed a thin, crumpled windbreaker and gave it to Ruth.

"Thanks. Do we have any more paper towels?"

He extracted the plastic bag and found two paper towels to give her. To his consternation, she unbuttoned her blouse. Leaning toward him, she shrugged herself from it. Turning away a little, she used one paper towel to dry her hair and the other to work over her arms and chest. He observed the swell of her left breast, clinging to her flesh-toned bra, as it moved under her ministrations.

"Here, work on my back." She handed Paul the dampish paper towels and presented her back for drying. He regarded the muscles of her back, the ridges of her spine, her freckles, and he shivered again. Beginning his attentions at her shoulders, he moved down past her bra strap. A man of poor impulse control might have unhooked that strap. He imagined his hands sharing her bra cups, his fingers gliding around her soft breasts, squeezing her flesh, but either trouble or mortification would be the result. Releasing the thought, he continued down, rubbing in a circular motion, stopping where the elastic of her skirt flared over her waist.

Ruth put an arm through the sleeve and leaned forward to wrestle the jacket on in their restricted space. "That feels better." She zipped up the jacket, and gave her blouse to him. He pressed the water out and folded it into his backpack. The mass of dark clouds had scudded by. Between the stragglers, blue appeared. "It's ending," she noted. The sun was seen again and the birds heard. The rain had moved on, leaving water dripping from tree branches and from the leaves of the bushes.

"As a child I wondered why they never smiled." He pointed at the rainbow, arching between the clouds like a petulant mouth between two bulbous, gloomy cheeks.

"You were an odd child. Aren't rainbows supposed to make you happy? My heart leaps up, that sort of thing." She sat up. "Can we get moving? My legs are wobbly, holding me on the slope."

Graceless, they slid to the trail. The rain hadn't lasted long enough to make the trail muddy. The path was easy, undulating and tending downward. They'd gone less than thirty yards when they heard crashing in the undergrowth above them. "There aren't any bears around here, are there?" he asked.

"Black bears, for sure. You don't have your gun with you?"

"Not today," he said, wishing he could turn her bantering to surprise. He'd never held a gun, but he saw the scene; the cold steel in his hand as he faced the towering seven-foot animal that recognized his lack of fear and meekly turned from them.

A white-tailed deer broke from the bushes. It leapt the trail a few feet before them and bounded on below. "Wow, he was a handsome buck!" exclaimed Ruth. "I've only seen does and fawns, but he had antlers that must have been two feet long."

"Good thing he didn't trample us. Where there's one there's probably more." He examined the slope above them as they walked.

"The lightning brought down a tree," Ruth said, pointing.

The blackened tree, still smoldering, had split in two. 'Bifurcated' he thought, vexed at the annoying word, cracking open in his head. The marred scene made him uneasy. They were a few feet from the tree before Paul understood it was a doe tangled in the limbs. He dropped to his knees.

"Oh, the poor thing," Ruth said. "We've got to get her out."

The doe twitched her right ear, turned her large brown eyes to him and slightly raised her slender neck to flare her nostrils. Tired, she laid her head down, her pink tongue poking out. Stoically waiting, she watched Paul. The tree had been substantial. Much of it had fallen above on the slope and its limbs had thrashed the trail, enmeshing the deer. "It doesn't look as if she's under any major branch," he said. He broke off a covering tangle of small branches and saw it was hopeless for her. Looking up at Ruth, he painfully shook his head.

"What? Let me see," she said and knelt beside him. One of the large scaffold branches of the tree had missed the doe but a smaller branch descending from it had pierced her haunches. She lay pinned to the earth. "Oh, no," moaned Ruth, "what can we do?"

Paul was seized by thoughts of his mother, her functioning as randomly shut down. At her end, she could only blink at him. Impaled by a pain grinding through his guts, he wanted no responsibility for this dying creature, but he wrenched himself from his frozen memories, saying, "If we had a saw we could cut through the branch." Really, nothing would work. They couldn't leave the doe, didn't have a saw, and they couldn't heal her. Freeing his breath, he said, "We'll have to kill her."

"How?" she asked.

Paul thought of pushing a branch through to her heart, incongruously seeing the doe's disdain at his inept efforts to penetrate her and find her heart. Bashing her with a branch was too intimate to contemplate, repeatedly beating at her until he was spent. "I'll have to crush her with a rock."

"Can you do that?" Ruth asked doubtfully.

"If it's big enough, and I can lift it, I think so."

They returned along the trail looking for something heavy. Ruth spotted a boulder buried in the earth above the trail. Paul snapped a fallen branch across his thigh and they used the two sticks to dig around the rock. After ten minutes of exhausting work, they paused to rest. Paul feared he wasn't able to carry the boulder twenty yards, even supposing they could dislodge it. "Let's get above and use our branches as levers and see if we can budge it," he said.

With their joint heave, the bolder broke free and crashed to the trail. Over a foot in diameter, it was circular enough that, laboring together, they could roll it, pitching down the trail. The doe seemed worse, her tongue lolled further from her mouth, her breath barely perceptible. "She's dying. Maybe we should wait," he suggested.

"She's suffering."

Paul nodded. He had to try. He positioned the stone two feet from the doe's face, squatted, grasped the stone and lifted it above his knees. Rising, he hefted it to his chest. Pausing a moment to summon his strength, he lifted the weight to his face and heaved it down. Before it left his hands, he knew he'd failed. The stone thudded to the earth beside her delicate neck. He dropped to his knees in despair.

"Let me help you," Ruth said.

"No. Give me a second to rest, I can do this." He lightly stroked the warm doe's neck and apologized, "Sorry, girl." After a few heartbeats, he reached for the boulder. The doe's beautiful brown eyes fixed on him as he brought the stone above his shoulders. With all the vigor left in him, he hurled it at her head. Recoiling, he leapt back and Ruth pushed into him. Accepting her hug, he patted her shoulder.

Looking anywhere but on the lifeless creature, they climbed over the tree. Somber, they walked on to the temple. The sun shone. Ruth unzipped her jacket, warming her chest and drying her bra.

In killing a fellow being, Paul was removed from his realm, translated to a home where much of his childhood intersected with his failing mother, erratically erased from his life. When Mrs. Jenks, full of life, had moved next-door, how he'd yearned for that mother to be his. When he should have been in bed, he collected scenes, transforming them into his own family story. In all the years that passed, never entering that house, he experienced family events at a tangent: the meals, the birthdays, their daughter's high-school graduation, and Mr. Jenks' death in a hunting accident.

"Here we are," she said, zipping up her jacket. They had reached the opening where the trail arrived at the temple. Paul returned from his self-absorption, wistfully thinking that the boy should have had more care and that he needed more care too, or from his twisted roots he'd grow bent and gnarled. "You were miles away," Ruth said.

"Sorry," he said, looking back at her, realizing he'd walked two miles without noticing. "I was thinking of my childhood family."

"That's nice. Did you have a good childhood?"

"Tolerable. My mother died of MS while I was in middle school. She was in a wheelchair for a while, but she lay in bed her last few years. Dad crumbled with it. He took to drinking."

"Oh, Paul, that's so sad."

"Should we say goodbye to Mr. Robson?"

"He'll be meditating," she said. "Let's not disturb him. I'll say your goodbyes when I see him on Sunday." They cleaned themselves with old paper napkins they found stuffed in the glove compartment. Driving down the mountain, Ruth said, "I'd like to get a cup of coffee. Are you up for it?"

"I don't know. I'm kind of tired. The afternoon turned out stressful."

"All the more reason. Don't go home and poop out. We'll go to the Joyful Spirit Cafe. You need something to pick you up."

Suppressing his desire for solitude, he agreed. On their return to Lexington, Ruth found a parking spot on Main Street near the cafe. Inside, he looked despairingly at the rows and columns on the menu board, the snacks and wraps, desserts and coffee-types, endlessly permuted. He lacked the energy for it. An indecisive donkey, equally spaced between piles of carrot-cake, he'd starve to death. Ruth went first, allowing more time for the blank space in his mind to enlarge. At his turn he said, "A regular coffee, please."

"With cream?"

"That's fine."

"Get something to eat," Ruth prompted. Paul asked if they had carrot-cake, and that's what he ordered. The lady behind the counter said he could pay when they finished eating.

"Paul, how wonderful!" came from behind. Paul turned to greet Pat and Rudy.

"Ruth Thompson," he said, introducing her, "this is Pat Brazier and Rudy. I'm sorry, Rudy, I don't know your last name."

"It's 'Price'," Rudy said.

"There's a table by the front window," Pat said. "Let's sit together, okay?" While Ruth went to the bathroom, and the others placed their orders, Paul sat, dispirited. Lovely as Pat was, her energy would empty him like a draining bathtub. Typical introvert, he thought, determined to fight it. Rudy and Pat finished ordering and sat with Paul. "What a storm last week!" exclaimed Pat dramatically. "And the wind! The house got a fierce lashing. You and Rudy covered the car window just in time. It was bad of you, leaving without saying goodbye. You must have been drowned in that rain."

Ruth returned from the bathroom and asked, "So, how do you know each other?"

"We met last Saturday," Pat replied. "Paul defended my car against a pair of delinquents. Did you see the article in yesterday's News Gazette?"

"That's why your name sounded familiar. We were proud of Paul at work."

"You work at the library?" asked Rudy.

"At the circulation desk. The newspaper was full of Paul's praise, though it did embarrass him. The reporter came by the library on Monday, and Paul clammed up."

"No matter," Pat said. "He interviewed me, and I set him straight. If I exaggerated a point or two, think of me as chief cheerleader on Team Paul." She winked at Paul.

Ruth described their traumatic hike, extolling Paul for his big-hearted willingness to help the injured deer. "It's right out of the Good Samaritan, isn't it," Pat said.

Rudy humorously pointed his finger at Paul's brow. "A bullet between the eyes would've been more humane."

"Do you have a gun?" asked Ruth.

"Not on me, but I travel with one. The world isn't safe, and we've a right to defend ourselves."

Their conversation paused, until Pat exclaimed, "How it rained this afternoon! Last Saturday we saw Paul and it poured. Today it pours and we see him again. Did you two get soaked on your hike?"

"My blouse got wet," Ruth said, "but Paul swapped it for his jacket."

"That must have been entertaining," Rudy said.

Pat kicked Rudy's chair leg. "Rudy, behave. Marry him, Ruth. That's my advice. Paul's close to perfect."

Ruth looked sympathetically at Paul. "You may be right, but every time we build him up, he shrinks a little more. Soon there'll be nothing left to admire." The victim of their focus squirmed, wishing he could vanish like a genie transported home, but living in a bottle brought unwelcome associations with his father.

The waitress came and distributed their food and coffee. Ruth had a vegetarian wrap, Rudy a roast beef on ciabatta roll, and Pat only a coffee. She sighed theatrically, "Always on a diet. There's too much of me to admire."

"No, you look great," Ruth said.

Pat, resuming earlier thoughts, said, "I'll try to be a more restrained cheerleader, Paul. Anyway, at my age, who wants me frisking around like a cheerleader?" After a bit she said, "Rudy, you missed your cue, you were supposed to say, 'I do'."

"I've said, 'I do,' too many times before," he said, playfully leering at Pat, "but frisk with me any time you want."

"I know it's politically incorrect in the same thought as 'frisking,' but did you hear about the attempted rape?" asked Pat. "Rudy was out of town. I have the police radio on in the background when I'm alone. It's mostly drugs and domestic disputes, or alcohol and car crashes, but last night it was a man wearing a ski-mask. He had a knife and dragged a young woman into an alley. She managed to scream, and he ran off."

"As I said," responded Rudy. "No place is safe. But you're safe with me around."

"It's surprising for Lexington," Ruth said. "We're having a rash of crimes lately."

Despite his aim to socialize, Paul was a boulder in the conversational stream. Leading him on to talk, Pat said, "The church Vestry wants me to give sixty-thousand dollars, to pull up the carpet, re-do the floors, replace the pew cushions with acoustic ones. What do you think?"

Happy to leave the topic of his supposed virtues, Paul replied, "The pew cushions are too thick. It makes me feel like a kid when I can't get my feet to the ground."

"A lot of money so you can grow up," retorted Rudy.

"And the church is dead. If the sound bounced more I'm sure the service would improve," Paul added.

"Hardly seems worth it," Rudy commented. "For an extra echo."

"I'll think about it," Pat said. "Paul, you aren't eating much of your cake. Can I share a few crumbs from the edge?" He pushed his plate closer and Pat used her coffee spoon to scoop a large piece into her mouth. "Umm, delicious," she said, licking the spoon. "If you'll excuse me, I need to wash my hands."

After Pat left, Rudy said, "The church has plenty, like the government, but they're both happy spending anything more they can get. Don't encourage Pat to waste her money is my advice." Some of the town merchants had moved stalls onto the sidewalks to attract the tourists, and from their window-nook Paul and Ruth watched the activities on the street until Pat's return.

"Shall I pay, Rudy?" asked Pat.

Paul took advantage of the small pause to leap in before Rudy. "No, Pat, let me get the bill for all of us." A tussle ensued, which Pat allowed Paul to win, and he went to the counter to pay.

Everyone was standing by the table when he returned. "Pat says there's wine-tasting at the Washington Street Purveyors this evening," Ruth said. "It's just around the corner. Can we go for a while?"

Pat left a tip on the table, and they ventured off. On the old brick sidewalk, there wasn't room for them all abreast. Pat and Paul came together in the lead, leaving Rudy able to chat with Ruth. "Honestly, Pat could lose a few pounds," Rudy said, "but you're very ship-shape."

"Do you have a nautical background?"

"A figure of speech, my dear. I was an executive in the drug industry. The competition took us over, so I retired early."

"Have you retired to Lexington?"

"I'm the carefree sort, so it's hard to tell. I have family connections here, but Lexington's a little isolated for my tastes. Although remote has its advantages."

"That's true. It's idyllic," Ruth said.

At the wine shop, they ducked, stepping down into the store. The small front door, checkered with diamond-shaped panes, had the aura of a much earlier century accommodating smaller people. The wide-planked flooring, the barrels and rough crates, reinforced the impression of a bygone time. They followed Pat into the tasting room. Paul pleasurably inhaled the wood-flavored air as they navigated the narrow aisles. "Hi Jeff," Pat said. "These are my friends, Ruth, Paul and Rudy. Jeff's the owner of this dungeon."

Jeff set out glasses and poured from his first selection. "This is a Sauvignon Blanc from South Australia. We're down to our last few dozen bottles. I've tried to buy more, but none's to be had. This sells for twenty-two dollars a bottle."

In an undertone to Ruth and Paul, Pat said, "Don't feel guilty about drinking Jeff's wine. I'll buy plenty to make up for it." Paul wasn't overly fond of white wine and this one had a grassy, sour taste. Sipping hers, Ruth made a face. Paul gestured with his glass, and she poured her wine into his. He tossed it down his throat, refraining from the next offering, a sweeter white. Paul had noticed Rudy observe him sharply. He guessed Rudy disapproved of his swigging the wine. He found Rudy disconcerting, unsuited to Pat's easy ways, but, no doubt, she found him enjoyably passionate. "I like that sweeter one, Jeff," Pat said.

"They're by the counter in the next room on your way out," he replied.

Rudy had intercepted a group of young people milling into the tasting room. He spoke to one of them. After a quick discussion, the group left. On Rudy's return, Pat asked him, "What was that about?"

"That was my nephew, Todd. My sister Jane's boy. She gets upset with his binge drinking. I warned him off. To sweeten it, I gave him money to take his friends to the movies."

"That was good of you, but you should have introduced us," she complained. "If I don't get to visit your family soon, I'll think you're ashamed of me."

Paul knew Todd from somewhere, but much of the population looked that way. He probably came into the library occasionally. They resumed their drinking, with Paul enjoying more enthusiasm as they progressed into the reds. Regardless of Pat's thoughtful comment, he amassed sufficient guilt for one bottle of red wine, buying the cheapest he could find. Pat purchased a variety of good to excellent bottles, and, when they stood outside the shop, she said to Paul and Ruth, "I insist you come to my house very soon. We'll do a wine tasting, and we won't limit the quantities. I'm in the phonebook. Give me a call." They said their farewells and parted.

At Ruth's car, Paul laid the picnic containers on the back seat, hung her blouse from a hook in the car and put the wine bottle into his backpack. "Thanks for the afternoon. It was different," he said, smiling with quick diffidence. "I'm fine walking back to the library to get my bike." He gave her a small wave and set off briskly, leaving her to observe his retreating back.

CHAPTER 4   FRIDAY

Paul set out for the evening to wander through the Maury Heights area of town. In passing near Willow Avenue his mind inescapably returned to five years earlier when he and Amanda lived there in a small block of apartments. He was content then, having someone to share the apartment with, but, disinclined to let any happy thought go unalloyed, he remembered how annoyingly bossy Amanda had been.

Their street was less attractive than its name, lined with aging gray apartment blocks, each separated by wire fencing, and no willow trees. One morning, the sky still gray, he'd gone out to find Spook. Not wanting to disturb the neighbors, he called softly for her. A shower was running. Glancing through the vine-covered wire fence, he located the sound through a bathroom window open about six inches. Spook came, and, bending to stroke her, he looked into the bathroom through the horizontal slit. The shower was turned off and a woman's leg stepped into view. How exciting that discovery had been! Foolish, he knew. More female flesh could be seen in town on any summer's day, and, judged by her sinewy thigh, the lady wasn't young. Yet he was moved by that forbidden and intimate contact. Spook would allow his caresses for only a moment before she leapt from his arms, heading for the apartment. He was left crouching without purpose on the concrete path, the power of his situation waning as his vulnerability mounted with the rising light, and he had gone in to breakfast.

Quickened by that small incident, Paul's criminal career grew, not visibly, but underground, waiting and feeding on sap as the cicada does. Not until the restless evenings that followed his separation from Amanda did he discover the balm he sought in his dark prowls.

A poorer section of town, Maury Heights was, in times past, a black neighborhood, but such distinctions had been breaking down for several decades with black and white families mingled in relative harmony, each group needing only the separation of their churches. Here were small, wooden, single-story houses with narrow front porches, the grassy borders of their properties demarcated by bushes or trees. Lacking alleyways, Paul's strategy required that he walk between darkened houses and amble along the rear boundaries. Occasionally, a dog barked, and he moved along, but nobody had ever challenged his right to be where he shouldn't be.

His mind of an orderly cast and in need of ambitious work, Paul had fixed on becoming an encyclopedia of the seven thousand residents of his town. An assiduous researcher with a retentive memory, he had ready access to the City Directory, to property tax records and to numerous local histories. In the evening, he explored Internet sites and memorized the names and connections of the families in the streets he'd visit. Having no family and, he must acknowledge, no real friends, he needed that social outlet, and his task, he was proud to think, was an undertaking of some intellectual breadth. Depending on the weather, he liked to sit on the grass, protected by a bush, or to lean against the trunk of a tree, ideally with a vantage over several houses. Having found a suitable covert, he contemplated the vastness of the stars, or the flecks of memory inside the infinitesimal speck of his own being, or, with harm to none, he watched events unfold within the surrounding houses.

Sitting in the shelter of a low hedge where, over time, he'd worn a comfortable curvature in the ground, Paul watched a young family. The children ran in and out of the kitchen while their mother cooked. Making a pie, he thought. The boy was around eight and Paul imagined himself there, with sisters, a mother who baked and a father who sat in the kitchen, talking.

"Who do we have here, then?" asked a deep, confident voice. Startled, moving to panic, Paul turned his shocked face to the half-seen figure of his interrogator. His incoherent, shambled excuses were truncated with, "My little joke. Been watching you, and we're up to the same lark." Dropping to a squat, with his hands on the ground before him, his inquisitor said in a youthful voice, "Rolf's my name. Rolf Sprunt."

Paul had been panicked by an affected authority, for this young man, with his compact body, receding chin, low forehead, pointy nose and fine long fingers splayed on the grass, was Spook's shrew come alive. Paul could even make whiskers grow from the shadows of his face. "Who are you?" Paul asked, beginning to believe, but uncertain of this creature fallen from the pages of Wind in the Willows. Serious as this was, he marveled at his urge to look around for Badger, Mole, or Toad.

"Fair's fair, what's your handle?" asked Rolf.

"My name's Paul. Can we keep our voices down, please," he begged.

"Anxious sort, are we?" Rolf whispered. "But sure thing, mate." From his accent, Paul knew this was an Australian shrew.

Paul started to rise. "Where are we going?" Rolf asked.

"I'm going home."

"No way to make a pal," complained Rolf. "It's still early. Let's find something more interesting." He pulled Paul to his feet and headed off between the houses, with Paul nervously lagging behind.

Reaching the street, Paul said, "I should go home."

Looking at him knowingly, Rolf said cheerily, "You're not done in. I watched you yesterday, and you'll be up for another hour."

Paul thought back over the previous evening, finding no hint of observation. "I don't like being followed," he said indignantly.

"Just my point. We'll team up," Rolf said, his confident tone turning to a question.

A Joey in a manic kangaroo's pouch, Paul needed stability. He crossed the street to a park bench, and Rolf accompanied him. The miniscule park, a flat strip of grass that fell off precipitously into a ravine of mimosas and other trees and bushes too dark to distinguish, had a fine view over the lights of the town and came with one decorative lamp-post offering a pale romantic glow sufficient to see each other by. Anyone observing them would have seen a pair of lovers.

"I work alone," Paul said.

"Doesn't mean you have to like it." Rolf lifted his legs onto the bench, wrapped his arms around them, and put his chin on his knees.

"So what's your story, Rolf? What's an Australian doing here?"

"I'm the proverbial remittance man, but in reverse."

Struggling to make sense of that, Paul finally asked, "How in reverse?"

"You know. The limey gentry sent their black sheep to Australia with a pittance to keep them there. My so very proper family got rid of me, but they sent me out of Oz. To another colony. So that's more like sideways than in reverse." Rolf snorted at his humor.

"Why Lexington?"

"As far as you can get from home, I'd say," Rolf said disgustedly. "But really because my aunt Regina's here. I'm staying with her. She's married to a professor at the Virginia Military Institute. They expect him to straighten me out."

"Is it working?" asked Paul rhetorically.

"Course not. But I'm not that bad. Dropped out of school and got my girlfriend preggers, but that was fixed up."

"I see," Paul said. "What's your uncle's name?"

"Seth Hopewell."

After a moment, Paul said, "22 Smith Street?"

Rolf showed his surprise. "How'd you know that?"

"I'll tell you later," Paul said, enjoying his small omniscience. "How old are you?"

"Nineteen."

"I take it you like to look at women?"

"Too right, mate. Bondi Beach, now that's a place I miss, topless beauties to wear your neck out with looking."

"Did you play games of doctor and nurse growing up?" asked Paul laughing.

Rolf nodded. "Always been a peeper. Here, let me think of a good one to tell you." Almost shyly, he continued, "One time, I was seven and my Mum and I went to visit a friend of hers. They had a very nice girl, Cynthia I think she was, must have been eleven. I saw her go off to the shower, and I hid under her bed. She came back wrapped in a towel and closed her door. It was only the two of us in her bedroom. I really wanted to touch her but I just lay there looking at her, seeing how pretty she was. She tossed her towel on the bed and she was starkers. I saw her brown nipples and the little mound between her legs. I couldn't stop myself from moving and she screamed. I got such a hiding. But it was worth it." He smiled fondly. "Have you got one for me?"

Paul delved for something significant to impress Rolf. "I was about seven, too. My parents took me to a beach, mostly pebbles I remember. There was a lady in front of me with her family. Can't have been any place to change because she was struggling with a towel draped around her. She didn't know, or care, that I was behind her. She was making a poor job of it, and I saw her naked back and all her rear-end as she squirmed into her swimsuit."

"That's it? Not much, is it?"

"I suppose not," Paul said, conceding to Rolf's precocious talent. "Though it's vivid in my memory."

"You'd see that much in a hospital ward," Rolf scoffed.

Paul was uneasy, but he had enjoyed sharing their unshareable stories. He vacillated as to leaving. Having engaged in conversation, he couldn't easily break from someone who had embarrassing knowledge of him. A quarter-moon had risen above the town. They looked over the pleasing view.

"Homos," came the taunt. "Queers. Fuckin' fags." Alarmed, they jerked to their feet as three men, one white, two black, descended the curve of the road, nearly upon them. Shoulders together, Paul and Rolf waited to see how bad this would get. "Homos, retards, fags, flamin' preverts," jeered the men as they circled Paul and Rolf who had backed against the bench.

"You twinkie pooftas," Rolf roared. "I'd like to arsehole you, you bunch of moron gits."

Paul's adrenaline spiked. Shaking with fear, he followed Rolf's lead and barked his imprecations. "Pin-headed thugs. Wouldn't know your rear-ends from trap-doors."

His words proved effective, for the three attacked. Two went for Rolf. The smaller white youth came at Paul. Rolf kneed one in the groin and spun away. His victim collapsed on the grass. Paul ducked at his assailant's charge, and his attacker's face crunched into Paul's skull. "Fuckin' broke m' nose," he screamed and slumped to the ground.

Rolf jumped onto and over the bench. "Quick man, run," he urged. They tore down the hill. After a few blocks, hearing no pursuit, they slowed. "We were great. What a team," Rolf exulted. "I'm around the corner, let's go." They trotted to the corner of Smith Street and walked the rest of the way to number 22. "Come in and clean the blood off," Rolf said. They went up the wooden steps to the house. Rolf opened the front door calling out, "Auntie Reggie, I'm home. Brought a friend. Be there in a minute." Rolf took Paul to the bathroom, ran to get paper towels and returned to help Paul rinse his hair under the tap and dry off before they went to Aunt Regina and Uncle Seth.

As they entered the living room, Seth reached for the remote and turned the TV off. Expecting a parade sergeant, Paul saw that. Seth was fiftyish, well tanned, with fair, buzz-cut hair and blue eyes, his solid build turning to stomach fat. "What have you been up to, Rolf?" Seth asked, his tone accusatory. Regina, plump, with a pleasingly round face and a family resemblance to Rolf in her fine black hair and brown eyes, sat on the couch, benignly smiling at them.

"Nothing," Rolf said. "Paul and I were sitting on a bench, talking. Three guys took us for pooftas and came belting at us. We ran, but not before Paul head-butted one of them." He grinned.

"I hate to see you getting into trouble," Regina said.

"Not our fault, Auntie Reg. We were just sitting there."

"Should we ring the police?" Regina asked.

"The rats are in their holes by now," Paul said. "Let's let it go."

"Good to see you boys fighting back, anyway," Seth said.

"Please sit down, Paul," Regina said, patting the couch.

Paul chose a hard-backed chair for the inevitable questions. Rolf dropped to the floor in front of him.

"What do you do, Paul?" asked Seth.

"I'm a librarian at the public library."

"And how did you two meet?" asked Regina.

"At the library," Rolf said. "I was working on a paper." Paul admired the speed of Rolf's invention but he hoped Rolf had finished fabricating.

"You're probably aware that Rolf audits English classes at the University?" Paul slightly nodded, indicating either attention or agreement. "I know an English professor who was obliging. Rolf can certainly do with learning some English," he laughed. "If I wasn't married to his aunt I'd only be guessing at what he says half the time."

"That's not true," objected Regina, "It's just a few words like that. Everyone in Australia sees so many American films. It's like a second language, talking American."

Rolf rose from the floor, "C'mon, Paul. I'll run you home."

"Okay, thanks," Paul said, standing. "It was great meeting you both."

"The pleasure was ours," Regina smiled at him. "We're thrilled that Rolf has found a friend. He so needs a mature influence in his life. Come again."

"Good night," Paul said, and he and Rolf headed outside. "That's it?" Paul asked, in dismay, of the car Rolf had stopped beside.

"Too proud, are we? You can bloody-well walk, mate."

"No, no, but you'd have to admit it's past its prime."

Rolf kicked the car affectionately. "The car's had so many prangs she must have been owned by a neg-driving-genius. There's more dents on her than car. But she runs okay. Hop in." Rolf, it proved, was disposed to stray from the center of his lane. Observing Paul flinch as they swished by parked cars with molecules of air to spare, Rolf said, "I'm not used to driving on this side of the road."

"How long have you been here?"

"Two months. I went for my license a few weeks ago when I bought the car. Funny story--the DMV man who tested me told me to turn left, so I make a left turn into the left lane and he says, 'what color stripe's in the middle of the road?' so I tell him it's yellow, and he says, 'what side of the road are we on?' Well, I can take a hint like the next fellow. Didn't have the foggiest notion what the color was to anything, but I move into the right lane. When we get back, he barrels off into the office with me trotting behind like I'm attached. Before he disappears, he looks back and says, 'You passed.' Blimey, that was a shocker. I was sure I'd failed, but I figure he liked my accent. Kind of surprising he didn't put his hand on my knee."

They stopped outside his apartment, and Paul exited the car, giving Rolf a small wave. "Let's do this again soon, mate," Rolf said. Paul shut the car door, stepping away with relief.

CHAPTER 5   SATURDAY

Paul was helping a patron when he saw Rolf come into the library. He concentrated on his task, but Rolf's presence was relentless, pawing through books, seemingly at random, glancing about, shifting position and repeating his doings. Excusing himself, Paul said, "I'll leave you to your research."

He returned to the reference desk to wait for Rolf's approach. Close by, Tim was talking with a high school student. She was asking about girls' sports, and Paul heard Tim's feeble answer. It was awkward, admitting he'd listened. Tim resented correction and intruding would lead to embarrassment, his own most of all. In his fine calculus of feelings, immediate action was impossible. He observed the young woman for a minute, walked over, and asked if she was finding what she needed. He suggested she try the U.S. Code nearby.

Tim was standing by the reference desk, ready with his remark. "You really wanted to check her out. I saw you watching her. The girls will get you in trouble someday."

"I was seeing if she needed help, that's all."

"She didn't. I gave her what she wanted."

While they spoke, Rolf had sidled to the reference desk. "You haven't got what she wants, mate," he said.

"What do you mean by that crack?" asked Tim, tilting back in amazement.

"A little chinwag, Paul?" asked Rolf, leaning against the chest-high counter. Aside to Tim he said, "Don't get your knickers in a knot. Meant no harm." He turned to Paul, "We both of us know you're a larrikin, so I'm thinking we go stickybeaking tonight."

"I don't know," demurred Paul.

"Sure, we'll have fun. I'll show you mine and you show me yours." Rolf winked at Tim. "Remember, I know a thing or two." Being obscurely threatened didn't make Paul happy, but, with Tim agog, he was grateful for Rolf's indirection. He nodded. "Okay, great," Rolf said. "I'll be round your place at nine tonight." Rolf turned. "Bye, matey," he said to Tim, and headed for the door.

"A strange creature," Tim said.

"He just puts it on for an audience."

Tim's face screwed up in bewilderment. Paul visualized the scattered pins of Tim's mental faculties. "What was he talking about?" Tim asked.

"He has feelings for me," he informed Tim, amusing himself.

A few minutes later the lights flashed. It was almost one o'clock and the library was closing.

Paul cycled home through the town cemetery. An old place, its chief tourist interest was the tomb of General Stonewall Jackson, famous lemon-eating oddball from the Civil War. The cemetery paths radiated from the General's statue and Paul zipped a circle around him, randomly venturing down the hill. The headstones on their hillside faced the hospital and rescue squad on the opposing hill. Not for the first time, Paul found the symmetry striking. On one side was the struggle to be born and to live, and on the other, the peace of death. Some of the cemetery occupants he knew. Some he recognized from genealogical research. The lives of others he re-created from their few carved words; the pathos of the infant's small headstone, the old woman outlasting those around her, always some variant of the thought that we live and fade like a ripple on a pond, or a lightening-bug flashing for its mate and gone. He imagined sleeping below, and others standing over him. Vastly better being the observer than the observed.

After lunch, Paul sat to re-read Jane Austin's 'Emma.' Through an uninterrupted Saturday afternoon and into early evening he joined the embrace of Jane's close community and the eternal awareness of her neighborly spies. He laid his book aside before eight o'clock and went outside to view the clouds turn red and purple and gray as the earth rotated him away from the sun. "Hello, Spook," he said. "Coming in?" and he and Spook went in for dinner.

As the hour approached 9:00, dressed in dark clothes, he fluttered about the room like a dull moth fearfully drawn to a bright exuberance. To calm his misgivings he settled in his armchair, endeavoring to observe his breathing and to still his mind, but he failed to divorce himself from the evening ahead and the tapping on his window came as a relief.

Rolf looked around the living room and was immediately insulting. "Dreary digs," he said.

Paul couldn't disagree. When he separated from Amanda, he had little cash and the cheap bits of furniture he'd purchased remained with him. "The overhead light's too dim," he said. "The apartment's better in the daylight. I've been thinking of looking for something better."

"You think too much," was Rolf's trenchant reply. "So, what are we up to tonight?"

"How about a game of chess?" Paul asked, contrite as he spoke. He was being superior, assuming Rolf couldn't play.

Rolf snorted, "Mate, I'd take you on, but not tonight. I've got a prime spot to show you. You pay me back with your favorite peep-show. What do you say?"

"Okay. Promise me you'll stay quiet and won't get us in trouble."

"I'll be as meek as a choirboy. And a lot quieter."

They discussed the logistics of their foray. Paul's offering began around 10:00, and Rolf's, half an hour later. With ample time, the two strolled out. They climbed Diamond Street to the higher parts of town and stopped at a park by the middle school to watch two young men toss a ball through a basketball hoop. "Two on two," called one of them.

Rolf scampered over, shouting back at Paul, "Come on man, we can take them." Paul ran over, willing to give his best. A constant walker and cyclist, he was fit, but his opponents were younger, taller, faster and better with the ball. Vanquished, to nobody's dissatisfaction, after half-an-hour Paul and Rolf parted from their momentary buddies, going around the block to Hart Lane. They pushed through a privacy hedge at the rear of a single-story house and sat on the grass under a beech tree, their backs against a wooden shed. One streetlight glowed dimly in the lane, its light screened by a large boxwood bush to their right. Had anyone opened the back door of the house, light spilling down the garden path to the shed might have revealed movement of theirs to an observer. If they were overheard, a neighbor with a flashlight might have picked them out over the wooden fence. All this Paul softly mentioned to Rolf.

"Right-o, mate," Rolf whispered back at his nervous friend. "I reckon we're as cozy as castled kings in this corner,"

The lights were off in both rooms at the rear of the house. To the left of the house, light shone on the narrow walkway running beside the fence.

"Anything happening?" asked Rolf of his guide.

"Hush. It will." The side window light disappeared, replaced by a hall light seen through the translucent glass in the back door. In turn, the room to their right was illuminated. Someone had moved from one room to another turning off lights as they went. Paul stood and reached to pull Rolf up. "It's better if we stand," he said. "Only be quiet. That's her bedroom. She's mostly punctual. A single lady of forty-three. Rita's her name. She bought this house four years ago, and I haven't seen any men friends. Sometimes the shade's up when she first comes to the bedroom, and I can tell you she's a fine looker with a great figure. Maybe she's shy. I'm sure she's lonely."

"You think if I knocked she'd have me in?" asked Rolf.

"Shhh!"

"But the shade's down. What are we supposed to see?"

"Patience," whispered Paul. "In a minute."

The bedroom light shone brightly through the lacy shade, illuminating blades of grass ten feet from the house but falling short of their shelter. Paul gripped Rolf's arm in anticipation as Rita came to stand before the window shade. In the sharpest of silhouettes, she pulled up and off her blouse, her hair falling back in profusion.

"What color's her hair," whispered Rolf.

"She's straw blonde, a mass of tight curls."

"Oh geez!" exhaled Rolf.

Bending, she removed her shoes. "What a pair of knockers," sighed Rolf.

Rita unhooked her skirt, unzipped it and stepped out of it. "That's her bed she's laying it on," Paul said. "She's between her bed and the window." Reaching behind, she unhooked her bra. Bending over, she placed it on the bed. Her breasts hung from her, and Rolf groaned. She stood on one leg, then the other, removing her panties. "She's naked now," Paul said softly. She picked up her nightgown, and one by one, her arms entered the sleeves. Upstretched, she let the nightgown slide over her breasts and envelop her body.

"Oh God, I'd like to touch her now," Rolf said. "Feel the cloth over her breasts and her nipples and stroke down to her belly. She'd like it too." Rita picked up her clothes from the bed, walked out of sight and turned off her light. Paul sat down. Rolf did likewise. "Wouldn't have believed it," Rolf said.

"Behind the shade? I know. It's frustrating."

"My dong's as hard as that tree," Rolf said. "It's painful."

"Funny world," whispered Paul. "We're in the dirt outside her window. She's getting in bed, not twenty feet from us, probably wants some man to touch her, and we're here, horny as toads." The two sat, contemplating the contrary ways of the universe.

A rustling came from the boxwood on the other side of the fence. Paul grabbed Rolf's arm. Two eyes glinted over the fence. "Time to scarper," Rolf said. As they leapt to their feet, a cat jumped from the fence, meowing at them. The large tabby rubbed against Paul's legs. It had one defective ear collapsed against its head from some misadventure of the night. "You gave us a fright, didn't you kitty," whispered Paul as he raked his fingers over the cat's arching back.

"We should go," Rolf said. Watched by the curious cat, Rolf led off in the direction of his Aunt Regina's house. "You haven't discovered anything spicy in Haven Lane?" Rolf asked anxiously.

"Don't think so." Paul's answer would have been the same whether he had or not.

The lights were out at Rolf's house as they passed. "They go to bed early and are up hours before me. We live in different time zones."

"No trouble with your being out late?" asked Paul.

"It's not said, but the nagging's there. I need to find a job and move out. Aunt Reggie's nice, but it's no fun living with parental-types." Paul agreed. For an instant, he thought of their finding an apartment or house together, but he backed from the thought as too audacious and troublesome.

"What I'm showing you," Rolf said, "reminds me of when I dumped school and went as a trainee with the telephone company in Sydney. One of their big customers was a chemical plant with thousands of phones. I'd trot around behind the technician, me not knowing what the hell I'm doing. Half our time was in the office, chatting up the receptionists. One of them wore real short skirts. Don't remember anything about her, just her legs and those skirts. They'd sit me down on a low bench by the wall. I'm short anyway, and she's forever swiveling around on her seat, talking, and I'm at her crotch level fixed on the playing field. She had white panties, always white. At sixteen you get erections from nothing at all, a bit of friction in your pants. Whenever she'd turn to me, I'd be up, and we'd go on like she was a ship chugging to and fro on the river and me the bridge that's lifting as she passes."

"Must have amused her."

"Suppose so. Women will just play with you."

At the bottom of the street, Haven Lane was directly below, but it lacked an easy way down. Following the street entailed a considerable detour so they dropped from the road into the brush and tall weeds. It was an unruly patch, ill lit, making for treacherous footing. Any slip would tumble them into thorny clumps of wild rose. Clutching in desperation at a bush to maintain his balance, Paul gasped, "Next time, let's take the road."

"Keep low and follow me. I've done this before." After a couple of minutes, they found their way to flat ground. Paul pulled the barbs from his hands and brushed the dirt from his pants. Like cautious deer at the forest's edge, keeping the rough hillside close beside them, they headed toward the secluded dead-end of the lane. Between the final two houses, they stopped at a lilac bush, turning with their backs to the bush and the street. The angle between the bush and the house was as black as any prowler's wish.

Five feet across and eight feet tall, the lilac had begun to bloom. The cloying fragrance spoke to Paul of spring's past and found its route to a place of happy memory. He was in a fine, big park, not far from his home, with fields and flowerbeds and a stand of trees. The park was, at his age, a woodland of vast expanse. The leaves, acorns, moss, insects, squirrels, birds, and trees were all that heaven needs. To his later shame, he delighted in hunting birds' eggs. How lovely, those robins' eggs. Blue as the morning sky, merged with the ocean's green--a miniature world resting in a straw bowl--perfection enough for a boy. He'd cradle the exquisite eggs home, poke each end with a pin and suck out their contents. He needed an older boy to correct his method, advising him to blow instead.

"Wake up," Rolf said, nudging him. "The show starts soon."

"Which house is it?"

"That one," Rolf said, pointing to their left.

"What's the street number?"

"How's that to anything?" responded Rolf testily.

Paul walked to the street and checked the mailbox. Returning he said, "I know who lives there."

"You'll really know her soon."

"It's the Hopewells. Your uncle Seth's brother. He's with the police department. She's a nurse at the hospital. Am I right?"

"So? They're not blood relatives of mine. It's not like she's my mother."

"What's the situation, then?" asked Paul.

"When Sergeant Hopewell's on duty and she's home, they're at it by 10:30. He gets off work at midnight, but they're done well before then."

"Who are? With what?"

"You be patient now," gloated Rolf. "Quiet," he whispered. "We're a few feet from him, and he'll hear us. Though not when it gets noisy." He chortled at his obscure joke.

Each of the houses had a rear glass sunroom. A light came on in the sunroom to their left. "Here we go," breathed Rolf. A tall, slender woman in her mid-thirties came into view, her long dark hair gathered by a blue scarf at the nape of her neck. "Her name's Celia," whispered Rolf. She was naked, carrying a cello. Her left hand grasped its neck, and the fingers of her right hand balanced the "C" of the cellos' mid-section. She stopped in front of a chair, turned to face her house, swung the cello out from her body and sat, spreading her legs. Her spectators had no trouble discovering her dark pubic hair, or her perfect white breasts that, while not large, were generous on her slim body. The cello swung back between her thighs. It had no spike. Celia held and supported it between her legs. The fingers of her left hand positioned over the strings, her right wrist arched over her bow, and she began playing a mournful, dreamy nocturne at a moderate volume.

"She's talented," Paul said.

"Loaded with it," agreed Rolf.

Fascinated, Paul observed her beautifully defined muscles. Her left hand vibrated the strings against the fingerboard, transferring motion to the muscle and fat of her upper arm. The sinews of her forearm tensed and released as her fingers played over the strings. He moved up her arm, gliding over the ripples of fat between skin and biceps to where the light shone on the flawlessly rounded ball of her shoulder. He was enamored with the form and functionality of that arm. Playing high on the fingerboard, she revealed a dark patch of underarm hair. It was endearing, as if he was privy to a small, but shameful, idiosyncrasy of hers.

"Don't you adore those perky tits?" sighed Rolf. "What we can see of them." Celia leaned forward with her ear close to her cello's neck and their view of her chest was blocked, but when she sat erect, her left breast became visible. "I'd love to eat them," moaned Rolf. "It's like some dessert-chef made them." Paul saw his point; a delightful pink nipple arranged in its pale brown aureole, set in milky flesh.

"Someone's smoking," Paul said, detecting the unpleasant, acrid smell of cigarette smoke.

"That's lover-boy. Move to your left and you'll see him."

Paul did, seeing the glowing red tip of a cigarette in the sunroom to his right. He stepped back beside Rolf. "You mean she's doing this for him?"

"You got it. She plays, and he watches. The perfect pair. The lucky bugger's got the best view of her boobies."

Paul mentally stroked her long leg from knee to buttocks and caressed her side, into her waist, over her ribcage to her underarm, touching the hair under her arm. Celia played pizzicato, smiling as she plucked the strings, seemingly happy.

A car sped down the lane and shuddered to a stop. Car doors slammed. Someone called, "Look around back."

The music stopped. Rolf whispered urgently, "Sounds like trouble." Looking around the bush he said, "Bloody-hell! It's hubby. Best nick off mate, or we're mincemeat." He took off, running past the sunrooms toward the dark hill.

"There he is." Then a second voice called, "There are two of them." Paul had been spotted, chasing after Rolf. As he sprinted past the sunroom, Paul glimpsed Celia entering the main part of the house with her cello. He was glad she'd made a decent exit.

"Police …stop … or I'll shoot," was shouted. Paul and Rolf zigzagged the last few feet before the hill. Paul imagined himself shot and simmering in a cooking pot. No shots came, and they disappeared like rabbits into a briar patch.

Dispatch had received a call from an elderly lady on Haven Lane who reported what she thought were prowlers. Sergeant Brian Hopewell and Officer Simon Pruett gave little credence to the hesitant caller, but it was Brian's street, and they were motivated to be quick, the attempted rapist from a couple of nights before was still uncaught. Parking tickets, drunk and disorderly, and domestic altercations offered little excitement compared with chasing real criminals. The officers rushed to the hillside to capture these malefactors.

Paul and Rolf slithered to the left, from one bush to another, scraping and banging themselves. Rolf spooned against Paul as they squeezed under a bush, panting, listening to the direction of pursuit. They heard thrashing in the bushes and saw the beams of flashlights, but the police had chosen, for now, to head straight up the hill. "Let's cut back to the street," suggested Paul.

"Too risky. We'd be seen if reinforcements come."

"Okay. Keep angling up the slope," whispered Paul. "I know where to go if we get past the hill."

Wriggling along the ground was too slow. More police arriving would surround them. Sliding out of their shelter, they scrambled as quietly and speedily as they could over the roots and through the scrubland. Low amongst the bushes, in darkness like burrowing blind mole rats, Paul ate the dirt kicked up by Rolf above him, but he needed that contact with his friend. He even had the wild notion that capturing the debris in his mouth would stop it screeing down the slope and revealing their path.

Paul reached up and grabbed Rolf's leg. They both froze. The flailing to their right came closer. A flashlight's beam passed over them. "Anything yet?" called a distant voice.

"Nothing," said the nearby officer. "I'll head this way and flush 'em to you if they're here." Paul recognized the voice of Officer Pruett. He was just above and to the right of them. While Officer Pruett scanned the distance with his light they were undetected, but in a moment, he would swing his beam down and see them. Paul fervently desired to be unseen. Reluctantly, he left his sheltering bush and scrambled up the slope to tackle Officer Pruett about the legs. As if in consort, Rolf, more at the officer's level on the hill, lunged out and shoved him in the chest. Officer Pruett lost his footing on the steep slope, fell against and over Paul's crouching form and tumbled hard down the slope. His momentum absorbed by a thicket of bramble bushes, he screamed in pain.

"What happened?" shouted his partner.

"I'm down. I'm caught by these damn thorns. I've lost my gun. Come quick!"

While Officer Pruett fought to detach himself from the painful tangle of razor barbs that dug into his uniform and skin, his partner thundered toward him like a rhino. Paul and Rolf abandoned guile. Opting for agility, they raced up the hill like a pair of monkeys, gaining confidence and speed as the pale light from the street above allowed them to see more of their way. Near the top, Paul came even with Rolf, panting out, "Stay down off the street. Follow me." They continued to force their way through the bushes ten feet below and parallel with the street. The brush thinned and eventually became scrubby grass, the ground sloping to a storm drain. Running down and up on the other side of the culvert they heard a siren on the road above, but no pursuit threatened. They followed a gentler up-hill slope to the backs of houses and walked out on the street.

"Whoopee! Now that was something," exulted Rolf.

"Hush," pleaded Paul. "We don't want to be seen or heard. Policemen threatening to shoot us is totally not fun."

"Where to now?"

"My ex is on the next street. They're away and I've got a key to their house. She lives there with her partner, Susan."

"Ouch!" commiserated Rolf. "Hard to compete with breasts."

They walked around the corner to Wilmer Road where Amanda and Susan lived in their old two-story brick house. Any passing car, Paul vowed to treat as hostile. He evaluated his escape as they approached each house, calculating where he'd dive and hide, slowing by dense hedges and low brick walls, speeding up past exposed rail fences. Likely, they couldn't be identified, but two young men, scratched and dirty, were more than suspicious and separating could be advantageous. No cars came, and their passage went unnoticed.

Amanda and Susan had left on Thursday for Susan's teachers' conference and would return Sunday evening. In their absence, as usual, Amanda wanted Paul to look in on Susan's cats, though she hadn't asked, just informed him they'd be gone and the cats expected him. The Siamese, like an ex-wife, was a whiner. The ginger cat had a perpetual grudge and, much like an ex-wife, didn't mind using her claws. They needed little attention, going as they pleased through their own cat-door in the side door of the house, but Amanda appreciated the removal of rabbit, bird and mice remains. One time, she'd stepped into the downstairs bathroom, turned on the light and found at her feet an eviscerated rabbit, dark blood, innards and feces spread across the floor. The rabbit, in her telling, was larger than her cats. Now and then, Paul thought himself into the mind of that poor rabbit, traumatized in the cat door, one cat pulling from inside and the other shoving from outside.

"We can clean up and wait for the excitement to die away," Paul said, "but we shouldn't stay long." He opened the side door and they walked through the laundry room into the kitchen. He topped-up the water bowl and checked about for kidneys, feathers or bloody fur, finding none. The cats had come into the kitchen from the living-room couch, rubbing against Paul, vociferous for their treats. From a bag in the pantry, Paul was permitted to give each cat six little crunchy treats a day.

Rolf looked at the baskets arrayed on top of the cupboards and the copper pots hanging above the island in the kitchen. "You can really tell they're dykes, can't you."

"Not me, apparently. Amanda had the same stuff when I married her."

Investigating the refrigerator, Rolf pulled out a bottle of beer. "This is a bit of alright. Want one?"

"I don't think you should," Paul said. He urged himself to loosen up, but it was counsel he knew he'd disregard.

"She got them all counted?"

"Wouldn't surprise me," Paul responded morosely.

Rolf twisted off the cap and slugged back the beer with evident relish. Checking the refrigerator again, he said, "I'm peckish. There's sandwich makings. Some mayo and roast-beef slices. I'll make you one."

Paul did feel in need of an energy boost. "I'll make a peanut-butter sandwich when I get back." Taking the paper-towel roll from the kitchen, he went to the bathroom, wiped the dirt from his clothes and scrubbed his hands and face. By the time he returned, Rolf had made him a peanut-butter sandwich. The dirt on Rolf's hands made Paul wish he hadn't. "Thanks," he said.

"No problem, mate." Rolf carried his sandwich off to the bathroom, and Paul cleaned away the evidence of their presence. He sat between the sleeping cats on the couch to finish his sandwich. Rolf returned, less scruffy, though, Paul was certain, nothing that Amanda wanted on her living-room carpet. Rolf whisked to the far corner of the room, opened the glass cabinet and picked out a figurine, tossing it from hand to hand.

"Be careful," begged Paul.

Rolf immediately dropped it, catching the statuette before it struck the floor. "Just teasing," he grinned. He took a better look. "Ugly, isn't it. A gnome singing from a book." Poking further, he said, "And here's one with two girl pixies. You know they belong to lesbos."

"They're mine," Paul said. "Those are Tom Clark gnomes. I used to collect them. There are several more in the cabinet. When we split, Amanda thought they'd be safer with her."

Rolf made a "tsk" noise. Paul couldn't tell if that was disapproval of gnomes, Amanda, or him. Having ample self-disapproval, he didn't need Rolf's augmentation. "Best off away from her is my thought," Rolf said.

"Jury's still out. Haven't made much of my opportunity so far," Paul replied pensively.

A great fidgeter, Rolf prowled into the TV room, picking up and examining books, ornaments and pictures. Paul trailed him. Rolf held up a framed photograph. "This them?"

"That's Amanda on the left, Susan on the right."

"She's a knock-out," Rolf said. Paul assumed he meant Susan. An oval-faced redhead with perfectly regular features, she was undeniably cute. Dressed in a school uniform she'd look no older than sixteen. He was sure that appealed to Rolf. He didn't find it unappealing himself. Amanda was more butch looking, attractive, but in a robust way.

He would have been more alert to Rolf's intrusions had he been less distracted, mulling the remnants of his relationship with Amanda. On that, as usual, he came to no conclusion, other than wishing his ex lived in some other town. Rolf was leaping up the steps, two at a time. "Don't go upstairs," Paul protested.

Disappearing on the landing above, Rolf called down, "When do I get to perv on the lives of two lesbians?" He turned the lights on upstairs, and Paul hurried after him.

Rolf had wandered into the main bedroom, a room dominated by the large bed that had been Paul and Amanda's marital bed. It was Amanda's choice. He'd suggested that the heavy-timbered frame and extra tall king-sized mattress overwhelmed the small bedroom in their old apartment, but Amanda liked the spacious bed, saying that she flailed around in the night and needed plenty of separation. The bed was better accommodated in this larger room. Rolf sat at the dressing table tugging at his hair with a silver hairbrush. "I'm a mess," he laughed. With his bruised cheek and plentiful scratches, he looked like a rat-king who'd fought for supremacy of the pack.

"You took the worst of the bushes leading us up the hill. Thanks," Paul said.

"Any time," Rolf modestly replied. He adjusted potions and lotions on the dressing table and picked up a perfume bottle, spraying it into the air. Rising, he sniffed and gulped at the particles. "Yummy, that's good. Very female."

"Let's not shift anything around. I'll get in trouble with Amanda. We shouldn't be up here."

"Not terribly consistent. We'll perv on women, but not on their stuff."

"I guess you're right. Only, don't disturb things."

Rolf went to the chest of drawers, picked up a picture in both hands, held it at arm's length and examined Susan in her sleeveless white summer dress. She smiled from the picture, her golden tan reflecting the sun. "Oh my! Her bod and that perfume are stirring me up." Rolf brought her to his lips and kissed her face.

Paul was amused at his antics. "She wouldn't be at all interested in you."

"I know, but something kinky about that." He put the picture back on the chest of drawers, opened the top drawer and rummaged in its contents, picking up panties and sniffing them. He rubbed a pair of stockings over his face, murmuring, "Hmmm," lasciviously. "Feels lovely." Opening the drawer below, he said, "Even better, much prettier." He held up a small, white lacy bra that Paul knew would belong to Susan. Pretending to wear it, he turned coquettishly to Paul. "Wouldn't it be fun to dress up?" Paul frowned at him. "Some other time," Rolf said. Investigating further, he pulled out a gray, silky-looking pair of panties, stroked his face and moaned as he rubbed it over his lips. He unzipped his trousers, pushed down his underwear and held his penis.

Paul was shocked. Other than a dog dragging itself on a carpet, if that counted, he'd never seen anyone masturbating. He'd done it himself, of course, but he'd never cared to look, and didn't care to now. With sharp distress, he remembered his invitation by the high school in-crowd to a party that turned into a masturbation event. They crowded into a bedroom and sat on the floor, each with a wad of tissues. When the lights went out, their zippers came down. Groaning and moaning, one by one the guys yelled they were coming, until, unable to contain his pleasure, he yelled out. The lights came on and everyone watched him squirt into his tissues. Looking around at the snickering crowd, he saw that nobody else had done anything, that he was the party joke.

Rolf had finished. An onset of weakness had him supporting himself with his right hand on the chest of drawers. His left hand cradled his penis in its silk nest. "Phew! That was great." Grinning at Paul, he said, "I'd have dumped you for her, too." Paul didn't find himself annoyed, rather he was pleased to have finally become one of the guys. Rolf folded the panties inside out, encasing his ejaculation. He wiped himself with the padded crotch area. "Should I put them back in the drawer?" he asked.

"We'll take them with us. They won't miss one pair," Paul said, entertained, if a little uneasy. Rolf went to the bathroom to finish cleaning himself and Paul stood back against the wall contemplating the bed. He felt a sexual tension within himself. There hadn't been much sex when he and Amanda occupied that bed, and, thinking so, brought back the last time he'd experienced sex there, indirectly, summertime, five years earlier.

It was Saturday morning, and he'd gone into work, but a scheduling error had two librarians on at the same time, so he worked for a couple of hours and came home. Amanda was out. She'd gone to the mall, a forty-minute drive away, and wasn't planning to return until around 1:00. For a while, he'd been meaning to weed through clothes he never wore and make a Goodwill bag. Around 11:00, he was in the small walk-in closet in the bedroom, tossing shirts on the floor, when he heard Amanda come into the apartment, laughing and chatting with someone. When Amanda said, "Paul won't be home for a couple of hours, we're alone, with only ourselves to please," he followed some instinct, and, instead of calling to her, he turned off the closet light and slid the door. The pocket door was six inches open when Amanda came into the bedroom with her friend Susan.

He reproached himself for a fool. In front of Susan, how could he explain being in a dark closet? In trepidation he watched, hopeful Amanda would show her purchases and leave. Visualizing the scene if Amanda came to hang them in the closet, sweat started from his skin.

"That was fun," Amanda said. "I'm glad you asked me to go. We should get together more often. You're great with colors. Paul's like some useless glum ox in a store, and I think he's color blind."

"I'm sorry if I cut your fun short, suggesting we come back," Susan said.

"No. Coming home for coffee and lunch is great. We can talk and be cozier than in a mall cafeteria."

"So, how are you and Paul getting along? It's been weeks, but the last time we talked things weren't so hot."

The question added misery to his shame. He was frustrated at times, with both Amanda and himself, but he hadn't known they were unhappy.

"I can't seem to tell him." Amanda said gloomily. "It'd be like kicking a faithful dog and seeing its hurt look. He's a good person, but he thinks before he acts, won't do things spontaneously. I've given up changing him. We're basically not a good match."

"And the sex?" asked Susan.

"It's a dud. My fault really, I can't get any enthusiasm. And at my age! What will I be like when I'm forty? I need excitement, and dear Paul is just quietly dull."

Quietly he sat on his pile of shirts, tears gently dripping off his nose, which, in his closeted circumstance, was the greatest exuberance allowed his sorrows. Always, he thought of honesty as a guiding principle, but this was an excess of truth and too suddenly imparted. He wiped the back of his bare left arm over his face to clear moisture from his eyes. In a blurry fashion, he looked at Amanda and Susan sitting on the end of the bed.

"So how's romance for you?" asked Amanda.

"Some dates, but no sparks."

"They should be flocking. You're so beautiful. Your red hair is gorgeous." She ran a hand down Susan's hair following it to where it turned wavy on her shoulders.

"Thanks. Your short haircut is cute, too."

"Should I try on the blouse?"

"Yes, do," Susan said. Amanda pulled a shiny dark green shirt from her shopping bag and held it before her. "It would look great with a push-up bra," Susan suggested.

"I'll try that." Amanda slid from the bed and opened her underwear drawer. The bedroom didn't have space to fully open the drawer while standing between the dresser and the bed, so Amanda fished around at the back until she found it. Susan had unbuttoned the new blouse and laid it on the bed. Amanda pulled her top over her head and stood before them in her purple bra.

"A Victoria's Secret bra, isn't it? I wish my boobs were that stunning. Mine are so tiny."

"Oh, no, yours are perfect. Everyone must notice you don't have a bra on, yours stand out so firmly." She smiled at Susan. "When I'm fifty, mine will be drooping on the ground and yours will still be pointing upwards."

"Nonsense. Anyway, now's now." Scooting over on the bed to kneel behind Amanda, she said, "I'll give you a hand." She unhooked the bra and rubbed Amanda's shoulders.

"That feels so good," Amanda murmured. She leaned back against the bed, shrugging out of her bra.

"You must be tense."

Watching them, he thought how warm two women could be together, natural and easy, as he never seemed to be. He had absorbed the first blow of Amanda's judgment. A prisoner shocked by the verdict, he dully accepted that life for him must change.

Amanda groaned as Susan kneaded her shoulders. She leaned forward, her breasts hanging down. An arresting picture that he kneeled to watch. Susan ran her palms in slow circular motions up Amanda's back, over her shoulders and down her sides. Amanda mewled at the soothing touch. Sliding her hands up Amanda's sides, Susan cupped each breast and her fingers extended to caress the nipples. His breath held at the eroticism of it. Amanda, too, was still. He waited for the shrug that would send Susan's hands away. Instead, Amanda slowly turned. Susan's hands traveled over Amanda's skin, not leaving her body. The girls faced each other. Still kneeling on the bed, Susan gripped onto Amanda who leaned toward her, burying her face in the cascade of Susan's hair. "Don't stop," she mumbled into Susan's shoulder.

He had lost his future, and now, in a nightmare of watchfulness, must suffer his wife's seduction. To thrust the closet door open would reveal the absurd cuckold and unforgivably assail their privacy. He did nothing but look, hoping for a quick end to his torment.

Unbuttoning her yellow dress, Susan tossed it to the edge of the bed, pulled off her sandals and threw them on the floor. Amanda pulled down her black skirt, bent to take off her shoes and climbed onto the bed. Each girl wore only white panties. Helplessly he watched Susan. How could a man look at her lithe, pliant body and not feel pleasure? And he was to understand that Amanda felt that same way? They came together kneeling on the bed, each kissing the other's face, fresh as two daffodils swaying and touching together. On Amanda's face a look of wondrous discovery, of a joy he supposed she had never known with him. It was more than enough. Curling down on his bed of discarded shirts, he clasped his hands over his ears and any moans that escaped his cocoon were drowned by the sounds of enjoyment given up by the girls.

"What are you up to?" asked Rolf. "I go to the toilet for a minute, and you've turned into a mealybug."

Paul found himself sitting on the floor with his knees against his chest and his arms gripped around his legs. He relaxed with a sigh. "Just dreaming, Rolf. Not too pleasantly."

"What's the point of daydreaming if it's not about half-naked women getting fully naked?"

"True enough," Paul said, standing up. "I need to mend my daydreams. But let's move, before the neighbors get nosy."

Paul checked the downstairs bathroom and decided it needed cleaning. Rolf wandered off but soon returned, shouting over the noise of the vacuum cleaner, "Someone's bashing on the front door."

"I'll go," Paul said. "If there's trouble, you hide. I don't want us seen together."

Opening the front door, Paul stood before Officer Pruett. "Mr. Paul Kirk, isn't it? We meet again."

"That's right. Sorry if I kept you. I was vacuuming and didn't hear the door for a while."

"You usually vacuum at 11:30 at night?"

"No, officer. The cats made a mess on the floor and I was cleaning up. Can I help you?"

"We've had a report of lights on in the house and people moving around, but the occupants are away, so we're told. Been other disturbances in the area tonight, so I'm checking into it. You're not away, though, I see."

"I don't live here. This is my ex-wife's house, Amanda Paris and her partner. They're out of town until tomorrow evening, so I'm looking after their cats."

"An odd time to feed cats, isn't it, sir?"

"That's true. I was at home and realized I'd forgotten to come by earlier."

"I see. Are you alone?"

Paul hesitated. "The cats are here, too."

"Where did you get the scratches on your face, if you don't mind my asking?"

Paul felt his face. Officer Pruett stood directly under the harsh porch light with dried blood streaked from his left ear to his jaw. His jowly cheeks were pocked red by briar thorns. Would an innocent citizen comment, 'You're in a worse state than me,' or suppress that observation? Deciding to stay clear of the topic, he answered Officer Pruett's question. "Cycling through the cemetery. My tire hit something and I tumbled over the handlebars. Landed face-first in the gravel." He was impressed at how easily that piece of mendacity came to him.

"The cemetery residents playing a trick on you," said Officer Pruett, smiling ghoulishly. "We remember your help at Mrs. Brazier's last week, so no suspicion, but, so I can write my report, do you object to my looking around?"

Having no choice, Paul said, "Of course not," fearful that Rolf would bring disaster.

Officer Pruett checked each room downstairs and clumped upstairs with Paul trailing behind. He opened a few closets, declared himself satisfied and prepared to leave. "Better if there's no more noise tonight."

"I'll put the vacuum away and go," Paul assured him.

"Goodnight, sir."

Relieved to have no more trouble, Paul watched Officer Pruett get into his car and drive away. Closing the door he called, "Rolf?" Wandering back to the kitchen he continued calling until he found Rolf, grinning, poking his head out of a tall basket in the laundry room.

"An ingenious hiding place," Paul said, laughing at Rolf who, doubtless for the effect, had surfaced with a pair of panties on top of his head.

"Lots of interesting smells down there," Rolf reported.

CHAPTER 6   SUNDAY

The church rituals, Paul hoped, would be soothing and enable him to think on his troubles. Being a jot away from jail and humiliation was no foundation for a rational life.

The day was sunny and crisp, the trees in blossom, the sky with a few high clouds. Cycling the streets of Lexington on such a spring morning contrasted agreeably with his evening commotion. But a life without peaks and valleys is a world that's flat and gray; in a decade, would he remember his tumultuous evening with Rolf or his morning at church? He was confident he knew the answer.

His arrival timed for a few minutes before church began, he entered, nodding to the robed choir members gathering in the vestibule. Making his way down the center aisle, he saw that the post-Easter congregation was small in number. He preferred not being crowded in the pew. When it came to the part of the Episcopal service that he disliked, the passing of the peace, he was happiest with nobody around him to offer their hand and wish him, 'Peace,' and expect likewise from him. He had little talent for society and forced conviviality was especially uncongenial.

Attracted by its sparse population, he walked to the front of the church, selected the third row on the left and sat beside the center aisle. Having barricaded his pew against incursion, he composed himself before the service began. The organist played the prelude, the sound of which, as he'd told Pat, might improve with the carpet's removal, but then, it could be the old organist that needed removing. He 'tsked' at his uncharitable thought. The cool, dim atmosphere, the stained-glass windows, the dark-timbered vaulted ceiling, the vast range of the organ filling the cavernous space, all combined to an other-worldliness conducive, he hoped, to soul searching. He did wish the ceiling lights, with their long pendulous light-shades rounding to a point, were not so phallic, and trusted he wasn't the only one to find them so.

The choir and officiants processed to the opening hymn. Prayer, Gloria, prayer, each flowed about him as the hum of nectar-laden bees on a summer morn. The congregation rose and descended. The light, sloping through the stained glass, thinned and colored as the clouds obscured or revealed the sun. Only partly aware of the motion about him, he achieved some serenity. "I will reform myself," he thought, feeling that Buddhism's unattached philosophy should be his guide.

The elderly lay-reader walked to the lectern, placed her finger at the beginning of her passage, cleared her throat and began, "The reading for today is from the First Letter of Peter, Chapter three, Verses eight to eighteen. 'Finally, all of you, have unity of spirit, sympathy, love of the brethren, a tender heart....'" Too far from the microphone, her voice droned. Paul's attention was, in the main, diffuse, but some words burrowed into receptive ground. "'Let him turn away from evil and do right; let him seek peace and pursue it.'" I will seek peace, he determined. He thought of King David. How he spied the loveliness of Bathsheba from the vantage of his roof; how he sent for her and lay with her. 'Lucky devil,' was his instant thought. Wrestling with himself, he imagined placidly looking on Bathsheba and her beauty. Taking pleasure in the sight, but remaining composed, unflustered, turning from her to pursue his daily round without clinging to thoughts of her. He approved of the notion, but it was confusing, as theoretically he approved of passion, not thwarted, but running free, as it were, to the sea.

Hearing movement behind him, he glanced to the right. Ten minutes into the service, latecomers would normally tiptoe into seats at the rear of the church, but two ladies progressed toward him along the center aisle. One was Mrs. Stickley, who lived on Borden Road. She was heading to her accustomed pew. Without conspicuous attention, he couldn't turn again to examine her companion. Surreptitiously, he watched as they came almost even with him. Mrs. Stickley stumbled, cried out, and would have fallen had Paul's arm not been thrust out to steady her, and Paul himself, standing before her a second later, been able to support her.

"Oh, my ankle," she moaned.

The reading halted. The congregation focused on this interesting misadventure. Had he been conscious of those many eyes, Paul's functioning would have been impaired, but, oblivious, he helped Mrs. Stickley to her second-row pew. He turned, then, to the lady standing erect in the aisle. A folded white cane hung from her right arm. "Allow me," he said, stepping from the pew. He touched her left arm, suggesting that she sit. Old Doc Haverson had come down the side aisle to sit beside Mrs. Stickley. Relieved of responsibility, Paul returned to his place across the aisle. The reading resumed. After a few moments, deciding that nothing needed doing with the injury, or that nothing could be done with Mrs. Stickley, the doctor retired to his seat.

In cogitating on such a disturbing event, Paul would normally have disappeared into himself, and certainly the music, song and chant that solaces the soul was nothing to him now, but not because he dwelt inwardly. A hunger to capture her every line devoured him. Like an intrepid adventurer, who one last time looks on his loved one's treasured face and figure, he memorized each feature, fault and plane. She was a dignified woman, a Penelope, scanning for her unseen Odysseus. When not leaning toward Mrs. Stickley, commiserating with her, she sat erect. Paul rotated his body a few degrees until he was looking across the aisle, nearly full on her profile. She would never see his attention. No glance of anger, irritation or amusement would come from her, inquiring as to his right to look. There was something Grecian about her olive skin, her broad full mouth, those dark eyebrows and her black lustrous hair. She wasn't slender or stocky but shaped in a compact form. About his own age, he conjectured. When others stood to sing, she sat, perhaps in deference to her companion, unable to stand. He, too, sat unmoving, hardly blinking, pleased when he detected her smile, or when, to track a sound, her face turned toward him. All through the priest's sermon, she sat attentive, while he heard not a word.

The priest said "The Peace of the Lord be always with you," and the people responded, "And also with you." Several came to gather about the second row, offering their peace and their sympathy for her injury to Mrs. Stickley and companion. As the small group receded in the seconds before the service resumed, Paul thought of striding to her, and softly, close to her ear, offering his peace to her. He didn't, but it did seem that she looked, encouraging him. Had he done so, she would have given him her hand. 'Consistency is the hobgoblin of little minds,' he thought, in mild self-loathing. If he objected to this enforced group hug, was it reasonable to object when it gained what he desired?

At communion, he wondered if she would go to the altar or stay and have the bread and chalice brought to her. The usher came to her row. Paul watched Mrs. Stickley speak to her. With her white cane extended, she rose and stepped into the aisle. Released to stand, Paul moved beside her. "May I help?" he bravely asked.

"Thank you," she said.

He was ennobled by her words. A knight in the lists so favored by his lady, empowered to battle for her, would go forward with no more joyful heart than Paul then possessed. He crooked his arm, touched it to hers, and she placed her hand on his forearm to be led. Approaching the chancel steps that led to the altar rail, he whispered, "Two steps up." He canvassed her large brown eyes, her long black lashes. Even her slightly bigish nose was a picture of loveliness. Her plain brown dress, cinched at the waist, showed off her figure, and the neckline over her full breasts offered a little cleavage. Unaware of the top step, he lurched badly, pulling her forward. Instantly, his arm crossed to her waist, steadying her. "I'm so sorry," he whispered in embarrassment.

She chuckled and whispered back, "Concentrate." Remorseful, Paul guided her to the railing. As they knelt together at the altar, he busily puzzled on their path. Normally the traffic flowed back by the side aisles, but Mrs. Stickley was an impediment in her pew. He must boldly make a way for his companion through the lines of waiting parishioners in the center aisle. After they received their communion he touched his arm to hers, escorting her through the waiting lines, saying, "Excuse me, excuse me," until she was safely returned. He crossed to his pew, proud to have accomplished his deed and feeling wonderfully useful.

With the lines of communicants served, the priest and deacon descended from the chancel, offering communion to those unable to reach the front. The priest gave a wafer to Mrs. Stickley, the deacon held the chalice to her. Dipping her wafer, she ate it. All that remained of that memorable service was the post communion prayer, the blessing and the dismissal. His lady stood for these, as he did, and then sat, as he did. The organist played a postlude, and the people noisily crowded to the exit.

"Young man," called Mrs. Stickley. "Young man," she called again before Paul realized she wanted him. He jumped up and went to her pew. "Assist us, if you please," she said.

"Of course," Paul said, glad to help, especially with the church emptying.

"Bronwyn, let this nice young man help me to my feet." Bronwyn moved from the pew. He sat on her vacated seat, aware of its warmth, of the heat transferring from her body into his. "What is your name?" asked Mrs. Stickley.

"It's Paul."

"Paul, you were heaven-sent for catching me. I spoke to the warden only yesterday about the simply shameful state of these carpets. 'Frayed and disreputable,' I said. No wonder anyone would trip."

"If the carpet was removed, the acoustics would be better," offered Paul, venturing some conversation.

"Nonsense! Think of us older folk falling and breaking a hip. Bad as these carpets are, they're softer than the bare floor." Unable to counter her argument, he held out his arm, and Mrs. Stickley pulled herself upright. "I'm fine," she said, holding onto the pew in front of her. "Go and help Bronwyn. I'll be there in a moment for you to give us an arm each."

Paul moved into the aisle, doubtful his arm was truly wanted by Bronwyn and, if so, which one and how to communicate his hesitation. She smiled at him. As if divining his uncertainty, she said, "Give me your right arm. We'll leave my aunt your left." So directed, he escorted the ladies out of the church to the closing notes of the organ.

Exiting the dimly lit church, blinking in the noon sunshine, Paul reported to Bronwyn, "Five steps down."

"Thanks, Paul."

"Help me to a seat and we'll stay for the coffee hour," said Mrs. Stickley.

"Don't worry about me," Bronwyn said. She unfolded her cane and made her way down the steps. Paul stiffened his arm for Mrs. Stickley to hold. They slowly descended the gray stone steps to the flagstone patio, making for the iron bench-seat.

A heavy woman, in her mid-sixties, Mrs. Stickley wheezed with exertion. Her ankle looked normal, and she appeared not to be in pain, but she leaned forcefully on him. When he had her seated, Mrs. Stickley suggested he sit. Deficient in conversation, he normally avoided these communal gatherings, but sitting with her aunt and learning something about Bronwyn was advantageous. Had he been tempted to approach Bronwyn he would only have stood invisible outside her happy circle.

"I'm Josie Stickley, by the way."

"Paul Kirk," he replied. "I know it's been a few months since I saw it in the News Gazette, but my condolences on the passing of your sister."

"Why thank you! Think of you being interested in obituaries and remembering that! Phyllis was my younger sister and quite the eccentric. She was diagnosed one month and, a shock to everyone, we buried her the next."

"I'm sorry," Paul said politely.

"An aggressive cancer they said, though everyone knows these doctors are better at detecting things after events."

"Is Bronwyn her daughter?"

"She's my brother Robert's child. Phyllis never married. She left her house to Bronwyn, which is why Bronwyn's come to Lexington. What a pair they were," she said, sighing. "The summers Bronwyn was here as a girl, I was forever mending the trouble she and Phyllis got into. You wouldn't believe it, but the caretaker at the cemetery threatened to have the City Council ban them. Chased them half way down Main Street for leapfrogging his headstones. But that was Phyllis. Just loved cemeteries. Soon enough, in my view, without going voluntarily. I had an earful from Rita Phelps, who's gone to join her husband there now, bless her soul. Spitting mad she was over the girls hiding Easter eggs around the tombstones in July. Called it disrespectful. And Phyllis was in her forties then!"

"I see," Paul said.

"You're not a frequent attender at church?"

"I'm afraid not."

"You need the right motivation. If you'd as many years as I in which to sin and as few left, you'd be more eager to make friends with heaven. Then there's my niece, you'll find her at church every Sunday, although she's more sinned against."

"Her blindness, you mean?"

"She's adjusted well, but it's a blessing I'm able to help her."

"I'm sure she's grateful."

"She is an exceptionally good child."

"May I ask how Bronwyn lost her sight?"

"It was her last year of college. Too much studying late at night is my belief. Very tragic in such a young person." While conversing with her aunt, he watched Bronwyn when he politely could, noting her happiness, chatting with those seeking her acquaintance, not the model of her aunt's tragic picture.

"Would you mind getting me a glass of lemonade? The sun is strong today."

"Of course," he said, leaping to his feet.

Heading to the lemonade table, he passed behind Bronwyn. She turned and asked, "Paul?"

"That's amazing. How did you know?"

Smiling at his bemusement, she said, "Trade secret. I also do card tricks. Can you join us?"

"No. I'm on a mission for your aunt. Would you like a glass of lemonade?"

"Yes, please."

He returned swiftly with the lemonades and heard the Junior Warden say to Bronwyn, "I was appointed the task of organizing the church picnic. My committee and I chose Lake Robinson for next Saturday. Might I perhaps invite you to come? I'd be extremely happy to bring you."

Paul interposed, "Your drink," before Bronwyn could respond. Bronwyn turned and thanked him. He carefully placed the plastic tumbler in her hands, watchful not to touch his skin to hers, lest she think him presumptuous.

She sipped her drink and said, "You'd better go to my aunt." Paul agreed, regretfully leaving her to John Wardle's question.

"Here you are," Paul said, handing the drink to Mrs. Stickley, who gulped it thirstily.

"I saw you talking to my niece. A charming girl, isn't she?"

"Yes, indeed."

"There's quite a group around her. She's only been here two weeks. It's good that she's getting to know people."

"And how are you doing, Josie?" asked the rector, ambling toward them. Dexter Forbes was their benign and jovial minister. With his round face, thick glasses and large belly he possessed an idiosyncratic air. A minister who delivers sermons without notes, elucidating with reference to the Hebrew and Greek, is bound to be a memorable sort. "Good thing our Paul was there to save you," he said.

"Paul's specialty," Pat said, as she and Rudy joined the group.

Paul stood to greet her, "Hello, Pat, Rudy."

"A more than usually entertaining service," Rudy said.

"You liked my joke about the Pope having arthritis?" asked the rector, winking at Paul.

"Any dig at the Catholics is fine with me," Rudy said.

"I had hoped the sermon was somewhat more on the topic of tolerance and not judging people by their appearance. What did you think, Paul?"

Paul was embarrassed. He thought of deflecting the question and saying, "I think I heard the joke before," which might have been so, but he answered, "Father Dexter, I'm afraid I was elsewhere at the time."

"Ah, yes," the rector sighed and smiled, "So many bodies, so few minds."

"Dexter, let me say firmly that the carpet must be replaced," said Josie. "I twisted my ankle this time but without Paul's intervention it would have been worse."

"Very true," said the rector. "We can be grateful for God's mercy, but we are hopeful, too, of financial assistance. The vestry is working on the issue, Josie. I trust you are not still in pain."

"It's tolerable," she replied. "That old quack Haverson tried to put his hands on me. God preserve me from doctors is what I say. Ah, here's my niece, come to liven us up." The group expanded the semi-circle standing about the seated Josie. John Wardle and Bronwyn inserted themselves between Rudy and the rector.

"Have you been enjoying yourself, child?" asked Josie.

"Oh yes, Aunt Josie, everyone is welcoming. My devilish childhood is absolved. Mrs. Armory reminded me of my larcenous ways with her apple tree, but she forgives me. I'll bake an apple pie for her, as penance."

"I like a girl with some devil in her," Rudy said. "Don't completely reform."

"No," replied Bronwyn. "And you are?"

"Rudy Price."

"And I'm Pat Brazier," Pat said, introducing herself. "It's a pleasure to meet you. I was speaking to John's mother, Pam Wardle, who's a friend of your aunt Josie, and she was telling me all about you. I'd love to have you over for dinner, once you're settled in."

"Thanks. I'll look forward to that."

"If I can be of help, please call me. I plan to have Paul over, too." Pat spoke in a determined fashion, looking at Paul. "I think he's avoiding me, but I owe him a dinner."

"It is good to bring the young people of the church together," said the rector. "Paul and Bronwyn, are you aware of the church picnic at Lake Robinson next Saturday? The pavilion is booked from noon and we eat at one o'clock. It's a covered-dish, so bring food or drink if you can but if not, come anyway. Some of our parishioners will have boats, and there's a trail around the lake. It should be fun."

"Thanks," Bronwyn said. "John mentioned it. I believe I will come. I'll ask my cousin, Sam, to bring me if that's okay? I know he'd have a great time."

"Sam will be happy to," said Mrs. Stickley.

"And you, Paul?" asked the rector.

"I'll be there," Paul said, pleased that Bronwyn wouldn't be going with John Wardle.

"That's understandable, having Sam take you," John said. "You haven't seen much of him."

"That's true. I haven't been back to Lexington in years." Laughingly she added, "Even if I had, I wouldn't have seen Sam."

"I suppose he was off at graduate school much of the time," John replied. "Ah," he paused, "you refer to your blindness, of course."

"I shouldn't tease you. I want people to use 'see' around me. It's natural, and if everyone has to watch every word then things get stilted, and people on stilts aren't very comfortable. As much as possible, I want to be one of the crowd."

"You could never be just one of the crowd, Bronwyn," John said fervently.

"Thank you for your gallantry, sir."

This chitchat irritated Paul. "I'll do my best to ignore you," he said, immediately aware of the abrupt confusion of his words and that any elaboration would make a bleating sheep of him.

"No more so than you ignore others, I hope," replied Bronwyn.

"I believe," Pat interjected, "that our Paul wants to be sinewy, like old beef jerky, but he's actually a soft-centered chocolate, from somewhere like Belgium or Switzerland."

"Maybe solid dark chocolate with nuts and raisins," suggested Bronwyn.

There was a small pause as the group waited for a new conversational direction. Rudy asked, "Are you totally blind?"

"I am. I lost my sight during my last two years of college. I was twenty-one, twenty-two. In the beginning, I'd see wiggly black lines in my left eye that went away. Then a month later, it was more like a nest of snakes. It went away, too, but the vision in that eye turned cloudy. The doctors didn't know why, but my retina was hemorrhaging. I had my good eye for a few months, but then one morning I woke and it was cloudy too. That was a terrifying day. I knew then I was going blind. With each blood vessel lost, each scar on the retina, I lost more vision. They tried to stabilize it with laser surgery but, as you see, without success. Within two years all my vision was gone."

An awkward lapse in conversation followed that grim tale, until Bronwyn said, "A horse-drawn carriage." The others looked and saw the covered carriage drawn slowly up the hill by a single horse.

"It's the tourists come to inspect us," Rudy said. "Did your hearing improve after you went blind?"

"Not in the slightest, but I became more attentive to sound, more aware of all my senses really." Paul thought of her as a panther in the jungle. She might have liked him to say that, but he didn't.

"My dear, I'm sure you're tired from your outing, and meeting new people. We should take you home. My ankle is sufficiently rested."

"Of course, Aunt Josie. I'm not tired, but if you're ready, we should certainly go."

Mrs. Stickley rose and took Bronwyn's arm. "Goodbye, everybody," Bronwyn said. "I look forward to seeing you again."

After Bronwyn and Josie left, the group drifted apart. Paul retrieved his bicycle from the parking area behind the church. As he walked past the front patio, Pat waved to him and came over with Rudy. "Bronwyn is a wonderful person, don't you think?"

"Uh, huh," Paul agreed, exhibiting none of his interest.

"Vulnerable, though," Rudy said thoughtfully. "A young woman with her looks. Anything might happen, her being so defenseless"

"That's why Lexington is wonderful for her," Pat said. "Everyone will watch out for her. I mean to. I'll have her for dinner soon. And you, too, Paul. If I'm not wrong, you wouldn't object to seeing Bronwyn again."

Paul thanked Pat and pedaled off. He worked at recollecting the last name of Mrs. Stickley's sister, which finally came to him as he pedaled slowly uphill toward the cemetery. It was 'Heathcote,' which must be Bronwyn's name. "Bronwyn Heathcote," he said aloud several times. It had a solid, earthen feel. Paul cycled to the newer section of the cemetery and located Phyllis' grave. He spent a few minutes talking with her, but he feared that she saw through him and mistrusted what she saw. Before leaving, Paul looked around. With nobody watching, he made his best frog-leap over her headstone.

Josie drove slowly from church to Bronwyn's house. With minor resentment, Bronwyn thought that her aunt's speed was suited to an invalid like herself. Josie ran the car up on the curb and bumped back down on the street, signaling their arrival. After the death of her husband, Willis, she'd come late to driving and her skills were notably deficient. Given freedom of choice, Bronwyn would have preferred walking to church with Nigel.

"Nigel," Bronwyn called, entering the house. She knelt, greeting a wet nose pushed into her palms. Stroking her hand over Nigel's back, she felt his tail wag and heard it swish. "I missed you too, boy." They walked along the hallway into the living room. Bronwyn and her aunt sat on the couch, and Nigel lay beside Bronwyn's feet. The house had a simple design, a comfortable workingman's cottage, Bronwyn thought it. The central passage from the front door passed between the bedrooms, Bronwyn's on the left, two smaller bedrooms on the right, and opened into the living room. The bathroom, laundry and kitchen were to the left. In recent years, her aunt Phyllis had modernized the back half of the house, taking out walls and doors, so the kitchen and living room formed one open area with a chunky "L" shape. French doors led to the patio, which Bronwyn thought the best feature of her house. Imagining the pageant of light gave her pleasure, and, with the doors open, she lived among the garden smells, the hum of bees and insects, and the touch of the breeze. Bronwyn bounced up from the couch and opened the doors wide. Nigel rubbed past her, eager to sniff the garden. Contentment occupied her as she inhaled deeply through her nose, identifying delicious mown grass and sweet apple blossom scents from a neighbor's property. Stepping onto the gravel path, she knelt, ran her fingers through the pea-gravel and sniffed with pleasure the biting scent of stirred-up gravel dust. I can learn so much from Nigel, she thought with delight, as she returned to her aunt.

"What are you up to, child?"

"Sorry to neglect you. I was pretending to be Nigel."

"Whatever makes you happy, dear, but you'll let the flies in."

That the room opened directly onto the outdoors reminded Bronwyn of her last years of high school; happy years with her father in Portugal. He was the commercial attaché at the U.S. Embassy in Lisbon, and they had rented a bungalow with French windows opening onto a grassy slope running down to a pond. She enjoyed sitting at his desk facing outdoors, dreaming of adventure and of a husband and children. Each day for the blind is an adventure, but not the adventure her seventeen-year-old self would have imagined. She trusted that Lexington would offer more than days filled with avoiding falls and bruises. She was ready for romance. Not desperate, she urged herself, quite picky really, but definitely ready.

"Could I have a glass of water?" asked her aunt. Bronwyn obliged, happy to be active. Josie sipped and said, "You had your share of admirers this morning."

Bronwyn smiled coyly at her aunt. "Did I?"

"John Wardle is a nice looking man, only a few years older than you. Pam and I discussed for years how suitable the match would be. You were undisciplined as a girl, and John would have been a calming influence. Mind you, I blame your father, traipsing you from country to country. Not enough continuity for a growing girl. Pam has been quiet on the subject since your blindness, though I still consider John an excellent catch for you. I can appreciate Pam's viewpoint, of course. I'd be none too happy if Sam came home with a blind girl. Not that I'm prejudiced, you understand, it's the practicalities."

"I see that. Oh, I'll be right back," Bronwyn said, hearing a knock on the front door. She returned a minute later with Sam.

"Hi Mom," Sam said. "I saw your car, but I came in anyway."

"Nice of you to visit your cousin, but don't forget you've a mother who needs visiting sometimes, too."

"I'll come over for dinner this week, if you promise not to annoy me about food or sneak meat onto my plate."

"You're too skinny, Sam. I have a right to worry. I've worried for thirty years, and I've no plans to stop."

"Your mother and I have been discussing my potential lovers at church this morning. We're partial to John Wardle but haven't covered the others yet."

"Not surprising if there were dozens, a looker like you," Sam said.

"And I have property. It's universally acknowledged that a good looking woman in possession of a house must be in want of a man."

"I wouldn't go for John, if I were you, cousin. Far too righteous. One of those who wanted Harry Potter banned at the library, the pompous ass."

"Plainly you won't be marrying John, but I'll consider him. He has the advantage of strong support from your mother. Aunt Josie, what other admirers did you see making up to me this morning?"

"There was that Rudy character. He kept sneaking looks at you. Down your dress, I'd have said. A heart-breaker, if ever there was one."

"Women love that in a man?" queried Sam.

"So they say. If you were a little more dangerous, Sam, the girls would be moths to your light," teased Bronwyn.

"Ships warned off the rocks by my light, more likely. There's Mandy, my current girlfriend, I'd say the rocks are looming on that relationship."

"Oh, I'm sorry," Bronwyn said.

Josie shuddered. "That girl has a tattoo on her wrist and a stud in her tongue. I want to close my eyes when I look at her. Sam can do lots better."

"Thanks, Mom. So who's this Rudy?"

57

"Jane Mercer is his sister," said Josie. "She's beaten down with useless men. Her husband won't keep a job, and her son, Todd, is a juvenile delinquent. Before this morning, it's been a good twenty years since I've seen Rudy. He couldn't wait to get to the big city to make his fortune."

"He'd be too old for Bronwyn?" asked Sam.

"Maybe forty-five. A fifteen year difference isn't bad in a man," said Josie.

"Mature and dangerous. A heady combination," Bronwyn said. "But we'll place him second in the running, unless of course he did make his fortune. Aunt Josie, what about Paul?"

"He was helpful. But he's so quiet."

"Neither mature nor dangerous. But maybe he's a late bloomer," Bronwyn said hopefully. "He might be our dark horse contender."

"Someone who doesn't talk is a poor match for someone who doesn't see," observed Sam.

"Shall we sit out in the back?" suggested Bronwyn. "I'll bring iced-tea."

"Go ahead," said Josie. "It's too sunny for me. I'll stay inside by the door and talk to you. I have my glass of water."

Sam moved a chair to the door for his mother while Bronwyn retrieved a jug of tea from the refrigerator. She took it to the small, glass-topped table on her patio and Sam brought glasses with ice. Bronwyn took off her shoes, and Nigel, who'd come from the end of the garden, laid his head on her feet. She wiggled her toes to scratch him and bent to caress his ears, whispering, "You don't say much either, do you boy."

"I may have to go to church to check out Bronwyn's potential lovers," Sam said. "Who is Paul?"

"I don't know about his family," said Josie. "He comes to church, now and then. I've seen him at the public library. He works there."

"A quiet librarian. Not promising," laughed Sam. "But he can read to you, Bronwyn."

"I've got Braille books, audio-books and my computer. I don't need a man for that. In fact, I don't need a man at all," she said with asperity, "so we'll just drop the subject."

"Sam's father was a nuisance around the house after his retirement, but I miss him," said Josie with a sigh. "There are great advantages to a man, when it comes to things like washers and wrenches. I think I'll ask Pam and John Wardle over for dinner and have you too, Bronwyn."

Bronwyn nudged Nigel's head off her feet and stood. "Aunt Josie, don't you think this is a wonderful place?" She walked a couple of steps along the garden path curling her toes in the pea-gravel and twirling as child-like as anyone walking barefoot on a gritty sand beach. "I was thinking of giving it a name, 'Heather Cottage at Cherry Lane.' Isn't that idyllic?"

"It is, my dear. These brick walls give lots of privacy, and Phyllis prided herself on her garden. She had such delightful flowers, but you'll prick yourself on those roses against the sidewall. I'll come and prune them for you. Better yet, we'll take them down. Something more sedate would suit your needs. Hollyhocks, I think."

"Just for now, I'd like to keep things the way Aunt Phyllis had them."

"Of course dear, but remember that Phyllis herself made changes. As children, we'd visit our grandparents here, not thinking about it then, of course, but this house was dark. It's wonderful what Phyllis has done to brighten it. The windows and glass doors are beautiful, though I never did understand where the money came from. It's not as if Phyllis had a real job. She'd paint, and, now and then, sell some of her artwork. You couldn't accuse her of spending lavishly, but she always had plenty of money."

"Maybe she was someone's mistress," Sam said mischievously.

"Sam, show respect," said Josie. "Your aunt never had a thing to do with men, as far as I could see."

"Maybe not a man, then," jabbed Sam, which induced his mother's usual impatient response.

"Your frivolity is just annoying. I should head home now. I'm late for my Sunday afternoon nap."

Bronwyn and Sam stood by the front door as Josie drove to the bottom of the hill, turning right to circle back on Laurel Lane to Main Street. "At least your neighbors' cars are safe," Sam said.

"Sam, can you come out to the back lane with me? I'd like to see what condition it's in."

Sam followed Bronwyn to the back of her garden. He watched as she struggled with the bolt on the gate. "I'll help, when you want. Next time I'll bring some oil."

"Thanks. Almost got it." With a grunt, Bronwyn opened the gate and stepped into the lane.

"You're brave, going there barefoot," Sam said, following her out. "Actually it's not too bad. Let's see, the house across the lane from yours has wooden fencing, made of horizontal boards. It's overgrown with vegetation. Downhill, the path is concrete with dirt borders for twenty yards. Then the lane changes to grass and the vines choke the path. I wouldn't try going there. Uphill the lane is clear. It turns to the right and heads out to your road."

"Much as it used to be. What's in the dirt border behind my wall?"

"Hostas maybe, and a bunch of taller weedy-looking things."

Bronwyn stooped, felt the plants near her and scooped some dirt, rolling it in her palm. "Okay. I'll come out soon and clear the weeds. Maybe plant some mums. Sam, can I ask a favor?"

"Sure."

"Can you take me to the church picnic next Saturday at Lake Robinson? We eat at one o'clock, but we should go a little earlier to meet people. I think you'd have fun. We might go out on a boat."

"That's asking a lot, dragging me to a church outing."

"John Wardle asked me to go with him. I said you'd take me."

"No further argument. Saturday it is."

Chapter 7   Monday

At work, Paul was still replaying his few words with Bronwyn from the previous day, wishing he'd shown more brilliance or even coherence. The faces of the young women who visited the library paled beside the image of her dark beauty. He was afraid that he was in a process of idealizing her. At around eleven o'clock, he looked up, saw her, and knew he wasn't wrong. In a crowded room, she would have signaled through any din to him. He leapt to his feet. His heart hammered, perspiration prickled the backs of his hands. He moved swiftly to her. "Hello," he said. She, and her yellow lab guide dog, stopped. "I'm Paul. We met yesterday."

"Nice to meet you again, Paul."

"Can I help you find something? I work here."

"Thanks. I checked your online catalog, and this is a print-out of some audio books I'd like." She held out her papers to him.

"The audio books are toward the back on the right wall. If I lead, will your dog follow?"

"Yes, please. Go, Nigel."

As he pulled her requests from the shelves, he worked at maintaining a conversation. "Your computer reads out the web pages and allows you to navigate the links?"

"It's not as fast as seeing the page, but I get there."

"You like Nineteenth Century English literature, if you don't mind my noticing what you're reading."

"Your saying that, reminds me of a story I heard somewhere. Would you like to hear it?"

"Certainly."

"This perfect English butler knocks on the bedroom door of the mistress of the house and enters. She's standing undressed in the middle of the room ready to step into her bath. Maybe it was one of those old copper tubs and a bevy of maids had labored to carry once-steaming hot water upstairs to fill it. He was a stately butler, not at all used to seeing his mistress unclothed. He could have closed his eyes, profusely debased himself and backed out of the door with deep apologies. That would have sadly humiliated his mistress and irreparably embarrassed their relationship. Not hesitating in his course, treating everything as in proper order, he fluffed the pillows, or whatever butlers do, handed his mistress the soap, and asked, 'Will there be anything else M'lady?' And with no flicker of interest in her breasts, he departed."

"Must have given him a happy recollection in old age," Paul said.

"I had a point to that story, what was it?" mused Bronwyn.

"Was it about my noticing you?"

"You were? No, it was about apologizing for noticing what I was reading. You couldn't help but notice. Apologizing only brings noticing to a level of importance that's embarrassing. The butler would never have said, 'If you don't mind my noticing, M'lady.'"

"I feel I should apologize. Though that seems a denigrated course, and I'm not sure what I'd be apologizing for."

Bronwyn laughed. "Me either. And yes, I like Nineteenth Century English literature."

"Me too," Paul said, happily in accord with her. "Should we go and check these out?"

"Thanks. I'm between clients. I need to get back soon."

"Hmmm," he said thoughtfully. "If my name was Sherlock, I'd determine from the ink-stain on your thumb and the callous on your pointer finger that you're a stenographer."

"Better stick with Paul the Librarian. Actually, the university hired me for their counseling center. It's been great so far. My clients take one look at me, and their problems seem less monumental."

"I'm not supposed to pet a guide dog, am I?"

"No. Approval comes from me while he's in harness, but you can put your hand out for him to sniff. Good boy, Nigel. This is Paul, he's a friend."

He escorted Bronwyn and Nigel to the circulation desk and put the audio books on the counter. "Ruth, this is Bronwyn, she's new to the area. Bronwyn, I'll leave Ruth to help you. Someone's waiting for me at the reference desk." She thanked him. By the time he'd finished assisting the patron, Bronwyn was gone.

At one o'clock, Paul shared the lunchroom with Ruth, who said, "Bronwyn and I talked a little. She's an attractive person, isn't she? She gets along well with her blindness."

"You're right," he reacted with uncharacteristic swiftness and force. "She's not bowed down by it, at all. We met at church yesterday, and I was immediately struck by her dignity." His excitement signaled like smoke and ash from a dormant volcano.

Ruth responded to Paul's burst of life by graciously suggesting, "Perhaps you should try to see her again." Paul nodded.

After lunch, he returned to the reference desk intending to use his computer to access Bronwyn's library record. That implicated a moral debate. On each approach to the issue, the same result obtained. Using his professional position to snoop into private information was unethical. Each time, he countered that he wanted only her address, which would be published information had Bronwyn been in town longer. In the end, he looked because he wanted to and had to. Her patron record gave him the information he needed. She lived at 6 Cherry Lane.

Boiled Peanuts

The rest of the afternoon passed swiftly. Sitting at his station a little after four o'clock, the light angling through the magazine area's tall windows smote him, suffusing him with heat. Dust danced in the light beams, and he was filled with such dreams as he could not have described; not of words or images, but color, as if he lay in a tropic sea bathed by changing greens and golds, flashing silvers and the deepest blues. Such reveries, far from his normal workday fare, were unfitting to his surroundings, but they came despite him.

Something about the youth that passed him drew Paul from his trance. He stood to watch the young man walk toward the back of the library and turn into the science-fiction section. He hesitated to actively spy on a library user and saw no reason to now, but an alarm jangled in his mind. As slowly as he reasonably could, he strolled past the fiction area. Nothing in the young man's profile made sense of his concerns. Reversing at the back wall, he turned left into European history and travel. Feeling foolish, he squatted and pulled a Greek travel guide from the shelf. Pretending to read, he examined the young man in the adjacent aisle, but his poor up-close surveillance skills led to his rapid detection. He was snared, mesmerized by a hostile returned stare. The young man spoke angrily, "What'ya want? You some kind of pervert?" Exposed, he was a grub on open ground with a sparrow pecking at him. What defense was there? He replaced the book on its shelf, stood, and slowly walked to his accuser, inwardly focused on his disordered emotions. Despite a false premise, the conclusion was correct. The young man spoke the truth. He was a pervert. Almost blind to his surroundings, he stopped before the youth. "What's wrong with you, Mister?"

Suddenly, waking to his knowledge, Paul said, "I know you! Yes. Saturday, a week ago, on Oakland Drive, you and another man smashed the window of a car and ran. You'd have stolen the contents of the car if I hadn't come along."

"Wasn't me."

"Oh, it was. I recognize you now. I'm calling the police."

"No. It's not like you think. We was told to do it."

Paul gripped the young man's shoulder. "What do you mean, 'told to'?"

"Todd said the man that owned the car wanted it broken into. We weren't to take nothing. Just run when he shouted at us. Some insurance scam, Todd said."

"This Todd, that's Rudy Price's nephew?"

"That's him. It was only fun. I wasn't out to make trouble for nobody."

"Alright. We won't involve the police for now. What's Todd's last name?"

"It's Todd Mercer." Paul released him. The young man squeezed past in the aisle and hurried from the library. Paul returned to the reference desk and looked up Todd's library record. He lived at 11 Oriole Court. Checking the City Directory, Paul saw that Jane and Steven Mercer lived there. At the wine shop, Rudy had said that Jane was his sister.

In the time before the library closed, Paul considered what he knew. He hadn't recognized Todd in the wine shop, but his glimpse of the young men outside Pat's house had been fleeting. It was surprising he'd recognized one of them this afternoon. He felt sure of Todd's involvement. Did that entangle Rudy in a plot? It must. Rudy would hear the rock crash through the car window, even know the time it would occur, give futile chase and be covered in glory for his attempt. Could Rudy have crafted such a paltry scheme to better himself in Pat's esteem? Paul feared so.

While cycling home, and during the early evening, his ruminations never strayed far from his problem. He could warn Pat, but his chain of flimsy evidence was anchored in unreliable testimony and arranging to smash a car window to enhance a second date seemed ludicrous. Pat was infatuated with Rudy. She'd reject any accusations with anger. Dropping the matter made sense but to save a shrew in Spook's mouth he'd give chase, for the kind and trusting Pat he must do what he could.

After dinner, with an hour before darkness and no definite plan, he ventured out on his bicycle. He cycled to Cherry Lane. The house on the right at the top of the street fronted on Main Street, behind it was a lane, and three houses farther down was Bronwyn's house. With no car in front, he stopped at her curb, exposed to observation by the neighbors. To allay suspicion, but diminishing his idiocy not a bit, he crossed his arms over his handlebars and placed his left cheek down on them, as if resting. At a ninety-degree angle, he inspected Bronwyn's home. It was a charming single-story house of whitish brick, with varying flecks of brown, black and red throughout. Its tin-roof was silver, its wood trim dark red. Close to the road, the house was separated from the sidewalk by a low brick wall surmounted by an old black wrought-iron fence; white gravel covered the small area from the wall to the house; the house was fronted by two rooms, their window-blinds closed; a brick walkway led to the front door.

His depiction complete, he cycled to the bottom of the road and turned right onto Glen Park Road. The houses there enjoyed a view of the park with its slide and swings. Paul crossed the street, stood his bike next to a park bench, and sat for a few minutes. He watched a mother push her youngster on a swing, admiring her grace as she bent to her task. He was taken with the greedy shouts to be pushed and the lively arcing of the swing in the orange-yellow glow of the late afternoon light. He reflected that Bronwyn was alive in the world and lived above him on the hill, and he felt a thrill of anticipation that he could not justify, an expectation of the boundless scope of life that exceeded his reasonable prospects. He sighed over his lapse into the ecstatic, re-mounted his bike and toiled back up Cherry Lane. He turned into the narrow alley two houses past Bronwyn's, followed its turn downhill and stopped behind her house. On each side of the lane were single-story houses with either wooden fences or brick walls. Many of the wooden fences were poorly tended and overgrown with bushes and creepers. Bronwyn's was a seven-foot high brick wall with an equally high and sturdy gate painted the same dark red as the trim on her house. Paul marveled at its security-minded or privacy-minded builder. He was happy that she lived in a fortress free from prying eyes.

With Bronwyn's geography set in his mind, he cycled to Pat's house. He had no intention of stopping. Being seen would be embarrassing. Pat's car, its window fixed, was parked outside her house. Seeing nothing else of interest, he cycled on, heading to Rolf's house. Regina answered his knock, expressing her delight at seeing him. "Rolf's in his room. Go on up. First on the right."

Paul tapped on Rolf's door. Getting no response, he called, "You there, Rolf?" He played with the notion of walking in, finding Rolf naked in the middle of the floor and totally ignoring his nudity. He couldn't see pulling it off with aplomb. Hearing movement, he tapped lightly on the door again. "It's Paul."

The door opened. Rolf was zipping his jeans, having trouble containing the bulge. "Hi cobber," he said.

"Geez, remind me not to shake hands with you, ever."

Rolf went to his bed and smoothed the sheets. He removed a pair of panties from under his pillow and put them beneath a layer of his own underwear in the top dresser drawer.

"Susan's?"

"Silky smooth, mate. Nothing better for buffing the old donger. Be super if I had a picture of her, though." He looked regretfully at Paul.

"Forget it. You've had enough from Amanda's." Paul looked around Rolf's small domain. The floral wallpaper testified to its once being a girl's room. He would have liked to open the window and release the old sock smell but that seemed indelicate in one seeking a favor. "I need your help."

"All ears, mate."

"There's this nice lady I know on Oakland that's being charmed by a sleazebag. I need to find out what he's up to."

"This is like a rival for your affections?"

"Nothing like that. This is serious. I'm worried about her. He could even be dangerous. What I'm thinking is, you can help me spy on him, maybe follow him, see what he's up to. What do you think?"

"Count me in. When do we start?" They discussed the situation and arranged to meet at Paul's apartment before dusk the following evening.

CHAPTER 8   TUESDAY

After dinner, to fill the time until Rolf arrived, Paul set out by bike to survey the territory of his interests. Outside Pat's house was a white Chevy Malibu with Florida plates that he assumed belonged to Rudy. That morning he'd checked Rudy's name in the library's patron database and in the City Directory and, not surprisingly, found nothing. Rudy could be staying at his sister's, but the straightforward route was to follow him when he left Pat's house. Satisfied that he knew Rudy's location, he cycled to Bronwyn's street.

Nothing was significantly different from his previous time there. He cycled slowly down the hill, turned right on Glen Park Road, then right on Laurel Lane, planning to circle around to Bronwyn's house. Laurel Lane was as steep as Cherry Lane. By the time he was almost to the top, his leg muscles ached. He stopped, approximately behind Bronwyn's house, at a "Randolph Realty, House for Rent" sign. Leaving his bike at the curb, he went to investigate. It was a single story house. Peering in the front window, he verified it was empty. He opened the side gate and walked beside the house into its small backyard. To the right, close to the house, an old shed sat among profusely grown weeds and creepers. The wooden fence that faced the back lane leaned disreputably inwards, burdened by, or possibly supported by, its ivy. Over the fence, he saw the top of Bronwyn's dark red gate and her brick wall.

Paul returned to his bike and completed his circuit to Bronwyn's street. Coasting down to her house, he passed a parked truck. Angling toward the curb he suddenly came beside Bronwyn and Nigel. He let an, "Oh," escape him. Disconcerted, he allowed his pedal to touch the curb and tip his bike. He landed at Bronwyn's feet, scraping his arm, grunting in pain. Nigel watched him, and Bronwyn held her arm down to him. "Are you hurt?"

"I don't usually do that."

"Paul, is that you?"

"Yes. I'm sorry to be so clumsy."

"Let me help you up."

"No, no. My hands are dirty. But thanks, I'll be fine." He stood and picked up his bike.

"Is your bike damaged?"

Rolling it, he said, "It's fine. Like me, a little scraped, but we're okay."

"My house is here. Come in. We'll get you patched up. Go home, Nigel." Paul followed like an awkward child in need of a band-aid, but it was the first day of a new school and the loveliest girl in class had noticed him.

Her hallway floor was made of old wide planking that squeaked a little. Glancing into the first door on the left, he saw the same bare dark boards extending into that room. Covered with a checkered yellow and brown quilt, was her bed. To the right were two closed doors. The passage opened into a light-filled room. "This is very pleasant," he said, looking out at Bronwyn's garden.

"Yes. I think it is. There, I've taken off Nigel's harness. He's lost his super-powers. He's an ordinary citizen dog now. Come to the kitchen sink, and we'll clean your scrapes."

Paul washed his hands and dried with paper towels. Bronwyn retrieved antibiotic cream and asked him to put her fingers on his scrape. He gently took her proffered hand and touched her fingers to the hairs of his right arm, just above the wrist. "From there to the elbow," he said. He closed his eyes and focused intensely on her fingertips sliding up his arm, tracing the furrows and ridges of his minor injury.

"Does that hurt?"

"Not at all."

"You're not a very satisfactory patient. You have to moan a lot. Then express your immense gratitude when my attentions ease your pain."

"I am feeling less pain."

"But I've done nothing. I'm the one moaning, and you're laughing at me." She vigorously rubbed in the ointment.

"No, indeed," he said, delighted at this conversational back and forth. "Can you tell me something? Outside the church, you knew I was behind you. I wanted to know how you did that."

"You wouldn't ask a magician to reveal a trick of the trade, would you?

"True, but disappointing."

"If I tell you, you'll be disappointed, and say, 'of course, that's so obvious.' The world is full of wonderful secrets when we're children, then knowledge makes adults of us and we spend our lives wishing we were children again. So, do you really want to know?"

"A little maturity can't hurt me."

"When you walked us out of church your Sunday shoes clicked a little, and you smelled of Irish Spring soap. When you came behind me on the patio, it was like your signature.

"Of course, that is so obvious."

Bronwyn swatted at him, but he stepped outside her range. "Go and sit," she commanded.

He went toward the couch but dropped to the floor beside Nigel. He held his hand to be sniffed, and he scratched behind Nigel's ears. He looked up at Bronwyn. "I expect you'd snap at me if I asked if you'd mind if I asked, so I'll just ask. Is everything black for you? I mean, if I close my eyes, I might see spots of orange or white or yellow. Do you see any colors?"

"I can picture colors. I remember what the sky looks like, but they say that fades over time, and it's important to keep visualizing images so the memories stay alive. Actually, I don't see black at all. Everything is gray, which is friendlier than eternal blackness."

"That's good."

"Were you going somewhere on your bike?"

"Only riding around town. I have someone coming over soon, so I'm afraid I need to leave, but could I look at your garden before I go?" Bronwyn led the way, standing aside so he could walk on the gravel path. "Nigel is staying beside me," he said.

"He likes going out, and I'm glad he likes you, too."

"If only we were on the outside trying to find our way in, this could be the Secret Garden with its high walls."

"You'd be Dickon to teach me about plants, and I'd be the curious girl come from India."

"I'm more like the poor crippled boy who knows nothing about gardening."

"Strangely enough, I did live in India. My father works for the State Department. We spent two years in Delhi when I was around six. I still recall the heat and the fragrant smells, the curries, flowers and incense. And the cologne my mother wore. She was alive then."

"I'm sorry. Did she die young?"

"When I was nine. We were traveling from Greece via the Suez Canal. Nobody saw her fall. She was never found. She vanished overboard."

"How terrible for you. I really hate to go if you want to talk about it, but I should leave."

"I'm fine, really. It was long ago. Come again. Nigel and I like visitors."

He left, satisfied that he'd functioned well at an important task. He wanted naturalness, but asking a few questions got him through. He cycled to his apartment. Rolf was sitting on the front steps. "Sorry I'm late," Paul apologized. "I went by Pat's house, and I'm sure Rudy's car was outside. Hopefully we can follow him tonight."

"Do we have a plan?"

"I wish I did. Hopefully something will happen."

Rolf drove them. They arrived without scraped metal and parked across the street from Pat's house. "I need a cigarette," Rolf said.

"Yuk, they'll kill you, and I hate the smell."

"Easy mate, I don't smoke. Where's your imagination? Two jaded private-eyes at a stake-out in their junky car, drinking cold coffee and smoking."

"Those aren't appealing roles. We have to take this seriously and be extremely careful. Rudy let it drop that he owns a gun."

"Came prepared," Rolf said proudly. "Look in the glove box."

Paul opened the latch. "Jesus! What are you thinking?"

"It's my Uncle Seth's. There are plenty in the gun cabinet. He won't miss one.

"Just what we need," moaned Paul. "We'll be caught loitering with a stolen gun. Don't even think about touching it."

The lights came on in Pat's house as twilight arrived. Five minutes later Pat and Rudy came down the steps.

Afraid of being seen, Paul sank low against Rolf. "That's him," he said.

"Don't get too cozy down there, matey," Rolf said to Paul. "She's kissing him goodbye," he reported. "He looks like a gigolo. Now there's a job I'd take a pay-cut to have."

Across the road, the car started up. A few seconds later, they were in pursuit.

Bronwyn enjoyed thinking about Paul. She liked his voice. It was strong and warm. He was diffident and quirky but responded politely to her poking at him. He was stiff as a butler, but she thought he'd loosen up, and, most important, she suspected he liked her. Things weren't ordained. Her blindness was no punishment from God. She was like a ball on a celestial pool table making her way, nudging and careening against the other balls. But that was only one idea. Her mind was too large to lack contradictory notions. For Paul to have randomly cycled by and been hurled at her feet was too much like direct intervention not to think it a happy portent.

She listened to a chapter from George Eliot's Middlemarch and planned to begin a book on sexual identity that she'd brought from the office. None of the books at the counseling center or at the university library were in Braille, but she could scan pages into her computer and have it read them to her. Some loss of independence was inevitable for the blind, but she was proud of this and any other autonomy she could assert. The phone rang before she began her task. She sat on the couch and picked up the phone. "Dad, this is a surprise," she exclaimed.

"You thought I was dead then? I'm sorry it's been so long. I've been out of communication." She'd long ceased asking her father for details of his life. She assumed he worked for the CIA, although he denied it. How else explain that she couldn't call him, and he rarely called her. "Listen. I'm getting married again. It's been a long time since your mother. I'm retiring soon, and I need someone to look after me in my old age. I've been seeing Agatha for a few years. She lives in Athens. It's that attraction I have for Greek women. Your mother was the loveliest creature to ever walk the dust of Crete, at least since goddesses lived there."

"That's good news, Dad. When's the wedding? Can I come?"

"No need. We'll have a small civil thing in a few weeks. We'll come back to the U.S. for a visit, and you can meet. Then I'll retire to Greece. A sun-drenched villa, overlooking the wine dark sea. Funny really, it's my business promoting American interests, but I've been gone so long I don't even feel American. How are you getting along in tiny Lexington?"

"Its small compass suits me. I've been thinking, Dad, about Aunt Phyllis. On Sunday, Aunt Josie implied that Aunt Phyllis didn't have much income. Did she ever have a job?"

"I don't think so. She was an artist in her small way, but unsuccessful. Remember, Josie and I were nearly ten years older than Phyllis. When I went to college, Phyllis was eight years old. We've had little contact over the years. Fallings-out happen in families. Phyllis and I barely spoke in the thirty years before her death.

"Why didn't you speak?"

"It's not important now. Maybe it never was, and I'm not going to rake it up. There was an argument over your mother."

"Didn't you treat her well?"

"Of course I did. Your mother was young, the same age as Phyllis. I was focused on my career. You know how it is."

"Aunt Phyllis left me this house but how did she come to own it? Wasn't it split with you and Josie as well?"

"Why this sudden interest in the family?"

"If I'm to be a fixture in Lexington, I want to know how I fit. How did she come to own this house?"

"I need to go, Bronwyn. Ask Josie your questions. She saw more of Phyllis than I did. My Grandma Ellen owned the house until her death in the mid-seventies. Phyllis lived with her in her last few years. With just the two of them, it's natural, Grandma leaving the house to Phyllis. Anyway, I'd say let it fade, like the ancient history it is. Goodbye for now, Bronwyn, I'll tell you when you have a stepmother."

Bronwyn slowly replaced the phone. Calls from her father sucked the air from the room. She'd never be more than a demoted Pluto in his solar system. Drying her moist eyes, she picked up the phone again, asked directory assistance for Pat Brazier's number and called her.

"Pat? This is Bronwyn Heathcote. We met after church."

"How nice of you to call."

"I'm looking for a favor, if you have time."

"Anything you want is fine with me, just ask."

"My Aunt Phyllis died last October and left me her house and possessions. As far as I know, the house was locked up and everything she had is still here. I'd like help donating books to a library, and I'd love to know more about my aunt. I thought there might be papers or a diary. Any clue as to how she spent her life. I know you're an almost complete stranger, but you did offer, and you're a woman."

"Wouldn't your other aunt be more appropriate?"

"My difficulty is that Aunt Josie thinks she's superior to Aunt Phyllis."

"Okay. If we find your aunt was a train robber, or the mayor's mistress, you can rely on my discretion. I love poking into other people's lives. I hope that doesn't diminish your trust in me."

Bronwyn laughed, comfortable with Pat as her choice. "I'm at 6 Cherry Lane. Could you do it some evening?"

"I'm busy tomorrow with book club. Thursday is fine. At seven?"

Chapter 9   Wednesday

By bedtime, Paul had decided to contact the realtor about renting the house. Such an upheaval felt as if he occupied a house slid from its foundations floating on a swollen river to the sea. He was unaware why his viewpoint had changed, but, by morning, he felt empowered, as if rushing through white-water rapids he'd found a paddle to steer by. He cycled to the Randolph Realty office on his way to work and arranged to meet with their representative at one o'clock at the house.

It was mid-morning when Paul saw Rolf approaching. Tim, who was chatting with Ruth at the circulation desk, stopped to watch Rolf move past, and he whispered in Ruth's ear. While there might be conspicuous reasons to disparage Rolf, Tim just made Paul angry.

"G'day, mate."

"G'day to you, Rolf."

Rolf looked around, ensuring privacy for their conspiratorial dialog. "I've got a plan."

"Wait a second, it's too public here." Paul walked over to the circulation desk. "Tim, can you watch the reference desk for a few minutes? I'll be with Rolf in the little conference room. He needs some help." Tim agreed.

Paul took Rolf into the small glassed-in office area used by literacy trainers. "What's your idea?" Paul asked.

"If we only watch tonight, we'll miss out on whatever our guy's up to today." Paul nodded. "I'm thinking I'll go now and stake out the house we followed him to. What'ya think?"

"You won't touch the gun, will you?"

"Course not, scares me more than it would him."

"I looked up the address this morning. Monique Newcomb owns it. We need to know his relationship with her. As late as we stayed, and his still being there, it looks like he's romancing Pat and she's another girlfriend."

"I could take compromising pictures."

"We need to clue Pat in without getting ourselves in trouble. You'd be too conspicuous. It's not like we need evidence for a court. Seeing a passionate kiss is enough to report to Pat."

"Always wanted to work for one of those magazines in the supermarket. 'Ace reporter uncovers scumbag boyfriend's love nest,' that sort of thing."

"They make those stories up. We need the truth. Monique may be a relative and Rudy perfectly innocent."

" Okey-dokey. If something happens I'll report back to you."

"Just watch from your car. Don't do anything silly. Here, let me give you a book. That way, if anyone comes by and asks what you're doing, tell them you're whiling away time, reading before you have to meet someone." Paul grabbed a remedial reading book, and they walked to the circulation desk. "Have you got a library card?"

"Not likely, mate."

Paul handed the book to Ruth and had her check the book out in his own name. Paul walked Rolf to his car and cautioned him again about doing anything rash. When he returned to the library, Ruth said, "That was nice of you."

"What was?"

"Helping him with his reading and checking the book out for him. It's sad when someone his age can't read well."

Paul smiled at her. "He's smarter than he looks."

In his available time during the morning, Paul looked for additional information on Monique but found little. She'd come from Florida, a possible connection to Rudy, and owned the house for three years. None of the Lexington church directories listed her, nor did the directories of the two universities. She had no local connections that he could discover.

At lunchtime, Paul met Troy Carter, Randolph Realty's rental agent, at Laurel Lane. Paul inspected the house, knowing it was acceptable in any condition. Troy apologized, explaining that the previous tenants were university students. "You can see how they left it. I think they dropped out of school. More interested in partying than studying. Probably shouldn't say this, but we tried to persuade the owner to renovate, and she wouldn't go for it, so the rent's reasonable. Let in some light, open things up to get rid of the cigarette smell. Not that I said this, you understand, it's not my business encouraging tenants to make improvements, but there are cans of paint in the shed. Clean down these walls, touch up the paintwork, and the house will be like new."

Paul agreed to all that Troy said and completed the rental application forms. "I'd like to move in as soon as possible."

"You don't have to give notice where you are?"

"I do. I'll pay double rent for a month, but that's okay."

"I have to run a credit check. I'll call you at work this afternoon to let you know everything's in order. Let's see, tomorrow's April 29th, if we start the lease from then, maybe I can persuade the owner to throw in a couple of free days and you can pay from May 1st. Come by the office before five, and you can pick up the key and move in tomorrow."

"Thanks. I'm off work tomorrow afternoon. I'll come by then and get the key."

During his afternoon at work, Paul was repeatedly drawn to mental images of himself at the tiller of a small boat in plunging waves. Sometimes Bronwyn was there, gripping the gunwales with white knuckles, other times he was alone.

At around 6:00, after a quick dinner, he walked to Sellers Avenue. In case Rolf needed dinner, he brought a bag with a small bottle of water, an apple and a peanut-butter sandwich. Rolf's car was just down the street from Monique Newcomb's house on her side of the street. Rudy's car was across the street. Rolf wasn't in sight, which was unsettling. His car was unlocked so Paul sat in the passenger seat to wait. He observed the house, watched squirrels chase each other around the trees and glanced in his book at the adventures of John, Wendy and their dog Rory at the beach.

Shortly before 7:00, Rudy, and a woman he assumed was Monique, came out of the house and walked to Rudy's car. Paul sank down, invisibly watching them. Monique's figure was curvaceous. In her thirties, with a short black dress and long blond hair, she was arresting. Dressed-up, they were probably going to a nice restaurant.

As Rudy drove away, there was movement in the front window of the house. Rolf was looking up and down the street. Paul got out of the car and self-consciously walked to the house. The threat of observant neighbors made every footstep difficult, as though he wore gigantic shoes. Rolf opened the front door, beckoned to him and backed into the hallway. "Rolf, get out of there," Paul said urgently.

"Come on in. Safe as houses. They're gone."

Paul fought against glancing about for the twitching curtains of concerned citizens. Coming into the house he said roughly, "You idiot, what are you doing?"

"Unruffle your feathers, mate. I'm investigating. Bloody-hell but I'm good at it." Rolf trotted into the first room off the hall and threw himself onto the bed.

"So, tell me." Paul demanded, following him, "We can't stay."

Rolf stopped his bouncing. "When I got here his car wasn't outside so I snooped around and saw this side window open. I was ready to skedaddle if I heard a peep. I pulled a rubbish bin from around the back to climb on." Slowly, Rolf drew something red from his pocket, "Another souvenir," he said gleefully, brandishing a pair of red panties.

"Stop going off on tangents and stick to the point," Paul said, irritated.

"Haven't left the bus, mate. If you close your trap and stick with me, we'll get there."

"I'm sorry. Tell me about the panties."

"There was nobody home, and I'm in her bedroom, so crikey, I figure, make the most of it. Her dresser's filled with these sexy things." Rolf giggled, twirling the panties around his finger. "Like a magpie I went for the brightest one. That's when I heard them at the front door. I shut the dresser drawer and barely had time to get in the closet. Give it a try. You can see everything."

Paul glanced at the closet's louvered doors. "I believe you. Then what?"

"They start to make out."

"Ah, we were right."

"She's kicking off her shoes, he's unzipping her dress, and he tosses her half naked on the bed. He's licking her like a jam tart. She's squealing and kicking like she doesn't love it. He pulls her bra and panties off, and in the raw she's something, I can tell you."

"I imagine," Paul said, feeling a little aroused at Rolf's description.

"He strips, and they lie there, him stroking her, and they're talking. A Sheila like that in your hands, can you see just talking! Better they weren't going at it hammers and tongs. I got to look at her bod, and I did my best to listen."

"Did they say anything incriminating?"

"For sure. But when you've got a throb in your knob it's not anyone's fault you can't concentrate properly."

"Okay. So what did you hear?"

"She was snarky at being left to rot in Lexington. I'm with her on that one. He's in trouble with some Mafia types and needs someplace safe. He's working on this investment deal."

"What kind of investment?"

"Something about selling land on the edge of growing cities. Sounds like a moneymaker to me. And they're off to Acapulco soon."

"Anything else?"

"They got to business. He's got no frigid digit down there I can tell you. Anyone could learn a thing or two from him."

"I'm pretty sure he'll make off with the cash," Paul said thoughtfully. He was aware that a car had stopped across the street. Someone trotted up the front steps. "Oh, God, he's back. Quick ..."

They dashed down the corridor. As they turned into the kitchen, the front door opened, and Rudy bellowed at them, "You damn punks. I'll get you."

Paul fumbled desperately with the bolt on the outside door of the kitchen. "Let me," Rolf tried to push him aside.

"Got it," Paul said with relief, and they tumbled down the steps. They raced straight at the back fence and scrambled over, falling to the other side. Wood splintered around them. Rudy was shooting at them. Paul gasped, "Make for the gate." With the speed of a hare, Paul was first at the gate. Its latch was a simple lever, and they barreled through with bullets striking the wood, ricocheting around them, whining off the brick of the house. The houses across the street, and on the street beyond, were unfenced. They fled until they collapsed under a bush. Huddled together, their chests shuddered with stress.

"Doesn't look like he chased us," heaved Paul. "Don't think he saw us clearly. I hope those shots were just meant to scare us."

"Scared me," Rolf said.

"Better not go back and get your car tonight. If your aunt and uncle ask, tell them it wouldn't start and you'll try again tomorrow."

"Okay. I'll walk. You going home?"

"I'm going by Pat's house. I've got to say something to her, though I can't tell her you broke into the house."

"Hope not. She could tell Rudy, and he'd come after me."

"Not to worry. Stay clear of Rudy in case he got a glimpse of you. We've enough evidence, so our spying job's done. And Rolf, thanks. You maybe went overboard, but you made it happen."

"That's what pals are for."

The two friends separated. Paul began rehearsing his arguments. Soon confused, he stopped under a tree to marshal his facts. The more he thought, the less persuasive he felt. He continued his reluctant way to Oakland Drive. Nobody was home at Pat's house, and he resolved to talk with her in the morning.

CHAPTER 10   THURSDAY

His rental contract had been accepted, and Paul knew he'd smack of a pathetic stalker if Bronwyn discovered he'd occupied the house behind hers based on their small acquaintance. And Pat, when she knew he'd watched her house and followed her lover, would surely spurn him. He cringed at these thoughts of denunciation, but he couldn't deviate from his course.

He set off at 8:17. Early enough to see Pat before work, but late enough to offer an excuse to leave Pat's quickly. He cycled up Oakland Drive, saw Rudy's car parked in the street and cycled on with his face averted. By the time he arrived at work he'd chivvied himself into permitting no further delay. Possessed of some quirks, Paul numbered among them a dislike of phones. His home phone he kept for emergencies and his work phone he was required to tolerate, but, if he could, he'd walk across town to avoid using the instrument. But call he must, so he looked up Pat's number and dialed.

"Pat?"

"Yes, who's calling?"

"I know this is peculiar. Please don't say my name aloud. This is Paul. I have information about Rudy that makes me doubt his honesty. All I'm asking is, don't do anything like investing money with him until after I've seen you."

Pat's reply came slowly, "Nothing has happened, and you're off track I'm sure. But I'll wait to hear from you."

"Thank you," he said, and hung up. The conversation was unsatisfactory. Accusations were useless if Rudy hadn't pressed her for money. He knew Pat must think poorly of him. Before anyone came to work and could overhear, he attempted another avenue. He called David Pryor at the law school. Over the years, they'd developed an amicable relationship. Usually he needed information from David, but occasionally the public library had a book or database not available at the University, and he worked hard to balance the score. David answered the phone, and Paul prefaced his request with an apology for bothering him with something he might dislike doing. "I can't give you much detail, but there's a man, Rudy Price, or I presume that's Rudolph, who's in town from Florida and I'm convinced he's running a financial scam. I don't have enough evidence to involve the police, but I'm worried about a woman who may become his victim."

"It's outside my line," replied David. "What were you thinking I'd do?"

"I know you've got Lexis and Westlaw databases that have information about people, like criminal record files."

"I can try. We can't use these databases to pry into personal information for self-satisfaction. This is a serious matter?"

"It is. And thanks for whatever you can find. I don't have an address, but I noted the license plate number of his car, would that help?"

"Possibly."

Paul gave him the plate information, thanked David again and expressed understanding if he couldn't find anything.

With his morning spent in a state of suppressed agitation, it wasn't surprising that Ruth showed concern. "Is everything okay, Paul? You're not your usual self."

"I'm fine, thanks. A couple of things looming are making me nervous, but everything will be fine." Paul was worried that Pat would come looking for him. Thoughts of an explosive discussion with Pat at his place of work suffused him with a hot, self-conscious embarrassment. Surely Spook never felt that way. It seemed unfair that imagination made you suffer the consequences of non-existent events.

After a couple of hours, David called back. "Some snippets for you. Mr. Price used to live in Pompano Beach, Broward County. He sold a house four years back for around $600,000 and there's no other trace of him since. I couldn't find any record that he owns any other real estate in Florida. There are a couple of criminal convictions, though."

"Ah, that's more promising."

"I'm not sure. He may not be law-abiding, but he only got probation. The first was in 1987 for sex with an under-age girl, then four years later for conspiracy to deliver drugs. It doesn't say what kind of drugs. He got two years probation for each offense." Paul thanked him. The information added disreputable lines to Rudy's picture but suggested no action plan.

When lunchtime arrived, he happily left his worries for the day. Only Troy Carter at Randolph Realty knew where to find him. He was a slate wiped clean of chalk, free of anyone who wanted to lay their troubles on him. Pat, Amanda, Rudy, Rolf, none of them could find him. He collected his key from the realtor's office and went to pack his apartment and take apart his furniture. Four trips in his old Ford Taurus station wagon sufficed, and on the fifth, he swept the apartment broom-clean and retrieved his complaining prisoner from the empty bedroom. "This is it, Spook. You'll like your new alleyway to prowl in. I'm hoping it will lead to something for me, too." With Spook cradled in his arms, he gave a last look at his apartment. He was ready for the romance of a new direction. "Let's go, Spook," he said excitedly.

Busy with tasks in his new home, the afternoon passed swiftly. He threw open windows, scrubbed floors, washed the walls, kitchen cabinets and drawers. By six o'clock, he'd lined and filled the kitchen cabinets and reassembled his bed, desk and small dining table. After dinner, in the hour before sunset, he investigated the backyard. With garden-clippers in hand, he pacified the riotous weeds and briars. He took a break after twenty minutes of slaughtering vegetation and wandered down the lane. He turned back when the brambles tore at him, and he came to stand in the lane by his dilapidated fence. Once he cleared the ivy, he would stand the fence upright and plant flowers in the strip of dirt between the path and fence.

Over Bronwyn's wall, he heard talking. Moving closer, he listened. He recognized Pat's voice, "The garden is beautiful. Thanks so much for inviting me."

Bronwyn answered, "I'm glad to make friends. It can be so hard. At parties, I have to stand and wait for someone to speak to me, and people are uneasy around the blind. No one likes to be reminded of their own vulnerability."

"You're probably right. Although in your own home you don't seem blind at all." Feet crunched on the gravel path close to the gate. Pat asked, "Do you mind if I look outside?" The bolt grated. He ought to speak to Pat, but, before the gate opened, he dashed behind his own fence. Too late, he realized that Pat could look in at his open gate. Probably she would, and she'd find him, obviously listening. He escaped into his doorless shed, joining the cobweb colonies and the rusty paint cans that chiefly occupied its gloomy interior. Brushing sticky strands from his hair, he peered through a slit in the boards. Pat appeared at his gate. "It's amazing," she said, "all the laneways in Lexington. We don't know half of them exist. I suppose sanitation workers used them to clean outhouses in centuries past." She left and he heard Bronwyn's gate shut. He stayed a while longer with the dust, rust and spiders, listening after the sounds of conversation had gone.

Bronwyn's living room was filled with the warmth of evening sunlight and the delight of the ladies with each other's company. Pat was gently curious about Bronwyn's life of blindness, which Bronwyn assured her was healthier than avoidance. "How do you do that without it spilling?" Pat asked, as Bronwyn poured a glass of red wine.

"By myself, I stop pouring when my fingertip gets wet. I'm guessing you wouldn't like that, so I listen as it splashes in. I can hear how full the glass is."

Bronwyn sat on the couch with Nigel at her feet and Pat beside her. "Tell me about your aunt," Pat said.

"Okay. Quick family history. My father, Robert, and my Aunt Josie are twins, born in 1945. Their sister, Phyllis, came along ten years later. Sam is Aunt Josie's only child, and he still lives in Lexington. I'm an only-child, too. Aunt Phyllis never married."

"Were you and Sam close?"

"Considering how little I was here. Sam and I were born in Lexington in 1980, but after a few months Dad was carting Mom and me around the world. When Mom died, Dad needed somewhere for me to come, so I spent a few summers in Lexington from the age of twelve onwards. Supposedly, I stayed with Aunt Josie, but mostly I was with Aunt Phyllis. Aunt Josie seemed a lot older."

"Phyllis was about twenty-five years older than you? Not close to your age."

"But she was fun. The summer I was twelve, we moved the furniture to the middle of my bedroom, covered the floor with an oilcloth and Aunt Phyllis gave me a painting orgy. It was the craziest thing. Dressed in swimsuits we painted any colors and shapes I wanted on the walls."

"Is your art work still here?"

"Sam told me it got painted over. My aunt thought I wouldn't miss it."

"Stop me if I'm nosy, but Sam didn't inherit anything?"

"I'm sure Aunt Phyllis loved him, but she must have thought I needed the house more. Aunt Josie said that Aunt Phyllis had about $10,000 in the bank when she died, which was enough to bury her and pay her bills. There's some mystery there. Aunt Phyllis had money, but it had no substantial source."

"So you'd like to find account books, check records, that sort of thing?"

"Or anything about her life. There are built-in bookcases in the bedrooms. There might be something personal among them, and, as I said on the phone, I'd like to donate books to a library. We could make piles, and I'll ask Paul to look at them."

Pat smiled and said, "Where should we start?"

"The sideboard in this room has some drawers. I think there are photo-albums, at least. Then we can work through the bedrooms."

The photographs, they soon agreed, were best looked at by a family member. Moving from bedroom to bedroom, they left much of the history and biography on the shelves and stacked art books in the corners of the room.

"In my younger days, I was an art teacher," Pat said. "There are some beautiful books here. Worth money. Wouldn't you like to find a buyer for them?"

"No. I'd prefer to give them away. Please take any you want."

"Only if we find romantic comedies. Froth and trivia's my style these days."

It was getting late in the evening when Pat, standing on a dining-chair to reach the highest shelves, said, "Here's something!"

"What is it?"

"Stacked behind other books up here ... I'll do some shifting."

"Well?" Bronwyn asked impatiently, hearing shuffling from one shelf to another.

"A dozen books were at the back of the shelf. They look like diaries. I've moved them down in the same order I found them."

Bronwyn felt over the books and pulled the first one from the shelf. Holding it out, she said, excitedly, "See if it's a diary."

Pat flipped the pages, back to front, stopping at the first page. "It's a journal with printed lines. Whoever wrote in it dated each entry. The first is August 9, 1970. If it's Phyllis she was around fifteen then."

"Please, read the first entry for me."

Sun., Aug. 9, 1970. Mom and dad have been gone a week today. I'm lonely without them. They gave me this book on my last birthday and I thought then, who keeps a diary? But I'll start it now and see if I like it.

"My grandparents died in a train crash. How sad it must have been for Phyllis. This is a wonderful find, but it's getting late, and I need to be up for work in the morning. Would you help read tomorrow evening if I made you dinner?"

"You couldn't keep me away," Pat said. "What time?"

"Let's say at 6:00? The microwave and I will team up to make lasagna."

Chapter 11   Friday

Eager to get the diaries transcribed, Bronwyn numbered twelve sticky notes, inserted them in sequence in the books and put the books in her backpack. "Come along, Nigel. Go to work." With Nigel at her side, she had few problems moving around town. She followed Nigel's lead at curbs and traffic lights, and Nigel guided her around bikes lying in their path. Nigel knew the way to her work, up Cherry Lane to Main Street, across seven intersections to Nelson Street, left and past one street to the counseling center. She trusted Nigel, but she also carried a mental map, counting crossroads, identifying buildings by smell or the echoes of her footsteps.

She and Nigel stopped at the corner of Main and Nelson while she used her phone to call operator assistance. On Jefferson Street, around the corner from her work, there was a print shop. Connected to them, she explained her situation and asked if they could look out in three minutes and tell her when she reached their doorway. Nigel guided her across Jefferson Street and instead of going the half-block to her office, she directed him left. A minute later she heard, "Hi. I'm Dave Hickman. This is the Jefferson Print Shop. It's up the steps to your right." Dave trotted up four wooden steps. "I'm holding the door open," he said. "The counter is to your right." She removed the journals from her backpack and placed them on the counter.

"You've been kind," she said. To set him at ease, she smiled and said, "You probably don't have many blind customers."

"I can safely say you're our very first."

"These are my aunt's diaries. She passed away last October. They're very important to me. I wanted photocopies made of all the pages and," she said apologetically, "I was hoping to get that done today."

Dave had been glancing through the volumes as she spoke. He said, "If we include facing pages in each copy then it's probably a two hour job. We can do it this morning for about $120. Is that too much?"

"No. That's fine. I'll come back at lunchtime to get them. I have another request. If you can't do it, perhaps you might suggest someone. I need the diaries transcribed into a text file so my computer can read them to me. I'm also concerned about my aunt's privacy. She lived in Lexington for a long time. I was hoping whoever transcribes the diaries would have no personal interest in their content."

"Hmmm," Dave hesitated. "We could find you a service out of town. It's self-serving, so shoot it down if you want, but my sister, Irene, is a secretary. She's laid off from the school system up in Staunton. She's a fast typist, and I know she'd like the income. What do you think?"

"That's great, if she'd do it."

"I'm out on a limb, but maybe it's a week's work? I think she'd be happy with $600. I'm having dinner with her tonight. If it's something you're both comfortable with, I'll arrange it." Bronwyn readily agreed. Relieved to have her needs met, she went happily on to work.

Paul knocked on Pat's door in mild dread.

"Good morning. Please come in." Pat's neutral tone chilled him. She indicated the front room. He sat in the most unyielding chair the room offered.

"I'm listening, Paul."

He pressed his knees together, clasped his hands on his lap and commenced his story. "I truly wouldn't interfere, except that I'm worried about you." Pat nodded. Feeling slightly encouraged, he continued, "On Monday, in the library, I recognized one of the men who attacked your car. I threatened him with the police, and he told me that Rudy's nephew, Todd, instigated the vandalism. He thought for some insurance scam."

"What was the young man's name?"

"I didn't ask him."

"But you believe this no-name person, who'd say anything to get out of trouble? Even if it was Rudy's nephew, you can't hold Rudy responsible. He knows Todd's a troublemaker. That's partly why Rudy's in Lexington, to be a role model for the boy."

"I did think Rudy was involved and in some way a danger to you, so I followed him the next evening when he left your house." Pat frowned at this. He'd known it would displease her. "He went directly from your house to a house owned by Monique Newcomb."

"I don't know the name. You believe they're lovers?" Paul nodded. "It's more likely she's a relative, wouldn't you think," Pat suggested forcefully.

"I can't give you proof, but it's not like that."

"I'm trying not to be angry with you, but I am disappointed. When I was a middle-school principal, I had a situation with students following a teacher home. They hid behind bushes and cars, watching her house. It was juvenile, but threatening. I had to put a stop to it. Even if your motive is good, you can't be hanging around my house watching. You do understand that?"

"I do." Desperately wanting to leave, he pushed on with his message. "Please, let me say what I came to say and then I'll go." She nodded, and he went on in quiet hopelessness. "He has a criminal record. Back in the late eighties and early nineties he was convicted of having sex with a minor and dealing in drugs."

"This won't do. Rudy has been open about his history. A girl who looked twenty was only sixteen. She was the police chief's niece, and from then the police were out to get him. They planted marijuana in his house and got him in trouble. When he left the county, he left that behind. Is there anything else?"

Roiling with embarrassment and frustration, Paul sat stiffly erect on his chair. "This involves a friend, so I can't tell you the source, but I believe Rudy has a scheme to defraud investors. I'm worried he'll ask you to invest. He pretends to represent a company that buys land around expanding cities and resells at a profit. There'd be nothing wrong if it was honest, but I'm afraid he means to steal from his investors."

"Enough, Paul. There's not a speck of proof in any of this, is there?" Paul shook his head sadly. "You've been consumed by a fantasy. I appreciate your interest in my welfare. For that reason, I'll defer judgment. Rudy is taking me tomorrow to the church picnic at the lake. I'll ask his advice. Tell him I'm unhappy with my investments. If he offers his 'scheme,' as you call it, I'll dig for details. Will that satisfy you?"

Paul stood, relieved to have the interview done. "Thanks. I'm truly sorry if I offended you." He left, emotionally exhausted, and was oblivious to his surroundings until he found himself cycling up to the back door of the library. "If I keep on this way I'll need a psychologist," Paul grumbled.

He revisited the confrontation many times that morning, finally concluding that he'd done what needed doing. As Pat had assumed responsibility, he cheered up and wasn't surprised when Ruth asked him, "Things looking up today?" and he could honestly say they were.

Bronwyn and Nigel left the counseling office on a pleasant spring afternoon. They walked into Hopkins Green, a tiny square of grass in the center of town bordered by a path and a few benches. Nigel followed his regular pattern and circled the grassy area to select his toilet spot. Bronwyn felt Nigel's back and pointed her toe toward his rear. When he moved away, she followed the line of her foot and retrieved the poop into a plastic bag. They walked to the corner of the park and deposited the bag in a bin. "Good boy, Nigel," Bronwyn said.

"I always wondered how that was done."

"Mr. Wardle?" asked Bronwyn.

"Yes, but please, it's 'John.' I hope we can be informal."

"'John' it is. Were you watching me?"

"It was nothing intentional, I assure you. You may not know this, but it's traditional in the Episcopal Church for the vestry to give the responsibility for the church building to the office of Junior Warden, which, of course, is my position, and--"

"And part of your office is observing ladies in the park?"

"We're getting along well enough for you to tease me," he said, laughing. "No, I was justifying my viewing you. It's because I'm by trade a builder that I was appointed to the office of Junior Warden, and you can't see it, of course, but my ladder is across the street. The bookstore there is concerned about the condition of the molding under their eaves, and they definitely are quite unsound."

"With my clients I have to be more circumspect in discussing their condition with strangers in the park. Builders have no confidential duty in regard to their client's unsound molding?"

"Goodness, I wouldn't have thought of that. You believe there's a privacy issue? I'll have to think on that, but then, we're not strangers, are we? Would you like to sit with me for a minute?"

Bronwyn agreed, and they sat on a nearby bench. "You were on your ladder when you saw me?" prompted Bronwyn.

"I was. And I couldn't help but see you and your dog."

"We were defecating."

"Yes. I came down to speak to you, and I admired its precision. A man like myself takes pleasure in the tenon fitting precisely in the mortise. That's a woodworking metaphor."

"Thank you, John, I appreciate the clarification. Many females would be unaware of the mortise and tenon joint."

"Exactly. Like any specialist I enjoy the language of my trade, although, of course, jargon can obscure the point for those not in the know."

"Are you a professional builder, licensed and insured?"

"I am. I can say honestly that my reputation is second to none in Lexington."

"Do you take small jobs? There are a few things I'd like done at my house."

"I'd be happy to help you. I can come on the weekend or early some evening?"

"What about Sunday? If I made you a sandwich for lunch, it wouldn't be like working on Sunday. You could visit, look at the house, and give me some suggestions?" They agreed to meet after church. John returned to his ladder and Bronwyn and Nigel continued home.

Pat arrived promptly at 6:00. "Can you give me a hand with dinner?" Bronwyn asked, "I'll get the lasagna going if you cut the bread. The table's set. There's nothing else to do but pour the wine." With their few preparations done, and while the lasagna was heating, they sat at the dining table to talk and sip wine.

"I never knew your Aunt Phyllis," Pat said regretfully. "I've been in Lexington for six years, but we never met. Of course, in small towns, without similar interests to bring you together, you might see someone frequently on the street and never know it. Did your aunt belong to any groups?"

"I wish I knew. During my summers here, she was devoted to entertaining me."

Over dinner, they chatted amiably about their backgrounds. For Pat it was a life in Kalispell, Montana, rising through the school system until her unhappy, but profitable, marriage brought her an early retirement. "With its snow-capped mountains, that part of Montana is truly beautiful, but it's cold much of the year. That's why I came to Lexington. We have mountains here, and it's not too hot or cold. Just right, as Baby Bear says."

Bronwyn explained her nomadic childhood. "My upbringing was like a U.N. meeting. I had a Greek mother. My first three years were in Brazil. My dad worked for the State Department. Every few years we'd be stationed somewhere else. After Brazil, it was Argentina, India, and then Egypt. When I was nine we traveled by boat from Egypt to Pakistan and my mother was lost at sea."

"How awful for you. At such a young age."

"We never knew what happened. She just vanished." Bronwyn paused, remembering. "No home, no mother, and I wasn't used to relying on dad. There was a Pakistani mother on the boat, going home to Lahore. She added me to her brood. I'd be far more neurotic if it wasn't for her and her girls. When I turned eleven, Dad shipped me to boarding school in England. I had a summer with Dad in London and three summers in Lexington. The last three years of high school, I was with Dad in Lisbon. He was making up for years of neglect and wasn't available much even then, but it was more than I'd had before. I loved it."

"What a varied upbringing! Quite the contrast to a small Virginia town and--forgive my saying so--to your more limited life now."

"That's true, although it's not like I'm under a dark blanket. It's easy to feel pity, my not seeing the sunset, never seeing my baby, if I have one, but a lot's left. I even astound people. Paul was amazed on Sunday when I knew it was him, walking behind me."

"Ah! Paul, now there's an interesting character, speaking of neurotic."

"Really?" asked Bronwyn with a lively interest. "I like him. I think he likes me too."

"Oh, he does. I saw him looking at you after church on Sunday."

Bronwyn smiled, "In that case we'll forgive him a few small neuroses."

"It's not my place to interfere, but I'd doubt his maturity level."

"Men are boys, aren't they," agreed Bronwyn. "I'm finished with dinner. Are you? I'd love to get on to Aunt Phyllis' diaries." They cleared up, refilled their wine glasses and sat on the couch. Pat re-read the first entry from August 9th. "I can read the diaries myself in another week," Bronwyn said. "Just zip past entries that don't catch your eye."

"Okay. Here's one a few days later."

Sat., Aug. 15, 1970. Josie and her blob of a husband Willis came by this afternoon. He patted me on the head. He's such an idiot. Josie said there wasn't enough to pay for our parent's funeral. Ever since dad hurt his back he hadn't worked, and Josie said they were poor. Willis said he'd give more than his share and patted my head again. I swatted him one. It's not my parents fault. They loved me and didn't mean to leave me. Nanny Ellen said it would be okay. Anyway, with Nanny I don't feel poor.

"Just as well you didn't have your Aunt Josie read the diaries," Pat said.

Bronwyn nodded. "My aunt's opinion of Willis is quite plain. From what I remember, she felt the same toward Aunt Josie."

"Is Willis still alive?"

"He died of an aneurysm about five years ago."

"Clue me in. Who was living here in the house with your Aunt Phyllis?"

"Let me think … Ellen's husband, my great-grandfather Daniel, died in the mid-sixties, and Ellen lived here alone. My grandfather had his accident on the building site, and he, my grandmother, and Phyllis moved in with Ellen."

"Okay," said Pat, "So three generations lived here. Then Phyllis' parents died in the train crash, and Phyllis was left to her grandmother. Did you ever know Ellen?"

"I wish I had. She died a few years before I was born."

Pat turned a few pages and read on.

Fri., Aug. 21, 1970. My parents won't ever have another birthday. It was Nanny Ellen's 70th birthday today. I made poppy-seed cake. Old ladies from the church came for tea in the afternoon. Nanny said poppy-seeds weren't good for their dentures, but she liked the cake. She complained it's hard outliving your son. She must have forgot he was my dad, too. I don't plan on getting married so I won't have to worry about losing anyone. It's a good thing we have each other, even if Nanny does put her teeth in a glass and it's gross.

Wed., Sept. 9, 1970. Clarence Perkins asked me out. Nanny Ellen says he's all angles and bones, and she's about right. He came running after me when school let out, so eager and pathetic that I said I'd go with him to Shelly Huffman's party on Friday. Shelly's pretty, and her crowd will be there. I hope nobody thinks I shouldn't go, a month after my parents died.

Fri., Sept. 11, 1970. I didn't wear black. People would just say they were sorry. Clarence doesn't drive, so we walked to Shelly's, about six blocks away on Lee Avenue. A tall brick home built before one of those old wars. Shelly had a ring of stones in the backyard and the boys kept the fire going with branches. Clarence roasted a marshmallow for me. The more he spun his stick in the air the more it flamed. The hiss and flare circles in my mind now. It was like a spacecraft from Mars, all squished and charred when it landed. But I picked it up and ate it and any little doomed Martians inside. We went up the staircase to the third floor looking at the old paintings on the walls. I wanted to see the faces of the dead people. Clarence pulled me into a bedroom on the top floor and closed the door. I knew what he wanted and I was curious too. I jumped on the bed and watched him. When his underwear came off it was like a wrinkled worm in a nest and I laughed. Clarence said that wasn't helpful. He got on the bed and as I glanced down at his worm he sucked my nose. I got the giggles and Clarence was mad. I wouldn't take my clothes off. I learned that boys don't grow bigger when they're laughed at.

"Phyllis had a poor introduction," Pat said. "My first attempt wasn't any better. Once his hands were on my breasts, his ejaculation was all over me. Now that's pretty messy," she laughed. "The nice thing with boys that age is they're ready again in ten minutes, so he got what he wanted after I showered."

With Pat twice her own age, Bronwyn found their girlish intimacy strange, but Pat was an odd mixture of experience and youthful fervor. Imagining her Aunt Phyllis there, and them all talking about boys, Bronwyn said, "My first was in Lisbon. He was eighteen and I was sixteen. It was on a couch like this. I spent an hour after, soaping and scrubbing so Dad wouldn't see any evidence."

"Was it enjoyable?"

"It was scary and contorted, but thankfully fast. If I'd been sensible, I would have put a towel down, but, sensible, I wouldn't have done it then at all. We hadn't gone out much before I got angry with him for eyeing everything in a skirt."

"Rudy's like that. But at least he's focused on the right fifty-percent."

"Not very discriminating, though," Bronwyn said. "You don't have personal experience of lovers turning out gay, do you?"

"Not myself. In another week, I'm booked on an Alaska cruise with an old girlfriend. She had two children with her husband before he announced he was gay. They divorced, but they get along famously. Gay guys make best friends, but it's wasteful marrying one."

"I'll keep that in mind," Bronwyn smiled, "and only go for men who ogle women. You said Paul was staring at me. That's a start."

Pat returned to flipping through pages.

Wed., Sept. 16, 1970. I wish mom and dad could be here for my 16th birthday. Josie brought a make-up case and said she'd show me how to use it, but she's a know-it-all big sister trying to take mom's place. If this were my house I wouldn't have to answer the door when she came. I got brushes, paper and watercolor paints from Nanny Ellen, which was great. It wasn't a surprise as we got them in Charlottesville last week. And Nanny took me to get my driver's permit so I can drive soon.

Sat., Sept. 19, 1970. Nanny Ellen made me have a birthday party. I wanted girls but she said some boys too, so I asked Jason and Clarence. I put two cups of Nanny's vodka in the ginger-ale punch and two cups of water in Nanny's vodka bottle. The boys got in a fight. Jason said Clarence had a small weener. Clarence said only fags look in the locker room, and anyway Jason's was the small weener. After cake and punch we played Monopoly. The boys got in a fight again and I kicked them out. Next time I'll just have girls. We decided when men lose their land and railroads their thingies shrivel and look like boiled peanuts.

Tue., Oct. 27, 1970. The art prize I won yesterday was taken back today and my entry was disqualified. Valerie and I had already spent the five dollar prize, so they couldn't get that back. It's not to go on my record anymore and Stephanie Coulter's dumb painting of a tulip won. Mine was a painting of boiled peanuts in their shells, soft and grub-like, brown and lumpy. There was one for each boy in art class. Valerie, Helen and I were in hysterics over who they belonged to. I didn't say which one was Clarence. Helen guessed. So how did she know? It went around school and I got called into the vice-principal's office. I said it was a painting of boiled peanuts and he got red in the face, but what could he say? A lot of fuss over peanuts, but it shows how art's important. Valerie said I was brave. It's Helen that blabbed. Next time I'll paint two pumpkins that have rotted a week past Halloween and I'll whisper that they're Helen's boobs.

"The girl's got fire," Pat said.
"What happened to it? I mean, in the summers I was here she was an oddball, but otherwise I've the impression her life was monastic. Like someone said 'get thee to a nunnery,' and she retired behind these high walls."
"The promise of our youth isn't always fulfilled."
"Sad, if that was true for Aunt Phyllis," Bronwyn said somberly. "It's as if at sixteen we're deciding her life will be a failure. I just hate it."
"There are more pages in her life. Let's not bemoan her fate yet," advised Pat.
"I'm getting tired. Could we read more another day? Will we see each other at the church picnic tomorrow afternoon?"
"Oh yes, I'll be there."
"Maybe we could pick up again the day after, on Sunday afternoon? Say around 3:00?"
"Love to," Pat agreed.

Chapter 12   Saturday

Planning to take bread to the picnic, Bronwyn had borrowed sourdough starter from her aunt Josie. She'd fed it flour, warm water and a pinch of sugar and left it to activate on the kitchen counter. The previous evening, after Pat left, she'd gently kneaded flour with the spongy liquid, rolled the result into a slightly tacky ball and set it in a bowl to rise overnight.

"What do you think makes it so satisfying?" she asked Nigel, working the dough through another kneading. She was confident he looked attentive. Her talks with Nigel were frequent and full of sympathy, but somewhat lacking in understanding. She divided the dough into two bread pans, covered each with plastic wrap and let them rise in the sunshine. A couple of hours later the dough was above the tops of the bread pans. The pungent sour yeast smell filled the kitchen, activating memories of her mother, happy in a kitchen. "You're here now, aren't you, Mom." Bronwyn listened, as if to the breath of her departed mother. "What fun we'd have," she sighed.

Aunt Phyllis' old oven exactly suited Bronwyn. Aunt Josie had shown her the settings on each knob and she had no trouble controlling the temperature and the timer. When Sam arrived, the bread had been baking for thirty-five minutes. "Smells great," he said. "I'm starving. Can I have a slice before we go?"

"You'll have to wait. There's no way I'm bringing a partly eaten loaf. Mentioning slices brings up something I've wanted to ask. Can you tell me something honestly?"

"Maybe. If it's about my eating your slice of mom's rhubarb pie when we were fourteen, I deny it."

"This is serious. It's about Aunt Phyllis. I want to know if you or your mother are upset that she left everything to me."

"Ummm," Sam responded. "Honestly? Mom was angry. Aunt Phyllis was smart, leaving her will with the attorney. Mom would have torn it up if she'd found it. I can understand her feelings, with her brother's child being favored over her own."

"How about you?"

"It hurt. But the house was all Aunt Phyllis had to leave, and she'd naturally think of your needs.

"Did you feel that Aunt Phyllis loved me more?"

Sam laughed. "There you go, psychoanalyzing me. We got along. She was fond of me, but she loved you. When you called or wrote, it was all she'd talk about."

"I do wish I'd understood that better. I hate it, that I neglected her after my blindness. It's a catalog of excuses. I was pretty depressed for a year, then I focused on my masters degree and starting out in practice. I was too self-absorbed." She began crying quietly.

"Oh Bronwyn, don't. Please."

"I'm sorry. I can't roll back the years and make it right. Everything gets taken away."

Sam put a tissue in her hand. "Give yourself a shake. There's plenty to be thankful for. And I haven't gone anywhere."

Bronwyn licked the tears from her lip and gave him a wobbly smile. "Sorry to do that in front of you."

Diverting to safer ground, Sam asked, "Is Mom going to the picnic?"

"Yes. She's riding with Pam Wardle and John."

The bell on the stove rang. Bronwyn put the loaves on a wire rack to cool. Sam helped her pack and, after a few minutes, they left for the lake.

It was nearly one o'clock when Sam drove onto the gravel parking area below the pavilion. "Will any of your other lovers be here, or is it just John?" he asked.

"I'm devaluing Rudy as an admirer. He and Pat seem to be an item, so his looking at my breasts seems less of a positive. I hope Paul is coming. Maybe there's some way to leave him a seat between us?" she asked shyly.

Sam smiled at her discomfort. "Sure, we can spread ourselves on a bench and take up room for three. I'll make growling noises so only your true love will dare approach."

"Thanks, Sam, but don't over-do chasing away suitors. We'll leave the growls to Nigel. Can you describe where we are?"

"Parking lot here. Straight ahead is the pavilion. To our right is the swimming pool, but probably it's not open for the season yet." As they walked up the small incline to the pavilion, Sam continued, "There are two rows of picnic tables in the shelter, around sixteen tables I think. The food's on a row of tables on the far side of the pavilion. Toilets are at the left end of the pavilion, men's to the left, women's to the right." Sam led Nigel and Bronwyn past the picnic tables and made room for their cutting board on the food table.

"Hello, Bronwyn. It's a pleasure to have you at our gathering. Dexter Forbes here."

"Yes, of course, Father Forbes. Your voice is quite distinctive."

"Is it, my dear? Loud, you mean."

"Oh, no. Deep as a purring Rolls-Royce, that could roar if it wished."

"You have an excellent auditory imagination, Bronwyn. To complete the picture, you may visualize me as stately as a Rolls, if somewhat on the portly side. It's nice to see you here, Sam. Thanks for bringing Bronwyn."

"My pleasure, Father Forbes."

The rector turned to Pat and Rudy, who had joined them. "Pat, Rudy, welcome. It's wonderful how we come to gravitate in front of the food." Jiggling his belly up and down he said, "Speaking just for myself, the food has come to gravitate in front of me." Bronwyn laughed, and he thanked her for tolerating his joke. "We have an excellent turn-out today. There must be a hundred hungry souls. Everyone, I suspect, is politely waiting for my blessing before they rush the food, so if you'll excuse me." He went to stand in the center of the pavilion and in an energetic voice said, "The Lord be with you." The congregation responded. He led them in a short prayer then commanded everyone to eat and have a good time.

"Clever of us, to be at the head of the food line," Rudy said, as they moved to the salad end of the table.

"Start us, then," Pat urged. "Bronwyn, can we sit with you?"

"Of course, I'd love that."

"There you are, Sam," said Josie breathlessly. "That hill is unreasonably steep. We're late because John wanted to bring his boat to take Bronwyn out on the water. A nice idea, but not well thought out. It took longer than we expected to hitch it to the car. Push yourself in there, John, can't you see that Bronwyn needs a plate."

"Certainly, Mrs. Stickley. Allow me, Bronwyn," John said, inserting himself beside her. "I'm holding your plate in front of you." Bronwyn felt for it and thanked him. "I'll describe the dishes," he said. "If you tell me what you like, I'll serve you." The group moved slowly down the food table with the congregation lining up behind them. "We have our choice of tables," John said. "If we head to the side near the parking, we'll be away from the food line."

"An excellent idea," said his mother.

John chose a table and turned to Bronwyn, "I'll sit at the end and you can sit next to me."

"No, no, John," his mother said. "Come on this side of the table between Josie and me. You can be opposite Bronwyn."

"Yes, of course, Mother," John replied and obediently went around the picnic bench.

"Sit where you are, Bronwyn. I'll be at the end," Sam said. He added in a whisper, "I'll use up the extra space between us. Put Nigel under the bench between us and you're well defended."

"Bronwyn, I'll sit here on your right. Rudy can squeeze next to me," Pat said.

Bronwyn leaned her head toward Pat and asked softly, "Have you seen Paul?"

"No. I wanted to speak to him myself. If I see him I'll drag him to our table."

"I'm so sorry, Bronwyn," exclaimed John. "I forgot your utensils." He rushed off to the food table. Returning, he laid them on the table with a flourish, saying, "Enjoy your food, Bronwyn."

"Thanks, John."

"Paul, Paul, come here," Pat called, seeing him hurry up the hill.

Paul came over. "Sorry I'm late," he apologized.

"We were afraid you weren't coming," Bronwyn said. "Here Sam, squeeze over and let Paul sit." She re-settled Nigel beneath her, finding room for Paul.

"The man needs to get his food," John observed.

"No point. Look at the line," rejoined Sam. "It'll be ten minutes before there's a path to the food."

Paul sat and explained that he'd worked at the library until one o'clock. "I sneaked out a little early and drove faster than I should have on those winding roads. I made good time. I hate being late."

"You weren't trying for the dramatic entrance?" asked Rudy.

"I'm overly punctual. I must have been punished for tardiness as a kid."

"Could be," Bronwyn said. "Our oddities usually trace to childhood."

"Introverted personality, I expect," Rudy said. "Not wanting to be noticed."

"That's a librarian trait, isn't it?" contributed John.

"I wouldn't say that wanting to be prompt is a negative," objected Sam.

"Sam, you haven't met Paul," Bronwyn said. "Paul, this is my cousin, Sam. His mother is my Aunt Josie."

"It's good to meet you," Paul said.

"Likewise. Happy to meet a friend of Bronwyn's."

Josie whispered to John, and he said, "Bronwyn, I understand you made this bread, it really is delicious. It's amazing that you can bake so well."

"You think so? Thanks. I enjoyed cooking before I was blind, and still do. Although in this case I'd say that anything with butter on it is going to taste good. Paul, I have a slice on my plate. I hate to think of you starving as we eat. Please, take it."

"Thanks. I am hungry." He took the slice and devoured it.

"And what do you think of the bread?" Pamela asked Paul.

It was an awkward question. In the ordinary way of admiration Paul would have liked to tell Bronwyn that he enjoyed her bread. However, in a competition, he wouldn't leap over John's compliment, even if easily accomplished. What came out was less than satisfactory. "To a starving man, everything tastes good."

Bronwyn laughed, "You certainly aren't talented with praise."

"Sadly, that's true. I've tasted sourdough bread before like this. It reminds me of the bread my mother baked when I was little."

"Now that's an excellent compliment," Bronwyn said.

"May I join you?" asked Dexter Forbes sitting down next to Josie. "Paul, you've no food. That needs rectifying."

"I was waiting for the stragglers to get to the trough. But they almost have. I'll go now."

"I've plenty of other good advice, if only my flock would listen." The rector sighed dramatically.

Paul left, and Pat leaned toward the rector saying quietly, "Father, I'd like to speak to you later about the carpets and pews."

"Yes, of course, Pat."

"I agree with you, Pat," interjected Josie. "No doubt you have in mind my nearly falling last Sunday. Those carpets are a menace."

"I'm sure a solution will be found, Josie," said the rector soothingly. "Let's not worry about it today." He turned toward John, "I'm told you brought your boat, John."

"I have. I was hoping Bronwyn would let me take her on the lake."

"And some of the other young people, I'm sure, would love to venture onto the water," the rector proposed. "Sam and Paul, I expect?"

"Yes, of course, Father Forbes," John replied. "The boat does seat four."

"We brought a boat too," Pat said. "Rudy is an experienced sailor. He borrowed his brother-in-law's boat. Would you like to come with us, Father?"

"You could calm the waters, if the waves blow," Rudy said.

"If only I could, but I must circulate among my flock on land. Another time, possibly."

Paul returned with a heaped plate and an extra plate with a slice of turkey. "Paul, John has invited you and Sam to go out on his boat with me," Bronwyn said.

"Thanks, John," Paul said. "Sounds like fun." To Bronwyn, he said quietly, "I brought extra turkey that I thought Nigel would enjoy."

Bronwyn hesitated. "He follows a strict eating routine. It means, if nothing else, that his toilet times are reliable. He'd certainly love you for it, and it's tempting, but I think not."

"Yes, of course. I didn't think it through. I should have asked first." Speaking to the table at large, Paul asked, "Would anyone like the turkey?"

"I'll take it from you," John said. Unopposed, he speared it with his fork.

"Bronwyn, I have an extra slice of bread on my plate, if you'd like it," Paul said.

"I'm sorry. It would interfere with my toilet time." She chuckled, "Just my lame joke. I'll take part of it."

Pleased that Bronwyn wanted to share his slice, he cut it in half and asked, "Should I put it on your plate?" Bronwyn offered her left hand, and he placed the bread on her palm. In removing his hand, the tip of his little finger, light as a dandelion seed, traversed the base of her thumb. His audacity stirred him, like a loitering street corner youth, to further rambunctious thoughts, and, searching for a means to serve her, he asked, "Would you like some water or lemonade, Bronwyn?"

"Please eat your lunch."

"Let me," John said, standing. "I'm going for a drink. Would you like something, Bronwyn?"

"Water, thanks, John."

Paul found John's officiousness irritating. Having a good appetite, and, not wanting to be dragging behind the group, he put his head down and engaged with his meal.

Pat and Rudy had left to put their boat on the water, the rector had gone to mingle, and Amanda and Susan had come to visit their table. "Hi Paul," Amanda said. His mouth stuffed, Paul nodded, acknowledging her presence. "This must be Bronwyn. I've been hearing about you. A partner of a friend of mine saw you professionally, but we won't say names. I was talking to Father Forbes a few days ago, and he was singing your praises."

"It's hopeless, looking for anonymity in Lexington," Bronwyn replied pleasantly.

"My partner, Susan, is next to you, Bronwyn," Amanda said.

Bronwyn exchanged greetings with Susan. "Did you know that Amanda is Paul's ex?" asked Susan.

"No, I didn't. That's interesting."

"That you're sandwiched between my two lovers?" Amanda joked.

"We don't need to go into that," said Josie.

"Some find it interesting," retorted Amanda.

"People are interested in lots of things best kept private," John responded.

"Do Amanda and Susan know everyone at the table?" asked Bronwyn. "Do you know my cousin, Sam?"

"Hi Sam," Amanda said. "You're Josie's son, aren't you? Your mother and I are on the Altar Guild together. We argue over carnations and lilies."

"You do exaggerate, Amanda. There are rules to follow. And I, for one, am allergic to lilies, and there are many of a similar mind."

"It's true, Josie," said Pamela. "We're alike in that."

"Bronwyn," asked John, "and Sam and Paul, would you like to walk down by the lake? There's a path leading to the boat ramp." He added apologetically, "I only have life-vests and seats for four,"

"An excellent idea," said Josie. "But you must look after Bronwyn on the rough spots in the path."

"In my son's hands she'll be as safe as an egg," said Pamela. "I'd like to come, too. A walk would be good after lunch."

"I'll join you," said Josie.

"Susan?" queried Amanda. "It's unanimous, then. We're all up for a hike."

Paul finished his lunch and stood to clear up. "I'll take your plate, Bronwyn," he said. In his eagerness, his arm knocked her cup, spilling it onto her lap. She stood quickly, brushing water off her jeans. He gasped, "I'm so sorry," and thrust a paper napkin from the table into her hands. "I need to watch what I'm doing."

"No problem. The cup was nearly empty."

"Let's go to the bathroom, Bronwyn," Susan said, "We'll dry you off."

Paul sat down, embarrassed at his awkwardness.

John chuckled. "We won't make you captain. If you can't keep a cup upright, you'd be bound to sink us." Paul nodded, agreeing with that wisdom. He picked Bronwyn's cup off the ground and busied himself clearing the table and trucking everything to the bin. Avoiding more conversation, he helped clear other tables.

Their group collected at the top of the grassy slope that led to the lake and watched the men play horseshoes and the children, croquet. When Bronwyn, Susan and Nigel returned from the bathroom, Paul joined the group. As they set off, he made his way beside Bronwyn. He had an impulse to apologize again but limited himself to asking if she was dry.

"Almost. I'll get wetter on the lake, and we won't worry about it then, so it's nothing now."

"Not to fear," John said from her other side. "The lake's perfectly calm today. I'll make sure you don't get wet, unless, of course, someone splashes you."

The path lay at the base of a moderately wooded hill with the lake a few feet to their right. Amanda and Susan strode ahead. The remaining group soon straggled apart. John stayed just ahead of Bronwyn and Nigel. When the path widened he'd drop back to offer solicitous help on the placement of her feet, otherwise he'd be turning to her, reporting on conditions. The path was safe and well maintained but the hard-packed dirt surface dipped and rose, and Bronwyn needed to concentrate. Paul and Sam strolled behind Bronwyn. Pamela and Josie struggled in the rear. The cause of their rough going they ascribed to their shoes, poorly designed for dirt trails.

Sam began an investigation of Paul with, "Bronwyn seems to like you a lot."

"Does she? She's a great person, although we should worry about her judgment if she likes me a lot."

"Bronwyn's very charitable. She puts up with me, but I'm her only cousin, so she doesn't have much choice."

"There's nobody on her mother's side?"

"I don't think so. If there is, her father hasn't been helpful. He basically cut off that side of the family."

"Family secrets, we all have them," Paul said. Then he asked, "What do you do for a living?" that being a question that moved a discussion along.

"I work for the Forestry Service. When you want to know which of these," Sam indicated the wooded slopes with a gesture, "are poplars and which are oaks, let me know."

"You could tell me anything, and I'd believe you."

"In that case, I'd say that you like Bronwyn a lot, too."

"Isn't that from Shakespeare? You tell me Bronwyn likes me, and you tell Bronwyn I like her, and before we know it, there's romance?"

Sam laughed. "Rebuke accepted. Tell me this, don't you find Bronwyn's blindness disturbing to deal with?"

"Psychologically? More in the abstract, I suppose. I've never known a blind person. I feel pity and hero worship at the same time, but it's hard to pity Bronwyn."

Ahead, Bronwyn and Nigel had stopped. Sam asked what the hold-up was. "Nigel won't move," Bronwyn said.

"It's a snake beside the path," Paul said excitedly. "A black snake, four feet in front of you, to your left. They're not harmful, I think."

John, who had unknowingly walked past the snake, came back. Perceiving the danger, he seized a broken branch from the hillside and warned Bronwyn back.

"Don't kill it," Paul appealed to him. "It's harmless."

"Its bite's nothing pleasant," John said tartly.

"Use your stick to nudge it up the hill," Sam advised.

"It's safer to kill it. It'll bite someone," responded John. Josie and Pamela had reached the group and added their voices to the verdict.

"Please, John, let it live," pleaded Bronwyn.

"Too dangerous," John said, in a passion to protect her and to wield his stick. "Some child will come along next and be bitten and, who knows, get infected." Before more protests could be heard, he raised the bough above his head and smashed it down on the snake. About four feet long, the snake lay extended, with its head beside the trail. John's blow crashed into its middle. The snake curled, but otherwise didn't try to escape. John hit it solidly three more times until the snake ceased moving, and the end of the branch splintered. Amanda and Susan had returned and stood behind John, safely beyond reach of his stick.

"Ugh!" said Susan, "It could have bitten us."

"Everyone's safe now," John said.

"There could be a nest of them," exclaimed Pamela. "Josie and I won't feel safe without you. Come and walk with us, John, and keep that branch with you."

"Oh, Mother, I'll stay ahead and keep a lookout."

"I insist, John."

John relinquished his position and moved back with his mother.

"Bronwyn, will you come and walk with us?" asked Amanda.

"There's not enough room for three," Susan said, moving past Bronwyn. "But we two lovers can walk together?" She entwined her arm through Paul's arm. He looked helplessly back at Sam, who waved him on.

Within minutes, the group had spread apart. Amanda took hold of Bronwyn's arm and they moved easily together in the lead. Susan's intent to talk with him astonished Paul. Their conversational existence had never been separate from Amanda, and the intimacy of interlocking arms was a surprise. To Paul's regret, his distance from Bronwyn increased as Susan talked.

Sam walked alone, politely lagging behind Paul and Susan so their conversation went unheard. Trailing the group, poorly rewarded for his bravery, John guarded Josie and his mother. His mother, in turn, guarded him from too close a proximity with blind Bronwyn.

Susan gripped Paul's arm, emphasizing her words. "Has Amanda talked to you about us?"

"Goodness! No."

"You were with Amanda for four years, and Amanda and I have been together four years."

"Are you having difficulties?"

"I don't know. I thought possibly you'd noticed something." She smiled at him, showing she meant no insult, "You're more observant than you seem. I remember how astounded Amanda was that you were onto her sexual orientation almost before she was."

"No credit to me, I assure you."

"Maybe I'm imagining things, but Amanda seems unhappy. And why would she have talked with the rector this week?"

"Perhaps she wanted help for a friend? You're very attractive, Susan, I'm sure it's nothing. Why don't you ask her?"

"You're probably right," she said. "You do think I'm attractive?"

"You're very cute."

"I wondered if you did. Amanda and I discussed you after our conference this past weekend. Amanda's convinced you're hankering for her still."

"Of course not!"

"That's what I said, but she was sure. Mrs. Stayton, our neighbor, told us there was a light on in our bedroom last Saturday. Not that we needed more evidence, men are terrible at putting toilet seats down."

Paul's face flushed. "It was the Siamese," he said. "She ran to the bedroom with a mouse in her mouth. I went to clean up."

"If you're inventing things, don't even bother. Amanda saw straightaway that her panties had been disturbed. Honestly, she found it amusing, thinking you were pining for her. I didn't tell her my drawer was messed up, too." Susan looked up sympathetically into Paul's face and patted his shoulder. "I can understand. Not having a girlfriend can get frustrating. It was my favorite pair of silk undies. I can imagine what you get up to with them, so I won't ask for them back." She smiled compassionately at him.

His hands prickled with perspiration. His mortification melded with a terrible memory from ninth grade when Joel Slifer had given him a folded note during class and whispered for him to pass it to Cindy Swisher. The note had said, 'Please lick my popsicle. Paul'. Cindy giggled at him, and the knowing kids, to the end of that school year, had called him 'Pops.' Paul averted his fiery face from Susan.

"I'll tell you honestly," Susan said, in a kindly, forgiving way, "I've done much the same. I was seventeen and had a crush on the girl who lived next door. I stole a pair of her panties off the washing line and wore them. Kinky, but there it is."

Fifty feet ahead, having culled Bronwyn from the group, Amanda was busy fulfilling her purpose. "I love your hair. It's so thick and glossy. You look in great shape, but if you ever think of joining the fitness center, let me know. I'm an instructor there. I'd love to work with you and get you familiar with the equipment."

"Thanks. I walk to work, but that's not enough exercise. I could do with getting my heart-rate up."

"Speaking of heart pounding, if you don't mind my asking, did you leave a boyfriend behind when you came here?"

"No. Boyfriends have been sparse. Blindness scares men away."

"Their loss," responded Amanda earnestly. "It's possible that I shouldn't say this, but Paul appears to like you. He likes looking at you, anyway."

Bronwyn felt a warmth about her face as she embraced the thought of Paul watching her. "He seems nice," she replied.

"Oh yeah, Paul's got a good heart. He's on the hopeless side, though. A mix between a clumsy puppy and an old hound dreaming in the sunshine."

"That's not too encouraging."

"I don't mean to run him down. I did marry him, after all. Although I did the asking. It's a poor reason for proposing, but he managed to organize a twenty-first birthday party for me. When I found out he'd spent his rent money on me, amazingly, I found that endearing. He was a penniless student, so, not what you'd call practical. In fact, I had to give the rent money to his roommate so he could lend it to Paul. I should have seen he'd want more guidance than I had patience for."

"You weren't compatible?"

"We were okay. Paul's too unoffending for us to have had arguments. It was mostly the sex. Surprising, but after four years of my putting up with him, it was Paul who left me. Would you believe that?" Amanda chuckled over the memory. "He said I wasn't happy. We sat to talk it over, and Paul asked if I wouldn't be happier with a woman. He was right! I'd just discovered it myself. So, he's more sensitive than I'd have thought."

"We've talked a little together, and I don't mind saying that I think highly of him."

"Ah, I thought that," Amanda said. "So maybe I'll give you this little caution. Last weekend, when Susan and I were away at her teachers' convention, Paul offered to look after our cats. When I opened my underwear drawer on Monday morning, it was obvious Paul had gone through them. I'm not too upset. It's a little flattering, but sad, too, don't you think?"

"Definitely something to keep in mind," Bronwyn said.

The path, which had been rising above the lake, took a turn inland and then curved down to a shingle-beach cove. As each group emerged from the trail, they made their way to the only boat at the small dock. Paul scrutinized John's boat, thankful it wasn't new or fancy. When John arrived, he passed life jackets up to Sam, and Paul helped Bronwyn on with hers. Stepping back onto the dock, John said, "Sam, if you'll get in and hold the boat steady, I'll help Bronwyn down." Supporting her, John said, "We'll put you up here in front. When we go fast the spray will get the guys in the back." Paul stepped down and Nigel leapt beside him. Paul and Sam sat in the rear.

"We're off, Mother. Enjoy your walk back," John said.

"Watch out for the rocks," cautioned his mother. "We'll see you at the pavilion."

"Amanda and I will walk on a little further," Susan said.

"Alright," said Josie. "We'll find our way back without you."

After several attempts, John got the engine started. Amanda and Susan untied the ropes and tossed them aboard. The boat slowly departed. John revved the engine and they roared onto the lake. After a few minutes, John stopped the engine, allowing them to drift toward the center of the lake. Bronwyn put her arm over the side and wriggled her fingers in the water. "Brhh! It's cold."

Urgently, Sam warned her, "The alligators will get you."

She jerked her hand out, realized Sam had fooled her, and sent a spray of water back to splash him.

"A shark's circling below," he warned again, earning himself another splash.

"There are black vultures circling above us," Paul said.

"And they'll descend to peck my eyes out," Bronwyn said, flicking water at Paul.

"It's not right, taking advantage of the fears of a blind person," complained John. "You should be ashamed of yourselves."

"Thank you for defending me, John. There are some noble guys left in the world."

"The world must be a fearful place without eyesight," John said. Turning to Sam and Paul, he continued gravely, "It's our duty not to add to the fear in the world."

"I do see that now, John. My apologies, Bronwyn," Sam said.

"Insincere, didn't you feel?" Bronwyn commented to her ally.

"I fear that you're right," agreed John.

Enjoying this repartee, Paul dissociated himself from the ill-intentioned Sam, grumbling, in a voice of maligned innocence, that he was truthfully reporting on the black vultures in the sky.

"They're turkey vultures, actually," corrected John.

"And no more foul-smelling poop imaginable," Sam said, leaning over the side and smacking the water. "One just missed you, Bronwyn," he shouted. "They've got you in their sights."

"Just ignore the both of them, Bronwyn," John advised.

"The vultures are beautiful," Paul said. "They're lazily circling on some updraft above us with their black wings stretched out wide, banking and turning. It must be wonderful, looking down on the lake and the woods. They don't care about us, or we about them, but together we're part of this beautiful scenery."

"Thank you for describing it," Bronwyn said.

John started the engine, shattering the poetic, and they sped across the water. He took them to one of the farthest coves of the lake where they drifted for a while.

"Surprising we didn't see Rudy's boat," John said. "They must have slipped past us." The breeze was freshening. The sun, warm when they first came on the water, was obscured by a mass of clouds. "We should move before the waves kick up," John said. He tried to start the engine several times without success. Sam and Paul looked at each other with concern. John let the engine rest and tried again. It struggled to life, and they roared across the lake. A couple of minutes later the engine suddenly idled.

"What happened?" asked Bronwyn nervously.

"I saw something," John said. He turned the boat to their left, slowly moving it forward. "It's Rudy," he said. Standing in a boat similar to their own, Rudy's arms were scissoring over his head.

Rudy hollered, "It won't start. We need gas."

John spoke over his shoulder, "There's a can in the storage bin." Paul retrieved the container as John brought the boats together.

"We expected you a long time ago," complained Rudy.

"I was so afraid we'd be stranded here all night," Pat said. "You're a welcome sight."

Rudy unscrewed the gas cap on his boat. Paul leaned down, his left hand straining as he tipped the heavy container. He restrained Rudy's boat with his right hand, preventing the boats from smacking together. When he'd poured a couple of gallons into the tank, Paul pushed himself off Rudy's boat, and John backed them away.

After a few tries, Rudy called out, "No luck. I'll let it sit for a minute." After the next series of attempts he called, "We'll need a tow."

John shouted back, "I don't have the equipment to tow you."

"There's a ring on the back of your boat," Rudy informed him, "and I've got a rope."

John, visibly perturbed, spoke doubtfully to his passengers. "We could pull the whole fiberglass back off our boat. We might sink."

"We can't leave them here," Bronwyn said.

After a moment's hesitation, John called, "Okay. Send over the rope."

Rudy clambered to the front of his boat, tied his end and tossed the rope. Paul caught it. Bending over the back of the boat, he attempted a knot. He wished he'd gone to camp as a child and learned knots. A slipknot was wanted, but he was too ignorant to tie one. General knowledge suited him to solving crossword puzzles and to little else in the actual world. He visualized the rope becoming taut and tried to tie something that tightened with the tension but could easily be untied at the dock. Having ventured his best, he signaled in a seaman-like fashion to the captain, who moved their craft. When the rope tightened, they settled to a steady speed. During the return trip, Paul was continuously nervous for his knot, like a proud parent who watches his child perform on stage, anxious that, as yet, nothing has disastrously flown apart.

"They're very intense," observed Sam. "Like young lovers totally absorbed in each other." Looking back at Rudy and Pat, Paul nodded. They were unaware of their surroundings, face-to-face, engrossed in conversation. Paul wasn't sure that love was the text of their discussion, but he had no reason to offer Sam disagreement.

The wind off the lake had strengthened and was blowing two-foot swells as they came to shore. Sam vaulted to the dock. Paul and John threw him a fore and an aft rope to secure the boat. Bronwyn and Nigel were helped up, and Paul bent to his knot. To his relief and surprise, yanking the end released the rope. Rudy tugged the rope back and tossed it to Sam who drew Rudy's boat toward the dock.

"I'm worried the wind will push them into us," John said. "Rudy," he shouted, "Tie off the back of your boat."

Ignorant of the danger, Rudy had jumped to the dock and was securing Sam's rope. The wind and waves pushed the rear of his boat outward, pivoting on the tied-off rope. In a few seconds, the back of Rudy's boat came around, prepared to smash their raised propellers. Paul leapt to the storage locker. He grabbed the engine housing with his left hand. Balanced on his left foot he thrust his right leg out to block Rudy's boat. Pat let out a shriek. Paul lost awareness of others in his concentration. Rudy's boat gyrated, whirled and sprang, again and again like a powerful beast hungry to destroy him. Exposed, his legs spread wide, he feared he'd fall and be crushed by the heaving boats. However long in wind and spray his battle raged in that mountain cove, it seemed an age to Paul, far longer than it took for Rudy to jump to his boat, scramble to the back and toss a rope to Sam who shouted to Paul, "I'm pulling her around." Slowly, the rear of Rudy's boat swung out from the dock and the distance increased between the boats. Paul's legs spread wider. In that final moment, when he must have fallen, an up-thrust of Rudy's boat toppled him back into his own. The plunging had deluged the boat with a foot of water. Seeing an oil-funnel floating in the boat, Paul attempted to bail with it, his hands and feet numb from the cold water, but his core fiercely warmed by his excited competence.

The crisis over, John backed his trailer down the ramp, Sam untied the ropes and John, up to his waist in the waves, cranked the boat onto his trailer. Paul hopped out onto the shingle and splashed to shore. John drove his boat up to the parking area, and Rudy took his turn on the ramp, winching his boat. "F-f-freezing," Rudy groaned as he stood in the choppy water.

"Would you believe that wind!" exclaimed Pat. "I never would have thought. Such a wind!"

Rudy and John, each having the foresight to bring extra clothes, left to put them on in the changing-room. When they were out of sight, Pat said, "Paul, I want to apologize for doubting you. I've been testing Rudy, and he pitched me the scheme you said he would. You persisted with your advice, despite my treating you badly, and I'm grateful." Turning to Bronwyn and Sam she said, "Paul has been warning me against Rudy. I didn't want to believe it, but I've been leading our conversation, probing his financial plans and his background, and, now that I see clearly, I agree with Paul."

"What has Rudy done?" asked Bronwyn.

"He's running a fraudulent investment scheme," Paul said. "If Pat invested she wouldn't see her money again."

"Damn, but the man was good in bed," bemoaned Pat, smiling ruefully. "Though smooth as he is, there've been cracks. Wednesday, when he took me out to dinner, he reached over after the meal and touched my hair. I was ready to melt with the romance of it. But he pulled a hair from my head! It was such a surprise that it didn't hurt. What came next was the kicker. He cleaned his teeth with it. Right there in the restaurant, he flossed. With my hair!"

"Memorable, certainly," Bronwyn said.

Sam laughed, "My dentist always complains I don't floss enough."

When John and Rudy rejoined them, Pat said to John, "I've been thinking about that sixty-thousand the vestry wants for the church, and I will give it."

"That's wonderful," John said. "It will be a long-lasting investment in the church. I can assure you that generations will benefit."

"That's no kind of investment," Rudy said, "They're guilting you into contributing. You need to put your assets into something that will grow. I can double your investment in a couple of years. Then you'll still have your money, and more. Give some away then, if you want. You can trust me to look after your interests and see to your money wisely."

Her wonted charity gone, she said, "I've concluded that I can't trust you. I was warned, and you've shown yourself a piece of fiction with an excuse for everything. We'll have no further dealings, financial or otherwise."

Rudy snarled at Paul, who had unconsciously been nodding in sympathy with Pat's words. "It was you, wasn't it? Sneaking around, working against me. I'd an idea it was you at the house. You'll regret messing with me. Guard what you love. I'll be taking it from you." Looking savagely around at the group, he spat on the ground and said, "To hell with the pack of you." Angrily striding to his car, he got in, slammed the door and roared up the hill.

"Wow!" said Sam. "Not what I expected at a church picnic."

"I lost my ride. Can you get me back to town, Paul?" asked Pat.

"Of course," Paul said. "I'm concerned he'll want to hurt you."

"I'll have a word with the police department. It's your safety we should worry about."

"He doesn't know where I live," Paul said with confidence. "I'll keep an eye out. I'll be fine."

Chapter 13   Sunday

On waking, Paul surveyed his previous afternoon. He'd survived his ordeal of social intercourse, done manly acts of seamanship and restored himself in Pat's esteem. He had cause to be unsettled, too. After the group had returned to the pavilion, Josie spoke to him of John's prosperity and of Bronwyn's attachment to John. Passions grow in the vacillation between hope and doubt, and Paul occupied that shaky ground.

He did want to go to church, but a desire to clean the backyard combined with his anti-social leaning to keep him home. The previous evening had been windy with rain showers, but today the breeze was soft and the sky bright blue with a few wispy clouds. Spook rubbed against him or sprawled on the ground observing him, but, after a busy night of hunting, she soon abandoned him to go inside. The sun was a worker's friend, warming to the back, but not overly hot. He weeded, cut the remaining brambles that climbed the shed and pulled the ivy from the fence. He'd purchased timber and two jacks to straighten the rear fence, and the remainder of his morning was occupied in slowly forcing the fence upright and setting braces. He was as happy as any boy digging in dirt.

At noon, after a sandwich and a glass of iced-tea, he worked in his shed. It reminded him of the many tumbled-down barns around the Shenandoah Valley. His old soldier, spare of flesh, with more story than substance, protected rusty cans of paint, ancient gardening implements and a rickety stepladder. In the corner closest to the house and the side fence were a few discarded snake skins, but no living snakes. Guiltily whacking at sticky cobwebs, a Goliath amid their small world, he disturbed the long-tenured residents. He stacked the shed's contents outside and stood the stepladder against the house. It was 12:30, and Paul came alert on hearing Bronwyn's French doors click open. She'd returned from church. He couldn't make out words, but he distinguished Bronwyn's cheerful tones and knew she spoke with a man. Paul walked to his rear gate, turned, and considered the stepladder against his house. By climbing a few steps, he might see over Bronwyn's wall.

Gripping the ladder, he halted. He could do Bronwyn no harm on his ladder, yet he hesitated. He lurched to the first rung and turned to face the lane. No fear of exposure there. With his back to the ladder, he pushed up a step. He could be seen from the lane, but the lane was largely abandoned. He could be seen from his neighbor's backyards, but only if their occupants came to the bottom of their gardens, and he would surely hear anyone before he was noticed. Ignoring misgivings, he pushed himself to the third step. He saw over Bronwyn's wall, but his view was too limited. Stabilizing himself with a hand on the roof of his shed, he pushed to the fourth step.

Bronwyn was entertaining John Wardle, which annoyed him. He was jealous and knew it. John stood easy, with a drink by the open door, talking to Bronwyn who worked in the kitchen. Paul stood on a wobbly ladder with his head disconcertingly exhibited. He thought a magical wish to swap them where they stood, delighting in John, transported, falling off the ladder in surprise. But, while he desired his own improving, becoming John was not the means. If John looked, his face might be picked out against the brick of the house, so Paul descended and lay on the ground staring at the sky, imagining what he couldn't see.

Bronwyn had lettuce, tomato and sliced bread on the cutting board and was microwaving the bacon. "I hope you don't mind veggie bacon strips," she said. "They're easy to prepare in the microwave."

"I'm one for the natural world," replied John. "It seems contrary to nature, concocting meat substitutes out of soy and whatever chemicals they use, although I do understand your particular need for simplicity."

"You're right of course, it's not nature's way, but there's plenty in nature to disapprove of. I hope you'll like them anyway." With good humor, John assured her he would.

"I felt sorry for Paul," John said, smiling, "plopping back to the pavilion yesterday in his squelching shoes. He's not much of a sailor I'm afraid. Of course, these things happen on boats in the water. When I go to the lake I always bring a complete change of clothes."

"Sometimes life just surprises us."

"Rudy's outburst was definitely a surprise. Mind you, I knew there was trouble coming when the boats approached the dock. That wind off the lake was too strong, and I doubted Rudy was the sailor Pat said he was. A man like that, it's no surprise he didn't care for Pat's generosity to the church, but to spit on the ground in front of the women! You couldn't see it, of course. Truly disgusting behavior."

"Your sandwich is ready. Let's go outside to eat," suggested Bronwyn.

In the garden, they enjoyed the sun's warmth. Nigel was at their feet, watchful for falling crumbs. Slowly ascending, above the angle of the wall, was in turn, hair, forehead, a pair of eyes, and then, like the pale moon in daylight hours, it sank below the horizon. Paul was essaying a look. He had stood on the ladder with his knees bent out and painfully, gradually, he'd straightened them, his head inching up the brick wall.

"Hellooo, hellooo!" It was Aunt Josie come to call.

"Hello, Mrs. Stickley," John said, as she hove into sight.

"It's a pleasure to see you young things together. I dropped in for a second to see how you were getting along. Then I'm off home for my nap. I'm not interrupting?"

"Oh no, Aunt Josie. I've finished eating, and John, I expect, has finished too?"

"I am. It hit the spot nicely. Now that your aunt can look after you, I'll get my tape-measure from the car and see about the jobs we discussed." He went about his tasks, leaving Josie to sit and have her curiosity satisfied.

"I had to park part-way down the hill, and I'm breathless, dear," she panted. "How have you and John been getting along? What have you got him doing?"

"Not so much. I asked him to put in a safety-bar in the shower. There are squeaky floorboards in the hall and the bedrooms to nail down. And I thought a chair-railing along each side of the hall, nothing too obtrusive, about waist-high, something I can hold onto if I get a bit wobbly."

"John's the right man for the job. His father, Wardle, Sr., was a builder too. He had skin cancer and passed away a couple of years ago. He wasn't young, mind you. It's not as if anything runs in that family. He was a good fifteen years older than Pam. About ten years ago, Phyllis had old Wardle renovate this house, and John worked with him. They knocked out walls and did something to move that wall," she pointed to the back wall of the living room, forgetting that Bronwyn couldn't see, "and put in all this splendid glass to the back."

"Maybe I'm beating on this Aunt Josie, but what did Aunt Phyllis do for a living? How could she afford these renovations?"

"You should talk to Kate Lavender at the Lavender Art Gallery. They were high school friends. When Phyllis needed money she did a painting for Kate, and, apparently, it's amazing how much tourists will pay for local art. Painting was never an interest of mine, although, had I tried my hand at it, I can see that it would be an easy life, selling a painting now and then."

"What kind of paintings did Aunt Phyllis do?"

"Even as a tiny thing she was an artist, and such a rebel in school, forever standing in the corner! They heated with coal those days, and the walls were grimy. I think Phyllis learned to draw with her face in the corner doing spit pictures on the wall. It was fields, tractors, hay-bales, that kind of thing when she was a teenager, but it's been an age since I've seen any. I'm a firm believer in constructive criticism, but Phyllis, I'm afraid, was overly sensitive. She wouldn't let me see her work."

"There were no paintings at her death?"

"Nothing. An empty easel, her brushes and paints.

John returned, saying he was swamped with business and would call in a few days to arrange the work for some evening. Bronwyn thanked him, reiterating that there was no rush. He said his goodbyes and left. "What a polite young man he is," said Josie. Bronwyn agreed and told her aunt she had invited Pat over for tea at three. "Did you? That's very generous of you. I feel badly for her. John was telling his mother and me on the way back to town yesterday how offensive that horrible man had been. Any man that will spit at you is a very low creature indeed."

Josie left, giving Bronwyn time to change her clothes and prepare. Pat arrived promptly at 3:00, and Bronwyn led her to the living room where cheese, crackers and an opened bottle of red wine waited. Nigel accepted Pat's affection and lay down on the floor to nap in the sunshine.

"Is there any news of Rudy?" Bronwyn asked.

"Not a peep. I don't expect to hear from him. Not enough motivation. Rudy knows where Paul works, so I'm a little concerned for him, though if Paul's right and Rudy can't find out where he lives--"

"Where does Paul live? Do you know?"

"I've no idea, but let's not worry about him, let's concentrate on Phyllis." Pat flipped through the photocopied pages. "The naughty girl had her art prize taken away, I remember. Here we go."

Tue., Nov. 3, 1970. Miss Wheeler put me on the basketball team. I'm not so great with the ball, but I am tall. We have cute little skirts and it's fun to look at the boys watching. We had practice after school. In the showers, the girls crowded around to see the cartoons I drew on the steamy tiles. I did Mr. Nichols, who's always scratching himself while he's teaching geography. He was naked with a potbelly and stick legs with his finger up his rear-end. It was a big hit. Miss Wheeler poked her head around to see what the fun was. All she found was a bunch of us rubbing our hands on the tiles making squeaky noises.

Tue., Dec. 2, 1970. I saw Nanny Ellen in her treasure box today. I wasn't spying. I just looked through the crack in the door and saw her. She was taking the box out of a secret compartment. I'll try to worm out of her what she's got. Probably old love letters, but maybe it is a treasure. I won't sneak and look, unless I have to.

"That's pretty interesting," Pat said. "Is it still hidden someplace?"

"Maybe Phyllis will tell us eventually. Probably it was personal stuff she didn't want a curious granddaughter getting into. But if there's a hidden compartment in the house, I'd definitely like to find it."

Fri., Dec. 25, 1970. Christmas today. Nanny Ellen put a stocking out for me by the fireplace, but I changed it and hung up a pillowcase instead. Nanny said I'd get coal for being greedy, and that's what I got. Santa brought me charcoal to draw with. Nanny is like a prune outside, with a sense of humor inside. She was upset with her present from me. I got Valerie's brother to buy me a bottle of vodka. I bet it tastes better than her old bottle that got watered down on my birthday but Nanny doesn't want me having anything to do with alcohol. The day felt sad and odd without mom and dad around.

Sat., Dec. 26, 1970. Nanny Ellen said I could, so I'm making the spare bedroom into a room for my painting. We pushed the bed against the wall and there's plenty of space for my things. The light could be better in wintertime, but it's not bad by the window. Nanny surprised me for Christmas, getting the art supply shop in Charlottesville to send me everything an artist needs. I've got books, canvas, stretching frames, gesso to prime the canvas, brushes, and oil paints. I'm so excited. I was thinking I'd do Clarence naked, though the painting might turn into a worm wriggling in a nest. I don't think I can do a whole person yet.

Sat., Jan. 23, 1971. It snowed today. Nanny's corgi Dozer is as dozy as they come. He's fat and doesn't like to move. Nanny was napping so I took Dozer for a walk down the back lane to where the brambles grow. Their arcs of ice and snow are pretty, but in the middle was something sad. A dead cardinal. Like bright blood in the snow, and I know about that as I got bloody from the thorns taking him out. I set him down on white paper on the floor by my easel and painted him dead in the snow.

Sun., Jan. 24, 1971. Nanny Ellen was mad at me. I'd left the cardinal, and Dozer had taken him. There were feathers all over the kitchen floor and a chewed bird waiting for us on the mat by the sink. Nanny got me out of bed so I could clean it all up. Great art is all about suffering.

Tue., Feb. 2, 1971. Had a driving lesson this afternoon. Shelly and Jason were making out in the back seat. Mr. Swartz was upset because I didn't concentrate on the road. He's a blind and deaf driving instructor. I could see Jason's hand in between Shelly's legs and his knee kept digging in the back of my seat. I slammed on the brakes at a crosswalk, and Shelly and Jason thumped into the front seats. They should learn to wear their seat belts. I told Mr. Swartz I thought I'd seen a mother duck and her ducklings crossing the road. He only nodded. You can say any random thing to grown-ups. They think you're weird anyway.

Mon., Feb. 8, 1971. Karen Pugh threw a wad of paper at Mrs. Tolley in Science today. Mrs. Tolley was writing on the blackboard and it hit her on the back of the head. Was she ever mad! She snapped around like a dragon and stared at me. Karen sits right in front of me and Mrs. Tolley thought I threw it. She stomped down to me and I smelled her bad breath. I went as stiff as the dead cardinal. She sent me to the vice-principal's office. Because I had a basketball game today he gave me detention after school tomorrow. He's a horribly unfair man.

Tue., Feb. 9, 1971. Detention was okay. I brought my painting book to study. There were six of us. Mr. Nichols was our teacher and when he'd walk up and down the aisles Jimmy Pufhal would half get out of his chair and scratch his rear end. I'm sure Mr. Nichols knew, but he kept quiet. I felt sorry for him.

Wed., Feb. 17, 1971. We played Staunton's team today and I got a couple of baskets, but we lost. Miss Wheeler told us not to worry because it was more important how we played the game. Who really thinks it's better to lose? Miss Wheeler tries hard but she isn't a great basketball coach. She's a wonderful art teacher and likes my work best in class. And she's good looking. She wears a gym skirt when she coaches us and with her long legs I can see why the principal made her do girls' basketball as well as art. The only thing is she attracts the wrong kind of men. Mr. Romano, the math teacher, is always hanging around after practice. Anyone would be better than him. Mr. Romano walks up and down in math class staring down at the girls with breasts.

Wed., Feb. 24, 1971. I've been thinking about God. Nanny Ellen believes in him, says they're old friends and they'll be shaking hands in a few years. Because Josie and Nanny think that way is no reason why I should. It's like the yellow jacket Josie gave me for my 16th birthday. It's big and the color's wrong and just because it was given to me doesn't mean I have to wear it.

"Becoming a free-thinking artist," Pat said, taking a short break to nibble on cheese and crackers.
"I hope Aunt Phyllis wouldn't have minded my looking at her diaries. It seems so invasive."
"Don't be concerned. From what you say, Phyllis loved you. My guess is she wants you interested in her life."

Sat., Feb. 27, 1971. I went to the movies and saw 'Love Story' with Valerie and Judy and we cried buckets. It's so romantic, loving and dying, like you're a bottle rocket exploding in the dark sky. For a moment you're the most beautiful thing there is. I want to shine like that. Afterwards, there was Miss Wheeler with a red teary face coming out holding onto Mr. Romano's arm. It's awful seeing them together!

"And she's a romantic too, but then everybody is at that age," Pat said. "She'll learn that we don't love and die. We love and get dumped." She went back to turning pages. "Ahh! Here's something about your treasure."

Sun., Mar. 14, 1971. I saw Nanny Ellen at her secret compartment. I pushed the door wider to look. It creaked but Nanny didn't notice. She's getting so she doesn't hear. Nanny had a book and was taking something out of it. I said "Nanny what's that?" She wasn't upset, but she put it back in the box and said I'd be old enough to be told on my 17th birthday. That's way off. I hope it's worth waiting for.

Fri., Mar. 26, 1971. I shouldn't have told everyone I was getting my driver's license. I failed the parallel parking. The officer wouldn't give me a fourth try. It's unfair. I bet I'd go days without having to park next to the curb, and I've seen real drivers give up on parking spots and go somewhere else. Nanny Ellen complains about her eyes. She doesn't drive at night any more. I'll take the test again next month and then I can drive her around.

Sat., Apr. 24, 1971. Miss Wheeler invited the art class out for a picnic and a painting session. She has a little farmhouse and a barn with a couple of horses. Valerie and Judy went with me in our car, but Nanny wouldn't let me drive. She dropped us off and said she'd come back at 3:00 to pick us up. The barn smelled of straw and leather and animal poop. Mr. Romano was in the kitchen making the salad. You'd have to torture me to make me eat anything he made. He's short, and I said to Valerie and Judy that he's a chimp wanting to mate with a human. We wished we could help Miss Wheeler.

Mon., May 3, 1971. I got invited to the Junior/Senior Prom! Ronald Lavender asked me. I barely know him but he seems harmless and I wanted to see everyone dressed up so I said I'd go. Turns out Valerie got asked by Calvin Ikenberry and she'd only go if we double-dated and he found someone for me. I was mad at Valerie, thinking it's not like I couldn't find my own date. Truthfully, nobody would have asked me. With a girly name like 'Lavender' he'd be odd, but he might be tougher than you'd think with kids teasing him. Anyway I'm strange myself, which is okay for an artist.

Fri., May 7, 1971. I passed my driving test today. Parallel parking was tricky but I got it on the third try. I wore my gym skirt to take the officer's mind off my driving. It's hard knowing what works and what doesn't. When I'm done with school I'm going to be an artist, then I'll be in charge of what works.

Wed., May 12, 1971. Valerie and Judy and I have been keeping an eye on Mr. Romano. If we see him do something nasty we can tell

Miss Wheeler. He lives close to the school. Across the football field then a couple of blocks to Summit Street. After school, Brandi Puckett was flirting with him. We were hiding on the top row of the stands, and she was fawning all over him in front of the football stands. She has a real crush. Judy thinks he's sort of handsome, in an oily kind of way. Brandi is a senior and everyone knows she's a slut. We were disappointed. We thought he'd take her home with him but they separated at Houston Street. He stood and watched her walk away so we think something will happen.

Thur., May 13, 1971. Nanny Ellen has been teaching me how to sew and she helped me with my dress. It's long and white with a ruffle around the neck and short puffy sleeves. Nanny cried. Dad took mom to the prom and it was her dress. It has yellow age-spots in the middle but a red sash around the waist covered that. Nanny said I looked elegant. It's old-fashioned but none of the girls will have one like it.

Sat., May 22, 1971. Ron borrowed his dad's new Ford Pinto. Ron and Calvin picked up Valerie and me. Nanny Ellen took pictures and cried. The gym had streamers and balloons and planets and stars and a sickle-moon hanging from the ceiling. Next year when I'm a junior I'll work on Prom decorations and they won't be so tacky. Mr. Romano was one of the chaperones. After a slow dance, Judy whispered to me that he'd followed Brandi out the side door. We told the boys we were off to the bathroom but we zipped outside and saw them heading under the stands. We told Miss Wheeler that Brandi and a boy were out there. She rushed out. We followed, sure she'd catch Mr. Romano with his hands where they shouldn't be. It didn't work. Ricky Jarvis loves Brandi and he'd followed them and was beating up on Mr. Romano. Ricky ran off and Mr. Romano, with a bloody nose, just plain lied. Everyone heard him whisper to Miss Wheeler that Brandi was a slut. He didn't lie about that part, even though it's mean saying it. He said he'd followed Ricky and Brandi out there. Miss Wheeler said he was brave and she helped him back to school. Brandi said Mr. Romano was a lying piece of shit and Valerie said he'd pinched her bottom. The rest of the night with the boys wasn't so interesting.

Tue., May 25, 1971. Valerie is adventuresome. She poked around outside Mr. Romano's house and found a key under the flowerpot on the front porch. She wanted to sneak in and look for love letters. I couldn't have Valerie think I'm a wimp so I knocked on the door and we ran beside the next house. He didn't answer so we took the key and opened the front door pretending we were nieces come to visit. We didn't find anything to use against him. A woman passing on the street looked at us through the front window, so we left.

Wed., May 26, 1971. After third period, I asked Brandi if we could talk to her about messing with Mr. Romano. Valerie and I met her behind the gym after school and went over our plan. Without Brandi it can't work, but Mr. Romano calling her a slut made her mad enough for anything. My plan's like something from a play.

Thur., May 27, 1971. Valerie and I went to Brandi's house at 7:00 PM and her mother let us in. Brandi lives in a nice house and her mother gave us brownies and milk. It makes you wonder if Brandi is as bad as kid's say. She's nice, except for wanting to drop Mr. Romano in a barrel of cement. Brandi called Mr. Romano and you'd have believed she was sick for him and just had to see him. She said if he came for a walk by the football stands at 8:00 she'd be there. We thought he couldn't resist. Miss Wheeler was trickier. I wasn't sure if she'd come. Valerie called, as her voice is fluty and we pretended she was Brandi's young sister. I'd written the script and Valerie read it quickly. She hung up before Miss Wheeler could ask hard questions. It went, 'Miss Wheeler, this is Brandi's little sister. I need help and I'm all alone. Brandi said I shouldn't tell, but she's doing something bad and I'm afraid for her. Mr. Romano asked her to come and Brandi has gone to his house and said she's going all the way with him. Brandi told me you're a nice teacher and I thought you'd go there and tell her not to. Thanks so much.' We called at 7:30 to give Miss Wheeler the right time to drive into town. Ricky met us at 7:50 and we watched Mr. Romano walk in the direction of the school. Then all we had to do was let Ricky and Brandi in. Valerie and I hid in the bushes. When Miss Wheeler drove up, Ricky and Brandi were at it, hot and heavy in full view in Mr. Romano's front room. Ricky's about the right size with the same dark hair. He's a good likeness if he keeps his face turned away. I hadn't thought what would happen after. For a few seconds Miss Wheeler looked at them then she pounded on the front door! They couldn't answer the door so they ran out the back and kept running. After they disappeared, Miss Wheeler drove off. I bet she wasn't feeling friendly with Mr. Romano.

"What a pickle! Hard to believe it won't have a bad ending," Bronwyn said. "How about we take a break?" They took Nigel for a walk. On their return, Bronwyn re-heated baked root-vegetables and scrambled some eggs for their dinner.

"Tuesday, I'm going on vacation," Pat said, "so I'll miss finding out about Phyllis. How about I come tomorrow evening with Chinese take-out?"

"I'd like that. You're a good friend." Grinning at Pat, she continued, "Even if you are motivated by nosiness."

"My great failing," lamented Pat. "Listen, I'll be back a week from Saturday. Come to my house for dinner that Sunday evening, and you can tell me how it works out for Phyllis. I'll be thinking about her while I'm away. I know she'll have a life to be proud of." Pleased with Pat's sympathy, Bronwyn agreed. She would have plenty of time to listen to the digital transcript. They cleared away the dishes and returned to the diaries.

Fri., May 28, 1971. Miss Wheeler didn't go home mad. She went to Brandi's house. Brandi doesn't have a sister, so things unraveled. Miss Wheeler waited with Brandi's mom. When Brandi came home with Ricky they made her tell. Nanny Ellen got a call from the principal this morning and we had to go to his office. It was scary. He talked about suspending Valerie and me from school, and Nanny looked sad. We got a week's detention and Valerie and I had to apologize to Mr. Romano and Miss Wheeler. Mr. Romano was all forgiving and came across as so kind, but he knows we know the creep he is. Miss Wheeler said she was terribly saddened by our dishonorable behavior and I cried. She won't want to be my friend anymore. The worst is oily Mr. Romano is cuddling up to her and she still thinks he's worth something.

Sat., June 12, 1971. School's out! I'll spend summer outdoors, learning how to paint. I bought a small easel and a folding chair and I've filled my backpack with supplies. I'll tramp around, and if I want to go far, hopefully Nanny Ellen will let me use the car. Today I hiked behind the high school and up the hill through the woods into the fields beyond. It's a slog, but worth it. I could see the Blue Ridge Mountains, and the universities and church spires in the dip below.

Mon., June 14, 1971. This morning I climbed a gate into a field but one of the cows charged me. I dropped my stuff and ran. Honestly I wasn't anywhere near her baby. I had to stand behind the fence and wait for them to move away, but it was good because it made me watch the cattle. An artist has to look carefully. It was fun seeing the calves scampering on their little stiff legs. I decided I'd ask permission to paint so I knocked on the farmhouse door and talked to the farmer's wife. She said I'd be fine if I stayed away from the cattle. The farmer came by in the afternoon to check me out. He's sinewy like rough wood grain and tall. He'd be interesting to paint, but I bet he wouldn't let me. Anyway, the painting would look like a fence post and he'd be angry with me for wasting his time.

Wed., June 16, 1971. The farmer's son came in his tractor to look me over. I think he liked what he saw, the big oaf. He said I could paint him if I wanted. He'd end up on canvas like an ox with a pinhead. I haven't done much with people or animals yet. Barns and plows and hay don't get impatient, so they're easier.

Fri., June 18, 1971. Nanny Ellen let me drive her car! I went swimming with Valerie and Judy at Goshen Pass. The road's snaky and the girls kept shrieking as we'd go round the bends, which wasn't helpful. The river is full of boulders and the water slides from a deep pool down a rock channel to a lower pool. The water runs fast and cold from the mountains, but you get used to it. We bought inner tubes at the tire-repair shop in town. They helped protect our rear ends from the rocks. The boys were another matter. When we landed in the lower pool and drifted down-river they'd surface like sharks and pinch us. I can see how a bottom sticking through a hole in a donut would be tempting to a lower order of human. Valerie kicked at Ron Lavender and gave him a bloody nose. I owed him for taking me to the Prom so I helped him clean up. His twin sister Kate introduced herself. She's a year older than me. I'd seen her at school but never talked to her. Later I did pencil sketches of rocks rising out of swirling water. Kate sat and watched. She said I've got talent. We could be friends.

Wed., July 7, 1971. Skip parades by on his tractor. I'm sure he feels manly, dominating over a weak female. I think of an old-time soldier wearing iron and mounted on a steaming horse and he falls off, with his legs and arms flailing like a beetle. I asked him how old he is and he's twenty-five. That's a bit old, but he does share his egg-salad sandwiches and lemonade with me and he's sort of handsome so he's kind of a sweetheart. Valerie keeps bragging over her doing it with Calvin, and I want to tell her I've done it too, but not today. I told Skip if he came by the field after sunset tomorrow he could have some fun with me.

Thur., July 8, 1971. I thought about what Skip would do if I changed my mind. The cattle make me nervous the same way. Small brains aren't predictable. Valerie said it hurts the first time. Hard to see how anything soft like Clarence's could hurt, but I knew they grew. I told Nanny Ellen I was going to stay out to see the moon rise. She said I could drive the car. I'd been watching for a few days and tonight the moon was full. My period just ended so it was perfect for my plan. I couldn't concentrate on painting so I wandered around the field looking at grasshoppers, ants and birds. I was sure they weren't anxious about sex, and they have smaller brains, so I didn't know what that meant. My brain was making me seasick. I lay down beside the haystack in the sunshine and when I woke it was dusk and I looked up at Skip towering over me. The bulge in his trousers was obvious. I'd worn a short-sleeved white top with no bra, a tiny brown skirt, white panties and sandals. 'Ready then are ya?' he said, his eyes fixed on my legs. My toes curled with the idea he'd start nibbling me from the toes up. I guessed he'd done it before, though maybe with the sheep, and that made me want to giggle, but with Clarence that was a no-no, so I snorted and sat up. 'Brought yer somethin,' he said. It was a small paper cup with white wine. I swallowed the sour stuff like medicine. Skip pulled straw from the haystack and spread a blanket on it. I liked him thinking about my comfort. I stepped out of my sandals and pulled my skirt down and sat on our scratchy bed. A few birds were calling their nighttime songs, the light was fading and the moon had risen large and yellow. I could see Skip, though some of the details were brushed away by the dark. He stripped to his underwear and I threw off my top. He stared at my breasts, his eyes glinty in the moonlight. Uncovering his thingy it shot out like a Jack-in-the box. I was surprised, but probably Skip's is bigger than Clarence's to start with. His big stick reached to the moon, like a giant candy-apple. I've never liked candy-apples. I was scared how the thing would fit in me, it seemed so unlikely. Skip bent down and pulled off my panties. He tickled me when he kissed my pube-hair. Straddling me he ran his hands all over and squeezed my breasts too hard. 'Sorry,' he said when I grunted. I was lying down, looking at the friendly face in the sky as Skip got between my legs poking at me. 'Too dry,' he said and licked a couple of fingers. He circled them around down there and pushed his fingers in and out until I was wet. I sure hoped his hands were washed before he did that. He pushed against my vagina and it was like the pleasure of an itch being scratched. When he shoved in me it hurt and I gasped. The moon was spectacular but Skip blocked my view. I shifted my head to the left so Luna's face would take my mind off the burning as Skip plowed into me.

"Not outstandingly successful," Bronwyn said.
"It'll get better. You'd have to wonder if someone else wouldn't be a better fit. Skip's someone who'd appeal more to me. Wow! He'd be about my age." Pat chuckled, "Maybe he's still in Lexington and I could replace Matilda the sheep in his affections."
"Someone's doing a lot of banging," Bronwyn said, listening to the hammering behind her house. "Not very neighborly, after dark on a Sunday."

Paul was perched on his shed with hammer and nails in hand. Earlier in the afternoon, he'd made a wooden, thirty-inch-square platform. Now it was dark and he couldn't be seen, he hammered it in place. The roof of the shed sloped from a central ridge, and his creation allowed him to sit on the high point of the roof with his back against the brick wall of the house. His hammering finished, Paul sat on his secured aerie looking over at Bronwyn and Pat. The ladies had moved to the kitchen. They spent a few minutes standing and talking before walking toward Bronwyn's front door.
Ten minutes passed before he saw her again. His heart raced with excitement. She emerged from the dark hallway like the goddess of a lake, entirely naked. He couldn't look long as she reached for the light-switch and turned the living area to gloom, and then walked to the kitchen light-switch and brought the house to darkness. Breathlessly privileged at being an intimate of her home, he sighed--a sigh of satisfaction, frustration, annoyance--a sigh encapsulating what was, could be and would never be. Of one thing he was certain, next time he'd bring a cushion to sit on.

CHAPTER 14   MONDAY

At a few minutes after 6:00 in the evening, Bronwyn opened her front door, sniffing the air. "No need to knock, your smell announced you."

"My new perfume," Pat said. "Goes straight to a man's heart. But there's only Nigel, and we're already sweethearts." In one hand, she carried a bag of Chinese food. With her other, she petted Nigel, who was having a good sniff of the bag. They moved to the living room. Bronwyn had the dining table prepared and the French-doors open.

"Shut the doors if it's too cool for you," Bronwyn said. "A cold front's supposed to be moving through."

From his stepladder, Paul, who had arrived home from work a few minutes earlier, watched Pat put the food onto the table. Having established Bronwyn's status and shared in the appetizing aroma of their Chinese food, he went to his own kitchen to prepare dinner.

"We don't have chopsticks, do we?" Bronwyn asked. She and Pat concurred in forks being essential. As Pat passed the containers, Bronwyn spooned from each into a different quadrant on her plate and lined the boxes neatly on the table.

"You're well organized," Pat said.

"It's a failing of the blind. Regularity will make an old maid of me before my time."

Easygoing jocularity continued through the meal, Bronwyn talking of the generalities of her work, and Pat anticipating her vacation. "This early in the year in Alaska there should be mini-icebergs. My girlfriend and I expect shipboard romances. I'm looking for someone with enough money for a balcony stateroom and we'll sip hot chocolate while he looks admiringly at me and I look off at the ice and the whales. That's what it's all about, pleasant surroundings, lovely food, good company and a little adoration. Of course, you can't let these men know you're too interested. Men are hunters by nature. Collapse on your back too quickly and they'll be off looking for other conquests."

"I'm not aware of many men shooting glances my way."

"Just shows that men are a hopeless lot," Pat said sympathetically.

On his stepladder, Paul watched Pat shut the doors to the garden. He went inside, put on a thick jacket and came back with a cushion and a large umbrella. The lights were on in Bronwyn's house. In the failing light, he felt secure. On his perch, he settled to a cross-legged, contemplative position with the handle of the umbrella resting on the point where his legs crossed.

BOILED PEANUTS

The rain fell in large plops, then assaulted in a steady downpour. It was noisy in his cave, but cozy.

"I'll speak up," Pat said, "so we aren't drowned by the noise of the rain on the roof."

Mon., Aug. 9, 1971. Skip's mad at me as I'm not ready to do it again. The big idiot paws at me, which isn't getting him anywhere. My period's late too, and I'm nervous. Mrs. Trilling in home-ec explained the cycle and how women are fertile in the middle part but we were right on the edge so that'd be pretty unfair. At least if anything happened I wouldn't have to disappoint mom. It's been a year since I started this diary. Their picture's by my bed otherwise their faces might start slipping from my memory.

Thur., Aug. 12, 1971. Nanny Ellen has been worried about me but I told her it was my period coming and I was sorry to be grouchy, which satisfied her. After worrying for a week, my period came yesterday. So I'm crampy but otherwise happy. For the past few days I've worked on this painting of a John Deere tractor sitting in the field. In honor of girl freedom I painted myself in the driver's bucket seat. I'm not too good with faces so the viewpoint's from behind my right shoulder and nobody can tell it's me. With imagination the girl's naked, but you can't see anything special. I bet Mr. Deere wouldn't use my painting in his magazine advertisements. Farmer Miller came by in the afternoon. He took a good look at my painting and sent me packing. I'm a bad influence on his son, he said. Summer's nearly over and I'm done with haystacks.

Sat., Aug. 21, 1971. School starts Monday. Brandi called this morning and said her best friend Tina is pregnant. She and Brandi had both been hot for Mr. Romano. When Brandi told her Mr. Romano was a slime-ball, Tina found that attractive! Mr. Romano spoke with the Principal, and because Tina graduated before he got her pregnant he was going to stay as a teacher. Brandi didn't know for sure if Tina and Mr. Romano were getting married. It was too late now and Brandi didn't see what else Tina could do.

Mon., Aug. 23, 1971. Mr. Romano had me come up front to demonstrate the properties of trapezoids. I knew enough to draw a triangle with its top cut off. I remembered third grade, needing to pee, but the teacher wouldn't let me, as it was my turn to stand and read. I couldn't hold it, and in front of everyone the pee ran down to my socks. I got sent home to change but Mommy wasn't there and I had to wait for her on the porch. I bet Mr. Romano wouldn't let me go to the bathroom. I didn't pee, but I didn't do the properties either. My trapezoid on the blackboard was nicely drawn but Mr. Romano said if I'd forgotten so much over the summer I should go to the office and arrange for a math tutor. He wants to embarrass me but a tutor's not a bad idea.

Wed., Aug. 25, 1971. During art class Miss Wheeler asked Valerie and me to stay after. When class let out Miss Wheeler sat us in the front row. Her skin was tanned like she'd been to the beach. She had a hint of delicious rose perfume. She knew about Mr. Romano, and said his libido was bigger than his brain. Miss Wheeler does use refined words. Miss Wheeler said she was sorry, and realized that Valerie and I did our best to help her. She wasn't saying it was okay to interfere but she was sorry she got mad and everything's forgiven.

Thur., Sept. 16, 1971. I'm 17 today. At breakfast I reminded Nanny Ellen that she'd promised to tell me about the hidden box. Nanny said she had to get me straight on family history. It's good to write it down here so I won't forget. Daniel Heathcote and Nanny are my dad's parents. Daniel was a ne'er-do-well who drank. He died of his liver in 1950. Four years before I was born, so we never met. Grandpa Daniel's father was Frederick Heathcote. He was born around the Civil War and the box belonged to him. Nanny pulled out the book to show me. It was large, and burned along the bottom edge. Nanny thought some of the stamp collection had come down from Frederick's father before him. Frederick had most every American stamp from the Nineteenth Century and some of the stamps with President's faces he had whole sheets. Nanny made me make a solemn promise not to ever tell about the burning. Nanny said that sometime in the 1920s her father-in-law Frederick went to bed tipsy and his cigarette burned the house down. The only property he saved was a photo album and the stamps. The house and contents were insured and the stamps were valuable by then. He took the insurance money but never told the insurance company that he'd saved the stamps from the fire. He used the money to buy this house and he hid the stamp album. Great-grandpa Frederick died in the 30's and his wife, whose name I've forgotten, sold a stamp when she needed money. She died in the 40's leaving the house to grandpa Daniel, but years before, she'd shown the stamps to my Nanny. Nanny says our family's women have more sense than the men. Nanny sold a stamp when she needed to, but as few as possible to keep them for the next generation. Nanny would have passed the secret to my mother if she hadn't died in the train crash, but now she's chosen me. I'm like an important female thread in the fabric of our family. I'm the keeper of a treasure.

"But Aunt Phyllis never passed anything on," Bronwyn mournfully complained. "Wouldn't she have chosen me?"

"Maybe there was nothing left, or she meant to, but didn't have time."

Bronwyn nodded. "She must have meant to. Aunt Phyllis knew she was sick at the end but she expected to live longer, so probably she was going to tell me. I'll have to be tapping on walls to find the secret compartment."

The rain had slowed to a drizzle, obscuring Paul's view. Pat turned pages, read a little and the ladies conversed. Inside his fleece jacket, under his domed roof, his accommodations dry and relatively snug, he was the occupant of a yurt on the steppes of Outer Mongolia. His mind drifted to the makeshift dwellings of early childhood; the tunnels under sheets draped over chairs, the outsized cardboard-box forts. Recollecting childhood scenes can pierce with a longing for what's past, and he ached for a wintry scene, a time when he was eight. On a waste strip in front of the park railings, a load of rough wood had been dumped. It seemed to him now that the snowflakes were a foot wide that floated down that winter as he carried each plank from flat ground up the knoll to build his house against the railings. It was a structure no taller than he was and surely hammered poorly, but inside was dry where he sat and watched the traffic and the falling snow. The hissing and spatting of rain encased him in a white noise little different from the batting of that long-ago snow. Sitting on the pinnacle of his shed in morose contemplation of his inner topography his older self looked out in wonder, that such a bare episode was a peak in his childhood.

"What would you do if you found the stamps?" asked Pat.

"I don't know. They belong, in theory, to some insurance company back in the 1920s, but that seems so lost in a far away land, and to give them up betrays my female ancestors who've guarded them for over eighty years."

"There's something devilish about a little immorality. And being a victimless crime, I'd go for it."

Bronwyn laughed at her co-conspirator, "It's wonderful when self-interest and inclination agree, and the devil's whispering in your ear."

"I wish I could treasure-hunt with you. It's an ill-timed vacation. You might ask your cousin, Sam, to look with you," and playing her devilish role she added, "Or Paul?"

"Let's get back to Aunt Phyllis for now. We don't have time for much more. After you're gone I might ask Sam." Smiling mischievously, she added, "Or Paul."

Wed., Sept. 29, 1971. I met with my math tutor today. The school counselor arranged it. She said I was privileged because he's a retired professor who's world famous and has written books and articles galore. Considering how dumb I am in math I was nervous, but I needn't have been. He's sweet. His name is Richard Vaughan. I'm sure it's something unpronounceable, coming from Hungary. We met in the school library right after school for an hour. He's got soft brown eyes the same color as Nanny Ellen's old rocking chair, hardly any hair, and an enormous forehead so you know he's super-smart. He asked about my family and I told him I was an orphan, thinking he'd go easy on me. He said he was too but that's kind of expected. He's even older than Nanny. He was pretty interested in me, so I told him about art and we didn't get to much math, but what we did was fun. He had me stand up to guess my weight. He was way off, like I was a baby elephant. He asked me if I knew about radio waves, and the light spectrum, and how they're all around. He said it's the same with math. Everything's made of numbers, even art. That was interesting, and it's true, like the eyes half way down the face and the mouth five-sixths down. I'm thinking of him as my math judo teacher. When I get bullied by Mr. Romano I can defend myself. Professor Vaughan said the school chairs weren't comfortable, so I asked if he'd like to come to my house next time and he could meet Nanny. He said he would. I thought they'd like each other.

Fri., Oct. 1, 1971. After school, we robbed the neighbors! Probably Mrs. Armory would have given us some, but it was more fun my way. She lives at number 12. You can see her apple tree from our back lane. I dared Clarence and Bill to climb over the wall. Valerie came to watch. The boys were spineless. They wouldn't go over the wall, so I had Clarence push me up. Clarence was going okay, but I had a short skirt and he got a full look up at me and his arms got weak. For all their strength, boys are pathetic. I dropped over the other side, pulled the bolt on the gate and everyone trooped in. Mrs. Armory would never have noticed the few apples we took, except she saw us from her back window. We ran. I don't think she knew it was me. I don't really like apples that much, but stolen apples are extra sweet.

"That makes me so angry with Aunt Phyllis. When I was fourteen, I robbed that same tree and she reamed me out. What a hypocrite! She said I'd have to make Mrs. Armory an apple pie, but I never did."

"You and your aunt were a pair," laughed Pat. "Your family's quite crime-ridden."

Wed., Nov. 3, 1971. Professor Vaughan was discussing proofs last week, and how they start with axioms that are obvious, and people don't have to prove them. He said there's a classic proof that all dogs have three tails. I sure couldn't prove it, but I pointed at Dozer who doesn't have three tails. Richard said 'No dog has two tails, you'd agree?' I thought about it and said yes. 'And all dogs have one more tail than no dog, you'd agree?' I said that sounded reasonable. He concluded, 'As no dog has two tails, and all dogs have one more tail than no dog, then all dogs have three tails.' Cool! That was my first math joke. Richard sure makes math interesting, he says it's like art, you get better with practice, and I do understand more in math class. For the past week I've been painting a dog that looks like Dozer except with three tails. I gave it to Richard and his eyes got misty. He said he'd treasure it always, which is sad to think about really, as that's not so very long.

Sat., Nov. 27, 1971. Christmas is coming. I drove over to Charlottesville with Nanny Ellen to go shopping. The fog on Afton Mountain was dense. I barely saw my hands gripped like death on the steering wheel. We made it safely and Nanny complimented my driving. Good thing I was driving. Nanny couldn't have seen her nose in that fog. We went to Miller & Rhoads, the department store, and the Christmas music made me cry, thinking of mom and dad taking me to see Santa. I got an abacus for Professor Vaughan that I hope he'll like and a yellow sweater for Josie. I'll get Nanny a bottle of vodka and maybe now she'll think I'm old enough. I figured out that Nanny's worried I'll become a ne'er-do-well.

Sun., Dec. 5, 1971. I confessed to Nanny Ellen this morning about the party at Valerie's last night. I probably should have kept quiet but I thought there'd be big trouble, and I'd better own-up first. Valerie's parents don't live together and as her mother's out of town and her father's clueless, she told him she was staying with a friend, but instead she threw a party at her mom's house. She had beer and the rest of us brought snacks. Valerie replaced the downstairs lights with purple light bulbs to make it like a college frat house. It was okay for a while but the music got louder and after a few beers the boys got gropier. Valerie, Judy and I went upstairs. We saw the police car's flashing blue lights. The music stopped and kids were streaming out like rats escaping the pest-control guy. We poured our beers down the sink and hid in a side attic, under where the roof slopes down. The police didn't find us. After an hour we snuck down and there was nobody in the house but us. The place was a mess so we cleaned up and went home. This morning Nanny made me go to the police station and I got cited for underage drinking. I called Valerie, worried I'd squealed on her, but she'd told her dad and the same thing happened to her.

Wed., Dec. 15, 1971. I gave Helen a Christmas present today. It was mean, but she deserved it for telling on my boiled peanuts picture. I got her a blouse for twenty cents at the thrift-store, and washed and starched it like new. It was the most hideous thing, with silvery threads running through it. I wrapped it in tissue paper and gave it to her in a Miller & Rhoads bag so it would look expensive. She loved it! She cried because she was happy I forgave her for tattling. She felt guilty ever since and was really sorry, and was glad we were friends again. So I guess we are. Helen doesn't feel guilty any more. Now it's me that feels guilty.

Mon., Feb. 21, 1972. Nanny Ellen and I went to Juvenile Court over my drinking beer at Valerie's party. We drank Valerie's mother's gin too, but none of us liked it so I didn't tell about that. I was worried, but Nanny said the judge wouldn't send me to juvenile corrections or anything like that. When we came up before the judge Nanny said I was a good girl and he sentenced me to community service for twenty hours. I have a form that lists the sort of work I can do and I took it to Mrs. Theriot. She said for my community service I could paint the backdrop for 'Oklahoma.'

Mon., Feb. 28, 1972. I started the backdrop after school. A surface so enormous is fun. The scrim is like cheesecloth and I let it down with thick ropes at the side of the stage. I'm not to use the big ladders so I let the scrim down to paint the top and pull it up as I paint downwards. My scene's a barn and cornfields with the sun shining through a misty morning. It looks like Farmer Miller's fields without the mountains.

Thur., Mar. 2, 1972. Mrs. Tolley in Science was mad at me. We were dissecting frogs and zapping them with electricity to see what happened to their muscles. For a frog, he was beautiful, and I wasn't going to cut him just for curiosity, so I refused. I said if she told me what happens I'd believe her. She wanted to know if I objected to cows being cut so I could have a hamburger. That was a pretty good argument. But I've got feelings and no arguing can make them go away. I had to talk with the vice-principal who's not as scary as he used to be, he said to tell Mrs. Tolley that I was excused from dissection.

Fri., Mar. 3, 1972. I went to the stage after school and my work was ruined. The bottom half of the scrim was painted over with a huge peace symbol and the words 'make love not war'. The lights in the auditorium were dim but I saw a girl walking up the center aisle toward the exit and I chased her. When I shouted, all she did was turn and face me. I crashed into her with my arms around her middle and knocked her paint can flying. We rolled around on the floor and I thumped her on the shoulder before she pinned me down. It was Kate Lavender sitting on me, breathing hard in my face. I was so angry with her, but I've forgiven her now. She was sorry it was my work she'd destroyed but she said people needed to hear that war wasn't right. We got to talking and I could see that her Vietnam protest was like frog dissection, only more important. Protesting was okay, but I had to repaint the backdrop. I told Kate I'd help do a more dramatic protest on opening night and she helped me repair the backdrop. Kate's good at painting so we got most of it fixed by the time the janitor made us leave.

Fri., Mar. 24, 1972. Kate came to my house for an anti-war conference. It was a lot like planning for a battle. In history, we'd learned about the gunpowder plot to blow up the British Parliament. I said we could burn something, like old leaves, in a garbage can underneath the stage so it would give off clouds of black smoke and in the confusion we'd shout out for peace. Kate said it was inventive, but dangerous. People might get trampled or we'd burn the school down. Kate had a better idea. She's been working with zinc-sulfide in her science class. It glows in the dark, and she thought I could mix the powder in paint and we'd make a glowing peace symbol appear during scene-change blackouts. Terrific, if it works. Kate will steal a cup-full from science lab and I'll talk to the stage lighting guys to see how the lights can help with our plan.

Thur., Apr. 6, 1972. During a break in rehearsals I went up to Frank and Joey at the lighting board. I didn't say anything about the zinc-sulfide. I asked if, theoretically, I wanted to display a peace symbol on the stage how I'd do that. Those guys know what they're doing. They argued technical stuff about gels and gobos and Joey said a pie plate would work. I nearly asked what kind of pie they wanted, but it was the aluminum. I'm supposed to cut my pattern into a pie plate to insert in a light. It didn't take bribing at all, they loved the idea.

Sun., Apr. 16, 1972. Last week I cut the pie plate to Frank and Joey's measurements. On Friday I mixed varnish with Kate's zinc-sulfide and after the dress rehearsal I was up there "touching up" the sun on the backdrop by painting on a varnish peace symbol. The performance on Saturday was monumental! When the lights came on there was my huge red Oklahoma sun with a bright white peace symbol on it from the pie-pan spotlight. Kate and I sat in the fourth row. We looked at each other as the buzz of excitement went up around the auditorium. At the first scene-change blackout, my beautiful sun kept on glowing its peace symbol in the dark. Our plan worked perfectly. Unfortunately, the guys didn't barricade the booth as they should have and by intermission someone made them turn off the spotlight. But the sun still shone its peace message through the blackouts. I'll get it on Monday, but they won't hear from me about Kate.

"Aunt Phyllis must have been in loads of trouble over that prank."

"Oh well, it didn't do any lasting harm," Pat said in amusement. "I'm sure someone had to paint over the sun, and the pie plate got taken away. Phyllis is a live-wire and I'd love to continue, but I'm flying to Vancouver early in the morning so I must get to bed."

"Sounds like the rain stopped," Bronwyn said. They rose from the couch and headed to the front door. "Have a safe trip and good luck with your male conquests," she said.

I'll miss you and Phyllis while I'm away. Remember, I've got you booked for dinner. I'll give you a call when I get back."

After fifteen minutes of watching from his station, Paul saw Bronwyn walk back into the living room. She did no more than turn the lights out there and in the kitchen before, he assumed, she went to bed. She was naked, but his view was blurred with rain fresh on the windows, and his heart didn't race as it had the previous night. Serenely happy, he called softly to her, "Good night, Bronwyn," before climbing down and going to bed.

Chapter 15   Tuesday

At 7:30 in the morning, Paul was on his stepladder anticipating Bronwyn's appearance. She came into view ten minutes later, smartly dressed in a dark blue skirt and white blouse. She fed Nigel and prepared her own breakfast. Paul's stomach growled as he watched Bronwyn sit to her egg, toast and orange juice. He wanted his breakfast but hung on to study her routines. She returned her dishes to the kitchen, opened the French doors and came out with Nigel on a leash. Her head moved from side to side as if she was glancing about. With her, Paul sniffed at the morning air: damp, grass, perhaps a whiff of manure. A crow's caw echoed "haw-haw" across the valley. His senses alert, he felt the mildly chill air riffle the hairs on his lower arms. "Do your job, boy," he heard. Nigel led Bronwyn to the grass below the angle of his view. They returned a couple of minutes later, Bronwyn knotting a plastic bag. Confident that she was preparing for work, he went inside and consumed a bowl of cereal. He sped through his shave, brushed his teeth, tossed his lunch ingredients in a bag and grabbed his backpack. Wheeling into the lane, he launched onto his bike and charged out to Bronwyn's road.

Bronwyn couldn't have completed her tasks and left for work, but he cycled to Main Street and coasted downhill, standing on his pedals to scout the distance. He didn't see her, as he knew he wouldn't. Turning his bike, he came back to the end of her lane, stopping a few feet in from the street, protected by the brick walls on each side of the lane. Sitting on his saddle, alert to street movement, he read his book on blindness. He was hoping that a trickle of confidence would seep from the book and give him a pool of chitchat and sensible questions. After twenty pages, unease percolated. She might have walked downhill on her street, taking the longer and hillier route to town. Soon he'd be late for work. But his worrying ceased as Bronwyn and Nigel crossed the lane before him. Part way across, they stopped. Nigel greeted him with a 'Wuff'. "What is it, Nigel?" asked Bronwyn. He froze, fearful she'd come toward him and would hear the blood pound in his chest. If the Goddess Diana turned her bow on him, he'd be like a hart, helpless to escape her arrow. "It's nothing, boy," she said. "Did you see a rabbit?" and they moved on.

Fumbling with his backpack's zipper, he stowed his book. He leaned on his handlebars waiting for his agitation to ebb. When equilibrium returned, he cycled after them. They were a few blocks ahead on Main Street. He reflected, as if surprised, that he had three choices; lag behind, come beside Bronwyn and speak to her, or cycle on by and fail to notice her. A fourth, was to turn on a side street and avoid the issue altogether. When that last pusillanimous evasion formed in his mind, he was so disgusted that he propelled his bike forward, ringing his bell lustily.

"Yo, there," he cried. Gratified with his spontaneity, he crossed to her side of the street calling from behind her, "It's Paul, Bronwyn."

Bronwyn turned her head to the street and smiled. It was wonderful that he appeared just as she was thinking of him. "Good morning, Paul. You're cycling to work?"

"I am."

"Where did you come from?"

"Back behind you."

She laughed at his nonsense, "I could have guessed that."

"You're going to work, too?" he said, happy with something simple for his part of the conversation. Cycling around a car he called out in frustration, "I'm sorry, I'm snaking around parked cars on the wrong side of the road. Shall I come on the sidewalk and walk my bike?"

"Please," she said. With Paul beside her she replied, "Yes, I'm off to work. I work nine to four. But that depends on my clients."

"You're lucky. I have to work until five. Sometimes I work Saturday mornings, but then I'm off an afternoon."

"I'm glad we bumped into each other. I have something to ask you." Feeling a slight trepidation, her words came in a rush. "I wanted to have you over tomorrow for dinner, if that's possible, I'm planning to ask Sam, too. I know he wants to get to know you better."

"Oh well, if Sam's coming, then of course I'd be happy to." The moment it was launched, he regretted his misdirected facetiousness.

Relieved he'd accepted, Bronwyn was a little nonplussed at his apparent slight of her. She decided he was insecure. Hoping his over-compensation poorly reflected his regard for her, she responded, "I expect Sam will say the same thing. 'Oh well, if Paul's coming, then of course I'd be happy to.' So I'll cook the meal and wait on you men, and you can bond, while I, your handmaiden, am ignored."

"Oh, goodness, no." he said, flustered.

"All in good fun. But if you find me dressed as a French maid, remember to give me an occasional 'merci,' for I work to be but noticed by you gentlemen."

"I see," he said doubtfully, unsure if this shoal needed navigating. "I'll look forward to it."

Bronwyn decided to tease him no more, for the moment.

Moving in front with his bicycle, he spoke over his shoulder, "The sidewalk's narrowing. There's a utility pole coming on the right." He failed to notice the guy-wire securing the pole to the pavement. Directly in line with the pole, it wasn't normally a hazard, but he looked back, his bike strayed toward the curb and, with his wheel on one side of the wire and him on the other, his impetus skewed the bike, forcing it to strike his legs. He fell, and his bike toppled on him.

Nigel brought Bronwyn to an immediate halt. "My goodness, are you okay?" she exclaimed.

"Umm, yes," he said weakly, trying to find a way to push the bicycle off, so he could stand. He wished his bike was less grubbily in contact with his work trousers. Getting a knee to the ground, he leveraged himself against the bicycle until they both stood. Bronwyn felt past his bicycle, found Paul's chest and felt her way to his shoulder.

"Are you hurt?"

Conscious of her arm anchored against him, he replied, "Shaken, but not stirred."

"Well, my fine hero, this is the second time I've found you on the ground beside your bike." She released her grip, allowing her arm to fall. "You'd better collect your wits around me before one or both of us are hurt." Chastened, he pushed onward with his bike. Nigel and Bronwyn followed. When the sidewalk widened, he came beside her and said he'd leave, to give himself time to clean up before work.

"Come at 6:00 tomorrow?" she asked. Paul promised he would. He mounted his bike, gave a cheery ring of his bell and pedaled off.

Bronwyn went on to work, light of foot, fearless of the uneven sidewalk bricks.

Paul pedaled fiercely, burning his thigh muscles. His legs were shaky when he arrived at the library. He hastened in with barely enough time to clean himself before the library opened. His morning had been stressful. He welcomed the coming absorption in his library routines.

After his day's work, Paul cycled home. He didn't stop at his house but continued down the hill to the park. He turned left, then left again on Bronwyn's street and labored up her hill. With her shades closed, there was no evidence of life at her house. He turned left into the lane and dismounted at her gate. Music played softly, maybe a Beethoven symphony, but he'd be guessing. Parking his bike in the shed, he climbed to the fourth rung of his stepladder. Bronwyn was sitting at her computer desk at the far left of her living room. Knowing where she was, he went inside to feed Spook and to prepare his own dinner.

It was a simple meal, a slice of toast, baked beans and a fried egg. He ate outside, sitting on a folding-chair by the shed. Spook lay under a bush, napping and watching him in her half-wakeful moments. The evening was warm for early May. He pleasantly moved between alert and drowsing states, reading his book and listening to the bees and the pastoral sounds of Bronwyn's music. He imagined balloons tied to his chair, drifting him over his fence and over Bronwyn's wall and gently landing him, with no volition on his part, in her garden, to the exclaim and joy of all. This led to the thought of moving his chair up to his eagle's nest on the shed, but he abandoned the idea when he visualized a chair-leg slipping off the platform and his noisy tumble to the ground.

After cleaning up from dinner, he couldn't resist climbing to his perch. He knew it was dangerous in the evening light. Wearing a short-sleeved pale blue top, Bronwyn worked in her kitchen. She was singing, or perhaps talking to Nigel. Watching her industry infused him with delight. She's preparing something for my dinner tomorrow, he thought. True or not, it was pleasing. He prided himself on facing the truth, but, on occasion, he wasn't averse to besting reality if it seemed deficient.

"Evening, Paul," came from his neighbor's backyard. "What are you up to?"

Paul was aghast. His focus on Bronwyn had diminished his peripheral awareness and allowed Mrs. Marmion from next door to imperil him. She was a small lady of advanced years and nothing to menace anyone, but his position teetered so, and could so easily fall to embarrassment and shame. He lunged to his left, hammering with his clenched right fist on the side of the roof that sloped from her. His left hand reached back and jerked the cushion off the platform so it slid down the roof. His pretend hammer hidden from her sight, he replied at a level calibrated to be inaudible over Bronwyn's wall, "I'm repairing the roof, Mrs. Marmion."

"You're baring it, you say?"

Fearful his voice would carry too far, he turned his face full on her and projected more firmly in her direction. "Re-pairing, Mrs. Marmion. I'm fixing the roof." With vigor, he bent to his work of noisily hammering the roof.

Mrs. Marmion hadn't moved. He gave up hammering because his hand hurt. "Paul, you've got a tile missing from this side that needs replacing," she said.

"Thanks, Mrs. Marmion. I'll get to it, but I'm finished now." He turned about on the roof, clumsy with the need to keep his hammer invisibly below the ridge. He climbed down, thinking it was good he wasn't sitting up there on a chair.

Bronwyn heard the hammering. At least it wasn't late on a Sunday evening. Shortly after, she answered a knock at her front door. It was John Wardle, who'd popped by for a moment to apologize for being too busy to get to her building tasks. She invited him in, and he agreed to a cup of coffee. As they went back to her living room, Bronwyn said, "I was about to make a pot, so it's no trouble. We'll have it ready shortly."

"Can I give you a hand to make it more efficient?"

She laughed, "A builder would look for efficiency."

"Forgive me. It's in my blood to take over any little job and I'm always finished before the next man. You're certainly not one to run around a track, but in my younger days, I was fast. 'Flash', that was me. Some of the locals still call me that."

"'Flash' has a dashing air to it," she said, smiling at him, "but I'll call you 'John,' if I may?"

"Dear Bronwyn, I hope you will, often."

"We're settled then, John. Here's the carafe, if you'll fill it to the four-cup line, I'll put two scoops in the filter and it will only take a few minutes of your time."

"I'm sorry I need to rush off. I'm interviewing a couple of guys this evening who want to be my assistants. Young men are all the same these days. They start work with enthusiasm, then before you know it their aunt Mildred needs a ride to the hospital, their car's broken down, or they've got the sniffles."

"You're not so far from a young man yourself."

"True, but I had a spine. These youngsters are soft and idle."

Along with his mug of coffee, Bronwyn fed him chocolate-chip cookies. They continued talking of John's business, a subject he was clearly happy to discourse on.

Paul sat on his folding chair for a few minutes before re-ascending his stepladder. He hoped Mrs. Marmion wouldn't greet him as he peeked over the shed's roof. She was gone. He turned to Bronwyn's house and the unwelcome sight of John Wardle inhabiting her kitchen. At a height gauged to minimize exposure, he watched their cozy familiarity. Fearful of detection, he descended after several minutes to sit in his chair. His legs, stressfully bent to maintain his precise elevation on the ladder, were a source of discomfort. He was in as foul a temper as any snapping turtle might be supposed to be. He imagined Bronwyn a round of delectable cheese and he a feeble mouse forlornly looking on while Mr. Rat, no friend to mouse or cheese, perambulated with his drooling grin about the toothsome feast. Paul shook himself and slapped his arms about himself as if to animate in that shabby husk of a man the will to stand, and fight and die. He did stand, and, opening his gate, he propelled himself along the lane at a furious clip.

It was well into twilight when he returned to his gate. He was accosted there by a figure rushing up the lane who grabbed his left arm and shouted gleefully, "Geez, Paul, it's you." Paul beheld no rat, but a far more kindly shrew who, he guiltily knew, he'd neglected for nearly a week.

"Rolf! You surprised me. I'd ask what you're doing, but I guess I know."

"Too true. I was exploring this alley, but it's the gloomiest of tunnels with not much to see. I discover it, and you're here before me." Paul pushed his gate open and Rolf exclaimed, "But you live here, don't you! That's wonderful. I went twice to your flat this weekend, and it was all dark. I was going to winkle you out at the library, but now there's no need."

"Yes, I should have told you. Come in," Paul said hospitably.

"Is that you, Paul?" Bronwyn's voice came from over the wall.

Paul groaned quietly at this disaster.

"Who's that, then?" asked Rolf.

"Paul, I can't pull the bolt. Can you help?"

"I can climb over, if you want me to," he called through the gate.

"Please."

Paul turned to Rolf. "She's a neighbor. It's important," he pleaded quietly. "Behave yourself." He raised his leg and Rolf pushed against his shin, sending him high enough to get a foot on the gate and a hand on the wall. "I'm coming over, Bronwyn. Step back." He rolled his chest onto the brick wall and slowly lowered himself beside the gate. Yanking on the bolt, he pulled it open. "Needs oiling," he said.

"But Paul, how strange to find you here. And who are you with?"

Paul opened the gate, and Rolf came in, looking around at the garden. "S'truth, you've got high walls around here. I'm Rolf," he said, holding out his hand.

"Good to meet you. I'm Bronwyn. Come in, both of you, and we'll talk." She turned and walked to the house.

Rolf bent to offer the back of his hand to Nigel. In an undertone he said, "She not into shaking hands?"

"She's blind, you idiot."

"Blimey. Poor girl. You soft on her, are you?"

"Be quiet, Rolf. Let's go in."

They followed Bronwyn into the kitchen. "Would you like a drink, Rolf?" she asked, getting out glasses. "There's no beer, but I have red wine."

"Anything's a bit of all right with me, Bronwyn."

"Is it? I may have some cod-liver oil about."

"Not close enough to turps for me. I can see you're a joker, like me. I'll have to watch it."

Bronwyn poured the glasses and handed them around. "So, tell me, what were you doing behind my house?"

"Paul's house too," Rolf said.

"What! Paul said he lives here?"

"No, no," Paul responded, considerably perturbed. "I live behind you."

"Across the lane? I don't understand. Why didn't you say anything before?"

"I didn't want to presume. You know, by being a neighbor, to make you think you had to be hospitable, or anything."

"Makes you want to chunder, 'im being such a sensitive bloke. You'd think he liked the other half, but you can trust me, he's no pansy."

"I see. Thank you, Rolf."

"Mind if I have a go at your loo?"

"Sure. First door on the right," Bronwyn said.

After Rolf closed the door, Paul said, "Sorry about that."

"Now I understand why you said, 'Back behind you,' this morning. It's not clear to me who's stranger, you, or your friend Rolf." They sipped their drinks for a minute. Bronwyn broke the awkward silence, "We're on for dinner tomorrow evening. I asked Sam and he's happy to come."

The toilet flushed and Rolf reappeared saying, "Lovely smells. A woman's toilet's like being in paradise."

"So, Rolf, how long have you known Paul?"

"Not long, but seems like it. He's a bonzer mate. Good to have beside you in a scrape."

"And you get in scrapes together?"

"Too right! I could tell you tales. You being a Sheila, I won't of course."

As soon as they finished their drinks, Paul insisted that he and Rolf needed to leave. Bronwyn walked to the gate with them. "Goodnight, Paul. It was nice meeting you, Rolf. I'll look forward to hearing more about you and Paul."

Rolf came into Paul's house and looked around. "Got prospects, but a little bare," he said.

"I'll get more furniture eventually. My needs aren't great."

"Hard to entertain your lady friend, though. The ladies'll want more comfort."

"I don't know if that's going to happen," Paul said disconsolately.

"You need cheering up, mate. Come and see the sights."

"No thanks. I am feeling low. I'll get some sleep."

Rolf left him for pleasures of the night. Paul went to bed, curling up to circle the black hole that had materialized in his stomach.

CHAPTER 16   WEDNESDAY

Paul arrived home from work with more than thirty minutes to prepare for Bronwyn's dinner, which was plenty of time. In his nervous condition, it was too much time. He took a shower to relax, dried forcefully and applied deodorant. He dressed in a pair of jeans and a casual red shirt. He shaved, splashed on after-shave, then a little more, then decided too much was worse than too little and scrubbed his face with soap and water until he was red, hoping that was more a reflection of his shirt than anything embarrassing. He walked out his front door and around the block to Bronwyn's front door.

Sam answered his knock. Paul was relieved that Sam had arrived before him. After his feeble explanation of the previous evening, he and Bronwyn alone might have known a constraint. He was anxious that the evening's conversation avoid the topic of his relocation behind Bronwyn's house. He feared the casual question that was death to him, 'How long, Paul, have you lived in your house?' The truth would lead Bronwyn's quick mind to question him, which would surely culminate in his disastrous confession.

Paul greeted Bronwyn and pulled a bottle of wine from his backpack. "I've brought a contribution." Remembering that she couldn't see it, he added hastily, "A bottle of red wine."

Bronwyn felt around in a drawer and held out a corkscrew. "Open it then. We'll get started."

Sam laughed, "Did you need to bring your backpack to carry one bottle of wine?"

"I have something else, but honestly I may not be comfortable bringing it out. So, please don't press me."

"A man of mystery," Bronwyn said.

"I would have carried the wine in the backpack anyway. It's a sad family story."

"Please tell us," Bronwyn said. "I know nothing of your family."

"Okay. My uncle--that's my mother's brother--died when I was nine. He only visited once or twice a year, but I was fond of him. He liked to laugh. Anyway, he was walking home from the liquor store, and he collapsed. He slid down the wall clutching his bottle, protecting it like a baby. People went by, not bothering, thinking him a drunk with his bottle. By the time he was noticed it was too late, the damage was done to his brain. After a few days in a coma he died. Ever since, if I carry a bottle of alcohol in my arms I think of my uncle, and I fear I'll drop the way he did."

"Wow, you're one neurotic guy," Sam said. "He really needs you, Bronwyn."

"Paul is an interesting case. My advice is to hold the bottle and think of your uncle. Imagine him alive and laughing, and after a while, it will get easier. It pays to fight these irrational fears, or you can reasonably say, to heck with it, what's one more little neurosis in a sea of 'em.'"

"Let's find a more cheerful subject," suggested Sam.

"Where are your parents, Paul?" she asked.

"That's not too cheerful. My mother died of MS when I was eleven. My father was a drunkard by then. He's living, if you can call it that, in Pittsburgh, where I grew up."

"I'm sorry. We both lost our mother's young. I'd like to talk more about that. But let's eat now. That should be safe. I don't remember if you know this, Paul, but Sam's a vegetarian, a vegetarian atheist. As odd as one gets in our society, but we love even his frailties."

"I'm not vegetarian," Paul said, "but I don't eat much meat."

"No hope of your becoming somewhat atheist, too?" asked Sam.

"I'm open to persuasion. There's an old American political word, 'mugwump.' I'm vague on its origin, but it could apply to me, a fence-sitter, with my mug on one side of the fence and my wump on the other.

"Neurotic and indecisive, the catalog grows," Sam said triumphantly.

Pulling the pan from the oven, Bronwyn said, "I prepared manicotti from scratch last night, which I wouldn't do for just anyone. I like cooking, but frozen convenience is more usual."

Her guests frequently remarked on the excellence of the meal, and they were well into their second bottle of wine when Paul suddenly thought that Sam and Ruth, both outdoorsy, would be a good match. "Do you have a girlfriend?" he asked.

"Mandy, the girl I've been dating, quite sensibly dumped me a week ago, so, not right now."

"I know these things aren't served up like steak from a menu, but I know someone you might like. Her name's Ruth Thompson. She works with me, at the circulation desk. She's a very kind girl and a committed vegetarian. She's Buddhist, which seems similar to being an atheist, and she likes mountains and forests. But I'll stop, before I'm accused of puffing her up."

"I think I've noticed her," Sam said. "Tall, long black hair?"

"That's her," Paul confirmed. "Give her a call, or I'll sound her out if you like."

"And me, Mr. Cupid? Is there someone on the menu for me," asked Bronwyn, opening a splendid avenue for Paul's self-advocacy.

"I thought, perhaps," he hesitated in confusion, "that you and John Wardle? Sam's mother was hinting that."

Sam snorted, "Don't listen to my mother. She's in her second childhood and believes in fairy tales. We have to add 'gullible' to your catalog of faults." While Paul appreciated Sam's quick rebuttal, he wished the denial had come from Bronwyn. "But thanks," Sam said. "I will call Ruth."

The meal finished, Sam put on coffee, and they busied themselves tidying the kitchen. "So, Paul, how long have you lived in your house?" asked Sam.

There it was. The innocent question that would test him. He should have prepared his words. Should he say, 'It was six days ago. In all honesty I moved to stalk a blind woman I barely knew.' The truth would end his hopes, but he couldn't lie. Clenching the edge of the kitchen counter, he said, "I'm renting the house." In his agitation, he kicked the backpack he'd stowed under the counter. It let out a clucking noise.

"Whatever was that?" exclaimed Bronwyn.

"Oh, um, sorry," said Paul, retrieving his backpack. "I wasn't sure if this was extremely silly so I was reluctant to bring them out."

"You've got chicks in there?" asked Sam incredulously.

"Eggs. Sort of. They're electronic eggs. It's silly, I know, and past Easter, but I thought that Bronwyn couldn't hunt for Easter eggs and this way she could. You throw the switch and the eggs make little cheeps and clucks."

"A romantic! Another fault to add to your catalog," crowed Sam.

Paul reached into his backpack, found the offending egg and turned it off. "I thought, only if we're in the mood, that we could compete blindfolded against Bronwyn."

"You guys are toast," Bronwyn said. "But Paul, when did you have time to get these?"

"On Sunday," he answered in embarrassment. "I ordered them on the Internet."

"I see," Bronwyn said. "That was extremely thoughtful. Sam, go to the hall closet, will you. You'll find scarves there. I'll get a couple of grocery bags."

With Sam blindfolded, and Bronwyn beside him in the hallway, Paul turned on the eggs and placed them about the kitchen and the living room. "Go," he called and both raced in with their bags in hand.

"How many?" asked Bronwyn, when the chirping eggs were all quieted in their bags.

"Seven for me," reported Sam.

"So, Bronwyn has thirteen," Paul said.

At his turn, Paul was determined to compete. He didn't want Bronwyn thinking he'd let her win, nor did he want to be trounced. Racing for the final egg, in their eagerness to contend, they tumbled together, rolling over each other on the floor. Both lost their bags and Bronwyn ended on top of him. From her superior position, she lunged for the egg under a pillow on the couch. Jubilant she shouted, "Got it." Paul pulled off his blindfold and handed over her bag. Bronwyn counted. "Only eight! What a let-down."

"It's a shell game, Bronwyn. Paul's a con-man. He pulled a switch-a-roo on the bags."

"You're right, Sam. The bags do look the same," Paul said contritely. "I agree. I couldn't be that good."

"I'm not so sure," she said. "I'm declaring Paul and I tied. That was a lot of fun. Shall we have coffee now? I want to tell you about Aunt Phyllis."

Settling down with their coffee, Sam and Bronwyn on the couch and Paul in the armchair, Bronwyn said, "You see the photocopies on the table beside the couch. Those are Aunt Phyllis' diaries. I'm getting the originals transcribed so I can hear them on my computer. Pat was reading to me, but she's on vacation, and I was thinking you two might help." Assured of their interest, Bronwyn related the gist of what she'd learned from the diaries and from talking with her father and Aunt Josie. "There's the potential for Aladdin's Cave behind these walls if the stamp collection still exists. Aunt Phyllis was supposed to be a fine artist, and it's a mystery to me why she gave up painting, or if she didn't, then what became of her paintings. I'm hoping the diaries will tell us. I've been thinking about going by the Lavender Art Gallery and talking to Kate Lavender. She was a school friend of Aunt Phyllis and apparently sold her work."

"I'm not working tomorrow afternoon," Paul said. "I could go with you, if you'd like?"

"That's great. I'll call the gallery in the morning and call you at the library to confirm."

"We can have a wall-tapping party on the weekend," Sam said.

"Yes, lets," agreed Bronwyn.

"So where are you in the diaries?" asked Sam.

"The middle of April, 1972. Phyllis is seventeen, a junior in high school and she's into mischief. She's just painted a glow-in-the-dark peace symbol on the backdrop of her school's spring musical. I'll read it thoroughly later, Sam, but if you'd skim along and read a few highlights."

Sam flipped pages to April 1972 and read onwards as time passed for Phyllis.

Mon., May 29, 1972. On Saturday I finished my painting of Miss Wheeler. It was a two-month project, watching Miss Wheeler in class, coming home and working on it. It's the best I've ever done that wasn't a tractor. She's a goddess in a glade, and the sun's striking her through the leaves. She's wearing something like a gym skirt and nothing else. Her back is so pretty and I can barely see her left breast as she looks back at me. She isn't offended that I'm looking at her. I wrapped the painting in brown paper and carried it around all day, until after school was out I took it by Miss Wheeler's room and gave it to her. I was in agony watching her. She looked between it and me for a long time and said it was the loveliest painting anybody had ever given her and I was the most talented student she's ever going to have, which made me glow. She decided to accept it but asked me never to paint her again without her permission. She'd noticed me watching her and said it's common for girls to get attached to younger female teachers that way and it was something that would pass. I cried and Miss Wheeler cried some too. It's like Skip and Miss Wheeler are on different planets and I'd rather live on Miss Wheeler's.

"Who's Skip?" asked Paul.

"He's her first sexual experience," explained Bronwyn. "But she's thinking of Miss Wheeler as a goddess and him as a clod. Miss Wheeler's right, a straight young woman may become emotionally attached to a slightly older woman and be sexually confused, but it straightens itself out after a while."

"Do tell more," Sam said.

"You men!"

"Just the way we're made. Right, Paul?"

Paul nodded. "It was one of the Greeks who said, in old age, how glad he was to be done with the tyranny of sex. Like a slave who'd escaped a savage master."

"Not making me look forward to old age," Sam said. "There's something to it though. A sex drive is like being a slave to a mistress you adore."

"Women like being admired," Bronwyn said, "but I'd guess the goddess would be offended. Aunt Phyllis would have been turned to stone or torn apart by her dogs. Goddesses aren't as kind as Miss Wheeler."

Wed., May 31, 1972. Richard specializes in number theory, which is what, I'm not sure. Today he was telling me how I'd make a fortune if I proved 'Goldbach's conjecture', which seems a suitable name if it's worth a mint. I don't need money anyway. I know where Nanny

Ellen hid her gold. It's the end of the school year almost, and Richard has helped me survive math class. Mr. Romano got fired this week. The rumor is he faked his credentials and didn't have the degrees he said he did, which doesn't surprise me.

Sat., Aug. 5, 1972. I wish mom could see me. This summer, instead of fields, I've been painting buildings. Yesterday I set up my easel on Main Street across from the old courthouse square. I'm a tourist attraction. Sometimes I'll have six people behind me, staring. Sounds scary, but I don't mind. I'm confident when I'm painting. The shop owners like me! They bring me drinks and snacks during the day. A man and his wife offered me $50 for my painting, which wasn't bad for a day's work. I hated doing it, but I said they could have it. It was on a stretching frame so they were only buying the canvas, and they'd have to pick it up after 4:00. I told them I'd leave it at the framing shop across the street. I checked back today and the lady in the frame shop was pleased. She gave me the $50 the couple paid. They had her frame it, so she said it was a good arrangement if I wanted to do that again.

"At least we know Aunt Phyllis made some money in her painting career," Sam said.
"It does seem tough," Paul said, "spending your day working and the results are taken away. But then, that's our workdays too, so I won't feel so bad for her."

Mon., Sept. 4, 1972. Nanny Ellen gave me an early birthday present this year. Nanny paid for it and Miss Wheeler arranged it with the art department. I get to take an art class at the university during my senior year of high school! I go twice a week on Tuesday and Thursday at three in the afternoon. Nanny says I can take the car to school every day now because she isn't driving much. Nanny doesn't see too well any more. She's all I have, unless you count Josie, which I'd only do if I had to.

"Aunt Phyllis didn't get along too well with my mom," commented Sam. "I don't blame her."

145

Thur., Oct. 5, 1972. I'm painting nudes at the university. Today was a shock. Richard's wife, Victoria, was our model. Richard and Victoria had me over for dinner a couple of month's back and she made chicken salad and homemade rosemary bread. Yum! People are so different without their clothes. She's crumpled, like a balloon losing its air. I told her after class it was weird seeing her like that. She said she enjoyed being looked at as long as the room wasn't cold, and artists need to see the world the way it is. We can romanticize if we want, but we have to know what's underneath. I've been thinking about that, and underneath her dried-up-apple skin there's still Victoria. Richard's big and outgoing and she's small and quiet, but they're matching bookends lucky to be together on the same shelf. The underneath layer is still physical and we're going to die.

"There's something God-like," Sam said, "and being an atheist I say 'like,' to watching a life unfurl that you know has already closed. It doesn't take much imagination to picture a future generation looking at us the same way. Makes me want to rush out and start a diary, or they'll be saying, 'He was in trees is all we know, and one tree, after all, is much like another.'"

"On that lugubrious note," Bronwyn said, "we should call it a night. Tomorrow we all labor in our various trees, and I, for one, am ready for bed."

Paul put the eggs in his backpack, Sam cleaned up the glasses, and they said their farewells to Bronwyn. Out on the street Sam said, "Goodnight. I'd give you a ride home but I expect you can manage one block. Good luck tomorrow at the art gallery."

Paul went home and immediately up on his shed. Bronwyn's lights were already out. Denied, he sat for ten minutes watching the unmoving darkness, nurturing a morose ache of loneliness that he took with him to bed.

CHAPTER 17   THURSDAY

Paul fried onions and mushrooms, scrambled in an egg, mixed it with salsa and cheese and wrapped the result in a large tortilla. With his breakfast burrito held in a paper towel, he climbed his ladder and looked into Bronwyn's domain. He wanted to see her naked, to feel his breath stilled and his heart race with excitement, but he knew she would come fully clothed and that familiarity was good, too, friendlier than a burst from his rapacious hormones. Perched uncomfortably on his ladder he enjoyed the warm distraction of his breakfast. After a few minutes, Bronwyn appeared, dressed in a lilac suit. He began enjoying the simple pleasure of expectation. Bronwyn could surprise him, but, with her limited morning tasks, he had a claim to know her movements in advance, 'Nigel is fed', 'The orange juice is poured' and 'Now Nigel's toilet'. Each of her tasks, he felt admiringly, was accomplished with a sureness and a serenity lacking in him, for all his vision.

He hoped to see Bronwyn in the afternoon, and, as accidental encounters would become suspicious, he cycled from the lane at 8:30, before she would complete her morning preparations but later than his usual departure time. That intentional small delay in his routine he likened to brushing his teeth with his left hand, something he intended to try soon. He wanted proof of his capacity to change.

Mid-morning his phone rang, "Paul Kirk," he said.

"Paul, this is Bronwyn." It was a thrilling experience. Her voice was slightly husky, like a deep bowl smote by a rubber mallet, mellowed with layered tones he hadn't noticed face to face. He shivered, anticipating more words. "I spoke with Kate at the gallery. She'd love to talk with us. Can you come to my office at four? I'm on the second floor. You know where I am?" Paul did. He agreed to meet her, and they hung up.

Scheduled to leave work at one o'clock, he was in no hurry and was fifteen minutes late by the time he went to the staff lounge to pick up his backpack and leave. Ruth stopped him. "I just talked with Sam Stickley. He said you suggested he call me."

Paul nodded warily. At the time of their hike, two weeks before, he'd become aware that Ruth was interested in him. But for the vision of Bronwyn the Sunday after, something might have happened. Ruth was appealingly unpretentious and, taken as a whole, was attractive. Despite his adequate good looks, and more than adequate intelligence, Paul acknowledged to himself the dearth of females interested in him. His chief fault, he supposed, was a predilection to lop off conversation, as if words were dollars and his budget was overspent. He imagined wading through molasses was more fun for a woman than tolerating a man given to monosyllabic answers who failed to have the basic decency to ask questions in return. "I thought you'd suit," he said.

"He seems very nice. He said he'd noticed me before, but it's difficult, starting something, when you don't know the other person's romantic status."

"He's a great guy," Paul said encouragingly.

Ruth examined her shoes. "I had thought … that you and I. But nothing happened." She lifted her face and said less bashfully, "But Sam seems sweet, doesn't he? He really likes you, which shows good judgment." Paul smiled, nodding. "He asked me to dinner tonight, to the Mexican restaurant." Paul said he hoped they'd have a good time.

He chose to cycle through the cemetery on his way home. "Hello, Phyllis," he said, standing at her grave. "Or may I call you Aunt Phyllis?" He read her headstone, "Born September 16 1954 Died October 5 2009 Remembered with Love." Probably it was Josie's doing, the wording, a bare and dull epithet for the likes of Phyllis. It was a shame she died relatively young, but if she hadn't died, Bronwyn wouldn't be in Lexington, and that was how things worked. He could only be grateful she'd died, which was no sentiment to feel in her presence, but surely she'd understand. Would she approve of him? He could understand her reservations. Too often, he saw himself as a badly baked loaf of bread, crusty on the outside and underdone inside. Too late to get back in the oven, but might he attempt to follow Bronwyn's advice and ease his negative neurotic replays? Today, he thought, I'll be a whole loaf. Crusty is inevitable, but a consistent bread of sweet and airy lightness. This amused him, as it sounded a mite ridiculous, but he thought he'd try. He turned his bike around and cycled back past the library to the grocery store where he bought grapes, a few varieties of cheese and a loaf of crusty French bread.

Later that afternoon, anxious not to be late, he set off for Bronwyn's building and was far too early. She might have a client who'd be embarrassed being seen outside the office door, so he cycled around the block. By his third go round, he wondered if the circuits, seemingly intended to soak up time, weren't really a magic ritual. A jumbled piece of poetry floated into his mind, 'Weave a circle round her thrice and drink the milk of paradise.'

Paul had passed the counseling offices many times in the past without truly noting the building, which he did now, as he pushed his bike up the curb and onto its front path. Adjacent to Hopkins Green, the old redbrick house jutted out in front with a wooden square-columned entryway that created a porch at both levels. In mini-waves, the brick path climbed and descended as it undulated through the grass leading to the lower porch's wooden steps. The porch and column paint had seen decay and been painted over for generations, which, together with the half-height basement windows, contributed to the slightly seedy impression of a building sinking into the earth. Leaning his bike against the side of the building, he sat on the front steps to wait. Sufficient time had passed, and he was ready to stand, when the front door opened and a gray-haired man in a suit came out.

"Do you need assistance finding anyone?" he asked pleasantly.

Paul squished against the handrail uprights, minimizing his presence on the steps. "No. Just fine thanks," he replied vacuously. He must seem afraid to go in. Paul watched him walk steadily off without a backward glance. He stood and made his way slowly to the second floor. Three rooms led from the landing. The third door, closest to the front of the building, had "Bronwyn Heathcote, LCSW" on a wooden plaque. It was a minute after four, but Paul was reluctant to enter, anxious not to disturb a client. For a minute, he heard only the creaks he made, shifting on the old floorboards. He'd appear foolish if someone came up the stairs or out of another office and saw him rooted there. Each second accumulated its weight until the load could be borne no more, and he advanced his hand to knock. The door was pulled inwards and Bronwyn stood before him.

"Paul?"

With his fist raised above her, he fixed on her face; not delicate, but strong; her long black eyelashes, those almond eyes looking at him, her golden skin, thick black eyebrows and a square chin; her hair brushed back, sunlit from the tall landing window. Dust motes danced about. Her dark hair had a few strands of lighter color. Tiny crinkles of her hair sparkled like the ocean. The makeup on her left cheekbone was darker than on her right. He'd love to help her in the mornings, if she only knew. Slowly he retracted his fist, staring at her.

"Paul?"

"Oh, yes, sorry, it's me."

"Come in then, you silly. I thought I heard someone out here, and my goodness, by now you're two minutes late."

Paul followed her. It was a large room with wide floor-planking that sloped downward a little toward the far wall, a dark brown desk and chairs, two comfy armchairs and a couch. A tall sash-window overlooked the street and let in plenty of light. Nigel lay on his bedding in the corner close to the window. He lazily bestirred himself to greet Paul.

"Hello Nigel, it's good to see you," Paul said, running his hand down Nigel's leg and shaking the offered paw.

"Nigel greets all my clients. He puts them at their ease. I don't see anybody pretending around a dog."

"Should I lie on the couch?" he asked, aiming for levity.

"No time at present, but I've a feeling you're a rich vein for exploration."

"Would that be gold or silver? Or else tin or coal?"

"Definitely I see darkness there. But not to worry, you've plenty of company, and you get a plus for acting well despite your faults."

Bronwyn retrieved Nigel's leash and harness and when he was uniformed for duty, they set off. Out on the street, privileged and amazed to be walking with this girl, Paul gave a few skips, thinking himself a light loaf, free of stodginess.

"What are you up to?" asked Bronwyn.

"Hopping over cracks so no evil comes to anyone."

"You're the one with cracks," she laughed.

Paul periodically shut his eyes as they walked along. It was horribly difficult to imagine never having the re-assurance of sight. Without help, it seemed impossible for Bronwyn to go the short distance from her office to the gallery, although certainly she'd have done it. 'Impossible deeds are my daily bread' she might have said. As they crossed the street, with the gallery a short walk ahead on the left, he saw someone looking out of the gallery door. Seeing them, she came onto the sidewalk.

"Hi," she said, "I'm Kate." She stepped aside. "Go on in."

It was a small gallery. The room they stood in branched to two smaller rooms. The front room displayed local nature scenes or Lexington buildings and there was one painting with a pink Cadillac in front of an old gas station. In her mid to late fifties, Kate was a trim figure with short-cropped hair.

"It's nice to see you, Bronwyn," Kate said. "Do you remember me at all? Since you called I've been thinking back, and you were in Lexington for three summers."

"That's right. I was between twelve and almost fifteen. I'm not sure if I do remember you, Kate. I'm sure I should."

"That's okay. Phyllis and I were close through the time of your birth. Less so, later. I expect galleries weren't on your summer entertainment list, but I saw you a few times. I was in my early forties then, slender, long blonde hair. The hair's white now and I'm wearing it short."

"Do you know Paul Kirk?" asked Bronwyn, by way of introduction.

"You've helped me at the public library, haven't you?"

"Now that you say that, I do remember. If you don't mind my revealing it, you were using our art database."

"I've no need for privacy. I expect I looked at images of some doubtfully decent art work, though."

"Kate, we came to talk to you about my Aunt Phyllis' art work."

"I'd hoped so. We could do a one woman show here, but, for Phyllis, we should arrange a showing in New York."

"No. That's it, we've nothing," Bronwyn said. "I was hoping you could tell us what happened."

"She left no paintings?" Kate was plainly shocked. "That would be tragic. Phyllis turned reclusive these past decades, but she was producing. I'd go to her house occasionally and she was secretive, but I knew from paint spatters and oil smells that she was working."

"You never sold any of her paintings?" asked Paul.

"Oh, I did. Phyllis helped enormously when I started this gallery. I was twenty-four and Phyllis a year younger. I was living on noodles and a dream. Phyllis saved me by supplying paintings my first few years. Those were the years that your mother was here."

"You knew her?"

"Very well. Sophie was a beautiful young woman. Your father was in some dangerous part of the world and he sent her here for the three years before your birth. He made one trip back, the Christmas before you came into the world."

"Can we talk about her sometime? She's been gone since I was nine. I'd love to hear about her as a young woman."

"Happy to. Sophie and Phyllis were a colorful pair. High-spirited to a fault. All these years I've longed for the world to discover Phyllis. There are residents in this county with early Phyllis Heathcote paintings. The paintings sold from my gallery could make them a fortune."

"Phyllis was that good?" asked Paul.

"Sureness, simplicity, style, she had it all. You can instantly identify Frank Sinatra. She was like that, an original. And she'd only have improved with the years."

"There's no basement? Or an attic space to look in?" asked Paul.

"There's no basement," Bronwyn replied, "and I can't look for an attic."

"I could help," Paul offered.

"Oh, please," Kate said. "Her later years weren't so happy. It would be such a sad end for Phyllis to leave nothing."

"Can you do that now, Paul?"

"Of course."

"Thanks, Kate," Bronwyn said. "I'm glad we renewed our acquaintance. I look forward to talking with you again."

As they walked onto the sidewalk, Kate said, "Let me know the instant you find anything."

Paul berated himself. Cycling was foolish. He should have realized there'd be an opportunity to walk Bronwyn home and now his bike was a nuisance.

"Can we go back by Hopkins Green?" Bronwyn asked, "Nigel is getting used to going there at 4:15. He needs punctuality as much as you do."

"That works well. I left my bike by your building."

At the park gates, Bronwyn and Nigel walked down the stone steps to the grass, and Paul went to retrieve his bike. By the time he wheeled his bike into the park, John Wardle was stationed beside Bronwyn.

"Hey, Paul," he said. "Isn't it still a workday for you?"

"Usually, but they let me out occasionally. Surprising, seeing you in the park with a paintbrush in hand."

"I'm making repairs across the way." Enthusiastic to point to his ladder he gestured over-strenuously and a line of white paint that erupted from his paintbrush came to adorn Paul's blue shirt. "Oh! I'm so sorry," John said.

"What is it?" asked Bronwyn.

"I spattered Paul's shirt with my paintbrush. Perhaps you should get home and put that in water," suggested John.

"Yes, do," Bronwyn said.

"No, it's nothing. It's an old shirt anyway."

"We'll get going," Bronwyn said. "John, will you be spending many more days across the street?"

"This one's a filler between larger jobs. Late afternoons are a good time, so unless an urgent matter comes up I'll be here several more days at this time. Perhaps I'll see you from my ladder another day?"

"It seems likely. We'd better leave and get Paul home to the wash." John said his farewells and crossed the street to his ladder. Exiting onto Jefferson Street, Bronwyn said, "Now be careful walking along. I'm not sure if your poor bike can take another fall."

Paul walked on the road with his bike, keeping beside Nigel and Bronwyn. When he came to a parked car, he moved briskly around it to arrive beside Bronwyn as she completed her shorter route. He was like the wind rushing over the curve of an airplane's wing causing an elevator effect. Acting out 'Bernoulli's principle' he thought, pleased at remembering its name. He should be creating a force that pulled Bronwyn toward him. It wasn't working, so he bumped up the curb with his bike and walked slightly ahead of her. 'Such nonsense' he thought irritably. He was coming up with a scientific name for magic. Twice today, he was guilty of invoking spells of enchantment.

As admonished, Paul walked carefully. He and his bike arrived unscathed at Bronwyn's house. He set his bike against the porch and followed her back to the living room. She released Nigel from his duties and opened the French doors. "Now," Bronwyn said, "Let's deal with this paint." She opened the hallway door into her small laundry room and retrieved detergent and a bucket. "Unbutton, and I'll help you, so you don't spread paint around." Paul didn't argue. When he indicated, she pulled his shirt off, put it in the bucket and went to the sink to rinse and soak it. He thought of that Sunday outside the church, barely a week and a half before, when he'd avoided touching her hand, afraid she'd think him presumptuous. Here he was, in her house, and her hands had touched his naked back. He could see the roof and upper brick wall of his house, and he wondered what that poor snooping wretch, Paul, would feel were he watching him now, half-naked in Bronwyn's house. 'Better me than him,' he thought. "I should go home and come back with another shirt," he said.

Bronwyn agreed. "What would the neighbors think, you standing around like that!"

Before he left, Paul had something he must say. "I was wondering if you might ..." he spoke with the hesitation of a man unaccomplished at asking a woman out, "since it's a pleasant evening, if you might want to take a picnic to the park?" Enlisting Nigel, he added, "I'm sure Nigel would like it. Wouldn't you, boy?"

"He would, of course. But I'm not well supplied for a picnic."

"No problem. I've got the makings at home. I'll bring them back."

"Do you? You're well prepared. In that case, yes please."

Nervously elated, Paul walked out through the back and, with some difficulty, opened the bolt on Bronwyn's gate. He went to his house and put on deodorant and a fresh shirt. From the refrigerator he retrieved grapes and cheese, and the egg-salad sandwiches he'd made that afternoon. The supplies he put in a small cooler, along with ice in plastic bags. Everything else was in a bag pre-marshaled for this moment. He returned quickly to Bronwyn, grabbing a can of oil and a flashlight on his way by the shed.

Bronwyn stood idly in the kitchen thinking how her hands would have liked to explore further. She knew his arms were hairy. She'd felt the fuzzy hair on his shoulders and in pulling the shirt from his trousers she'd touched thicker hair on his lower back. She wondered where else his hair grew and imagined slowly rubbing her fingers in circles over his chest. She felt a light tingling through her brain and a small ache between her legs where unpracticed muscles were tensing. Joel, her last real boyfriend, had dumped her when blindness came. Not that she entirely blamed him. Blindness, like the briars that choked Sleeping Beauty's castle, had formed an impenetrable social barrier. Only slowly had she woken to her new self, needing no hero's kiss for that, but oh, how wonderful it would be to feel Paul's firm arms around her and his warm breath on her lips. She gave a little shiver at the excitement of her daydream. Unlikely as Paul seemed for hero material, he'd be steadfast. Twice she'd met him by accident with his bike and both times he'd fallen. She smiled at the thought, amused at Paul, her hero, falling from his steed. She didn't see him flailing like a beetle, but pulling himself erect. He was definitely no clod, but far too formal in his language and his ways. He and his friend Rolf were a pair of misfits. She wondered if he had other friends and wouldn't be surprised if he didn't. Perhaps he was Sleeping Beauty, and she would hack through his briars and free him with a kiss.

"That was amazingly fast," she said, hearing him return.

"I've got everything, and I brought a can of oil. I'll work on your troublesome bolt if you give me something to clean up with."

"That's wonderful," Bronwyn said, handing him paper towels, "It's good having a man in the house." For so much of his life, he'd dreamed himself a part of other family circles. Being the man to lubricate the squeaky bolt was a narcotic to Paul. In a euphoria of domestic joy he oiled and thrust the bolt in and out, until it was as smooth as, well, he could only think of the smoothness of Bronwyn's skin. He sighed forlornly, but remonstrated with himself that he wasn't heavy and stodgy today, but a thing of air. He left the can beside the gravel path to retrieve later, and, recovering some of his joy, he returned to Bronwyn, redolent with the manly smell of oil.

"Should I look around for an attic?" he asked.

"Sounds good."

Paul checked the laundry room, bathroom and hallway. "There's nothing of interest there. We'll have a look in the first bedroom on the left." He went in and commented on the large skylight.

"This was Aunt Phyllis' studio."

"There it is," exclaimed Paul. "Pull-down steps in the corner behind the door." He walked over and tugged on the short cord. The top half of the ladder came down and he folded out the bottom half. "I brought a flashlight in the bag, but hopefully there's a light switch up there." He climbed partway up and called down, "It's here on a support beam." He turned on the switch and glanced around. "Do you want to come up? It's floored, but the headroom, except in the very center, is too low to stand."

"Go on up," Bronwyn said. "I'll stand on the ladder. You can tell me what's there."

Paul clambered into the attic. Crouching, he moved to the center of the house. Bronwyn's head appeared. "Anything?"

"Don't think so, an old bed-frame, a couple of sleds. Here's some boxes." He spent a minute investigating. "Sorry," he reported, "just old school books and art books. It's warm up here, so probably it isn't the best climate for storing artwork anyway. Some hand-puppets. They're very cute."

"I remember those. Aunt Phyllis put on puppet shows for me. I hadn't thought about that in years. So, that's all?"

"That's it," Paul confirmed. She backed down the steps. Paul descended and returned the steps to the ceiling.

"Disheartening," she said, "but the park will cheer us up."

Bronwyn got Nigel ready while Paul closed the French doors and retrieved his cooler and bag. "We'll need a blanket to sit on," she said.

"I have one in the bag."

"You thought of everything. I'm impressed."

They walked down the hill to the park and spread their blanket near the playground where a young mother was pushing her girl on a swing. Paul put out paper plates. "Grapes to your left, an assortment of cheese to your right," he said pulling off the plastic wrap.

"Yummy. I'm famished," she said.

"I'm cutting French bread for the cheese. Here's an egg-salad sandwich. I've put it by your right knee."

"I smell premeditation," Bronwyn said.

"Oh no, that's the mustard in the egg-salad."

"Maybe, but it's very sweet."

"I brought red wine. There may be a regulation against alcohol in the park, so I rinsed out an empty grape juice bottle and put the wine in there."

"You've the mind of a master criminal. The local police must be relieved you didn't take to a life of crime."

"I brought mugs for our wine. Not elegant, but they're more stable on uneven ground." Paul poured the wine. Bronwyn was sitting cross-legged, and he placed the cup within the triangle of her legs, against the inside of her right thigh. "I hope that's alright," he said.

"Good egg-salad sandwich," Bronwyn said, munching. "You've got talent, besides the criminal."

Paul looked at the mother and child. The girl was about four and super-active. There were a number of turtles or frogs on huge springs. From one to another she ran and bounced, or gleefully climbed the slide, or clambered on the jungle-gym with her anxious mother gripping her. The young mother's white-blonde hair attracted the sunshine and her movements were supple, but she aroused no ache of longing in him. He was amused, watching her deflect disasters from her girl. He and Bronwyn sat peacefully, at the center of life abounding in the park. The squirrels chased, the kingfisher fished, the crows hopped, he described the scene to Bronwyn, omitting the woman's prettiness.

"I visited your Aunt Phyllis," he said.

"You did?"

"When I cycled through the cemetery. We had a nice chat."

"Did she give you any useful information?"

"General advice. About gathering rosebuds while you may."

"Advice the dead are well qualified to give. Too bad for the roses, though." A moment later, they heard screaming. "What happened?" Bronwyn exclaimed.

"She fell from the jungle-gym. I'll see if I can help." He hurried over and returned to collect paper towels and a plastic bag of ice from the cooler. "A scraped face and a bloody nose. Back in a second." He rushed off and gave the mother a paper towel. He wrapped the bag of ice in more paper towels. Glancing back at Bronwyn, he saw a man standing over her. He thrust the ice at the mother. "Sorry, I've got to go." He ran. Quickly realizing that it was Rudy, he rocketed up the slope. Rudy was looking down on Bronwyn from his superior position.

"Hello, who's there, please?" she was asking, holding on to Nigel.

Breathless from exertion, and the fright and hostility that gripped his chest, Paul gasped, "What are you doing here?"

"Sir Galahad, rescuing the ladies, I see." Rudy bent to choose a piece of cheese and bread, and stood, casually chewing, contemplating Paul who was edging beside Bronwyn. "I followed you from town. Neither of you have eyes. Bronwyn, you and I would make a better team. He's not worth your time and no woman's ever complained of me."

"What do you want?" Paul asked in a quavering voice. "You're not welcome here."

Rudy smiled at Paul's agitation. "It'll be no picnic in the park when your throat's slit and you're breathing blood." He plucked a bunch of grapes from the plate. "See you in your nightmares," he said pleasantly. He strolled down the hill, stopping to offer his grapes to the mother and her tearful child.

"Phew!" exhaled Paul, sinking beside Bronwyn, putting his arm over her shoulders to comfort her. "That was scary. He's a real psycho." His chest heaved with agitation, and Bronwyn, who had been stroking Nigel, turned her attention to Paul. She placed her head on his chest until his heart was pacified and his breath calm.

"Should we contact the police?" she asked.

"It'd be like prodding an angry boar. I'll watch more carefully in the future. Who'd have thought a humble librarian would have enemies?"

"You are a humble and noble Sir Galahad," Bronwyn said.

"Our picnic is ruined," Paul said. "Can we go to your house and finish the wine in real glasses?" Bronwyn got Nigel ready while Paul packed up. He left most of their supplies in the grass for the crows to consume, not wanting to touch anything that Rudy had touched.

CHAPTER 18 FRIDAY

Paul was grateful that work diverted him from constant thoughts of Bronwyn, but he remained aware of the upcoming weekend and the possibility of further contact with her. The latches and hinges on both gates were oiled, and his was unbolted in readiness. He visualized an effortless intercourse, Bronwyn slipping between the houses, although, realistically, some action beyond oiling gates would be needed to further his ambitions. He hoped he'd be prepared when it happened.

During a lull in the morning's activity, Paul asked Ruth about her date with Sam. She was galvanized to an outpouring of thanks for his part in arranging it. He had never seen her so excited and voluble. "Sam asked me to go with him tomorrow to the llama show at the Horse Center. They're adorable. I'm really looking forward to it." Paul said how pleased he was that things looked promising, and they agreed that Sam was a wonderful person. "He switched from a business major to forestry," Ruth said. "There can't be any money in looking after trees. How true to himself a decision like that was."

Paul could understand Ruth finding the romance of the forest more attractive than the commonplace environment of the office. "He does seem to have a giving personality," he said, not knowing for sure if that was true but pleased to say something in tune with Ruth's enthusiasm. The workday passed with him the recipient of beatific smiles from Ruth. He hoped that Sam reciprocated her feelings, though he expected never to see such an expression of bliss on Sam's face.

That evening, he and Spook spent their time outside, as it was pleasantly warm. Spook alternated between resting and chasing butterflies, grasshoppers and imaginary insects. Paul, more sedate in his folding chair, read, and he listened for sounds from beyond his fence. A couple of times he was confident that Bronwyn walked on her gravel path. Hoping her gate would open, his breath stopped. When nothing happened, reluctantly he breathed again.

Engaged in a battle royal, he would lust for her like David on his roof, he would shield her from the ignominy of lustful watchers, he would abjure the climb to his shed. The battle pressed. Weakness, respect, desire, nobility, waged on their flinty ground a bloody struggle that none could tell the ending of. In the coming darkness he expected no abatement in this war, unless he should capitulate. Suddenly he stooped, snatched a rock and, half standing, hurled it at his stepladder. It thudded into the brick above the top rung, gashing the wall. If his aim was to strike his ladder, it gave no shudder. His irrational act shamed him.

He went inside and exchanged his shirt for a dark turtleneck that would keep him warm and safe from notice in the dark. Returning to the backyard, he prowled his small enclosure, watching the stars come out. Looking at the infinite expanse of the heavens, like anyone who does, he thought how puny a thing is man, how all his glorious battles are but dust in the air. That perspective, however accurate, was too arid to motivate him. He needed a view more nourishing of life. What was it that impelled the chaos through eons to culminate in a soul like Bronwyn? Desire, he thought, must be the impulse for all creatures--to fill themselves and survive. But are we purely physical? Bronwyn would want him nobler. But what harm was there to anyone, climbing to his perch, partaking of the knowledge it offered?

Paul was for some hours the ground of combat where armies swayed, assembling and re-assembling as the battle waged. All that was clear from each melee was that no force had yet propelled him from the earth. He paced in gathering fatigue, resolving to seek his bed and find his peace in sleep, but for another moment, he held. Flinging himself into his chair, he thought that Bronwyn would have gone to bed, but it was a Friday and she might still be awake. He might see her naked, if he looked.

A scraping in the lane killed all introspection. Every muscle he controlled went rigid with his fierce need to catalog the peril to its source. Another scuff outside his gate, and he thought of Rolf, but no, Rolf wouldn't lurk there. The latch lifted on Bronwyn's gate and clicked shut. The can of oil he'd left by her garden path was kicked across the gravel and he heard a muffled imprecation.

Bronwyn's gate was unlocked. Was this a welcome visitor? But from a dark lane? Wrenching free of immobility, quickly and silently he scaled his ladder. In the dimmest of light, as in the shadow of a poor candle's glow, a man's shape reached for the handle on the French door, opened it, entered the house and closed the door behind him. Paul's skin was fevered, his heart pounded, his breath sucked at air, but he could not breathe. Frantically uncertain, he fought to think. All done with such certitude! This man knew his entry was unbarred. Was Bronwyn eagerly expecting him, caressing him now in her soft embrace? His own bond with her, nothing more than hope on his part, gave him no claim. Did she have a lover? One who needed to be discrete? Why not? But yet, if he knew her, he doubted it. But did he know her? A man of simpler parts might have dived from his roost and battered through the intervening doors to assault this stranger, but Paul was etched with his role from childhood on, uncrossed are the circles of the watcher and the watched. And yet he knew Bronwyn, or he doubted that he did. Nigel barked and went silent, further proof of welcome. Nigel would protect his mistress from threat.

By any righteous judgment he'd be the envious assaulter of a rival lover, and how embarrassing, to thrust himself between the arms of lovers. The gate decided him. His mind traced back to yesterday. He'd oiled the hardware on the gate. Thinking to leave that way he'd left it unbolted. They'd returned from the park, had their wine, and he'd gone by Bronwyn's front door to cycle home. Was he at fault, leaving the way clear to her?

He tumbled down the ladder. Fumbling for the latches in the dark, he blundered through the gates. The lock wasn't clicked shut on the door to her house. He pushed, and the door swung quietly in. Creeping to the hallway, he strained to hear. At the murmur of lovers he could still retreat. A glimmer of light was under Bronwyn's bedroom door. Some kind of sack was in the corridor. He heard them active in the bedroom, but he could decide nothing. Not a sack, but Nigel, and that concluded his folly. With Nigel sleeping by her door there was no threat. He stopped. Desperate to hurry from the awful situation, something gripped him. It was Nigel. Nigel should have detected him. Ignoring the squeaking floor, he rushed forward. His hand came bloody from Nigel's fur. Roaring, he lunged at Bronwyn's door. His bloody hand slipped on the knob. It would not turn. Wailing, "Bronwyn," in a fury, he gripped behind the knob with his left hand, succeeded in turning it and erupted into the bedroom. He glimpsed Bronwyn, naked on the bed, lying on her back, blood on her forehead. A blow punched into his skull, and his momentum threw him over the bare floor, thudding his right shoulder against the bed. He half-stood, raised his arms to break the blows he knew would come, and a pain more cutting than any he'd ever known seared into his left arm. He fell against the bed, and a kick to his side dropped him to the floor.

Aware within his pain that the man had gone, he desperately needed to move, though his body ached to curl on the floor and moan. Painfully, clutching at the bedspread, he pulled himself up. He collapsed on the bed, his feet dragging on the floor, his left arm useless from the pain. Pushing, flopping, he came level with Bronwyn. His face by hers, he touched her injured forehead. She was breathing and, immense relief, her wound was only an abrasion from a blow. Sinking to the floor, he picked up the phone on the nightstand and called 911.

"Come quickly," he said to the operator. "There's been an intruder. I need police and ambulance. This is Paul Kirk. I'm at Bronwyn Heathcote's on Cherry Lane. I can't remember the number. My head's not working."

"That's alright, sir. The emergency phone system says number 6. Has the intruder gone? How are you hurt?"

"I think he's gone." Looking at the blood welling from his arm, he faintly said, "A knife, it must have been a knife. My arm's cut. Bronwyn has a head wound. She's unconscious."

"You'll have help shortly. I suggest you stay on the line."

"I've got to look after Bronwyn and her dog, but thanks," he said and hung up.

He struggled to the bathroom, wrapped a towel around his arm and carried a bathrobe to Bronwyn. Even with a pounding head and a useless screaming arm, he was aware of her splendid body, but he was pleased to cover her. In the hallway, Nigel's blood had formed a small pool. Relieved at detecting a movement of Nigel's chest, he went to the phone to call Spook's vet. Not finding a phonebook, he called directory assistance and asked for the number. His vet's answering machine directed him to an emergency vet, which he called.

"Rockbridge Animal Hospital. This is Melanie Shires."

"Melanie, this is Paul Kirk, it's an emergency. I'm at Bronwyn Heathcote's at 6 Cherry Lane in Lexington. Her seeing-eye dog has been stabbed." His words jostled together in support of each other. "Can you come and help."

"We don't normally make house calls."

"I can't bring Nigel. The police will be here soon, and I've been stabbed. He may be dying. He's a seeing-eye dog, very valuable, and he's so critical to Bronwyn. I beg you, please. It's so important. The police will be here when someone comes."

She hesitated and said, "Okay. I'm leaving now. Cherry Lane is off Main Street?"

"That's right. A bit south of the center of town. Number 6."

"Expect me in a few minutes."

Paul unlocked the front door and turned his attention to Bronwyn. He ran warm water in the bathroom to dampen a washcloth and applied it to her injured forehead. Her eyelids opened, and she groaned. Tenderly, barely touching her, he cupped her cheek with his hand. She turned her face into his palm, clamped on and viciously bit through his skin. He screamed in pain, "It's me, Paul." Bronwyn released him. There was blood on his hand.

"Paul?" she gasped. "Is he gone?"

"Yes, he's gone."

"Nigel?" she said in panic, "Where's Nigel?"

"He's injured, but alive. I've called a vet. They'll be here in a few minutes. The police too."

"Help me," she said, sitting up. The bathrobe dropped to her waist, and Paul glanced down at her breasts, at the small bumps on the brown aureoles surrounding her nipples, but, like an impassioned artist looking at a nude model, a higher purpose drove him. It was the need to assist her.

"Here's your bathrobe," he said, holding it up against her. "I can't help more. My left arm's hurt."

"Oh, Paul, you're injured?" She put on the bathrobe, not bothering to tie it, and felt her way up his arm to the towel.

"Ouch!" he said. "It's a knife wound, but I'm okay." In the aftermath of battle, to stand with his wound and proclaim it nothing, amazed him. "Nigel's around from the door. He's got a stab wound in his left shoulder and must have been knocked on the head."

They went to the hallway. Bronwyn, sobbing in distress, felt over Nigel's body. "He's breathing. Thank God!"

Her bathrobe gapped open. Paul avoided looking at her legs. The intensity of events and his utility to Bronwyn had temporarily made a firmer man of him. "The police are here. I see their blue flashing lights. Better tie your bathrobe."

"Thanks, Paul," she said.

He opened the front door to Sergeant Driscoll and Officer Pruett.

"Mr. Kirk," nodded the sergeant. "What's been happening? Injured yourself?" he asked, looking at Paul's arm.

"We had an intruder with a knife. He attacked Bronwyn," Paul said, gesturing down to where she knelt, her hand resting gently on Nigel.

"Where did the attack take place?"

"The bedroom here." Paul indicated Bronwyn's bedroom.

"Let's stay out of there for the moment. The dog was injured, too?"

"The vet should arrive shortly."

"The lady raped, was she?" asked Officer Pruett.

"I don't think so, but you should ask her," Paul said.

"Ma'am," said Sergeant Driscoll, drawing Bronwyn's focus from Nigel. "Ma'am, do you have physical injuries?"

"Only this bang on my head."

"Rescue squad's here," said Officer Pruett looking at the ambulance in the street, "and that'd be the vet."

Melanie Shires hurried into the hallway followed by the paramedics. She introduced herself and knelt beside Nigel and Bronwyn. "Will he live?" Bronwyn asked.

"The signs are good. He's breathing regularly," Melanie said soothingly.

"It's getting crowded," said Sergeant Driscoll, "and you two need attending. Is there a room where you can sit down? If we could get you to come, Ma'am, we'll leave the vet some room to work," he said sympathetically.

Paul helped Bronwyn to stand. She rubbed her face with the sleeve of her bathrobe and led them to the living room. Bronwyn and Paul sat on the couch while the paramedics worked on them.

"We should employ you in the Department, Mr. Kirk," said Sergeant Driscoll. "You're a busy man where there's trouble."

"Could you call me Paul? 'Mr. Kirk' makes me nervous."

"We seem to find you in various houses throughout the town. Is this where you live?"

"Oh no, officer, Bronwyn lives here."

"Can I have her name for my notes?" asked Officer Pruett.

"Bronwyn Heathcote," Paul said. "My house is immediately behind on Laurel Lane. I was sitting out, watching the stars, when I heard someone come down the lane and go through Bronwyn's gate."

"So you gave chase? Very brave of you," approved Officer Pruett.

Bronwyn touched her hand to Paul's side. "It was, wasn't it," she said, her voice catching and more tears flowing. Paul pointed to a box of tissues on the end-table, and one of the paramedics put it into her lap. She blew her nose and composed herself.

"So, Mr. Kirk, you heard this person. How long was it before you pursued him into the house?" asked Sergeant Driscoll. Paul hesitated. "Mr. Kirk?" the sergeant prompted.

"It was about four minutes."

"I see. A long time, it seems."

"Yes," Paul agreed.

"Sorry to interrupt," said the paramedic working on Paul. "We've finished here. He has a deep cut in his arm that I've bandaged, but it needs stitches, so we should take him to the hospital. The lady seems okay, but she should come along to check for concussion or fractures."

Melanie came down the hallway and said, "I need to take him to the hospital."

"Will Nigel be okay?" asked Bronwyn.

"It's a bad shoulder wound, and he'll need to sleep off the blow to his head. I'll check for fractures, but I think he'll recover in a few days. Do you have a sheet you could spare, to carry him out to my van? And a couple of men maybe, to help carry him?"

"Take any sheet you want from the hall linen closet," Bronwyn said.

"Would you guys mind helping?" Sergeant Driscoll asked the paramedics. "I'll finish a few preliminary questions with these two, and you can take them to the hospital."

The vet left with the paramedics and, at Officer Driscoll's raised eyebrow, Paul re-commenced his explanation. "It's true. I hesitated."

"Are you two lovers?" asked Officer Pruett.

"No, officer," Paul said.

"So you thought ... what?" asked the sergeant.

"Well," Paul hesitated, "that it was a liaison."

"Oh, Paul, you thought I had a lover?"

"I didn't think so. But yes, I guess I thought it might be."

"And what decided you to act," asked the sergeant.

"I'd been here the previous evening, having a glass of wine. I remembered I'd left the gate unbolted."

"Oh," said Bronwyn.

"I see," said Sergeant Driscoll. "Could either of you identify the assailant in any way?"

"His voice was muffled," Bronwyn said. "He had something like a ski mask covering his face."

"He was just a shape," Paul said. "I never saw him clearly."

"Think carefully, Miss Heathcote," said Officer Pruett. "Is there any chance that your assailant was Mr. Kirk?"

"Of course not," Bronwyn said, aghast.

"Would something about your assailant eliminate Mr. Kirk as a suspect?" asked Officer Pruett.

"No. But Paul couldn't do something like that. He rescued me, and he's injured."

"Just routine, you understand, Miss Heathcote," said the sergeant. "You've got a bite mark on your hand, Mr. Kirk. You sustained that here?"

"That was an accident. I mistook him for the intruder," Bronwyn explained. "It occurred after the attack."

"With a blow to the head," said Officer Pruett, "you may have confused the timeline. We're making no accusations, just trying to understand the situation."

The vet came back. "I'm off with Nigel," she said. "Don't worry too much. I think he'll be fine. I know how important he is to you. If you don't hear from me then everything's going well. Call me tomorrow, early afternoon, and I'll let you know how he's doing.

"Thank you," Bronwyn said. "Please look after him for me."

"We'll stay for a while if you don't mind, Miss Heathcote," said the sergeant. "Look over the place and check for fingerprints. We'll talk with you and Mr. Kirk again in the morning."

"Of course."

"Call us if you need a ride from the hospital," said the sergeant. "We'll be glad to assist."

The paramedics came back with stretchers. To Paul's protest, they responded that it was regulations, and he and Bronwyn were strapped in. Transported to the hospital, they were taken to separate rooms in the emergency department. A nurse came to check Paul's vital signs, and then, except for an occasional nurse who'd look in, he was ignored for the next hour. One nurse said there'd been a car crash. Some teenagers were being seen to, and sorry for the delay. He was dozing when the door opened, and Bronwyn was led in by a nurse.

"Brought you some company," the nurse said. "There we go, sweetie, here's a seat in the corner." Bronwyn sat down, and the nurse left them.

Paul sat up. "Are you okay?" he asked.

"Fine. The doctor didn't see any likelihood of a fracture. I refused further treatment, so I'm done. You haven't been seen yet?"

"Not yet. I'm sorry I delayed following him. I'm sorry about leaving the gate open, too. That was bad of me."

"Don't worry. He'd have climbed over the gate anyway. It was my fault for not locking the door to the house. As for you thinking I had a lover, that's understandable. We don't know each other very well. I haven't had one in years. Now you know that much about me."

"Did he hurt you?" asked Paul. "Other than knocking you on the head."

Bronwyn responded after a moment. "I woke when Nigel barked. He ran to the hall and there was a scuffle. I was out of bed when someone slammed the door. He threw me back on the bed and said he'd kill me if I made a sound. He had a knife across my throat and he struggled to take off a glove. Then he felt my breasts."

"You don't need to speak about it."

"It makes me shudder, but talking is good."

"Do you think it was Rudy?"

"His voice was muffled. It might have been, but I don't know. He said he was going to have fun with me. If you hadn't come, he would have raped me. He must have heard you in the hall, because he stopped groping and the knife came off my throat. He pressed his gloved hand over my mouth and that's when he hit me. I guess with the handle end of the knife."

The door opened, and a woman in a white coat walked in. "I'm Janet Owens, a physician's assistant. I'm going to stitch your arm, Paul." To Bronwyn, she said, "You can stay if you like."

"Yes, please. I'd like that."

"She wants to hear me scream," Paul said.

Janet cut off the bandage and said, "Local anesthetic does wonders." She jabbed around the wound to numb it. "This is a long, deep slice. It'll take a few stitches. You'll need to have them removed in a week, and you may have a scar." When she finished with his arm, Janet checked his other injuries. "Some ice for this nasty bump on your head. We'll get you to radiology to check it out." Paul winced as she felt around his left side. "A fractured rib here. I'll send a nurse in to look after you. Sorry I don't have more time," she said apologetically, "It's a busy night. Good to have met you both."

She hurried out. A few minutes later, a nurse came in that Paul hadn't seen before, although she looked familiar. Her dark hair knotted at the top of her head, she wore pink, blue and white floral scrubs. Going to the computer on the cart, she looked at his record and said, "Paul Kirk. You're Rolf's friend, right?"

Surprised, Paul answered, "Why, yes," realizing then who she was. He'd have known her instantly, had she been naked. He visualized her bare, well-formed arms, but chided himself for doing so in Bronwyn's presence and in that antiseptic environment.

"I'm Celia Hopewell. Rolf's aunt, a marriage or so removed."

"This is Bronwyn," Paul said. Nervously wondering how Celia knew of him.

She and Bronwyn exchanged greetings. She fetched bandages from a cupboard and said, "Drop the gown to your waist and I'll strap you." While she worked, she talked. "My neighbor told me he recognized Rolf leaving my performance a couple of weeks back, so I had a quiet word with Rolf. He confessed that you two had been watching me. It was naughty of you boys to come and not tell me. Although I see that you're far from being a boy."

"You play in an orchestra?" asked Bronwyn.

"The Rockbridge Symphony. I love to perform." Turning back to Paul she said, "Come and see me any time."

"I'd love to," replied Bronwyn.

Celia laughed. "That would be delightful." Her dark brown eyes looked at Paul, and she quirked an eyebrow at him in amusement.

"Rolf seems like a nice young man," Bronwyn said.

"He is a good boy," agreed Celia, turning to her, "but he needs watching."

"I'm sure Paul will be helpful there."

Celia gave the bandages a tug to tighten them. "Ouch," he complained.

"Be brave, young soldier. I'll have you taken to radiology in a moment."

"Paul," Bronwyn said. "I'll wait in reception for you. I'll give Sam a call and have him get us. Celia, could someone show me the way?"

"It's through the double doors, then left."

"I'm blind, you see. I couldn't find it on my own."

"Oh," said Celia. "I never realized. "Let's go. Paul, lie back down. Someone will fetch you."

An hour or so later, Paul was released. He found Sam and Bronwyn waiting for him.

"A relatively clean bill of health," Paul said. "The worst was that tetanus shot because of your bite. They'll have to test you for rabies."

"Humph!" Bronwyn grunted, not amused by his facetiousness. "When you froth at the mouth is when I worry about you, and not before. The police brought my purse. They locked the house so I wouldn't have had a key otherwise. We're to expect them at nine in the morning."

Sam drove them to Bronwyn's house. When the three sat in the living room, Paul said, "I was wondering if you'd let me sleep on the couch tonight?"

"Afraid to be alone, Paul? But it's a good idea," Sam said. "Or I will, if you prefer, Bronwyn."

"No harm if Paul's here when the police come to talk with us in the morning. There's a spare bedroom."

"I'll be comfortable on the couch," Paul said.

"I can trust you?" asked Sam. "Bronwyn tells me you're the prime suspect."

"That's just silly," Bronwyn scoffed. "I'm quite safe with Paul."

"Then I'll leave. I want to be fresh for my date with Ruth in the morning. We're going to the Horse Center."

"Bring her by for lunch, if you can," Bronwyn said.

Sam agreed to ask her, and he left. Bronwyn showed Paul the linen closet and got him a pillow.

"I hope you sleep well. I wish both Nigel and you could guard me tonight. Goodnight, Paul."

He settled down for what, with his injuries, must be an irritable night on a couch too short to stretch out on. He was still awake around two o'clock when the moon rose and immersed him in pale silvery light. Lying on his right side, looking out at the garden, he imagined Bronwyn tip-toeing down the hallway behind him. In a moment, she would kneel beside him, a moonlit naked angel. She'd touch his face and kiss him. The next he knew it was 7:30, and the moon was replaced by sunlight seeping through the gauze of a pallid, misty morning.

CHAPTER 19   SATURDAY

Paul collected cleaning supplies and a bucket from the laundry room and quietly scrubbed Nigel's bloodstain. He went to the hall bathroom to shower. By the time he emerged, Bronwyn, wrapped in her bathrobe, was at work in the kitchen.

"An emotional night," she said, by way of greeting.

"It was. Did you sleep well?"

"I woke a lot, worrying about Nigel, but surprisingly I did sleep. And you?"

"I was fine, thanks. The pain medicine helped. I think I'll go home now and change into clean clothes."

"Okay. Your omelet will be ready in ten minutes."

On his way by, he picked up the oilcan and returned it to the shed. He changed into jeans and a casual shirt. Returning past his stepladder, he thought, 'I've got no use for you today. I'll be there when Bronwyn pours the orange juice. I might even do it for her.'

"You were quick," she said.

"The breakfast smells are all here."

"What calls to a man," she sighed. They sat companionably at the table to eat. "It's nice, sharing breakfast, even though I miss Nigel."

"I'm a poor substitute, I know," he said. "If you want, you can take me to the end of the garden to do my morning business."

"A poor, messy joke, I'm afraid. This is Nigel's time. I wonder how you knew."

Paul regretted his inane remark, reproaching himself for displaying any knowledge of her habits. Split personalities may be okay if they don't intersect, but Mr. Hyde wasn't one to stay repressed. "If that was Rudy last night, hopefully he's done with his revenge," he said. "Setting the police on him is like poking a wasps' nest, but I suppose we must."

"We'd be even more his victims otherwise."

"You're right. I'm being wimpy. It's my personality, wanting to stay outside things and not be noticed."

"Paul, you've got to watch for that negative reinforcement. You're far more capable than you think. You helped Pat, and you helped me."

"I did, didn't I! However inadequately."

"There you go," Bronwyn said, laughing. "It's taken years to make you the mess you are, but I think you're slowly untangling yourself. Though let's not analyze you any more today, okay."

Paul hoped Bronwyn was right about the untangling. He wanted Bronwyn's approval. The problem was, he didn't overly admire himself and promoting defective goods was none too ethical. He salved his conscience with the thought that the package he offered was more than what he was. It included what he would become.

"How are your injuries today?" asked Bronwyn.

"The drugs are wearing off. My arm and side are a pair of nagging ex-wives. The worst, though, is that vicious bite on my hand, the unkindest cut of all."

"I wonder if the police are on to something?" Bronwyn mused teasingly. "You might have hidden the knife while I was unconscious. Anyway, you probably deserved the bite for something."

"You're absolutely right," Paul said.

"I'll try to protect you today from shrewish ex-wives. You stay on the couch, and I'll look after you, but now, if you'll excuse me, I need to shower and get dressed before the police arrive."

Paul picked up Phyllis' diary and soon found his interest engaged. When Bronwyn returned, he asked, "Shall I read from the diary until the police come?"

"Go ahead. I picked the transcript up from the print shop yesterday and loaded the disc on my computer. I searched for 'stamps' but didn't find anything useful." She explained to Paul the story behind the stamp collection.

> Wed. Oct. 25, 1972. I've turned 18 and being a senior, Nanny Ellen told me I had to apply to college. I refused, and she's mad at me. I enjoy the art classes at the university, but I know they'd make me do stuff like science and math. It's disloyal to Richard, but that really doesn't sound like fun. I want to paint. I talked with Richard about it today at our tutoring session, and he said he'd be happy to write me a recommendation letter to colleges if I changed my mind.

"Could be a negative side to those stamps," Bronwyn said, "Aunt Phyllis doesn't have financial pressures. But then, Kate Lavender said that her paintings sold, so probably Aunt Phyllis was right about her career."

> Tue., Dec. 12, 1972. Richard's wife Victoria died yesterday. Only a couple of months ago she was modeling at our art class, and she was so elegant. I went over to see him and he cried, so I held his hand. I didn't know what to do, but he wanted me there. He talked in Hungarian like I was her, from 60 years before. Richard's very old but he has kind of a baby face and if I'd been Victoria I could see

being excited about this wonderful man wanting me. I envy her. She had a great life, and who can say for me?

Fri., Dec. 15, 1972. Since I heard about Victoria, I've been doing a painting of Richard. He's handsome, dressed in a suit like he's accepting the Nobel Prize for solving Goldbach's conjecture and the world's in awe of him. Visitation was at the funeral home at 5:00 today, but I took the painting by after school. I peeked in and nobody was around. The coffin was in the room to the right with all the flowers, and there was a poster-board with pictures of Victoria from childhood on. I didn't spend time looking, as I shouldn't have been there. I felt sneaky, and it's spooky in a funeral home, but I opened the coffin and Victoria was like a wax doll with a pretty blue dress. I put Richard's painting on her chest and closed the coffin. I got goose bumps thinking of them buried together. When Nanny Ellen and I came for the visitation I was surprised to see the coffin open. I didn't know about that. Who'd want to see a dead body, that's creepy. I'd never been to a visitation before, except for my parents, and their coffins weren't open. There was a long line of people and when we got to Richard he cried out that I was the best of girls, and Victoria loved her present and was going to keep it with her. But he said I should have asked. I hope Victoria won't be cremated.

"Seems typical of Aunt Phyllis," Bronwyn said. "Good intentions, but over the top."
Paul flipped through more pages. "She graduates from high school in June of 1973. She told the boys she was naked under her graduation gown. She'd left buttons undone at the bottom of her gown and the boys nearly stood on their heads to look. Of course she was wearing shorts."
Bronwyn nodded. "Well intentioned and evil."
"And here she has a summer job," Paul said.

Mon., July 2, 1973. Last week I started work at the Potpourri. It's a job for the summer in a high-priced tourist shop. The manager pushes against me in the aisle. I know what's in his pants. If I see it, I'll lop it off with a kitchen knife. His dumb name is Izzy Cross. I call him Izzy Lizard in my head. The other sales lady is Brenda. She's fat and Izzy can't squeeze by her. She says things like, 'Mr. Cross you're so funny.' If he's funny I'm a rotten apple, so you know she's hot for him. I'm doing a painting of them as Jack Sprat and his wife. I can put up with the job. It's only for the summer.

Sat., July 7, 1973. Studying Izzy for his painting had its problems. The idiot thought I was interested in him. This morning I opened a large jar of peanut butter made from Virginia peanuts and spread it on the front of my apron. When Izzy slithered along the aisle I slid the apron around and it went all over the front of his trousers. He wouldn't have got in that mess if he hadn't tried shoving his thing up my rear. Maybe I shouldn't have laughed and said Brenda would lick it off for him. I got fired, and Nanny Ellen was disappointed with me.

"Not trying too hard to keep her job," Bronwyn said. "First ideas are often the best. I liked hers, about using the knife."
"Ouch!"
"Well you may cringe. Men should keep their libidos in check." Hearing a knock at the front door, Bronwyn said, "I'll get it. Stay seated." She came back with Sergeant Driscoll and Officer Pruett. Bronwyn sat beside Paul, the sergeant took the armchair, and Officer Pruett pulled over a chair from the dining table and opened his notebook.
"We came to no conclusions after you left," said the sergeant. "Sorry if we left anything disordered. We tried to clean up. I see that someone has scrubbed the dog's blood from the hall."
"Paul is always very helpful," Bronwyn said.
"Is there anything you can describe about your assailant, Miss Heathcote?" asked Officer Pruett.
"He wore gloves. He had garlic on his breath."
"No physical features? The kind of mask he wore?"
"Nigel is my seeing-eye dog, officer. I'm blind. Totally."
"It seems that we have the problem with seeing," said the sergeant. "I had no idea. And you, Mr. Kirk? You saw nothing?"
"He came from behind the door. I was concentrating on Bronwyn. He hit me almost immediately. After that it was a painful blur." Paul leaned forward, but his ribs complained, and he sat back against the couch. "We think we know who it was."
"Who is that, Mr. Kirk?" asked the sergeant.
"Rudy Price. You met him at Patricia Brazier's house when her car got broken into. Bronwyn and I were down at the park the day before yesterday, and he threatened me."

"Why would he do that?" asked Officer Pruett. "He threatened you, but he attacked Miss Heathcote?"

"He must have thought I lived here. I believe Rudy is floating some kind of Ponzi scheme. I warned Pat away from him, so Rudy's angry with me."

"How do you know that, about a Ponzi scheme?" asked the sergeant.

"I'd like to say, but I can't. I'd get a friend in trouble."

"Very well," said the sergeant. "It may come out later, but we won't pursue it for now. We find you, late at night, roughhousing in the streets with delinquents. Next, there's a complaint that you're behaving suspiciously in your ex-wife's house late at night and now, again late at night, you're involved with an assault. You're out a lot at night?"

"I like to watch the night sky."

"Too much watching will trip you up, Mr. Kirk," warned the sergeant. "You'd best be careful."

"How can we find Rudy Price?" asked Officer Pruett.

"He was seeing Pat Brazier, but he has a girlfriend on the side," Paul said. "Her name's Monique Newcomb, she lives on Sellers Avenue."

"Something you discovered while stargazing?" asked the sergeant rhetorically. "We'll find Mr. Price. Most likely there'll be more questions in the future. I hope your dog recovers soon, Miss Heathcote."

After the police left, Bronwyn asked, "What was that, about being at your ex-wife's house late at night?"

"Amanda and Susan were away for a few days and had me check on the cats. Their neighbor saw the light on and called the police."

Bronwyn remembered Amanda's warning that Paul had rifled her underwear drawer. She contemplated asking for an explanation but decided that would be ungrateful and presumed too much familiarity. "I see. No harm there. In my experience watchful neighbors are very handy."

"What's going to happen tonight? And until they catch this man?"

"I'll lock the back gate and the doors to the house, I'm sure I'll be fine. You can't sleep here every night."

His imagined response was far too risky to vocalize. "I suppose," he said. "I'll keep a look out for you."

"I've been thinking about how odd it was, your not saying you lived right behind me, and I do understand. When there's something you don't mention immediately, then it seems awkward to mention, and soon it's impossible, because it's so strange not having said anything before."

"Thank you," Paul said. "That sounds like a good justification. I do seem super-sensitive to embarrassment."

"Speaking of embarrassing, it's been fifteen years since I robbed Mrs. Armory down the street. It's past time I paid her back. Stay put and I'll bring you a bag of apples and a bowl. If you peel and core them, I'll get everything else ready for a pie. I have frozen pie crusts, so yours is the hard part."

"Do we have enough for an extra pie?"

Bronwyn laughed. "I think so. Forgive me for neglecting your stomach."

Mundane domesticity occupied their time until late in the morning when Bronwyn answered a knock on the front door. It was John Wardle.

"Hello, Bronwyn. I hope you don't mind my stopping by." Sniffing the air he said, "Oh my, that's appetizing."

"Come in and have some. We're offering apple pie to callers this morning."

When John walked into the living room, Paul, ensconced on his couch and delighted to be found in residence, greeted him. "Morning John." John sniffed. "We've made apple pie," Paul said. "I'll put on some coffee." He stood, a little stiffly, and unerringly located the coffee and filter papers.

"Where's Nigel?" John asked Bronwyn, "and what did you do to your head?"

"There was an intruder during the night," Bronwyn said. "Nigel defended me and got a knife wound for his bravery. He's at the vet's."

"Bronwyn! Were you hurt?"

"Thankfully, no more than a bump. Paul saw the man and rescued me."

In astonishment, John exclaimed, "Paul was here last night."

Paul would have liked John to retain the impression of his proprietary right to Bronwyn's company, but he was obliged to explain that he lived immediately behind Bronwyn and had heard the man enter from the lane.

"An amazing coincidence. You living right behind Bronwyn. How long have you lived there?"

"Not long," Paul said. His imprecision sounded evasive, and he was forced to be more definite. "Only since last month."

"I hadn't realized," Bronwyn said. "That is a coincidence. You must have moved in shortly before I did." Bronwyn's incorrect assumption relieved Paul's immediate anxiety, but he knew he'd effectively lied to her.

They had their coffee and pie, and John explained the purpose of his visit. "I've promised my time to too many people next week, so I was hoping you'd let me do your tasks tomorrow afternoon. I wouldn't normally suggest a Sunday, but otherwise I'll be putting off the work for another week."

"The jobs aren't urgent, but that's fine if you'd like to. If you run into late afternoon I'll make you dinner."

"Just for tomorrow, I think I can guarantee to move slowly," John said cheerfully.

A knocking at the front door was followed by, "Hellooo, hellooo!" called down the hallway.

Bronwyn called back, "We're here, Aunt Josie."

"How lovely to see you, John," said Josie, coming into the living room. "And Paul here, too! I was speaking to your mother only yesterday, John. She was telling me that you'd come by and how well your business was doing. You're a good boy, visiting your mother. My Sam, who is an irritant to me, only comes to see me when I nag him, which is tiresome for everyone. And how does the library business prosper, Paul?"

"I'm not sure that it ever truly prospers, Mrs. Stickley. Just sort of plods along."

"Yes, I imagine so," she replied. "I can't stay long, there's no space out there, so my car's double-parked. What I wanted to say, Bronwyn, was that I called Sam this morning at eight o'clock. He denied it, but I think I woke the lazy boy up. He told me about the awful attack on you last night. How could it have happened?" Bronwyn patiently explained the essential facts. "It was careless, leaving the gate open," Josie complained to Paul, "and I don't see why you didn't tackle the man outside the house and save Bronwyn from her anguish."

"Delay might have been fatal," concurred John.

"Believe me, I'm in agreement with you both," Paul said.

"It's my belief that you must have a burglar alarm, at once," said Josie.

"That's an excellent idea, Mrs. Stickley," John said, nodding approvingly. "I have experience installing them. I could certainly do that for you, Bronwyn."

"Thank you. I'll think about it."

"Until it's done," said Josie, "I insist that you stay with me. I'm just not comfortable with you in this house, helpless and alone. It's far too dangerous. Evidently this has turned into an unsafe neighborhood, although what can you expect with these back alleyways? They're an invitation to skulking men."

"Thanks, Aunt Josie, but I'll stay in my home. I'll be sure to lock up."

"And I'll keep an eye on her, Mrs. Stickley," Paul said, adding his reassurance.

"That's not at all comforting," said Josie.

"Please Bronwyn, let me install the alarms," pressed John. "I'd be happy to."

"Okay, John. It does make sense."

"Excellent. It will take a couple of days to get the parts. Mid-week I can work on it."

"I thought you had no time this week," Bronwyn said.

"This is urgent, and I'm more than willing to push back a few jobs for you, but now, you'll really have to excuse me, I must get back to work."

"I'll walk out with you, John," said Josie. "I'm very sorry you're determined to be stubborn about coming home with me, Bronwyn."

"Phew!" exhaled Bronwyn after they left. "My aunt is a know-it-all. Which doesn't mean she's always wrong."

"I will keep an eye out for you," Paul said.

"I know you will. Speaking of which, why don't you tell me your phone number." Paul did. Bronwyn recited it a few times until she had it memorized. Cheerily, she said, "Delivering pie is the perfect antidote. We'll throw our worries aside."

Paul carried the apple pie. Outside the front door, Bronwyn took hold of his left arm. "I'll hold gently," she said. "I know this arm hurts. It's odd to think of you and Nigel having knife wounds in a similar place from defending me."

"For the moment I'll be your substitute guide-person."

"When we get back we'll call the vet and make sure Nigel's okay."

They walked the short distance down the hill with Bronwyn chanting, "Simple Bronwyn met a pie-man going to the fair; said simple Bronwyn to the pie-man let me taste your ware."

Spontaneously exuberant, Paul responded, "I expect you've got no penny, so there'll be no licking on my pie. There's plenty to taste at the house." He became flustered, fearful of some awkward sexual undercurrent, but he was uncertain what exactly he'd implied and decided to ignore it.

Mrs. Armory was delighted to see them. "It's wonderful that you'd think to do this," she said. "And you young man, I've seen you at church, you're …?"

"Paul. A friend of Bronwyn's." He enjoyed saying that and mentally repeated it.

"I hope this shows my regret, Mrs. Armory, for stealing your apples all those years ago."

"Really, dear, you did no harm. There were more apples than I could ever use. It's a wonder you didn't hurt yourself climbing the wall. It would have been so much safer knocking on the front door and asking for some."

"Not so much fun," Bronwyn smiled.

"I'm afraid Bronwyn isn't sounding contrite," Paul said.

"No. Too much like her Aunt Phyllis." Mrs. Armory smiled in return. "Now there was a brazen thief. Really loved her apples, or it wouldn't surprise me if she sold them at the market. I'm sorry to say that my poor apple tree, after forty years, has hardly anything left in her. She and I have grown old together."

"I'll have to bake you another pie. To make up for my Aunt Phyllis."

"Oh, no, your aunt was a good neighbor, just a little wild in her teens, as so many are. She grew into herself when your mother came here to live. Such a lovely pair. Walking arm-in-arm, I remember. They just shone with health and happiness. But everything ends, as we all know," she said with a sigh. "After you were born, Bronwyn, your mother took you away, and I never saw her again. I know your Aunt Phyllis missed her. But what was I going to say?" She paused to think. "Oh yes, that your aunt gave me a painting of my apple tree. It's in the front room. Would you like to see it?"

"I'd love to, Mrs. Armory," Bronwyn said. "Paul can describe it to me."

"Yes of course, dear, sorry. Well, come on in." Mrs. Armory took them into her formal room and pulled open the curtains. "There it is on the wall. I'll go and put the pie in the kitchen."

"It's a pointillist painting like a Van Gogh," said Paul. "About two feet square, with an apple tree full of white blossoms and a yellowish-orange brick wall behind it. It's close to sunset. 'Heathcote' is in small orangey lettering on the bottom right. You know a breeze is blowing because blossoms are falling from the tree."

"Do you like it?" asked Mrs. Armory, coming back into the room.

"It's beautiful," exclaimed Paul.

"Thank you. She was at her peak then," said Mrs. Armory wistfully. "My tree, I mean."

"Hold on to the painting, Mrs. Armory. It may be worth a lot of money one day," Bronwyn said.

"Goodness, I'd never part with it. But dear, I have no children. I'll leave it to you when I go. It's a shame you can't see it, of course."

"Oh, Mrs. Armory, that's not necessary," Bronwyn said.

"All I have in the family is a nephew who never visits, and I'd far rather you, who'd feel its sentimental value, get to keep it. Especially if it's valuable."

Walking back up the street, Bronwyn said, "I feel so guilty."

"For taking the painting from the inconsiderate nephew?"

"No. Because I am that nephew." They'd reached Bronwyn's front door, and she began to weep.

"What is it? Please don't," he pleaded.

"I'm the inconsiderate niece," she spluttered. "I turned fifteen the end of my last summer in Lexington, and I never came back. Portugal, then college, then I was blinded, but none of it's any good for an excuse. I rarely wrote. I didn't call often enough. I let her down. And she loved me and left me her house, and I didn't deserve it." Paul uncomfortably put his right arm around her shoulder. Bronwyn didn't feel his shy stiffness, only his comfort. She moved into him, sobbing on his flannel shirt. Without thinking, she wiped her leaky nose on his shirt.

"I'm sorry to come apart on you," she mumbled.

Paul didn't like Bronwyn to suffer, but he was pleased to have his arm about her, and her wet face pressed into his chest was definitely to his liking.

"Hello, hello, what have we here?" Bronwyn and Paul separated. Turning, Paul saw Sam and Ruth loping down the hill. "Had to park on Main Street," Sam explained. "Got here in time to see some very suspicious activity going on at number 6. Looked a lot like cuddling to the observant eye."

"Sorry, officer, completely wrong," Bronwyn said. "I hope the rest of the police force have better detective skills. Just having a cry session. A nervous reaction to last night, I guess."

"Sam has been telling me about your terrible experience," Ruth said sympathetically. "Let's go in. We'll tidy you up."

Bronwyn and Ruth went to the bathroom. Paul and Sam walked down the hallway and stood in the living room.

"The llamas were cute?" asked Paul.

"Definitely. Llamas get a girl in a cuddlesome mood. I'd recommend watching the critters for anyone on a second date."

"If I get that far, I might try it."

"Not sure you need my help there. You're doing fine. So, what was Bronwyn crying about?"

"She's upset at not communicating more with her Aunt Phyllis," Paul said.

"She had a crying fit with me on that, too, but it's past fixing now. Let's do something useful and see what's for lunch." They were making lettuce, tomato and cheese sandwiches when Bronwyn and Ruth came down the hallway, laughing.

"Ruth and I are having a great time," Bronwyn said. "We're telling tales of worthless men we know."

"Just great," responded Sam grumpily. "Stay away from when I got shoved against Kelly Tolley and my braces caught in her sock."

"I did forget that," Bronwyn laughed delightedly. "That should be a highlight on the Sam tour. We were fourteen and hiking up House Mountain. Sam got pushed, and he toppled onto Kelly on the hill. She's kicking, and Sam's teeth are attached to her ankle like a tenacious attack dog."

"A metaphor for my life," responded Sam mournfully. "Women have been kicking me ever since."

"But that's enough of this woman-hater," Bronwyn said. "I'd like to call the vet. Paul, can you call the number for me? There should be a phonebook in the drawer under the phone."

When Paul heard the phone ring at the animal hospital, he passed the phone to Bronwyn who talked with the vet for a few minutes. To everyone's relief, Nigel was recovering. After she hung up, Bronwyn said, "The vet wants to keep Nigel for a few days. Paul, could you walk with me to work, at least Monday and Tuesday morning? I'm not confident walking the route without Nigel. I'll arrange for one of the people in my building to drive me home." Excited to be asked, he readily agreed. They had a carefree lunch, and Sam, leaving to take Ruth home, said he'd be back in an hour, and they'd try wall tapping.

"I'd like to go to the vets to visit Nigel. Could we do that now?" Bronwyn asked Paul. They walked through their gates and through Paul's house to his car. "You're so perfectly located," Bronwyn said, a sentiment he fully agreed with.

At the animal hospital, they were taken to Nigel, who lay on an old gray blanket in a space four-feet square between low concrete walls. His tail thumped up and down as Paul unlatched the wire gate. Bronwyn bent down and touched her way to Nigel. Paul left them together and went from cage to cage scratching the heads of excited, yipping dogs.

"Paul?" called Bronwyn.

He came to the cage entrance. "I'm just visiting my friends out here."

"Did you have a dog growing up?"

"Nope. I have my cat Spook now, but I never had a dog."

"We moved around too much for me to have one, but Nigel's making up for it, aren't you boy?"

Paul squeezed into the cage and petted Nigel. "I wonder if Spook and Nigel would get along?" he said.

"Let's try them together."

Bronwyn smelled clean, like linen dried in the sunshine. Separated from her by inches of insubstantial air, he had a powerful urge to touch his lips to her cheek. He imagined a rope over the Grand Canyon, the tightrope walker balanced and confident, but cautious. Just then, the voltage of his desire might have overcome his resistance, and a spark crossed that air barrier, had Melanie Shires not arrived. "A striking family picture," Melanie commented. "Too bad I don't have my camera or we'd have you in our New Year's calendar." Paul stood and helped Bronwyn to navigate from the cage. "Nigel's doing well," Melanie said. "He's not up to walking today but he'll be better tomorrow and the day after. Tuesday you can take him home."

Reassured, Bronwyn was content. They drove home, parked back on Paul's street and walked through his house and their neighborly pair of gates.

"Can we read more from the diary?" Bronwyn asked when they sat again on her couch. "I'd like to see if there's anything about my mother or the paintings."

Paul skimmed for a moment. "Your great-grandmother is dying."

Wed., Aug. 22, 1973. It was Nanny Ellen's birthday yesterday. She said she won't ever see another. At least she's got time to prepare for it. I've been seeing how slow she's getting, and thin. She has leukemia. I'll be all alone, except for Josie. We went to the bank this morning and now I can sign checks the same as Nanny. This afternoon we went to Charlottesville to sell a stamp. It's an old store with glass cases and trays of stamps laid out inside them. Nanny told the owner I'd be conducting our business in the future. Nanny told me we have plenty of money in the bank, but she sold a stamp to show me how.

Sat., Dec. 22, 1973. I've been sitting by Nanny Ellen's bed a lot. The nurse comes in a few hours each day, and she gives Nanny her drugs. While she was there, I went to visit Richard who isn't doing well since Victoria died. He likes to see me and while some of his math facts are interesting I don't need them any more since I graduated. Richard can't stop trying, because that's who he is. For a Christmas present, I brought him a painting of Victoria. I copied it from the nude one I did in art class but I made her younger and she has on a black top that goes nicely with her blonde hair. Richard put her painting on the sideboard just opposite his armchair. His old eyes were teary when I left.

Tue., Mar. 5, 1974. We had the funeral service for Nanny Ellen this morning. Lots of old people that I didn't know shook my hand. It's hard to imagine being inside that wooden box and not getting claustrophobic and wanting to bang your way out. The minister said the dead are focused on the eternal but personally I'd say they're just dead. It'll be lonely without Nanny. I've still got Dozer but he's very old in dog-years and won't be around much longer. Mr. Stikes the lawyer came by the house and ate the ham biscuits the old ladies brought. He has Nanny's will. He said everything's mine. I shouldn't worry about anything, and he'll get the house registered in my name. Robert won't care about not getting anything but I bet Josie will blame me for Nanny not leaving her anything.

"I'd guess Aunt Phyllis was right about Aunt Josie being resentful," Bronwyn said. "Sam said she was mad when Phyllis left everything to me and gave him nothing. There's a tradition forming around this property of slighting relatives and descendents."

Wed., May 1, 1974. I've sold a few paintings of local scenes at the artist co-op in town but I really hate working so hard and never seeing them again. I'll give one away though. I climbed on Mrs. Armory's wall this afternoon and sketched her apple tree. It's in blossom. Sheltered up against its wall it's the most beautiful thing. I need to get on well with my neighbors so this is my apology for the apples.

"That's the only Heathcote painting we're sure of the location of," Bronwyn said, "but, as Kate Lavender said, there must be others in houses around the county and some spread to who knows where by the tourists."

Sat., June 22, 1974. I went to Richard's funeral service this afternoon. He died suddenly, which was good. When Victoria died, his heart was broken and he wasn't interested in it healing. I wish I thought they were together, that would be comforting. But we can't believe things just to make ourselves comfortable. Some mathematicians came from Washington, D.C., and one gave a speech about Richard's work in number theory. Richard had written tons of books and articles so he must have been important but I'll remember him for the smile of a cherub and his patience with a dumb girl. The mathematician's talk was boring but I bet it was way closer to the truth than the Preacher's gospel, 'The Lord loves us. Say Amen to that.'

They heard a rapping on the front door and Sam called down the hallway that he was coming in. When he sat in the armchair, he asked immediately, "What did you think of Ruth?"

"She's great," Bronwyn answered. "She got straight into fixing my tearful face. She's a really interesting character and a genuine person. You couldn't do better than her for a girlfriend, if you like her."

From the warmth of Bronwyn's approval, Paul wondered why, in the two years he'd known Ruth, he hadn't been drawn to her. But a real match is needed to get shy tinder like that burning. He thought back to Amanda, who'd pursued him and, in retrospect, you could ask why she did. He was proud of his small self-promotions with Bronwyn, and he resolved to continue them, not promising dramatic leaps but trusting more to his tortoise-like nature.

"We've been hearing from Aunt Phyllis," Bronwyn explained to Sam. "Great-grandmother Ellen has died and so has Richard her math tutor."

Paul, who'd been flicking through pages, said, "There's something here about your mother."

> Tue., Feb. 25, 1975. Robert called early this afternoon. It's six hours later in Greece. They were at a bar celebrating with a noisy crowd so it was hard to hear. Typical of Robert, telling me he got married after it happened. Robert's thirty and Sophie isn't as old as me. Ten years older is a lot. Robert's not ugly, but her getting to be a U.S. citizen must be part of it. Sophie got on the phone but I couldn't understand what she said. Robert promised to bring her for a visit in May. I haven't seen him in years, so if he actually comes that'll be great. I have a spare bedroom for them, but maybe they'll want to stay with Josie and not me.

Paul looked ahead to May and said, "Yes, they did come. There are a few entries from the middle of May. They stayed with Josie for a week. Bronwyn, here's one about your mother."

> Fri., May 23, 1975. I told Robert they should stay with me, but he said Josie would get upset as they grew up together and I was the little sister. Sophie's English isn't so good but honestly you can't always understand what people are saying who were born here in this county. She's fun and always smiling. As brown as a cow-pie, but since she's exotic I should say she's more like nutmeg. Having written that, I went to the spice cupboard and Nanny Ellen had left whole nutmegs in a can. I scraped some curls off and chewed them. Nutmeg has a strong bite that stays in the memory of your mouth for

a long while. Sophie walked over from Josie's house this morning. It must be two and a half miles but she didn't think anything of it. She stood at the front door in her shorts and short-sleeved shirt with the sun behind her and the fine hairs on her arm glistened like dew. I dragged her into my studio in a passion to paint her but she wouldn't sit for me. We walked to town instead and looked at antique shops. I'll buy the brocaded rocking chair that Sophie liked and surprise her the next time she and Robert visit.

"That must be the rocking chair in the spare bedroom," Bronwyn said. "It'll be more special with a history"

"Is it time for treasure hunting?" asked Sam.

"Are we bored with furniture talk? Alright, let's do it," Bronwyn said, getting to her feet. "All we know from the diaries is that the room had a door to it. Probably, it's either the studio or one of the bedrooms. I had an impression of some depth to the room. The laundry or bathroom aren't likely."

"Let's do Bronwyn's bedroom first," Sam suggested. "That's the likeliest hiding place. Then the spare bedroom and the studio."

Sam assigned areas in the bedroom and they began tapping.

"The wainscot paneling seems likeliest," Paul said. "We'd see a line in the plaster if there's anything hidden behind the upper half of the walls. Behind the built-in bookcases is a possibility too." They pushed, prodded and tapped but no useful response came from the walls. "The wood is too solid," Paul said.

Sam and Paul moved Bronwyn's bed and dresser out from the wall and found nothing. They returned the room to order and moved on to the spare bedroom, which had the same wainscoting, but again their efforts failed. "Last chance," Paul said as they moved to the studio.

Three of the studio walls were plastered and one was entirely paneled. Sam said, "Paul and I can take the plaster walls, Bronwyn, if you'll try your luck on the paneled wall closest to the living room. Your ears are more sensitive than ours." The walls yielded nothing. Frustrated, they returned to the living room.

"John is coming tomorrow afternoon," Bronwyn said. "I'll ask him about removing the wainscoting. Maybe try my bedroom first."

"A wasted effort if the diaries reveal where the box is located," Paul said.

"That's true," Bronwyn replied. "There's no rush anyway. Paul, would you like to read some more? I'm especially interested in hearing about my mother. She was in Lexington for three years. Try from mid-1977 onwards."

Paul silently skimmed the diary. "Okay. Here we are around Christmas."

Thur., Dec. 22, 1977. Sophie comes tomorrow. Willis is picking her up from the airport. I don't know who she's staying with. Robert called Josie and she said Sophie could stay with her. Then he called me and I said she should live with me. She's staying all through Robert's tour of duty in Afghanistan. It's too dangerous for her there and he'll have no time for her anyway.

Fri., Dec. 23, 1977. Willis took Sophie to his house, which I'd expected, but it's a blow anyway. Sophie's nearly my age. Why would she want to be with Josie who's ten years older? She's married to Robert who's that much older, but that's different. I walked over to Josie's house after lunch. Not that I'd have walked that far to see Josie, but I wanted Sophie to know I could. Her English is hugely better than two years ago. She's the same otherwise; brown skin, brown eyes, slender, long legs, long black hair. I'd love to paint her. I'm thinking Lady Godiva on a white horse.

Sun., Dec. 25, 1977. Christmas today. I went to Josie's and we opened presents. Josie gave Sophie gloves and a scarf. She thought someone from Greece wouldn't have clothes for winter. Sophie gave Josie and me a bottle of retsina wine each. They're special because Sophie carried them all the way from Greece. Josie doesn't drink alcohol but I think she will, when nobody looks. Sophie's present was back at my house so she tried out her gloves and scarf and we hiked back here. My present was the brocaded rocking chair she'd admired in the antique store two years back. She rocked furiously on it and said she loved it. She's going to leave it here and visit, like shared custody. We drank my bottle of wine and I got to look at her and hear about Robert.

Sat., Dec. 31, 1977. Sophie moved in with me. I'm so happy. Willis drove her over with her bags. Her room was all ready for her. I'd bought a new cover for the spare bed and a large rug for the floor. Both are shades of light browns and grays to make her feel at home. I'm not sure if those are the colors of Greece but I did my best. Josie got annoyed with Sophie for being out late at night. Sophie wouldn't be spoken to like that and said she was used to being up late. I'll be mad too, if Sophie's out with boys. She's supposed to be married after all. And I usually go to bed early. I'll try siestas and see if that works.

Tue., Jan. 10, 1978. It snowed overnight and this morning we had four inches on the ground. I brought the sled down from the attic and mid-morning we put on layers of clothes and looked like a pair of ladybugs. We trudged over to Nelson Street to play on the hill behind the apartment buildings. We squished together like mating beetles and zoomed down to smack into the snowdrifts. I loved tumbling and rolling with Sophie till we'd crash together in the snow and look up at the endless sky. I may never be that happy again. One day's just got to be happiest. When it's gone, none are ever that good again.

Thurs., Feb. 23, 1978. Ever since October I've been modeling at the University. Victoria used to do it and when I saw the job notice, I thought, why not? I've got no problem showing my body to a roomful of students, and I like hearing the professor. Today was the first nude painting class for this semester and Sophie said she didn't like my doing it, which surprised me, coming from free-spirited Sophie. I'd stop, but I want to tease her more.

Thur., Mar. 2, 1978. I went to my nude class this afternoon. Sophie was mad at me. She likes to get her way. From hints, she and Robert get in fights, because he wants to be the boss. It's a lot better without a man around the house. There's a boy in the class who smiles at me and talks to me during the break. Not hard figuring him out. I told Sophie, and she said it wasn't decent showing myself to someone who's getting hot looking at me. I'm not responsible for what goes on inside him. He can look at the angles and roundness of me, the light and shade, and it doesn't hurt me. He's a sweet boy, very polite, and he'd be easy to seduce. I've been thinking how nice it would be, having a little girl. If he got me pregnant I wouldn't tell him, and the baby would be just mine.

"Did your Aunt Phyllis ever have a child?" asked Paul.

"Not as far as I know," Bronwyn said. "But anything's possible with my secretive family. My father won't tell me about Aunt Phyllis or my mother, and my Aunt Josie doesn't seem to have liked Aunt Phyllis very much."

"Mom was probably jealous," Sam said. "Older and younger-sister rivalry. Phyllis got the house and the art talent and didn't need a man to support her."

> Sat., Mar. 18, 1978. Sophie and I went to see, Aladdin, at the Henry Street Playhouse. The actors were university students and some town's people. Sophie loved it and wants to find her own treasure cave. I thought of telling her about my treasure but I'll keep the secret. If I ever have a girl, or if Sophie does, then I'll pass it on to her. I liked the parts in the play with the cute little children. Two young men dressed in loin cloths carried a treasure chest onto the stage and opened it to show the jewels. Up popped this adorable little girl, about three years old, looking very confused. She climbed out of the chest and ran off-stage crying. Her older brother in the performance must have played a trick and smuggled her on-stage.

"Aunt Phyllis wanted our family's treasure kept a secret," Bronwyn said. "She wouldn't even tell my mother. If she hadn't died suddenly, I'm sure she would have made me its keeper. It's bad that I've let knowledge of it slip from the female side. I messed-up my family tradition."

"We won't tell," Sam said. "Anyway, it's a very uncertain treasure that can't be found."

> Thur., Mar. 23, 1978. I persuaded Sophie to come model with me at the nude painting class. I'm not sure what made her do it. She hasn't even sat for me yet. I called Professor Paiva and he was delighted to have us for the price of one. He suggested a couple of sea-nymphs facing each other. When we took off our robes I really got to look at Sophie. I'm sure she'd never sat still so long before. We'd send each other messages with our eyes and little muscle twitches. What you can do with an eyebrow, and a look, and the corner of your mouth! We had fun. I do love Sophie. She's the sister I should have had. For

hours all I did was look at her and store her up for when I'll paint her.

Sat., Apr. 22, 1978. We haven't heard from Robert since Christmas. Sophie says she's used to it. With me she isn't lonely, and with her it's true for me too. I want Sophie to stay always. We went to Natural Bridge today, down in the caves. Sophie saw a tunnel running off to the right and we fell behind the tour group and ran back into it. We scrambled along with the tunnel getting darker and narrower. We were pushing against each other, neither of us wanting the other to get ahead. The roof angled down and we got wedged, pushing in the darkness like a couple of earth worms stuck together. You can't stay forever like that so we wriggled out and caught up with the tour.

Sun., Apr. 30, 1978. Sophie has been sitting for me the past couple of weeks. She doesn't like to sit long, but small intervals are enough. I can nearly visualize her when she isn't there. I'd been painting since the sun came up and I was tired, so in the middle of the afternoon when the sunshine warmed the cover on my bed I lay on it for a nap. I woke up when Sophie came and snuggled against me. It was delicious, the sun and Sophie comforting me, and I drowsed back off to sleep. Growing up, our cats Callie and Lucy would do that in the sunshine. I always wanted to come back as a cat, though I wouldn't eat mice. We read for the rest of the day. Sophie reads one chapter and I do the next. Right now it's 'Jane Eyre.' Sophie doesn't think much of Mr. Rochester, he's too domineering and old, she says, and just because nobody's loved her before doesn't mean Jane should fall for the first person who does.

Mon., May 1, 1978. It was another sunny afternoon and hoping Sophie would join me I took a nap. She did, and we drowsed together for a while. When I woke and turned over, she was looking at me, smiling. Her robe had fallen open and I traced my fingers over her collar bone thinking how lovely and how fragile. Sophie took my hand and lightly touched my fingers on her breast. A warm tingle spread below my belly. I kissed her mouth, realizing I'd wanted to taste her for months.

"Paul," Bronwyn interrupted.

"Umm," he responded vaguely.

"Let's stop now, okay?"

"Oh, right."

"So much for that family secret," Sam said.

"Thank you, both," Bronwyn said. "I'll read the diaries myself for a while."

Sam stood up. "Appears to be our hint to leave."

Paul bolted the back gate, and he and Sam left by the front door. They parted at Sam's car without further discussion. Paul walked home and made himself dinner. He took an apple for desert and climbed with it onto his shed. It would be daylight for hours, but he wanted to watch from his highest perch to maintain a vigil on Bronwyn and the surrounding alley and backyards. He was spying on Bronwyn but safeguarding her, in large part, justified his watching.

Chapter 20 Sunday

Through the night, Paul remained on his shed. Around midnight he retrieved the seat cushion from his armchair, a blanket and an extra pillow. He was intermittently able to sleep by dangling his legs on each side of the roof-slope and leaning back against the cushion. He appreciated why early ape-men came down from their trees and slept in caves. It was cold and uncomfortable up there. He longed for a horizontal position in his own cave.

He woke to a pale gray-blue sky behind Bronwyn's house and watched the unseen sun touch with purple fingers the ropy clouds lying just above the horizon. With the daylight, Bronwyn was safe. He went to bed and straight to sleep.

Waking, with barely time to cycle to church by 10:30, he did without a shower, dressed quickly in whatever clothes came to hand, put on his church jacket and pedaled off vigorously. He was in time to walk through the choir forming lines in the vestibule. He found his preferred seat, slightly behind and across the aisle from Bronwyn, who was sitting with her Aunt Josie. However, his thoughts of peacefully observing Bronwyn were dispelled by John Wardle who walked in and stood boldly by Bronwyn. Speaking to her aunt, John caused them to move over, and he sat in the seat Bronwyn had vacated.

Frustrated by this maneuver, Paul was out of tune with the church service and generally grumpy. At the passing of the peace, nobody was in arm's length to offer their hand and receive his churlishness. John, however, walked across the aisle to wish him "Peace." Paul responded indistinctly, which could be taken as its recipient chose.

After the service, he watched John leave, arm in arm with Bronwyn and her aunt. Josie's eyes had passed over him without recognition, and he'd felt himself shrink. He thought of escaping out the side exit, but an image came to him of Mr. Toad cycling home to Toad Hall. He sat until the last echo of the organ postlude died from the church then reluctantly walked to the main door. He stood on the steps in what seemed, after the dim light of the church, to be the glare of a spotlight. Nobody appeared to notice him as he descended to the patio. Near the lemonade table, Bronwyn, Josie and John were talking with the rector. Picking up a cup of lemonade Paul cleared his throat, prepared to say something but unaware what it would be.

"Is that Paul?" asked Bronwyn.

"It is," Paul replied, moving closer.

"You are here." She put her hand out and touched his chest for a second. "I asked if you were, but nobody seemed to know."

"Yes, I'm here."

"I see that you are," laughed Bronwyn.

"And looking haggard," John remarked.

Paul ran a palm over his cheek. "I was running late this morning and didn't shave."

"We're delighted to have you in any condition," said the rector.

Bronwyn put her hand up. Her fingers glided over Paul's shoulder, lit on his chin and felt his left cheek. Travelling to his right cheek, her fingers dropped away, leaving his lips tingling. "I didn't sleep so well myself," she said. "It's true, Paul. You are shamefully rugged. Now, John, I'm sure, came presentable to church." She found John's arm and, tracing her way to his face, put her palm to his cheek saying, "What a contrast! Beauty and the Beast."

John smiled contentedly. "Respect for our God, is all."

"And you smell respectful too," Bronwyn said, sniffing the aroma of John's after-shave lotion, which Paul thought far too strong.

"Well, I'm heading out," Paul said. He gulped his lemonade, discarded the paper cup, turned about and walked to where his bike waited for him behind the church. Bronwyn had shown clear favoritism, and he knew she planned to give John a Sunday dinner. He cycled home with a formless anger. Happily, the streets were largely free of traffic for his vision was obscured, as if a patch of fog had perversely fixed on accompanying him home.

He tried to read his book that afternoon, but the words skittered, running from him like marbles on a slope. Periodically, a strong urge rose in him to go to his ladder, but he resisted, determined to be worthy of Bronwyn's trust. She was in no danger. The only danger was to him, should John cut between him and his hopes.

Bronwyn was eager to understand more of her mother's relationship with Phyllis, but John, who arrived immediately after lunch, disturbed her reading. While he worked in the hallway, a lack of privacy checked her desire. Only when he moved into her bedroom was she released to play the diaries softly on her computer. She remained half-aware of sounds from her bedroom, not wanting John to find her crouched over whispering speakers.

It was far more than a touch and kiss. Her mother and aunt had lived in a state of supernal bliss. Outside the home, they acted as romping children. Within walls, their passion was the fiercer, knowing that strictures would flay their innocence bare should the community ever see clearly. Bronwyn herself was shocked, that her mother was unfaithful, and with Aunt Phyllis, very nearly her mother's sister. She brought to her mind the mother living in her memory and realized, as she never had before, that in contrast with these diaries, the mother she knew was unhappy.

Hearing John in the hallway, she closed the file and tried to meet his enthusiasm with interest. "The railings are in place," he said. "And the handles in the shower. I just started re-nailing your squeaky floorboards and I found this under the floor in your bedroom. Good thing I didn't just nail them down. I was curious why the boards weren't properly secured."

"Is it a box?"

"Yes, it's a metal box. I'll put it on the table."

Bronwyn felt around the box. "This is wonderful. It belonged to my Aunt Phyllis. I've been searching for it. You don't know how much this means to me. I'm so grateful."

"Well that's excellent. I'm very pleased to help. Do you know what's in it? Should I open it and tell you."

"I know what should be there. Maybe a quick peek. I'd like to make sure."

"It's not locked," John said, clicking it open. "It looks like a picture album."

"Thanks John. Let's not go any further. That's exactly what I'd hoped for."

"And a bundle of letters."

"Letters? Oh, that's even more exciting." She explored the box and touched around the thick bundle, running her fingertips over the smooth ribbon crossed both ways over the letters.

"Should I look and see who they're from?" offered John.

"No, thanks. I'd rather have someone in the family read them. I hope you understand."

"Of course. I'll get back to work. It'll take me about an hour and a half to nail all the boards."

Bronwyn understood that her excitement had pleased John and how deflated he was by her small rejection. "I'll have dinner for us after your hard work," she said. To comfort him she added, "I'm extremely happy you came today." John thanked her more cheerfully and returned to her bedroom, closing the door to diminish the noise of his banging. Bronwyn appreciated his thoughtfulness and returned to the diaries.

As she listened, she ceased being aware of the neutral tone of the text-to-speech software, hearing instead the soft voice of her Aunt Phyllis. Both had known their wonderful contentment would not last, but kept such thoughts from each other until the Christmas season of 1979 when Robert sundered their idyllic married life. Returning to Lexington on a one-week leave he naturally moved into the spare bedroom with Sophie, and, being an energetic man long-parted from his wife, he engaged in spirited sex while he could. Crouched in the hallway with her back to Sophie's wall, Phyllis suffered the bedsprings, the thrustings into her dear Sophie, and Robert's happy groans. She begged Sophie to disabuse Robert, but Sophie refused. Having married him, she was bound by her obligation. Could she tell the priest and her parents in Greece that she'd cast off a good man because she loved his sister? It was impossible, and she warned Phyllis never to say a word more.

When he left at the end of December, they had crept together, each giving the other their sadness, their longing and their pity. With the loss of their future, never again could their joy be as pure as their honeyed days. But yet, there was a year before Robert would come to carelessly wrest Sophie from her, and what a year of wonder it was, for Sophie was pregnant. Their hopes and dreams were carried forward by the child that lay between them. Their child, that grew and kicked, and wailingly came forth in a spurt of blood to be held so lovingly by Phyllis in that birthing room. She was theirs to cradle for three months together. On the afternoon of December 23rd, a day early, Robert entered the house and found them asleep together, Phyllis and Sophie naked, and the truth was clear to him. The tears and pleas of Phyllis were spent against the wall of his anger, and of Sophie's shame. He packed his family, and hers, taking them from her that afternoon.

Bronwyn felt the face of her wristwatch. She needed to make dinner. What she'd learned from the diaries was enough to digest. She was happy to close the file and turn her attention elsewhere. A large and a small potato went into the microwave and she brought out leftover chili to re-heat.

As Paul prepared his dinner, the phone rang. Calls were rare and definitely unexpected on Sunday evening. It was Rolf. Barely greeting Paul, he rushed on with his words. "I've only got a minute and this is my one call. I need your help, mate. The coppers have got me at the police station. They say I assaulted some lady, which is hogwash. They want to know where I was between 10:00 and 10:30 last night. Told them, of course, we were together at my aunt's listening to her cello playing so I need you to tell them I was and not wherever they want to say I was. Can you do that, mate?" Paul hesitated. This was deep water to drown in. "You comin', mate?"

"I'm sure we'll get it straightened out. I'll be there shortly."

Lying to the police was serious. If Rolf was in trouble, then, by association, he was too. If it went badly he might occupy a jail cell that night. He drove to the police department and pushed the buzzer on the door. A voice asked him his business, and he was buzzed in.

Paul walked straight to the counter. The officer looked up as he approached, "Paul Kirk?" He nodded. Paul focused on the other two occupants of the waiting room and saw, to his consternation, Rudy and

Monique. Rudy was holding Monique's hand. He grinned at Paul saying, "I thought you'd get flushed out with the other rat."

The officer turned to his left and called to someone Paul couldn't see, "Paul Kirk's here."

Sergeant Driscoll appeared, opened the flap in the counter and beckoned Paul through.

"You saw Miss Newcomb and Mr. Price?"

"Are you questioning them about the assault?" asked Paul.

The sergeant pointed to a small interview room. "Take a seat and I'll be along in a minute."

The room was bare except for a small table and three chairs. Paul chose to sit facing the door, his back securely against the wall. After a short wait, Sergeant Driscoll returned with Officer Pruett, the sergeant took the chair to Paul's left and Officer Pruett sat at his right.

"Do you mind an audio recording?" asked the sergeant.

"That's fine," Paul replied mechanically. Officer Pruett put the recording device on the table and pushed the start button.

The sergeant identified him for the recording and continued, speaking to Paul, "We're investigating a sexual assault. The victim has identified Rolf Sprunt as the assailant."

"That can't be right. Rolf's a little odd, but he's entirely harmless," Paul said.

"Maybe so," said the sergeant agreeably. "Rolf says he was with you around 10:30 last night when the attack took place. Is that so?"

Paul nodded a few times, waiting for whatever would come from his mouth. "Yes," he said.

"And where were you?" asked the sergeant patiently.

"We were at his Aunt Celia's house from about a quarter past ten until close to eleven o'clock."

"Excellent. That would be Celia Hopewell? She'll vouch for this?"

"Well, no. We were outside her house. She was playing the cello, and we were listening."

"Two weeks back, it was you two up the hill," exclaimed Officer Pruett angrily. "Two hours I crawled under thorn bushes to find my gun. You know how many damn thorns I had in me?" He stood in excitement. "Assaulting a police officer is a very serious offense."

"Simon," said the sergeant. "Enough for now. Why don't you take the other couple to an interview room and go over the facts of the assault again. And find out where he was at the time."

Officer Pruett cast a baleful look at Paul, and left, shutting the door.

Paul suddenly understood why Rudy and Monique were there. "Monique was the one assaulted?"

"Strange, isn't it," the sergeant mused. "You accuse Rudy of attempting to rape your girlfriend and now Rudy's girlfriend accuses your friend of the same thing. Something symmetrical about that, wouldn't you say?"

"I would. But Bronwyn's not my girlfriend."

"You've got your eye on her, right? I mean, you like her."

"I do."

Sergeant Driscoll stood and turned off the recording. He paced the small area between the table and the door. "Some parts of this are clear to me," he said. "I had an idea before, what you were up to after dark. Not very nice, spying on your friend's aunt. If I asked for details about last night I bet it wouldn't all match with Rolf's story. I'm thinking the alibi's invented, at least for last night." He frowned, appearing to forget that Paul was there. After a minute he resumed, "I believe you're more misguided than malicious. I'd like to help you. Would Rudy have known about your relationship with Rolf?"

"I don't see how, but he must have guessed."

"We examined Miss Newcomb's bedroom and found Rolf's fingerprints. You said, in regard to Rudy's financial scheme, that your source was a friend you didn't want to get in trouble. Is it possible that Rolf's fingerprints came there before yesterday?"

Paul nodded noncommittally.

"I don't know what precipitated the accusation last night, but I'm confident no attempted rape occurred. I've good cause to lock the pair of you up, but I believe you're repentant and can exercise control over your young friend. Would that be correct?"

"Most definitely."

Sergeant Driscoll nodded. "I'll release Rolf into your hands. I don't know how this will play out, but I'd be careful."

As Paul and Rolf walked outside to the parking lot, Paul gestured at the white Chevy Malibu. "Rudy's still here," he said.

"Should we let the air out of his tires?"

Paul snorted. "Tempting, but I promised Sergeant Driscoll we'd stay out of trouble. I thought you could stay with me for a few days."

"You're on, mate," Rolf said, clearly pleased.

Paul drove to Rolf's house for Rolf to pack some clothes and a toothbrush. The TV was on in the living room when they walked in the front door. Rolf dashed upstairs, shouting, "Paul's here." Paul walked in to say hello.

"Nice to see you again, Paul," Regina said as Seth turned off the TV.

"Thanks, Mrs. Hopewell. Mr. Hopewell," he replied. "I've asked Rolf to stay with me for a few days. Hopefully that's okay."

193

"Sounds great," Seth said.

"I'm short on bedding. Would you mind if we borrowed some for Rolf?"

Regina took Paul to the linen closet and filled his arms with sheets and blankets. She called up to Rolf to bring his pillow.

Rolf came down the stairs hugging his bag and pillow. "See ya, Aunt Reggie," he said with muffled affection.

"Have fun. Give us a kiss," she demanded, offering her cheek.

Rolf obediently kissed her. At Seth's request, Paul gave them his phone number.

On their way outside Rolf said, "I should have had your number. The operator said you're unlisted, so how's anybody supposed to find you? The police were good for something. They got your number for me."

"Sorry Rolf, I just keep the phone for emergencies."

"Bloody selfish, isn't it. What about other people's emergencies?"

They drove in separate cars to Paul's house. Depositing Rolf's bedding on the couch, Paul asked, "Before we do anything, tell me, what did happen last night?"

Rolf reported that, wanting a repeat view of Monique, he'd gone to her house and pulled the garbage can under her bedroom window. On mounting, his reward was the sight of Monique grinding away as she straddled Rudy. Rolf, seeing her titties waving at him, could hardly be expected not to join in the fun, but he became so focused on his own pleasure that he only noticed Monique staring at him seconds before Rudy jerked him from his perch. A totally naked Rudy, an exposed Rolf, both part-way erect, struggled to the front of the house. Monique came running in her bathrobe, but, before she could attack him, Rolf slipped from Rudy's grip and tore off.

"A pretty picture," Paul said. "Rudy may have glimpsed you at Monique's house when he chased and shot at us. He probably guessed I was the other person with you. After your escapade last night, he and Monique concocted the attempted rape to punish us. So far, that hasn't worked for them. Though it did confirm Rudy's suspicions."

"Where do I sleep?" asked Rolf.

"In the shed." At Rolf's surprised look, Paul held up his hand. "I'll be there too." He explained about Rudy following him to Bronwyn's house, the threat at the park and the attempted rape. "If it was Rudy who attacked Bronwyn, he might still believe I live at Bronwyn's or else he's figured out where I do live. Whichever, Bronwyn and I are in danger."

"So, I'm covering your back. That's cool." Rolf thought some more. "That's the reason you want me to stay with you?"

"No. I thought we'd help each other, but I've been realizing this evening that we should gang up against Rudy." Rolf accepted this. They went to the shed to inspect their headquarters. "We can bring out my mattress and all the sheets and blankets we have," Paul said. "And we'll take turns being awake." They brought to the shed anything useful as a weapon; flashlights, a baseball bat, kitchen knives, rope, and duct tape. The result was a cozy home, at least as much as befitted an encampment. As dusk came on, sitting on a cushion with his back against the doorframe, Paul felt eight years old again, looking on a world of promise and mystery from the makeshift house he'd built against the park railings. This time he had a friend to occupy the space with him. This time, and truly for the first time in his life, Paul believed that he was in control, not of the world around him, but of himself. A sense of thanksgiving, almost of rapture, rose through his body, welling in his brain. With time, he could shape himself. He hoped he'd have that time.

"We'll have to whisper," Paul said. "If he comes into the lane, we mustn't be heard. It'll be dark soon, so let me show you above." He pointed to the roof of the shed. He couldn't allow Rolf to see Bronwyn undressed, so he'd have Rolf take the first shift and he'd go up around 9:30.

"What a view!" Rolf whispered, looking down at Bronwyn working on her computer. "Keeping it all to yourself, were you?"

Paul, who had stayed on his stepladder, responded softly and slowly, "I can't do any more of this peeping business. It's all too serious. I'm in love with Bronwyn." Whispering to Rolf on the solemn night air, Paul confessed what he hadn't said plainly enough to himself, that he was indeed a man in love.

"Righty-o mate. Message understood."

"Once we're sure Bronwyn's gone to bed, we'll stay down in the shed. We should hear anyone in the lane."

"A pity the lane isn't gravel," whispered Rolf.

"What a great idea," Paul whispered back with enthusiasm. "You're right. Gravel's what we need. Come on down and give me a hand."

With Rolf's assistance, Paul climbed onto Bronwyn's wall. He rolled over the wall and quietly lowered himself into her garden. Kneeling by the gravel path, he formed a few mounds of gravel. He whispered through the gate for Rolf to step back and scooped up each mound, tossing the gravel over the gate. His fifth load rattled onto the concrete path as Bronwyn's door clicked open. Paul stepped back onto the grass, going completely still.

"Is anyone there?" Bronwyn called. She came forward hesitantly, stopping three feet from him. She must sense him, he thought; he'd twitch, or belch, or scratch, or gasp for air. His heart drummed in his body, and it seemed she must hear him, but she moved on to the gate. Checking the bolt and rubbing her shoes over the gravel, she whispered uncertainly, "Is anyone here?" Hesitating no more, she retreated to the house and locked the door.

Using the crossbeams on its inner side, Paul climbed the gate with ease. As he crunched onto the gravel Rolf said, "That her was it?"

"I made too much noise. I scared her."

"You should have opened her gate, just to spread the gravel."

Paul, who did think himself Rolf's intellectual superior, humbly admitted, "You're right. I should have done that."

Paul rested on the mattress until 9:30, when he relieved Rolf on the shed. "Get some sleep," Paul said, "so you'll be alert later." He didn't know exactly when Bronwyn went to bed. There were no lights on in her house. He sensed her presence at the computer from the ambient light, but between one time and the next, she was gone. Close to four in the morning the moon rose. Paul dozed and dreamed and watched. He allowed Rolf to sleep through the night. Wrapped in two blankets, he listened to Rolf snuffling and the occasional noise of animals in the night. He meditated, thinking that a good loaf needed fresh yeast, wholesome flour and the right application of heat. How that analogized, he wasn't sure, but with the inharmonious inputs of his life, it was unreasonable to expect a happy outcome. He was a disappointment to himself and to his baker. Softly, and a little sadly, he chuckled. It was 6:15 and daylight edged the sky. He climbed down and lay beside Rolf, drowsing for an hour, intermittently waking to check his watch. He had a commitment at 8:30 to walk Bronwyn to work.

Chapter 21   Monday

"What will you do today?" Paul asked.
"Can I use the Internet? I'd like to look for a job."
"Help yourself. What are you looking for?"
"The kind of job I'd be good at. I'll tell you if I get anything."

Paul was curious as to what Rolf was qualified to do, though he understood Rolf's desire not to be quizzed. He bolted the back gate and gave Rolf the spare house-key. At 8:25, he walked around the block to Bronwyn's house. She was ready at his knock, and they set out. Bronwyn held onto his right arm just above the elbow. On Main Street, with an easy path for a few blocks, Bronwyn said, "John was by yesterday. He means very well and has been extremely helpful to me."

It would be too much to expect that even a morally enlightened man would take such praise of a rival with a wholly even temper, and Paul responded, "But he's slightly pompous, isn't he?"

Bronwyn laughed and squeezed Paul's arm. "Dear Paul," she said, "He's as pompous as you're obtuse." Paul wasn't sure that he was obtuse, but it seemed unsafe ground to venture on. He didn't need to, as she kept talking. "There was an odd incident last night before I went to bed. I thought of calling you but decided not to. It was like someone was throwing the pebbles of my path up in a fountain. When I went out, there was nothing, although I felt some cavities in the gravel. It was strange."

Paul checked their progress. The muscles in his arm tensed as if he was connected to a lie detector. "What is it?" she asked.

More foolish than obtuse, she would think him, but he was helpless to abate the powerful flood of his confession. "I did it. I thought, with gravel on the lane, that I'd hear an intruder. So I tossed some over the wall." Bronwyn stopped walking. Her arm fell from him.

"When I went out? You were there?"
"I was," he said sadly.
"But how frightening! And you wouldn't speak?"
"It wasn't right. I was trespassing, and my instincts took over."
"Have you ever thought that you're too convoluted? Let's just move along, okay?" she said brusquely. "I need to get to work." She held out her hand, which he contacted with his elbow. They set out again, two continents separated by an isthmus of silence.

Bronwyn was right. He was too convoluted. After a few minutes of battling his inner core, of wanting to close up like a hedgehog, he abandoned his pride and ventured timidly, "I was quiet because I didn't want you to know how worried I am for you."

"That's scary," she said, "and sweet at the same time, too. Alright, I see that we aren't in a position of total openness with each other. I'll forgive you. In return I want you to be open with me if another decision like that comes up." Paul was relieved and readily agreed. Bronwyn was also eager to be mollified. His social aptitude was imperfect, yet she liked his qualities. Something in his childhood, she was sure, had thrown him into stormier weather than his young frame could handle and had tattered his sails. She wasn't aiming to overhaul him, but she hoped that in smoother waters he would set out again to be the fine ship he was meant to be.

"I have big news," she said, reverting to a cheerful topic. "John found Aunt Phyllis' box under the floorboards in my bedroom. And there's a bundle of letters in the box. The album's there. I haven't tried to discover if it has any stamps."

Paul wished that someone other than John had found it, but he was pleased for Bronwyn. "That's exciting. I'd love to help, of course."

"I was hoping you and Sam would come over tonight. I'll make dinner around 6:00?" He agreed, vastly thankful that Bronwyn was forgiving. They walked on to her workplace. Paul opened the front door and watched as she climbed the stairs. He walked slowly to work, his emotions engaged in blowing dandelion seeds; a puff for she loves me, a puff for she respects me not. Bronwyn might be persuaded to love him, but knowing him, would she respect him? For the five minutes up the hill to the library, his tides of elation and self-deprecation rose and fell, now to the sky, now in the mud. That he arrived at work two minutes late was of little concern. He would make it up from his lunch hour.

Except on rare occasions of illness, Paul's enthusiasm for his work was unfailing. During his workday, he felt symptomatic. Anticipating a cold kept him cocooned in a slightly depressed state but no sickness eventuated, and, by late afternoon, he was shaking off his malaise. He left work at 5:00 and went to visit Phyllis who was among the liveliest of the dead in the cemetery. His knowledge of her grew, as if she was capable of future discovery and change. Phyllis loved Bronwyn's mother and loved Bronwyn as her own. A plea to her wasn't wasted. Approaching in humbleness, kneeling on the grass above her grave, he said only, "I'm not worthy of her, I know." Purified by his declaration, thinking of nothing in particular, he stayed for a while, warmed by the spring sunshine, until he roused himself to walk home.

Rolf was preparing their dinner. "I bought mushrooms and eggs," he said proudly. "I'm making us a quiche."

"Oh, no! I should have called you. Bronwyn invited me to dinner at six o'clock."

"No matter. You can have some tomorrow, if it lasts that long." Paul was distressed that Rolf appeared low-spirited.

"How'd your job hunting go?"

"There's not much, but a few possibles. You'd better get a shower before you see your girl, and don't forget the deodorant." He did as Rolf advised. When he was ready to go, Rolf said, "I'll be on the Internet. Aunt Regina's computer has the X-rated sites filtered out, but yours is wide open."

Paul walked around the block, and Sam opened the door to him. "What have you got?" he asked, pointing to the book that Paul held.

"It's the Scott Catalogue of U.S. Stamps. I borrowed it, just in case it's needed."

As they went down the hallway, Sam called to Bronwyn, "Paul's brought a book with stamp prices. He's being optimistic."

"That's great," she said.

"I have to leave by seven," Sam apologized. "I promised Ruth we'd go out for a coffee."

"How are you two doing?" asked Paul.

"She's great. I've got her fooled into thinking I am, too. I really think we're going someplace."

"That's wonderful. She's a sweet girl," Paul said. Looking around he asked, "Where's your Aunt Phyllis' box?"

"It's hidden," Bronwyn smiled. "Until after your dinner, so you won't be tempted. Come and get your chow. It's just leftover chili. I added frozen corn and vegetable mix to stretch it. I think I put in too much chili powder, though."

Paul cut them each a slice of bread, and they dug into their bowls. "Wow!" complained Sam. "My scalp's rising with the heat."

"It's just right," Paul said, earning a grateful smile from Bronwyn, before he ruined it. "Providing you grew up in Calcutta."

"Humph!" Bronwyn grumped at her ungrateful guests.

"It's too bad you didn't get a chance to see Nigel today," Paul said.

"But I did! Sandy McCormick, from my office, drove me home. We went by the animal hospital. Nigel was so happy to see me. I'll bring him home after work tomorrow."

Over dinner, Bronwyn gave a synopsis of the relationship between her mother and Aunt Phyllis and of the day when she and her mother were taken from Aunt Phyllis.

"A delicate topic," Sam said. "It's hard to know where the rights and wrongs are."

"It is delicate. Can I ask you not to talk with anyone about it, for now?"

Sam and Paul agreed, and they all further agreed that eating every scrap of Bronwyn's dinner wasn't necessary. After they cleaned up, Bronwyn asked Sam to pull out the box from where she'd shoved it under the couch. He laid it on the dining table and opened it. "An album, and a bunch of letters in their envelopes," Sam reported.

"Sam or Paul, open it up, let's see what I'm the guardian of."

"Drum roll," Paul said, rat-a-tat-tatting on the table.

Sam opened the album and exhaled. "There they are," he said, carefully turning a few pages. "Mint condition, mostly. Just a few are cancelled by the Post Office. You've hit the jackpot," he said in awe.

Bronwyn nodded, taking the news without obvious excitement.

Eagerly Sam pushed the album to Paul, "Here, look in your book."

Paul flipped through the earlier pages of his price book and quickly identified several. "Here's a sheet of non-perforated Ben Franklins. These 5-cent ones are worth about $2,000 each, and you have a sheet of forty. These green George Washington's are worth about the same. The rest look like they're perforated sheets," he said glancing ahead a few pages. "The 24 cent Declaration of Independence ones go for around $3,000 each. Some of the later pages may be less valuable, but let's guess at $1,000 a stamp. You've got about 40 pages, and I'd say," he paused, looking again, "on average, over 20 stamps per page. That's …," he hesitated over the math, "approaching a million dollars."

They sat in silence for a moment until Bronwyn said, "It's a serious windfall, for sure, but let's put it away and worry about it later. I want to know who the letters are from. I can only imagine one person."

Sam removed the ribbon and examined the envelopes. Paul put the album and its box under the couch to free up table space. "They're addressed to Aunt Phyllis," Sam said, "all in the same hand. They're in chronological order, judging by the postmarks that are legible." Sam pulled out the sheet from the first envelope. "It's from your mother."

"No disrespect to you two but I'd prefer to read these myself. My blindness can be so frustrating."

"You can get them transcribed like the diaries," suggested Paul.

"I will. But can you just read the first one, Sam, and we'll see how it goes."

"Okay," Sam said.

January 10, 1981
Dear Heart,
    We are travelling by ship from New Orleans to Rio. Bronwyn is doing wonderfully well. Her legs grow chubbier by the

day. You must miss her terribly, as I miss you. She will have no memory of what we were to each other, and it's better she doesn't know. Robert forbids me from ever communicating with you, but the Purser assures me that a letter given to him will be mailed from San Juan when we dock there. I will write when I can, and send you pictures of our child. I beg you, never write to me. How cruel the world is. How happy, if we could have stayed behind our walls! How weak I am. Why could he not have stayed away?

It's a comfort, thinking of you in familiar little Lexington in the house where we loved too much. Robert may drag me about the world but my heart remains with you. Do not hope for more. We will never meet again my love.

You are strong. Go on being strong. I pray that your art will be your savior and Bronwyn mine.

"It's signed 'Sophie,'" Sam said. "The page is splotched. Who knows with whose tears."

"Let me feel," she said. Sam put the letter into her hands. Touching the small indents in the paper, Bronwyn cried her tears for this old sorrow and the freshness of her grief.

"Here," she said, passing the letter back to Sam, who put it carefully away.

Sam and Paul looked at each other, neither one immune from a prickling of tears. "Should we go?" asked Paul of Bronwyn.

"I need to," Sam said.

"That's fine, Sam. Thanks for being with me. Have a great time with Ruth."

Paul and Sam rose to leave, but Bronwyn said, "Can you stay, Paul?"

He sat and waved goodbye to Sam who was hurrying out, "Of course," he said.

"Paul, can I trust you?"

"If you haven't been able to, you can from here on."

Bronwyn nodded. "I'd like you to read the final letter please."

Paul reverently opened the last envelope and removed its one sheet of paper.

August 20, 1990
Dear Heart,

When I first wrote to you, it was from a ship and now again. We travel somewhere in the Red Sea, but there is only darkness out there and no consequence to me where we go. Robert is off gambling and Bronwyn asleep for the night in her bunk. So innocent, but she is so like you, mischief lies in her like a monkey! Next month she'll be 10 and I trust that soon you will see her and she will love you.

All that I am is Bronwyn and my thoughts of you. I dream of you and Bronwyn together, that my wrong may in part be corrected. Not in this world or the next will we be together, but I pray that God's mercy lets you come to know our child. Without me captive here Robert cannot care for Bronwyn, and he will surely send her back to Lexington.

Don't blame Robert. My body sleeps with you in sunshine, and he has taken a gloomy shadow for his wife. His pride would not allow it, but Oh, if he could have turned, and left us where he found us. What a life our little family would have had!

When I leave the cabin, I'll drop this letter in the mail slot at the Purser's Desk then slip over the side. A few quick gasps. Only a minor struggle beside the suffering of these 10 years without you.

Be hopeful, as I am, that good will come of this. I shall be at peace and you will fear for me no more. Goodbye, my love.

Paul had been reading with increasing difficulty, the words catching and tearing at his emotions. He felt Bronwyn's loss, almost as his own. "That's the end," he said. "Just her signature."

"She abandoned me."

"No. She'd been depressed for a long time. She loved you but found her situation intolerable. She imagined a happier solution for you, with Phyllis."

"How sad." She inhaled deeply to control her emotions. "I wish--" she floundered, "I wish--. If only Aunt Phyllis had told me. Paul, would you leave now, please. I have a desperate need to sob and it'd be better if you left."

"Of course," he said. Lacking the privilege to touch and comfort her, he folded the letter back in its envelope and left her.

CHAPTER 22   TUESDAY

Paul and Rolf sat at breakfast discussing the caller from the previous evening. While Paul was at Bronwyn's, Rolf had answered the phone. Rolf reported that the man spoke as if he had a cloth over his mouth. As Rolf recalled it, he'd said, "I've seen you watching her and I know about the cello lady, you pair of perverts. I'm watching you and you'll regret it if you keep spying, or I see you on that shed again."

"A pity you don't have caller-ID," Rolf said.

"Someone like that wouldn't use a traceable phone anyway. How do you suppose he got my phone number?"

"And how did he know about my Aunt Celia?"

"The police know that, thanks to your escapade. And the police know my phone number."

"Didn't sound like he was from the police station," Rolf said.

"No. Probably not the police," agreed Paul. "He must be sneaking into the lane after dark. If it's Rudy, I don't know how he's getting his information. Maybe it's somebody who doesn't like voyeurs and has been following us."

"Gives you the creeps, being watched like that doesn't it," Rolf said.

Paul nodded, smiling at him. "We weren't up on the shed last night, and we'll keep it that way. We'll need to be super-aware of movement in the lane."

Paul finished his morning routines, and, at 8:25, he left Rolf to his online job-hunting and walked to Bronwyn's house. She was waiting outside her front door, and they set out immediately. After they turned onto Main Street, he said, "With Nigel coming back to duty, I'll miss our walks."

"You probably miss cycling, too."

"That's true. Did you have a good cry last night?"

"I did. It's a terrible thing. Asleep in the cabin and my mother thinking those thoughts next to me, but I finally know what happened to her. Aunt Phyllis thought she was protecting me but it's such a loss. We would have been closer if she'd been more open with me."

"And the stamps? How does it feel being wealthy?"

"I'm not sure I want them," Bronwyn said. "Should I keep sneaking the sale of a few stamps each year?"

"So much time has passed. You could auction off the lot and be done with it, unless your family tradition of holding them for another generation appeals to you."

"I'm thinking that I won't keep them," Bronwyn said. "But I haven't thought through the alternative."

"That's good."

"It is?"

"I was only thinking that sudden wealth makes people different." Paul finished lamely with, "Inaccessible, that sort of thing."

"You think I won't like you if I have money?"

Snakes writhed in his belly. He was losing control of the conversation. "Step down in a few paces," he instructed, as they came to an intersection. "There's a car turning in front of us." They resumed walking across the street. Paul told her when to step up onto the curb.

"But I do like you, Paul. I like you a lot. And money wouldn't make any difference to that." She squeezed his arm. Wrapping her right arm through his, she allowed him to take some of her weight as she skipped a few paces.

Heat flushed through his arms, his hands were sweaty. This, he was sure, was the moment. He would stop, and she would obediently stop beside him. He would turn to her, putting his arm about her shoulders, supporting her, should she show weakness in her knees at his declaration of passionate fidelity and love.

The moment passed, and their walk continued. The problem was, she would inevitably find out his history. Matching Bronwyn with a pervert was nothing Paul wanted for her. A generous soul like Bronwyn might forgive him, but knowledge and forgiveness must come before the healing, and only then, if there was any hope, the declaration. His confession must come before everything. Paul's snakes roiled at the thought.

"You've gone quiet," Bronwyn said.

"Sorry."

"No problem, we're nearly there. Go on with your thinking."

At her workplace, Paul said goodbye and pensively headed to his work. He decided that, as no circumstance would ever arise to make the task attractive, he must schedule his confession. Today was too soon. He'd think some more on it, but, tomorrow evening at exactly 7:00, he would knock on her door, and Bronwyn would hear him.

At work, Paul was pleased with any diversion from his difficult thoughts. Ruth's conversation had narrowed to just one topic, but he actively attended to her praise of Sam. It was doubtful that Sam had a legitimate claim to all the honor and virtue that Ruth stuffed him with, but, as much of the pleasure of being in love is talking about it, he played his role and listened.

Tim spoke to him mid-morning and asked, "Did your uncle ever get you?"

"My uncle?"

"From Gary, Indiana. He called on Saturday morning. He said he'd lost track of you, so I looked you up in the staff directory and told him you'd moved to Laurel Lane. He said that explained it, and I gave him your phone number. I hope that was okay."

Having no uncle, Paul said, "Of course it was."

During the day, whenever he failed to avoid thoughts of his own troubles, Paul visualized the following evening's interview with Bronwyn. The scenarios he invented mostly turned out badly, and those that didn't weren't credible.

At moments of leisure during Bronwyn's workday, she joyfully anticipated her reunion with Nigel and was cautiously joyful, thinking that Paul would soon profess his fondness. She amused herself with the word 'tremulous.' It sounded so old-fashioned, but she was tremulous with desire. She would love to tell someone, but it was foolish to babble about the state of mind of someone as circumspect as Paul.

John had come by at noon to borrow her house-key. She had expressed her gratitude that he'd driven an hour to Roanoke the previous afternoon to pick up the parts for the burglar alarm system. When Bronwyn and Nigel were dropped off at home around 4:30, John was busy working, but he stopped for a minute to show her the alarm panel and to allow her to set a combination.

"Can you stay for dinner?" Bronwyn asked.

John hesitated. "I'd love to, but I promised Mother I'd have dinner with her tonight. Any other time would be great."

Bronwyn took Nigel for a walk. On her return, she fed Nigel and made herself a simple meal of macaroni and cheese. She ate at the dining table while John completed the wiring to the French doors.

"Honestly, if you'd stayed to dinner I would have given you something more appetizing," she said, shoveling the last spoonfuls into her mouth.

"It's very satisfying, isn't it--macaroni and cheese." Then, with evident satisfaction, he said, "There, I've finished." He packed up and took his stepladder and tools to his van, coming back to say goodbye. "I'm done. Your house-key is on the kitchen counter, just to the right of the sink. I'm glad you decided to have the alarm system installed. It's not safe for a woman alone without extra protection."

"Thanks, John. You've been very kind."

"It's just surprising your aunt didn't have one installed when my father and I made the alterations to the house a decade back. I'm sure Dad recommended it."

Bronwyn laughed. "She'd gone all those years without, why would she suddenly want one."

205

"It's usual with a vault."

"What vault?" asked Bronwyn in perplexity.

"In the studio. You don't know about it?" Taking her into the studio, he guided her hand up the paneling and showed her a slight indentation. She pressed and John said, "Move to your left a little. The wall comes out in ten seconds." She heard a mechanism click and a slight grinding noise. "It wants a touch of oil," John observed. "There's a gap of three feet at the left but otherwise most of the wall comes straight out to a distance of three feet. Just walk in behind the wall, and you'll find the racks your aunt had installed."

Bronwyn pushed the button. Ten seconds later, the wall closed.

"There's a trip bar," John said. "If you were in there, and it shut, it wouldn't crush you."

"That's comforting."

"It's strange that you didn't know about it, but I'm glad I could show you."

"I'm grateful to you, yet again," Bronwyn said as she walked him to the front door.

She returned to the living room and called Paul. The phone rang so long that she almost hung up thinking he wasn't home from work. Then he answered.

"Were you trying to decide if it was anyone you wanted to speak to?" asked Bronwyn.

"How did you know?"

"Paul, I need you. I have the most astonishing thing to show you. Come quickly by the lane."

She went out, opened the gate for him and ushered him into the studio, refusing to answer his questions. "Now," she told him. "Stand there."

Paul watched as she went to the left of the paneled wall, felt her way up above her head, and pressed. He heard a click. "Not astonishing so far," he said, then decided he'd spoken prematurely. The wall moved toward him. He stepped back, then again, waiting for it to stop. "I was wrong. That is astonishing."

"John knew all about it. He wasn't aware I didn't know. It's been amazing that he's solved all my Aunt Phyllis mysteries, don't you think?"

Paul didn't answer. Bronwyn smiled at him. "Come on! Tell me what's in there."

He walked in and said, "It's about three feet deep. It was bad of Sam and me, not noticing this room's shorter than it should have been. The storage area's about ten feet across, and floor to ceiling high. It's full of shelves, cubbies, slots, all shapes and sizes. What you want to know is that they're full. There are some paintings stacked vertically and framed, but the majority are rolled canvases." Paul pulled one out and carefully unrolled it.

"Very nice. A woman with long black hair. I haven't seen a picture of your mother, but this must be her."

Paul turned to Bronwyn and found her sitting on the floor, tears flooding her face. "Oh, no," he said, kneeling in front of her.

"I'm a wreck," she spluttered. "Help me to stand. We have to call Kate Lavender." Holding her hands, he pulled her up.

He found Kate's number in the phonebook and dialed, but she didn't answer at home. "It'll be frustrating if she isn't there," Bronwyn said.

"I'm trying the gallery," he said. Kate answered, and he passed the phone to Bronwyn who talked to Kate for a minute.

"She said she was putting on her jet-pack. She'll be outside before I've hung up." Bronwyn pretended to listen to the front door. "Late, it seems. I'm too excited to sit, let's stand by the front door and wait for her."

Five minutes later, Kate drove up to the house. She ran to them, more demonstrably excited even than Bronwyn. "Quick," she begged, "let me see."

An hour followed, in which paintings brought to the workbench were examined by Kate, described by Paul to Bronwyn, and returned to storage. Some were of local scenes, the buildings and streets of Lexington, the hills, fields and forests that surround it, but most were portraits.

"The ones of you as a girl are from photos," Kate explained, "but they just glow with spirit. And so many of Sophie! We're not a quarter of the way through, and it's obvious this is a monumental collection."

Bronwyn sighed. "I wish I could see them."

"A great pity," Kate said. "The paintings of your mother bring to mind Wyeth's Helga portraits. He worked in total secrecy for over six years, fitting a passive woman into a landscape. Phyllis painted for thirty years in seclusion. These are psychological studies: love, anger, torment, joy. Bronwyn, your mother will live forever in these portraits. They are, I'm positive, works of genius. The most intensely felt portraits I've ever seen. These will explode on the art world."

"Valuable then," Paul said.

"Incalculable. I have no idea how many millions of dollars these will fetch."

"This is all so overwhelming," Bronwyn said to Kate. "I don't like the idea of selling the anguish and intimacy that Aunt Phyllis put into these works. Aunt Phyllis never wanted to."

"I see what you mean," Kate said. "It's plain that Phyllis loved your mother, and you, too, but she preserved these paintings for some purpose. What was that? Surely, she wanted them seen. There are other options. What I'd suggest is a massive showing in New York. Sell only some, like the landscapes you're not personally invested in. I believe you'll be forced to, as there'll be tax ramifications from an inheritance of this magnitude. When Phyllis is justifiably famous, we can do exhibitions, tours going to places like the National Art Gallery. Sell prints, and books that catalog the collection. Museums will pay to exhibit them, trust me. We can keep the bulk of the collection together and let the world see it."

"Thanks, Kate. This is an immense responsibility. I need time to think. Can I talk to you in a couple of days?"

"Of course, whatever you wish. If you're concerned about the loss of family privacy I'd say that short of destroying the paintings, or closing up the wall and hiding them, there's no stopping it. The force and passion in these works reveals a compelling story, whatever your wishes."

They returned the last paintings from the workbench to their place in storage and Bronwyn closed the wall. "Goodbye," Kate said. "If you do call me, I'll happily spend a few days listing and photographing the collection. I'll always be grateful to Phyllis for the help she gave me in early days, and I'd love to launch her on the world. She wouldn't have wanted it in life, but I have a feeling she wants it now."

Kate left. Bronwyn and Paul moved to the living room where Bronwyn collapsed onto the couch. Paul sat in the armchair, watching her. "Aunt Phyllis keeps giving me things. What am I to do with it all?" she asked.

Paul walked into the kitchen. Rolf, who was cleaning up, said, "You must be hungry, going over there without your dinner. Or did she feed you?"

"No. I'm hungry."

Rolf made him a toasted-cheese sandwich, and an extra one for himself.

"A man who'll starve himself for a woman is a man in love," Rolf said.

"I'm not sure about your logic, but the conclusion's fair enough."

"Don't be running over there. As I see it, ignoring her will fuel her fire."

"I've been thinking, Rolf. I'm going to tell her about my peeping ways."

"Big mistake, mate. Girls don't want to know what they don't want to know. They think they do, but how many girls do you know that think clearly? They grow up twisted by romance stories thinking the world's full of princes. Did you ever see one? I bet even princes aren't princes."

"Your argument's good, but not very principled."

"Principles will lose you the Sheila. Would you tell Mary you're seeing Jane? Course not. Any fool can tell that honesty and girls don't mix."

"I'll think about it," Paul replied, not meaning it, but certainly attracted to Rolf's viewpoint. It made sense, letting glue set before delivering a shock to the bond.

"I applied for a job in Virginia Beach. They want me for an interview tomorrow afternoon. I gave them your name as a reference."

"Congratulations. What job is it?"

"I'll tell you more about it if the interview goes well."

After dinner, Paul changed into jeans and a dark shirt. Ineptly, but proudly, he brushed his teeth with his wrong hand. He sat out by the shed on his folding chair and read until 8:15 when the light failed. The stars blinked into being. A personal light show, just for me, he thought, diverted by his solipsism. That cold distance had always been the trouble with his life. Watching the stars didn't make them part of his existence.

Rolf came out around 9:00, and he and Paul quietly talked. Rolf had been exploring sex sites on the Internet and was willing to show Paul tomorrow. "Thanks," Paul whispered. "I should swear off until I see how it goes with Bronwyn."

"All that pressure," Rolf whispered back. "When your dick jabbers at you it takes over. If a woman can't stop chattering, you let her go shopping. Same with your dick. A little pleasure reduces the tension and you can think again."

At around 9:30, Rolf lay down in the shed. Paul promised to wake him in a couple of hours. He would have liked a quick peek at Bronwyn, to reassure himself, but you can't say you have principles if you make exceptions at every temptation. Nothing happened during his watch except an animal noise that caused him to freeze and listen. At 11:00, he woke Rolf and took his turn on the mattress.

The next he knew, Rolf was shaking him. Groggy, he thought he must have been asleep for an hour or so. Rolf's hand over his mouth signaled silence and woke him instantly. He followed Rolf from the shed.

A slight crunching on the gravel in the lane, a struggle on the wall, and, with a grunt, someone was on Bronwyn's wall. There was just enough light to detect his movement. Paul and Rolf held still while the intruder lowered himself on the other side of the wall. They grabbed their weapons, Paul slid the well-oiled bolt, opened his gate, and they stole into the lane. Paul wished he had a plan. The intruder certainly had one, and they should have prepared against someone better armed than they were. A cleared path across the pea-gravel would have helped to keep their presence a surprise. Moving to the right, Paul stayed on the dirt strip outside his fence. Rolf followed. When Paul judged they were beyond the gravel, he handed Rolf the baseball bat and whispered that he'd open the gate. He rushed at Bronwyn's wall, leaping with his foot extended. His eager momentum and his foot scrambling on the wall carried him quickly to the top. His enemy must have heard him. He dropped to the dirt and trampled the few low bushes in his dash to open the gate. Rolf moved in, shoved the bat at him and made off down the side wall. Paul threw himself on the grass and rolled to a crouch. Their enemy must be close to the house but, without movement, he was undetectable.

Paul heard a cracking noise, and a whine by his ear. A bullet smacked into the back wall. He sank lower, scuttled forward a few feet, another bullet whined by, burying itself in the ground behind him. His heart thumping, Paul edged to the right. He'd seen a slight muzzle flash a few feet from the house at the right corner of the garden. He moved his right fist, tightly gripping the bat, followed by his right leg, left hand and left leg. He was a club-footed crab without a shell. He was thinking of rushing the shooter, when Rolf, bravely or foolishly, threw a rock at their enemy and leapt forward. Then Rolf disastrously fell, crashing onto the stone patio outside the French doors and the shooter ran at him, to shoot him where he lay. Paul burst forward, the bat above his head. The intruder went down and struggled with Rolf for the gun. The gun spat twice at the garden wall. Before Paul could use his bat, he tripped, and he fell heavily onto the intruder. Rolling off, he struck with his bat at what he thought was an arm.

"Rolf?" gasped Paul.

"Hit him again," demanded Rolf. Paul did, connecting with something hard.

Clinging to each other for support, Rolf and Paul looked down at the shape below them. Nigel was barking in the house.

"You didn't kill him, did you?" asked Rolf. "Serve the bugger right."

"I don't think I hit him that hard." Paul peered into Bronwyn's living room. There were no lights and he couldn't see much. "Bronwyn," he shouted. "It's Paul. Open the door."

By the French doors, Nigel was barking furiously, his paws scratching the glass. Bronwyn, visible in her white bathrobe, bent to soothe Nigel. He called again, "Bronwyn, open the door, it's Paul."

"Paul?" she asked, clicking open the door. The burglar alarm rang with ear-damaging intensity. She rushed to the panel to turn it off and returned saying, "Sorry, I forgot it was on."

"Turn on the lights, will you," Paul said. "We've caught your attacker." He passed the bat to Rolf, went in and called the police. When he hung up, he took Bronwyn's hand and led her to Rolf and Nigel, who were guarding the still body of their intruder.

"Rolf's here, too," Paul said.

"Hush, Nigel," Bronwyn said. "Paul, who is it?"

"We don't know," Paul said. "He's wearing a ski mask. I think we should leave him until the police arrive."

Bronwyn went in to dress. Sirens approached a couple of minutes later. Bronwyn returned, followed by Sergeant Driscoll. Rushing down the hallway behind them was Officer Pruett with his gun raised.

"No need for the gun," the sergeant said, glancing about.

Officer Pruett put away his gun and knelt beside the intruder, feeling his neck. "He's alive," he said.

"The rescue squad should be here any minute." Sergeant Driscoll looked at Rolf, "Hit him with the bat did you, sir?"

"No. That was me," Paul said.

Officer Pruett looked at the gun. "I'll get a bag from the car to put that into." He left for his car. An ambulance siren approached.

"What happened with the rope?" asked the sergeant. Paul had been wondering as well. From the upright of the clothesline near the house, a rope stretched at calf height diagonally to the trunk of a small tree on the other side of the garden. It must have caused their attacker's fall, and his own, too.

"I tied it," Rolf said. "We've been watching from Paul's back garden and the rope was an extra surprise." Paul was astounded that Rolf had thought ahead so successfully and effected the trap while he slept.

"I see," the sergeant responded. "The pair of you expected this. Dangerous work. You should have called us instead of tackling him. We might be looking down at your dead bodies about now."

Two paramedics came back with Officer Pruett. One asked, "What happened?"

"He was shooting at us," Paul explained. "I hit him a couple times with a baseball bat. I think once on the arm and once on the head."

The paramedics carefully rolled the injured man onto his back. One went to get a stretcher. The other removed a pair of scissors from his bag and cut off the ski mask.

"It's Rudy," Paul said.

Rudy's sleeve was cut open, a tourniquet applied and an IV started. The other paramedic returned. They attached a neck brace, lifted him onto a board, and transferred him to a stretcher. Rudy groaned as he was strapped in, his eyes opened, he looked wildly around and then relaxed. "Damn termites brought down the tree," he said.

"Take him away," said Sergeant Driscoll.

"Just a bump on the head," Rudy said. "I've got something to say first." The paramedics hesitated.

"Speak then," said the sergeant, "but just for a minute. These guys need to do their job. You have the right to remain silent. Anything you say can and will be used against you in a court of law. You have the right to an attorney--"

"Got it chief," interrupted Rudy. "I've heard it before. Wanted to say, lady, that a roll in your hay would have been delicious." Rolf raised the bat as if to strike him. Officer Pruett pulled his arm down. "Would have been a pleasure, getting to your boyfriend. Figured he'd be watching, and I'd gut him, easy as hooking a fish in a fish farm. Your boy's a pervert. Classy thing like you can't know that. I'm doing you a favor. He's been watching you."

"He's been guarding me," Bronwyn said with indignation.

"Think again sweetheart. Gets his jollies watching you over your wall. What d'ya think he moved here for? Ask him and his friend Rolf about the cello lady they've been spying on. They're a pair of maggots. Just ask the police."

"What do you mean?" asked the sergeant. "Why would she ask the police?"

"Ask him," he said, looking at Officer Pruett. "Told me he chased them after he found them spying, but they attacked him and slithered away."

"This true?" asked the sergeant.

"Might've slipped out when I was interviewing him," Officer Pruett admitted sullenly.

"I've said what I'm saying. And put some damn ice on my head," moaned Rudy.

The paramedics lifted the stretcher across the threshold and wheeled Rudy toward the hall. The sergeant jerked his head at Officer Pruett. "Follow them and stay with him. I'll be along shortly."

"Paul?" queried Bronwyn.

"Let me interrupt, Miss Heathcote," said the sergeant. "Then I'll leave you. First, on Rudy. It will be hard to pin the earlier attempted rape on him. It's possible his girlfriend will be cooperative and may know something helpful. Doubtful I'd say, but we have him on trespass, assault with a deadly weapon and attempted murder. And we'll see what the FBI can do with this alleged financial fraud. Second, on these young men. I've had a quiet word with Mr. Kirk, and I can tell you he's remorseful. Twice he's prevented harm to you at significant risk to himself, and he deserves credit for that."
Speaking to Rolf and Paul, he said, "I'll need you two to sign a statement. Come by the Department tomorrow morning at nine o'clock."

Sergeant Driscoll left. Rolf went to the tree by the wall and untied his rope, saying, "Think I'll skedaddle."

"Have you been spying on me as well, Rolf?"

"No ma'am. Not that you're not something terrific. Any man would be happy looking at you. Paul wouldn't let me, you see."

"Then I thank you for risking your life for me."

"Welcome," said Rolf as he untied the other end of the rope. "I'll be off," he said, and rapidly removed himself to avoid witnessing his friend's drubbing.

"You've been brave and I should be falling into your arms. Had you been quirky and kind, I could have loved you ... Is it true? Have you been looking in windows at night?"

Agonizingly aware for several minutes that this moment was coming, Paul had used none of his time to prepare a defense. His mind was a wasteland. Sick, alone, in pain, he regretted that his barren way lacked all hospice. "Yes," he said, "it's true."

"How long have you been watching over my wall?"

He thought for a moment. "Since Sunday, a little over a week ago."

"And did you rent the house to spy on me?"

"To be close to you. It was later I found I could see into your house."

"I'm so disappointed. The trust I had in you--and all this while--is there nothing you can say?"

"I planned to tell you, but it's so difficult."

"You wormed your way into my heart like a parasite. It's you that raped me. Don't speak to me. Don't ever communicate with me. Please leave. And stop your detestable spying for the good of your own soul."

"I have. I will go. You're right to detest me." He turned and left quickly, clicking the gate shut behind him.

In a daze, Bronwyn walked to her gate and slid the bolt. She rested her head on the solid wooden gate and cried. The loss of her hopes overwhelmed her. She shuddered in distress. Nigel nudged her, she rubbed her sleeve over her face, and they went into the house.

Paul stood at the other side of the gate, his mind wintry with grief. He heard her suffering. He put his forehead on the gate to be near to her. He'd caused it. Bronwyn was lost, his chance of a new life gone. What was there for him? He fell to the gravel, penitently grateful for the gouging of his knees. Tears dropped, his diaphragm shuddered painfully and sobs racked him. After a few minutes, the spasms eased, and he mastered a calm semblance to take into Rolf.

CHAPTER 23   WEDNESDAY – FRIDAY

Not needing to watch over Bronwyn, they had moved the mattress back in from the shed. Rolf spent the night on the couch. Paul, in his own bed, found to his surprise that the day's emotional toil, which had left him exhausted, had benefited him with a good night's sleep. At 8:50, he called work, leaving a message that he was sick and wouldn't be in. In all his years, he had never taken an unjustified sick day, but today he was not entirely himself.

His old car was in better shape than Rolf's clunker, and Paul had offered it for the four-hour drive to Rolf's job interview. As there seemed barely enough time for the police interview before Rolf needed to set out for Virginia Beach, he and Paul drove to the police department in Paul's car, and Paul planned to walk home. They were nervous that questions would touch on their own criminality, but they had only to recite the facts of the evening, and their statements being non-confrontational, Rolf was soon on the highway and Paul walking toward home.

His usual route from that part of town would take him near the library. Having called in sick, it made sense to divert away from his workplace, so he walked to the east of town, by the hospital, in streets he knew by night, but had never walked by day. His pace slowed, for what would he do when he reached home? Gray and insubstantial as a shadow, flitting unnoticed through the streets, perpetually walking, looking and longing, Paul's imagination rebelled against this nonsensical melancholia. He smiled wryly. He could become a legend, forever wandering the streets of Lexington, grown aged and crippled in his pavement pounding, mothers pointing him out to their children, a warning to them of misspent youth.

He moved more rapidly, the idea growing in him, propelling him. He was the engineer of his train, but since childhood it was as if he'd slept and been carelessly shunted over many switches to a disused spur. Bronwyn was right to be distressed. She was the kick to his head, his heart, his groin, waking his soul to the danger, not of disaster, but its antithesis, a life of barren nullity.

Paul returned home and struggled with his armchair's bulk in moving it out to the back. He put it beside the shed and, coupled with his temptation, he sat to contemplate his life. His grief, the loss of Bronwyn, what he had done to Bronwyn, pounded through the floor of him. Time would blunt its force, he understood, but now he welcomed its pain, reveled in the extravagance of it. That he could feel such misery was a strange and fierce joy. Not since childhood had such a longing flooded him. The turbulent ocean had returned to wash over the mud flats of his estuary.

He took Mr. Robson for his guide, who'd observed at the Buddhist temple that 'our life is the creation of our own mind.' To Paul, this implied an active mind directing itself to worthy ends, and he worked diligently that day, determined that clear knowledge of his defects would be the ground on which to build anew. By no pretense can a day of study straighten the tilt of a bad foundation, but he had begun, and patient time that settles all faults would be his ally. He would not abandon hope.

At 4:30, he heard Bronwyn's French doors click open. He expected no more than that minimal contact. He would see her about town, but he would not bring himself to her notice. When he had proved himself, perhaps he could say to her, 'I'm that person you might have loved,' and, if she hadn't found someone else, she might smile at him.

Rolf returned at 8:30 that evening. Paul had made a quiche, anticipating that Rolf would be hungry. A contented belly is the enemy of effort, and Paul had eaten sparingly during the day. He was glad when Rolf said he was ravenous. They eagerly sat to eat, and, after they'd consumed two slices each, Rolf revealed that he had been runner-up in the New South Wales swim meet. It was this ability, he hoped, that would get him the job.

"It's at this huge time-share resort," he said, "with an Olympic pool, a kiddies' pool and a lagoon. Bloody silly, but there's a pirate ship smack in the middle of the lagoon. Anyways, it's a job for the season, being a life-guard."

"I can see how an Australian would be good at that," Paul said.

"Too right, mate. My family used to live around the corner from Dawn Fraser's pub."

"Did they?"

"Don't suppose you'd know of her, but she won gold, swimming at the Olympics. She's an Australian legend, and likes a schooner of beer too. Swimming and beer, that's Australians. This job's right up my alley. I can sit in the sunshine and perv on the shapely Sheilas, and I'll chat-up the barmaid and she'll slip me some beers, off-duty like."

Paul wished him luck and took himself to bed early. He was tired from struggling in a maze of confusion. He would have liked to convulse in sorrow, lashing himself with his pitiable condition, but Rolf's presence made that impossible, and such exuberance was inconsistent with his shrinking self-centeredness. However, he couldn't pass the entire night free of curling in a tight ball of lugubrious misfortune, but there's comfort in soaking a pillow with tears. He deserved to suffer, and if he didn't, could hardly claim he loved, so suffering had something noble in it.

The next morning he returned to work, telling those who asked, that it was a stomach problem. That was not far from the truth, his issues were intestinal. The weekly News Gazette came out that day, and he was glad that the night's happenings had missed the edition. He needed more time to adjust before he could talk about events with the curious or the sympathetic. During the day, he was like a backache sufferer who periodically sweeps his body to check his posture. He was checking for mindfulness. The more he thought on his problems, the more he realized the need to be galvanized from his routine, to be jolted and jolted again. He spoke kindly to Tim, listened with greater care to Ruth, interjected comments in the lunchroom conversation and thoughtfully interacted with the library patrons. His misery stayed with him, but he pictured a happy boat afloat on a sea of gloom. The sun would come out and the floods recede, but his boat would stay buoyed with the hope that Bronwyn, in this better universe, would not find John to her liking and would forgive him.

    Rolf assisted in the evenings. He listened patiently to Paul's ramblings, understanding that a mate's there to help. As he said, many times he'd lusted for a woman who'd rejected him, or didn't notice him, so he identified.

    On Friday, Rolf came by the library to tell Paul that he had the job. He intended to leave in the morning. Paul was happy for him and would miss him.

CHAPTER 24   SATURDAY

To see his friend well fed for the trip, Paul made a full breakfast of sausage and pancakes, coffee and orange juice. After breakfast, Rolf put his bags in the car while Paul made him a bag-lunch. He waved as Rolf drove up the hill to Main Street, glad that Rolf had a new direction, sad that he was leaving and not a little relieved at the breakup of their partnership.

The morning was beautifully sunny. To occupy himself, Paul opened the windows to the house, swept, vacuumed, washed and scrubbed. Spring-cleaning felt right, though it wasn't the house that needed it. Late in the morning, he took a cardboard box to the lane and collected Bronwyn's gravel. He heard a bolt drawn on a gate. His fanciful notion, that Bronwyn would appear, was superseded by the wrinkled face of Mrs. Marmion peeping out from her fence.

"Is that you, Paul?" she asked.

"Yes," he replied. "I'm picking up gravel."

She shuffled onto the concrete path. "Why thank you," she said, peering at his work. "That's thoughtful of you. I wouldn't want to fall."

"I'm nearly finished," he said. Mrs. Marmion stood over him, watching. Paul wished she wouldn't, but he talked with her, as she plainly wished him to, and he thanked her when she pointed at more specks for him to collect. After he'd completed the task to Mrs. Marmion's satisfaction, he would call Sam and ask him to get the gravel back onto Bronwyn's path.

Bronwyn was in her garden, walking on the gravel path. For no more purpose than to be heard, he reached into the box with both hands, picked up a substantial scoop and forcefully showered the gravel back into the box.

"Is that you, Paul?" Bronwyn responded from her side of the wall.

"Yes," he replied. He thought of enlarging on that. Much could be said, but Bronwyn had forbidden communication.

"What are you doing?"

He called back over her wall, "I'm putting your gravel in a box."

"That really was a good idea."

He thought she meant spreading the gravel in the first place. "That might have been Rolf's idea, or at least a joint idea."

"And spying? Was that Rolf's idea? Was he your leader?"

"He's only nineteen. It was my fault. I've been doing it for nearly as long as I can remember."

"Did you see me naked from your shed?"

Paul glanced at Mrs. Marmion who smiled benignly at him, cocking her head to hear more clearly. He smiled uncertainly at her and turned to Bronwyn's wall, "I did." Energetically, he added, "I wanted to be with you, to share in your life."

217

"You didn't get aroused?"

Paul hesitated. He looked again at Mrs. Marmion who, with great curiosity, was observing him speak to the wall. "It was exciting. You're exciting."

"So you weren't masturbating, watching me?"

"It was nothing like that. I wanted to know about your life, be a part of it."

Bronwyn slid back her bolt and stepped out. "You'd better bring the gravel in."

"Have you met Mrs. Marmion?" Paul asked. "She lives next door to me, to your left. Mrs. Marmion, this is Bronwyn Heathcote."

"Nice to meet you, dearie."

"I'm happy to meet you, Mrs. Marmion," replied Bronwyn.

"It's lovely that you and Paul are getting along this well. He's so thoughtful, picking up the gravel, but like all men, you've got to keep after him. Paul, you haven't replaced that tile on your shed roof yet."

"No, Mrs. Marmion. I'll get to that very soon."

Bronwyn said her goodbyes and turned back into her garden. Paul nodded to his neighbor, picked up the box and followed Bronwyn. She was sitting on the grass, chortling. Her laughter built, and she fell back, her amusement echoing between her high walls. While he spread the gravel on her path, she and Nigel gleefully rolled about. He put the empty box outside the gate. Mrs. Marmion was still standing in the lane. He waved to her and shut the gate. When Bronwyn and Nigel ceased their play, she sat up, and her chuckles abated.

"I'm glad my embarrassment with the neighbors is a source of hilarity to you," he said feeling irritated and awkward but overwhelmingly bewildered at his presence within her walls.

"Sit down," she told him, soberly. Paul sat on the grass in front of her. "Did you send Rolf here this morning?"

"Rolf was here?"

"He's hardly unimpeachable, is he, being the co-conspirator, but he thinks you're loyal and true. 'Dinky-di,' and such extravagant words of praise. I've been particularly concerned about something Amanda told me, that while she was away you'd gone through her underwear drawer."

"It didn't exactly happen like that," Paul said, "although I can see why she thought so."

"Don't worry. Rolf explained. And about his aunt Celia, the cello player, who didn't mind your being there. That's not an excuse of course, and I'm sure there've been others who would have minded. The thing is, you're not one that chops people up and dissolves them in acid in your bathtub, are you?"

"I don't have a bathtub."

"So, not knowing these other people, and knowing you, I've decided to care more for you than them."

Solid as he was on the earth, Paul levitated an inch above the ground. "You'll forgive me?"

"I have conditions. If you agree to them, we'll start again. One is honesty. I won't dig into your past, but you must be honest for the future."

"That's no problem."

"You'll go to a counselor. Not me, of course. I can recommend someone."

Paul hesitated. "That sounds unpleasant."

"It won't be, once you start. It just takes honesty. These needs of yours are rooted in childhood, and you'll want help dealing with them."

"I agree," Paul said.

"And you'll stop your peeping."

"Definitely."

"At everyone except me."

Paul smiled in gratitude. "I am fond of looking at you."

"Well, we don't need to exactly start over. Rolf tells me that you're besotted. Would Rolf be truthful, do you think?"

"I've found him so."

Bronwyn nodded, "I want to see you. Come here."

He scooted over beside her. She felt for his chest and undid the top buttons of his shirt. She circled her fingers over his chest. "Not bad," she said. Her fingers continued their exploration over his shoulders and up to his throat and cheeks. "Did you shave this morning?"

"Not thoroughly. I didn't know about this inspection."

"A little sand-papery is okay." Her fingertips brushed his lips, hovering there. His lips tingled intensely. He wanted to bite her fingers, but he just blew on them instead. She ran her fingers through his hair, descended to his forehead, over his eyelids, to his cheekbones and swirled over his ears. She stroked his cheeks and delivered her verdict, "Borderline attractive. How does it feel, being watched?"

"Oh, I love it."

She crossed her arms, pulled up her tee-shirt and dropped it beside her. "Of course, since you've seen me naked, this isn't very exciting," she said, reaching behind to unhook her bra.

"No, no, you're totally wrong." His breath had quickened, his heart beat fast, he was having trouble suppressing the stirrings in his jeans. Bronwyn's breasts in the sunshine were as intimately beautiful as anything he'd ever seen. For a comparison in loveliness, he thought of Celia's shoulder, but he quashed that thought. "How honest do you want me to be?" he asked.

"You mean like imperfections? Not very."

Paul touched her shoulders and softly kissed her neck. Barely touching her skin, his lips traveled down to her right breast and played with her nipple. She groaned and said, "Let's move to the bed."

He stood, helping her to rise. They hurried to her bedroom. Paul opened the blinds to let the sunshine fall on the bed covers. Bronwyn kicked off her shoes and hopped on the bed. "Do you have a condom?" she asked.

"Oh, no, I don't."

"Not at home?"

"No," he said. "You neither?"

"Now that's frustrating," Bronwyn groaned.

"Let's not worry," Paul said. "We'll build up the anticipation. Maybe it's just selfish, but for me, lying here in the sunshine, looking at your breasts, and arms, and shoulders, and touching you," he laughed at the memory that came to him, "it'd be as glorious as finding a nest of robin's eggs."

"That good!" exclaimed Bronwyn. As they spooned on the bed in the sunshine, Bronwyn thought of her mother and her Aunt Phyllis. She hoped they'd be happy for her.

Chapter 25   Sunday

Paul and Bronwyn shared their night together. Nigel lay on the floor at the foot of the bed, content with the new arrangement. In the morning, Bronwyn called Aunt Josie and told her that Paul would walk her to church. Their walk could scarcely have been more enjoyably playful, two bunnies scampering along, he nibbling on her neck and she on his. Arriving before the choir assembled, they walked arm-in-arm down the center aisle and Mrs. Stickley, seeing them, moved over on her pew.

"Well," she asked, "did you two have a pleasant walk?"

"It was just perfect, thanks, Aunt Josie," Bronwyn said.

When it came time for the passing of the peace, Paul was unable to say an intelligible, 'Peace,' but he shook hands and nodded in a pleasant manner. At the social hour on the church patio, Bronwyn held onto Paul's hand. John, noticing, said, "You're looking well, Paul. Remembered to shave this morning, I see." Having thus been satisfactorily introduced to their community as an attached couple they retired for the afternoon behind Bronwyn's walls, continuing their investigation of each other.

Late afternoon found them behind-schedule for Pat's party, but Paul knew Pat would forgive them. He checked Bronwyn's make-up and pronounced her lovely. When they arrived at Pat's house, Sam and Ruth were there. Pat had wine set out in the kitchen for their tasting and was her usual convivial self. "I can't wait to tell you all about my cruise. But wait! What have I missed?" she asked, looking at Paul and Bronwyn holding hands.

Paul raised Bronwyn's hand and kissed her fingers. "Bronwyn has decided to tolerate me."

They toasted the couple, and, not to be entirely out-shone, Sam said, "Ruth and I have been talking, and we may have an announcement soon."

"But you haven't known each other two weeks," Bronwyn complained.

"Sam is over-eager," Ruth said, laughing, looking at the floor in embarrassment. She raised her head and, in her diffident way, said, "Our tastes are similar, and we really like each other." Smiling at Sam, she said, "We feel so right about this."

"Love is in the air," Pat cheered. "Grab some bottles. I think we'll move to the living room and be comfortable." She carried the cheese platter and set it down on the coffee table. From experience, Paul knew to select the couch that he and Bronwyn could sink into together. Cozy in their nest, they listened to Pat's tale of her cruise.

"There was a wedding party on board," she said. "I was sitting on a couch near the bar, and the father of the bride sat down. We got to chatting.

He was escaping the party because he can't stand his ex-wife. He worked as a surgeon, but had problems with his hands and couldn't operate anymore. He just retired. One thing led to another, and I can tell you his hands work fine for my purpose. He's a couple of years younger than me, which is good. I'm too lively to want an older man. We talked on the phone last night, and he's visiting in early June, so I'm hopeful our ship-board romance will outlast the voyage."

Bronwyn explained to Ruth about the diaries and brought Pat and Ruth up to date on the discovery of the stamps and the paintings. "Kate Lavender has agreed to be my artistic business manager. I have money saved up, which Kate says we'll need for a while. I'm happy to spend it on Aunt Phyllis' work. I owe her that."

Serenely happy, Paul looked at those around him. Just for an instant, his felt his soul divide, hovering outside amid the magnolia tree, observing the family in their living room.

Epilogue

While not allowing it to ruin his contentment, Paul had an underlying concern that his seamy history must be revealed during Rudy's trial. Scrutiny of his past by the inhabitants of his small town would be harsh, but, as events unfolded, he escaped his deserved punishment. Sergeant Driscoll informed him that the FBI had relocated Rudy overseas. He'd squealed on his mobster associates and was living in fear of their long reach.

Rolf called Paul at the end of June, full of his news. He'd met a trio of British girls who worked at the resort, and they liked his easy-going ways. After the summer, the four planned to leave on a year-long back-packing trip around Australia.

It was July 4th when Bronwyn, Paul, Ruth and Sam again assembled at Pat's for dinner. Pat was eagerly telling them of her doctor friend who'd stayed in Lexington for a week and continued calling every day. "He wants to retire here," she said with restrained excitement.

"For a small town, Lexington has a lot to offer," Bronwyn said, smiling. "I hope it works out for the two of you."

Sam reached for Ruth's hand. Beaming at the room, he said, "Everyone, we have an announcement."

"Ahhh," said Paul, "Hardly a surprise. If you two glowed any brighter we'd--most of us--need sunglasses."

"There's no hurry," Ruth said. "We're enjoying things as they are. We thought we'd get married next May. We might scrape up a deposit for a house by then." Pat offered her congratulations, and Bronwyn leaned over and kissed Ruth, welcoming her to the family.

"Congratulations, Ruth," Paul said, "but isn't your religion an impediment?"

"Sam and I had a long talk with Mr. Robson this afternoon at the Buddhist temple. There's no pressure, but Sam feels enough sympathy with Buddhist ideals to give it a try."

"But with Buddhism, you're aiming to diminish attachments," Paul said in mock puzzlement. "How can you square that with being engaged?"

"Oh, stop teasing," laughed Ruth.

To complement Sam's announcement, the town's firework display began bursting in the sky. They trooped outside and stood in the backyard watching the rockets explode and shower downwards. Paul did his best to describe the show to Bronwyn. Pitying him, she told him just to watch, and she'd hold his arm and be happy sharing his pleasure.

When the finale's crescendo faded away, Bronwyn said, "This is the moment for me to announce something, too." She added hastily, "Don't get scared, Paul. I'm not announcing our engagement."

"Phew!" he said, laughing. "Though, except it would detract from this being Sam and Ruth's night, it's not a totally awful idea."

Bronwyn nodded. "It's about the stamp collection. It's been a tradition in the family for generations that they're passed down through the female side, so, I've decided to give them to Sam, with Ruth as their guardian."

"No, Bronwyn," objected Sam. "They're far too valuable."

"It's settled," Bronwyn said firmly. "This is the best thing for the family."

Paul was proud of her. He regretted only, for Bronwyn's sake, that their joint lifetime would be insufficient to soften all the stubborn bristles of his personality, but with Bronwyn at his side, and her family and friends about him, he was sure his proclivities would be quieted.

Boiled Peanuts

CPSIA information can be obtained at www.ICGtesting.com
264636BV00006B/1/P